No Rest for the Wicked

WENDY ROBERTSON

headline

Copyright © 2005 Wendy Robertson

The right of Wendy Robertson to be identified as the Author of
the Work has been asserted by her in accordance with
the Copyright, Designs and Patents Act 1988.

First published in 2005
by HEADLINE BOOK PUBLISHING

First published in paperback in 2006
by HEADLINE BOOK PUBLISHING

A HEADLINE paperback

1

ISBN 0 7553 0945 6

Typeset in Bembo by Avon DataSet Ltd,
Bidford-on-Avon, Warwickshire

Printed and bound in Great Britain by
Mackays of Chatham plc, Chatham, Kent

Headline's policy is to use papers that are natural, renewable and
recyclable products and made from wood grown in sustainable
forests. The logging and manufacturing processes are expected to
conform to the environmental regulations of the country of origin.

HEADLINE BOOK PUBLISHING
A division of Hodder Headline
338 Euston Road
London NW1 3BH

www.headline.co.uk
www.hodderheadline.com

For Virginia Hiller

Acknowledgements

Thank you to Gillian Wales, who manages Bishop Auckland Town Hall, which houses the present-day Eden Theatre. As well as supplying many sources on theatrical history, Gillian let me study the unique Eden Theatre Year Book of 1923, when Arthur Jefferson, father of Stan Laurel, was manager there. Mr Jefferson's succinct, often downbeat, comments on the week-by-week running of a small provincial theatre were an inspiration: a hotline to those times, invaluable to a novelist. I would thank Harriet Evans for her witty, creative and supportive editorship, and Yvonne Holland for her meticulous line editing, and both of these for their crucial understanding of the way I work. And I would thank my friend Juliet Burton in appreciation of a rapport which soars over and above the commonplace communication between writer and agent.

Palmer's Varieties

Owners: Mr & Mrs A. J. Palmer
Actor Manager: Mr A. J. Palmer
Financial Director: Mrs Hermione Palmer
Musical Director: Mrs Hermione Palmer
Wardrobe: Miss Abigail Wharton
Asst Wardrobe: Mlle Pippa Valois
Stage Manager/Carpenter etc.:
Josiah Barrington
And, For Your Delectation . . .
Miss Tesserina – Dancer of the Spheres
Professor Stefane Slater – Reader of Minds
Tom Merriman – The Stitch
Roy, Blaze and Marie, The Three
Divines – Aerial Elegance
Cameron Lake – World-Renowned Baritone
Lily Lambert – The Somerset Song Thrush
Cissie Barnard – Fun and Feminine Frolic
Madame Sophia Bunce and her Dancing
Pixies – Fine Formations

Paris 1923

Pippa

I was already late, having strayed out on to the *place*, attracted by the crowds waiting there for the funeral of a great actress. I know my mother saw her many times at the *Comédie-Française*. She had these two posters of her pasted up on the wall just by the *armoire* – one of the actress in *Gismonda* and another, stiffer image of her as Joan of Arc. Sarah Bernhardt. The Divine Sarah. My mother did not know this woman, but still she loved her. And these people now packed on to the Place Voltaire, held back by the *sergents de ville*, they did not know her, but they loved her too.

At first you might have mistaken them for a genial crowd at some kind of fête. The pavements were busy. There were couples canoodling, children playing with hoops and balls, maids in pairs hanging over shiny bassinets. And men – men of all shapes and sizes, all classes and kinds. Men smoking cigars or soft white cigarettes. Men wearing cloth caps and berets, work helmets and American fedoras. Men in tall hats, without cloaks or coats on this soft spring morning.

1

I wriggled my way to the front of the crowd. As I stood there the hum of talk and the laughter of the crowd to my left stilled, and we all became quiet, and then the people to our right became quiet. Respect swept the *place* like a soft broom.

The cortège was long, the followers dark-clad and sombre. But the spring sun was kind, illuminating the massed flowers, which seemed to glow with a light of their own: stage light without the artifice. All of those men, from the humblest to the most grand, raised their hats in the air. Some threw their caps right up, up into the blue sky. Some – women as well – threw white flowers in the way of the cortège, which itself was laden with white flowers. A voice behind me murmured, '*Ah, que des fleurs! Toutes, toutes blanches!*'

Honestly, you'd have thought it was a queen they were burying; even a president. Grown men were standing there, with tears in their eyes, hands trembling.

At last the cortège swayed on its way towards the leafy mists of the Père-Lachaise cemetery. All around me there was silence, a vacuum of disappointment. Then the crowd began to chatter and murmur, scrambling to retrieve its festive mood.

I squeezed my way back through the people and rushed on towards our lodgings, my canvas bag bulging with the day's bread for Miss Abigail. I turned the corner into the narrow alleyway – a customary short cut – only to be stopped in my tracks by yet another crowd. I pulled up and leaned against a crumbling stone wall. As you will see, I am always keen for a show.

The small boy was the first to throw a stone. He was standing in front of a gaggle of citizens crowded under an archway leading to a dusty courtyard. All these people – poor working people, by their dress – were staring goggle-eyed at a young woman who was whirling and dancing in the narrow alleyway. She wore no shift underneath her long gown and her limbs gleamed through the sheer green fabric. The bright shade of her dress was reflected in the dozens of ragged ribbons tied anyhow in her hair. As she danced her tapestry sack bag moved softly against her body.

We stood there watching her for quite a time. Some people in the crowd were laughing, nudging each other and pointing at her. Then suddenly, in the shadowy canyon of the alleyway, a beam of light fell upon the girl and she responded as though the paved roadway were a stage and the sunbeam a spotlight. She danced with her eyes closed, to some sinewy tune that only she could hear. Then she paused, swirled round slowly once more, raised her arm in a dramatic movement and paused again, very still for a second.

There in the blinding sunlight, for anyone to see, was the naked soft flesh of her underarm, the sharp incurve of her waist. Then, she swooped almost to the ground, before drawing herself upright again, hands raised up towards the narrow band of blue sky that squeezed itself between the tall, dusty tenements. A priestess making some kind of offering. On cue, a sharper slash of sunlight intensified the line between her breasts, and made her thighs gleam beneath the fine green silk of her dress.

The thought came to me that the girl must be mad, an escaped lunatic for certain.

Then the strangest thing happened. The amusement in the crowd suddenly soured in the air. One of the men started to crow like a cock and another whistled. A thin woman with the face of a pig shouted, 'Harlot!' and spat on the dusty ground before the dancer.

That was when the boy bent down, picked up the stone

and threw it towards her. It dropped at her feet, raising the dust, but still she danced on. The pig-faced woman picked up another stone and threw it quite softly, so that it skimmed the dancer's waist, making her stop mid-twirl. Her eyes stayed closed, thick lashes shadowing her full brown cheeks. A very thin man cheered the pig-faced woman's shot and she turned to drop him a parody of a curtsy.

A fine theatrical moment. I know my theatre.

Her eyes still closed, the dancer stroked a hand from her breasts right down over her belly and then slowly, slowly started her dance once more. Now the men began to jeer and shout in earnest. One of them stooped to pick up another stone and threw it towards the dancer with a good deal of force. Not to hit her, you understand. More in the fashion of a person throwing a stone at a cat to make it scat. The man next to him followed suit; his arm took the same exaggerated arc through the air, coming out of the darkness of the alley into the ray of sunlight within which the dancer moved. Then the boy copied him, as did the pig-faced woman. From within the crowd came a growling hum. This gaggle of poor people had become a hunting pack taking up a scent.

At last the dancer smelled this greater threat and stopped dancing. Her eyes flew open. She looked around, as though seeing these people for the first time. Then, clutching her bag to her side, she set off to run, her thin clothes flapping softly around her brown legs as they flashed in and out of the sun and shadow of the narrow street. The pack pursued her through the maze of back alleys that connected the fine boulevards of the city. In the end they cornered her against a blank wall of an old church.

I knew this place. My mother once lit candles there for a

cure. That was less than three weeks before she died. Who would believe in God?

The dancer stood very still for a second before a well-aimed stone hit her on the temple and felled her. The mob stopped in its tracks and became silent.

Breathing hard – she had taken some keeping up with – I now walked steadily through the crowd, pushing violently at the thin man and the pig-faced woman to make my passage. I kneeled in the dirt by the dancer's side, pulled her ribboned hair away from the bloody wound and looked up at the faces of the pack. The pig-faced woman had saliva at the corner of her mouth.

A stone fell by my skirt and raised dust on the ground. It was then that I shouted at them, screaming that they were dolts and curs to attack a harmless lunatic. Kneeling there by the church I brought down on them the curse of St Jude. The words and the style were very fine but they were not my own, merely an imitation, borrowed from a drama I once saw in performance. I don't know whether it was the power of the words themselves, my voice (very loud for such a small person), or their own doltish consciences, but the crowd of people began to melt away, disunited now and harmless.

The pig-faced woman, looking now no more malevolent than any poor street trader, sniffed, wiped her nose with the back of her hand and turned to slink away. The rest trailed behind her. The last one to go was the boy. He lingered for a second, then with a flourish of defiance he bent down, picked up a stone, jammed it into the pocket of his ragged breeches, and loped off.

The mad dancer and I watched her tormenters trickle away. Then she sat up, pulled her skirts down to her ankles and examined me carefully. Her arms were round and covered with fine, dark hair. Her eyebrows were like swallow's wings against her broad brow, dark despite the fairness of her hair. She was a beauty. No doubt about it.

'*Grazie, signorina, grazie,*' she said.

Italian. I've heard the lingo before. Our theatre director, Mr A. J. Palmer, once had this Italian tenor in his troupe but was obliged to pay him off in Bordeaux. The problem was that the tenor could not sing in English, nor yet in French, which would have been convenient here in France. Now, that *still* might not have mattered as we French, of high and low estate, are lovers of culture and would have taken to him no matter what language he sang in. But Mr A. J. Palmer sulked over him. I suspect the real reason for this was that the tenor was gallant with his wife, *Mrs* Palmer, even though she was no more handsome than a brightly plumed parrot. I had not then been with the troupe long enough to understand the sense of all this. The tenor was gone before I could test my theory and at that time I knew none of them well enough to be sure what had really happened.

Now, on hearing the lunatic's greeting, I jumped up, held out my hands and pulled her to her feet. She rose and rose and when she got to the sky she stopped. She loomed over me. I remember thinking, *mon Dieu*, this one is tall. This aspect of her hadn't occurred to me as I watched her dancing from a distance among the tall buildings. She was so beautifully in proportion: pleasing legs supporting a slender trunk; pleasing head set on a fine column of a neck. Not out of proportion at all. But now I could see she was as tall as any man, which made me think perhaps this was why those men in the crowd took such a dislike to her.

She stood in front of me, one hand clutching her sack

bag, the other hanging loosely by her side, looking so lost that I was certain that despite being beautiful and beautifully built she must indeed be a lunatic. What would become of her? What if at some point the music started up in her head again and she began to dance and another crowd came after her? At first they might watch her and like her. Then they would begin to hate her. It only took one small boy.

She would end up dead. I was sure of it.

'You will go home, *mademoiselle*?' I said hopefully.

She shook her head slowly from side to side. I was not certain whether this was because she didn't understand my admittedly accented English or whether she was refusing to go home. Or whether she didn't have a home to go to anyway. I tried my suggestion in French. '*Pouvez-vous aller chez vous, mademoiselle?*'

Again she shook her head, her eyes opaque.

Well, I'd tried my best. After all, she was a lunatic. I shrugged and turned to go. Then she touched me on my shoulder and made me turn back to face her. She touched her own breast, then mine, and hooked her hands together and made them walk. She would come with me. She told me this without words.

I shook my head. 'No, no, *mademoiselle*. You cannot come home with me. I have no home. Just the mattress on the floor of a crooked woman who sews like an angel.'

I walked on, away from her, but she ran after me and insisted on linking my arm and coming with me. The walking calmed me down and I stopped worrying about her. As we made our way through the streets I told her about the troupe. I spoke in French, thinking perhaps it would be nearer Italian than the English. Me, I know English very well. My dear *maman* was a good teacher. English is a very fine language even though it's a language of sticks and stones and false mirrors, and bears no relationship to French at all.

As we walked along I told the lunatic of Mr A. J. Palmer and his gaggle of strange English, who were now on their last week at a fourth-rate *cabaret* at the back of the Pigalle. I told her of the wonderful Miss Abigail Wharton, who had burned her hands and – looking for fresh sewing hands in M. Carnet's sweatshop in Toulouse – was delighted to hear me speak English, and on the spot made me her assistant wardrobe-mistress, seamstress, mender-and-maker all rolled into one.

I didn't bother to explain to the lunatic precisely how, even after Miss Abigail's hand had healed, I remained latched on to this funny English troupe. I hung on to Miss Abigail and the troupe when they finally came to Paris. We travelled via Bordeaux – you will remember the tenor left us there for some unfathomable reason.

Latching on to the troupe was not so hard to achieve, as its members had begun to make a pet of me, sending me on errands and giving me sweet things as rewards, telling each other what a dear little thing I was.

Me, I accepted all this attention and kept quiet. There was a brittleness about the affections of these theatrical people, which could, I may tell you, turn very sour. Look at the Italian tenor. Mrs Palmer had not shown an ounce of pity for him when he was dismissed, although he had been her devoted slave. So I kept my head down and *watched my ps and qs*, as Miss Abigail would say. It was worth it. Being in their company was infinitely better than M. Carnet's sweatshop. As well as this, I had my eye on England as a destination for more reasons than one.

As we hurried through the streets the lunatic nodded and

smiled at my stories, though I became sure she understood nothing. Still, such was the persuasion of those fine eyes in that dark face that in the end I abandoned my first intention to lose her, and took her hand and led her down back alleys, to the narrow court that smelled of old onions and privies, where the troupe had their lodgings. The downstairs *foyer* was empty and the stone staircase echoed with our hurrying steps. There was no one about. Our own comrades, some of whom also inhabited rooms here, would be asleep. Their routine was ironclad: late performances, late unwinding over cheap wine in cafés, late sleeping to be fresh for the noon call for places.

A. J. Palmer was very strict with his people. Theirs was a hard daily round; their only experience of glamour was when they were on the tiny stage in their finery: Mrs Palmer playing the piano in the gaslight for Lily Lambert (also called 'The Somerset Song Thrush'), and Cissie Barnard in their glittering costumes; Mr Palmer holding forth in some drama written by himself to show off his own dramatic powers; Tom Merriman strutting about the stage as a fine Spanish dancer before he fell over his feet and made everyone laugh. The troupers were always most themselves when they were on stage, any stage, even a narrow *cabaret* behind the Pigalle. They were least themselves when they were bickering in some flea-ridden lodgings with no inside tap.

Hand in hand, the dancer and I climbed the stone staircase to the fifth level, hauling ourselves to the very top of the building, to the long narrow room I shared with Miss Abigail. Well, not exactly *shared*! It was my habit to sleep on a rug on the floor by her bed, unless the night or our room was very cold. At such times I was obliged to creep in with Miss Abigail to get her warm again. It was no chore: more like warming a small chilled bird that has turned up on your doorstep on a very cold morning.

You may think I was chancing it, taking this lunatic woman to squeeze in with Miss Abigail and me. But if you said that, it would show that you didn't know my friend, the extraordinary Miss Abigail Wharton, one-time singer and dancer on the very best London stages, a woman with the hands of an angel and a heart as large as Paris.

Abigail

Abigail Wharton had started in the theatre as a child dancer, rented out at nine to a theatre dance master by a stage-struck mother, who afterwards returned to her home village in the North to hire herself as a farm domestic. As the years went by, Mrs Wharton was kept alive by the monthly London letter from her daughter, which always contained a small money order. She changed the order to hard cash, which she saved in an old creamware pot in her garret above the dairy. When the farmer's wife died with her son in childbirth, Mrs Wharton's savings jar added to her attractions for the grieving farmer. She married him strictly for their mutual convenience, had three sons with him, then slaved on just as she always had done, in the low farmhouse. At least then she had the warmth of her predecessor's deathbed, which was beside the chimneybreast.

As the years went on, Abigail's round, childish hand developed into a flourishing scrawl, and the frail notepaper was replaced by scented and stoutly prosperous parchment: an elegant missive from an unknown, glamorous world. The money orders, still enclosed in the envelopes, stopped the farmer husband scoffing about the dark immorality of the stage, and people who got above themselves.

In 1911, when she was thirty-seven years old, Abigail fell while dancing in a London music hall and broke both of her ankles. They were hobbled and tightly bound by a distracted surgeon who advised morphia for the pain. Unable to dance, Abigail went to her mother's house in the North to lick her wounds and consider any option in life that did not involve dancing.

In the months that followed, her mother and stepfamily scoffed at her cut-glass accent, but in the long evenings they relished her stories of the risky backstage life in London, which for them had all the mystic splendour of an Eastern bazaar. By the flickering fire they sat transfixed by Abigail's tales of nights when she danced before the royal princes, a foreign potentate and three prime ministers. The farmer's wife would demand intimate tales of her own favourite, Marie Lloyd, whom Abigail had met when Miss Lloyd was still calling herself Bella Delamare, before she became the naughty darling of the music hall.

As soon as Abigail was able to walk without sticks, even though her gait was awkward, rocking and ungainly, she was restless to be off. She knew there was no question of dancing again for a living, but still she looked towards the theatre. She thought perhaps she might get some kind of domestic work or sewing in a theatrical boarding house. In the end she was saved from this domestic drudgery by her old friend Hetty Palmer. Hetty was dancing at a theatre in York and came to visit Abigail at the farm on her Sunday off. She took one look at the low walls of the farm and the extensive piggery beyond and said that dear Abigail simply, simply must return with her. She must go back into the theatre. At that point Abigail kicked out a twisted ankle from under her long skirt.

'Oh, yes, I can dance, dear Hetty. Don't you see? Perfect legs.'

'There's more to us than dancing, my darling. My dear brother AJ has just set up this theatre troupe with some musical hussy from Sunderland. He was telling me he needs a wardrobe mistress who has what he called "some idea". Perfect place for you, my darling. Right in the middle of it all, but no dancing.'

'Wardrobe mistress? I know nothing of such things.'

'Ah! But, darling, aren't you the neatest, loveliest needle-woman? Who is it that sewed her own costume and mine when we were Corrigan's Babes and just ten years old? And look at that beautiful dress that you're wearing even now. You could have bought it in Bond Street and yet I'd wager you made it yourself. Go on, darling! Do join dear old AJ, and keep an eye on the Sunderland hussy for me.'

Abigail couldn't deny that she was tempted. She looked around her mother's low dwelling, contemplated the lashing rain that seemed only to occur in the country, said her tearful goodbyes to her mother and brothers, shook her stepfather by his grimy hand and went off with Hetty in the gig to the railway station.

So it was that Abigail Wharton became a member of Palmer's Varieties from the very beginning. She kept a promise to Hetty to exchange weekly letters, until Hetty went to America on tour, married a stockbroker and didn't come back. After that Abigail only heard from Hetty once in three months. She thoughtfully shared her letters with AJ. He declared himself too preoccupied to write to his sister but was still mildly interested in her affairs.

A. J. Palmer valued Abigail for her professional attitude to the demands of the company's wardrobe and respected her even more as a fellow professional who knew people in the business. His wife, Hermione – the 'Sunderland hussy' – also respected the wardrobe mistress, even though occasionally she liked to keep her in what she saw as 'her place'.

In joining the company Abigail met up again with Josiah Barrington, who acted as stage manager and carpenter. She had known and liked Josiah when they both worked in various London music halls. He was a quiet, intelligent man and knew when and when not to press his suit. The two of them had become close in their time together at Palmer's but he had kept a discreet distance since Abigail had taken young Pippa under her wing in Toulouse. He regretted the necessity, but he saw the new distraction of the French girl as his own fault. After the accident to her hands, Abigail had been quite distraught so he'd suggested that she visit a sewing workshop in the town, and 'buy' a pair of hands while her own healed. Even so, when Abigail turned up with the watchful sprite that was Pippa Valois, Josiah had been surprised. He'd envisaged some comfortable gesticulating French woman whom they could throw off in Bordeaux. He hadn't reckoned on Abigail taking to the girl, almost making her a daughter.

So, ever pragmatic, Josiah took a step back in Abigail's life. Abigail and Pippa were inseparable. Abigail was the child's teacher and mentor, her mother and friend. As the months passed she transformed Pippa from half-wild street child to sturdy professional, mostly cheerful but always with a street child's keen, watchful eye.

Josiah and Abigail still met each day for their glass of port. On holidays it was a bottle of champagne. But now at the end of the evening they went their separate ways to their own beds. Josiah swallowed his own disappointment and treasured their residual friendship. And he sat back and waited. After all, things never lasted very long in the theatre.

Pippa's Feeling for the Truth

If you never saw Miss Abigail Wharton walk – if you saw her drinking coffee in a café, or sitting in a boat on the Seine, her thick grey hair escaping her overdecorated hat and rioting about in a river breeze – you'd certainly take her as a fine woman of a certain age who had once been a beauty. But if you saw her walk, rocking from side to side like a toy horse, all sense of beauty would be replaced by pity, a pity that would have to make do with the beauty of her soul.

Mr Barrington, the Palmer's Varieties stage manager, knew all about the beauty of Miss Abigail's soul. He was her beau and had known her before she fell off the stage at Wilton's Music Hall and broke not one, but both of her ankles. He told me Miss Abigail had been a true beauty and in his eyes still was.

'It's still there, little Pippa. That beauty that comes from the inside, honey. I'm tellen yeh, from inside. Beauty. An' I don't say that lightly.'

He spoke very oddly, Mr Barrington: kind of soft and low and at the back of his throat. He explained this to me.

He came from the North of England where they have Viking ancestors, and they all speak like this, as if they are growling in the face of a north-east gale. In this soft speech he was unlike the rest of the players. With very little effort *they* could throw their voices down fifty feet of dusty music hall. Sometimes they would forget to turn this talent off, so that when they were beside you they might blow off your ear with a single passing comment.

Miss Abigail, like the others, naturally spoke clear stage-English, and thought at first that my own command of English was useful in the everyday sense. However, she considered my accent something of a joke, and set to work on it straight away.

I remember that first day at M. Carnet's workshop when she made me tell her how I came to be in the stews of Toulouse, and how I could speak English at all. So I told her my tale of a mother, a respectable teacher of English. I even mentioned my mother's brief meeting with an Englishman, a traveller of some sorts. Miss Abigail clicked her false teeth. The tale of my own subsequent birth without the benefit of a wedding mass brought mutters of disapproval. Then with my further tale of my father's brief return in officer's uniform during the Great War, she smiled.

'I was ten years old, then, madame, but all I can remember is the soiled smell of his uniform and the twinkle in his eye.'

Then, hearing of my father's re-desertion of us both, Miss Abigail shook her head. 'You've not been blessed, dear,' she said. 'But what of your mother? How can it be that you ended up in this dark sewing shop, pricking your fingers for a living?'

'By the time I was twelve the feeling against my mother in our small town in the South was too much, so we came to

Paris.' I took a breath then and told her the lie. 'My mother spent all our savings to take one trip to England in search of him and, *malheureusement*, never returned.' I went on with the truth. 'I met Monsieur Carnet when he was in Paris buying a new sewing machine. I was begging in the market so he brought me, as well as the machine, back here to Toulouse and very kindly allowed me to work for him.'

This lying about my mother was an old habit, going right back to Carcassonne, the ancient dusty city of the South, where the children in the street used to mock me about her. The truth would not do. Lies, even unnecessary lies, could act as a kind of cloak. I learned this in the streets.

'Poor little thing.' Miss Abigail's bandaged, claw-like hand clasped my arm. At that point she had glared across at M. Carnet, who was hovering in the doorway of the workshop underneath the sign that bore his name.

I shrugged then. 'I wished to save money to go to England like my mother. *Hélas*, Monsieur Carnet is a kind man but never pays more than what provides for rent and bread. That's why I am still here pricking my fingers, madame.'

Her hand tightened on my shoulder. 'You shall sew for me and save my poor old hands and then come with us to England to find your mother. I shall teach you the King's English proper. You may have grasped our lingo in your own way but you'll get nowhere in the world lisping like a little frog. The first thing you should learn is to bite your tongue when you say *th*, or you'll get nowhere, nowhere at all.'

A painful language, this English.

As I say, I am rather prone to telling stories. What I say is not always the truth. The tale about my mother going to find her long-lost love was *not quite* the truth. But had I told Miss

18

Abigail the real truth perhaps she would not have been so keen to be my *patronne*.

The truth is, my mother was an English teacher in the small town in the South where she was born, and as I grew she taught me English alongside her pupils. This, she told me in private, was in preparation for the day when I would meet my English father. But the shame of my birth lost her all of her pupils and she had to do what she could to make money. In the end she was driven from Carcassonne to Paris, where she kept us both by obliging gentlemen travellers with her superb, although somewhat exotic, English, her witty repartee and her warm bed.

There were many visitors to Carcassonne even then. People found their way there by accident en route through the Midi to Spain, or by design to visit this fine old town, with its swirling river and great square, haunted by the ghosts of crusaders who tried without success to breach the ancient bastion that looms above it.

When I was very small, as my mother was about her business I lay in a basket under the table. When I was older I hid in a little pantry off the corner of our small apartment. I have to admit that even when I was quite young I learned of the astonishing things that men and women do when they are together. But still these matters were never, ever mentioned between my mother and me. Not even as she was dying.

How could I tell Miss Abigail, who thought me a child, about all this? Far better for her to think of my dearest *maman* on her quest in the English shires than in the French cemetery after she died, overwhelmed by the gift of influenza from a gentleman who hailed from Southwold, in the English county of Suffolk.

So, in my months with Palmer's Varieties, tutored by the assiduous Miss Abigail, I had learned to bite my tongue on *th* and became a creative seamstress, skilled in the manufacture of exotic outfits from the most simple materials. In time I came to speak fluent English of the more stagy, cut-glass kind. I have even, from time to time, been allowed to speak a line on stage in one of A. J. Palmer's short dramas. As well as this, tutored by the robust Mr Barrington, I'm an expert in building and dismantling scenery, painting and touching up backdrops and doing the thing he calls 'fettling the lights'. I looked up the word 'fettling' in Miss Abigail's dictionary and it is something to do with horses. Miss Abigail told me not to worry about it as Mr Barrington used English in a different way.

One of Miss Abigail's sayings is that I have done well by her and she will do well by me. This is not hard for me. She is always very kind. So now perhaps you can see why I took the lunatic dancer up to our spare lodgings, confident that Miss Abigail would not throw her out on her ear.

Refuge

When the dancer and I arrived, Miss Abigail was sitting in a
fall of light from the window, darning some men's tights.
With her spectacles perched on her nose and the sunlight
transforming her thick, let-down hair to pure silver, she
looked very pretty. She put down her darning and surveyed
the dancer, whose head nearly reached the sloping ceiling of
our garret and whose presence shrank the size of our room to
a closet.

Miss Abigail looked me severely in the eye. 'So what's this,
my naughty little frog? A wounded deer?'

The dancer stood helplessly clutching her bag as the words
streamed from me. I told Miss Abigail of the woman's
wonderful dancing and how the crowd had pursued her with
their half-bricks and bloodcurdling yells, and how my own
great courage had secured her rescue. I knew the story was
good but was aware that it had a rather weak ending.

'I think she must be a lunatic and she has no one to help
her,' I said. 'She said, "*Grazie, signorina*" in the Italian lingo
but has said nothing since. She doesn't understand anything I

say, in English or French. She might be dumb or crazy, or both.'

Miss Abigail stood up, drew the girl towards her, then pushed her gently so that she was sitting on the bed. Then she pulled a stool from by the window and sat in front of her. She touched her own rather shrunken bosom and looked the woman deeply in the eyes. 'I am Abigail Wharton.' Louder. '*I am Abigail Wharton.*'

Then she touched the woman's breast, barely covered by the thin fabric of her gown. 'You?' she said, putting her pretty head on one side.

'Tesserina,' the woman lisped. She touched her own breast. 'Tesserina.'

Then they sat very still, staring at each other. I kneeled down by Miss Abigail's stool. I touched my rather flat chest. 'Pippa,' I said. 'Pippa.'

A faint smile crossed Tesserina's face. 'Pippastre*ll*a!' she said, her tongue lingering over the *ll* as though she was licking the word into the air. And she laughed as though she had made a joke.

(Later in our acquaintance I learned that she had made a pun. '*Pipistrello*' meant 'bat' in Italian.)

I shook my head vigorously. 'No, Pippa. *Pi-ppa*. Just that.'

She nodded her head gravely. '*Grazie, Pippa.*' She touched her own breast again. 'Tesserina.'

Miss Abigail relaxed and sat back on her stool. 'Well, that's a relief then.'

Now I tell you the truth when I say that in the next hour, there in that tiny cluttered room, Miss Abigail got a whole story out of Tesserina entirely by means of gesture. We learned that day that though the dancer might not talk, when she wanted to, she was a brilliant mime. In that little room she

22

showed us how she was taken to an asylum (*gesture 'very big building' which I think must be an asylum or a prison*) because a man attacked her with a knife (*terrible gargoyle expression and a plunging action into her lower stomach*). They both glanced at me at this point and I realised they were talking about more than just a knife. I reminded myself that these two knew nothing about my observations from the pantry in my mother's apartment. Anyway, it seemed that in this asylum a man with staring eyes had made Tesserina dance and cry and grimace with laughter and do something that involved writhing on a bed like a snake. Here Miss Abigail glanced at me again and shook her head vigorously.

Then on the narrow floor space in that tiny room Tesserina mimed her escape. She swept her hair up into an invisible cap. She mimed pulling on trousers, shrugging herself into a jacket, creeping through a gate, then a jaunty walk to freedom.

'But why dance in the street like that?' Miss Abigail danced two rocking steps and put her head on one side in query. Tesserina rubbed her thumb and forefinger together and tucked her hand deep in her bag.

'Usually people are kinder to her than they were today,' reported Miss Abigail. 'Usually they will give her money.'

'She was in the wrong street for kindness,' I said.

'Wrong street!' Miss Abigail suddenly laughed. 'But really, my dear, it was the right street because there in that street she found a little Pippa who was to be her saviour. And I will tell you here and now, she may be a dancer but she is no lunatic.'

I joined in her laughter and Tesserina looked from one of us to the other and she too began to laugh. Then she stood up from the bed, grabbed Miss Abigail with one hand and me with the other and pulled us round in a whirling dance until we were all gasping and patting each other on the back.

Gathering her breath Miss Abigail caught my eye. 'Well, dear little frog, today we have buried our dear Divine Sarah. Perhaps we have found another, a Divine Tesserina.'

My cue. I drew a deep breath and began to tell her about the funeral and all the white flowers and the men throwing their hats in the air.

The Lone Child

Abigail had not been surprised to find Pippa alone in Toulouse. All cities – in Abigail's experience – were infested by lone, deserted, orphaned or runaway children. In the 1880s, she herself had been a lone ten-year-old in London. Once her mother had taken Mr Corrigan's guinea, apart from the mechanical routines of rehearsal and performances, young Abigail was really on her own. You could hardly count as friends the other 'Corrigan's Babes'. Those children who couldn't stand the savage routine of rehearsing and performing six shows every week, fifty-two weeks a year, would run away. That was if they were not decanted on to the street, discarded by Madame Corrigan like last week's newspapers. Some Babes died of consumption or sheer exhaustion. Those left – those who survived being slapped by Madame for stumbles or other mistakes – were over-eager to please her and intensely jealous of each other.

Among the Babes, though, Abigail's friend Hetty Palmer had been the exception. Hetty's extended family – a hundred years in the profession – kept a close eye on her, and she had

Madame Corrigan's measure. After Hetty's arrival things looked up for Abigail. The two of them were a team and, despite the oppression of the Corrigans, they enjoyed their dancing. Then a new Babe, Dina Brooks, joined them and clung fast. When they were old enough, the three of them escaped from Madame Corrigan and graduated to the music-hall chorus. Dina and Hetty occasionally singled themselves out as soubrettes in musical dramas. But although she was a fine dancer and very striking-looking, Abigail had always been too reserved and modest to strike out on her own. She always preferred the robust comradeship of the chorus and cherished her friendships with Dina and Hetty.

These precious friendships came to Abigail's mind as she observed Pippa's delight in her new friend. It was true that the girl was years older than Pippa, as well as a foot taller. It was also true that she was strange: dumb (except for that exclaimed 'Pippastrella!') and quite possibly mad. The very sight of the two girls together was very comical: one tall as a beanpole and the other small and fine, dancing around her like a firefly.

Later, when she finally saw Tesserina move and dance, something else stirred in Abigail: the feeling that stirs a horse breeder when he sees a talented yearling run; the feeling a musician gets when he encounters a child with perfect pitch. Here was talent.

So, in those last weeks in Paris, Abigail kept Tesserina with her, dipping into her savings to pay for her keep and fending off suggestions from the Palmers and even Josiah that she was playing with fire, housing a dumb madwoman. They protested that whereas Pippa could show herself to be useful, organising costumes, pressing and washing, sewing where necessary, this tall stranger was nothing less than a burden and – with the cold logic of theatrical life – should be dumped as soon as possible.

But Abigail had a plan. Early in the mornings, in the opal light of the dusty deserted *cabaret*, she would place Tesserina centre stage and play music for her on a wind-up phonograph. First she let the girl just listen to the tune. Then by comical demonstration she got her to move to the sweep of the music. Then she began to push and pull, lead and demonstrate as well as her own difficult gait would allow. Within days Tesserina was liberated by the crackling tones of the music and began to get the sense of the space of the stage, so different from the narrow confines of the street.

Pippa sat out front and cheered and halloo'd every piece of progress and every innovation. Abigail wondered at Pippa's generosity and openness, comparing this exultant vision with the tight, watchful child she'd brought out of M. Carnet's workshop in Toulouse. She knew she'd done a good thing with Pippa, She knew that for sure. Perhaps she could do this good thing for Tesserina.

The test would surely be when they travelled back to England. Of course, that proposal was an issue with the Palmers. AJ laughed in Abigail's face when she suggested her protégées be included on the troupe's group ticket.

'My dear Miss Wharton!' he boomed. 'Let me relieve you of the notion that I have five-pound notes sewn into the lining of my coat. If you want your young ladies to come with you, I fear you must pay for them out of your own pocket.'

Really, Abigail knew she should have expected no less. Of course she would have to pay for them. They were her girls now, after all.

A Theatrical Life

Abigail Wharton had spent much of her early working life in London, in some low halls as well as the finer theatres. Although she had long loved the theatrical life, she thought the best and the worst of that life was the drudgery of the travelling. Travelling was an unavoidable part of the routine. The company would complete a hard engagement in some town, and whether they had done well or badly it was up sticks and on to another place. Of course, the best part of this was that the travelling ever onwards gave them a clean slate on which to draw their new performance, though one had to admit that the slate was only really clean if the previous show had not been an absolute disaster. If this was the case a company's reputation had a tendency to go before it. However, the Palmers ran a tight ship, and while their company's highs had never been too high, their lows were never low enough to ruin their reputation.

Abigail had always particularly enjoyed travelling to France for their seasons there – especially those during the war. These performances had an edge, a desperate enjoyment to them that made the whole thing more crucial. And then after the war they had kept going, encouraged by their popularity with French audiences. Abigail admired the skill with which the Palmers changed their approach to suit the French audience. Not many English companies could do this.

In her long career before joining Palmer's, Abigail had travelled even more widely, as far as Australia and South Africa with some of the great companies. In those days the sea voyages outwards and back were always a good rest, even though at times the company were called on to sing for their supper. It was not always obligatory. Abigail had been on board once on the way to Australia, when the great Marie Lloyd (unlike the rest of the performers) was travelling First Class. Miss Lloyd had been outraged at the condescension shown her by some of the first-class passengers. So, when asked to perform for them she refused. And this was when she'd already performed for the delight of the Second Class and even the steerage passengers. When asked by the purser to do her turn for the First Class, she'd flashed back at him that if she was not *bloody well* good enough to be their equal on the journey, she was damned if they were good enough for her to perform for them.

Compared with such adventures, this present trip across the English Channel was short, even though Abigail was aware that their trip onwards by train to their destination in the North would take nearly as long as the sea trip. She was looking forward to their day-stop in London when she would catch up with her old friend Dina Brooks. She'd written to her from Paris and was longing to see her today for more reasons than one.

Seasickness

My dear friend Tesserina does not relish sea travel. She reckons nothing to the vastness of the North Sea and the adventure of our journey. She has pulled a chair across to the very corner of the grand saloon and set it to face the wall. Despite much cajoling, she insists on sitting there with her eyes closed.

I try to explain her stubbornness to the steward and he shakes his head, then puts one finger, very strangely, to his nose.

'Never bother, miss,' he says. 'The sea gets to a person in all kinds of ways. I've seen worse than that, I'm tellen yer.'

He's a small man: small hands, small feet. But his head is rather large for his body. His eyes are mild and I trust him.

The other members of the troupe are scattered about the saloon, all about their own affairs. Mr and Mrs Palmer are holding court in one corner with their usual acolytes: Cameron Lake, the gentleman baritone, Cissie Barnard, the actress-comedienne with her hat with the nodding plume, and Lily Lambert, the singer. Two clerkish men – strangers – have joined them at their table. They are leaning forward, their eyes like saucers. What attraction these theatricals have for more sober folk!

Mrs Palmer is quite heavily made up, but Cissie and Lily have just a touch of cheek and lip rouge, and in the low lamplight of the saloon look much younger than their years: not a day over thirty. They are flirting and laughing with the two clerks, and now and then Lily reaches out to touch the younger man on the sleeve. Those two always flirt when we are out in the real world. Sometimes Lily might find herself a beau for a few days but it never lasts. Cissie never secures herself a beau, as she drinks twice as much as Lily and has a tendency to fall over before anyone can secure the pleasure of her company.

In another corner Miss Abigail and Mr Barrington are playing whist with the comic, Tom Merriman, and Roy Divine, the youngest acrobat from the Australian high-wire act called the Three Divines. These acrobats joined a French circus when it was touring Australia and travelled to Europe. When the circus folded through lack of money in Bordeaux, the Divines dazzled AJ with their skills and he took them on to give his troupe what he called 'an aerial dimension'.

In the saloon the other two Divines – a very glamorous brother and sister called Blaze and Marie – are drinking coffee with a burly man and his wife, both wide-eyed. I can see the attraction Blaze and Marie have for such people, as they are golden creatures who move with the grace of panthers. But why should the high-flyers bother with such dullards? Then I note the diamond pin in the burly man's broad tie and his wife's glittering necklace. Miss Abigail has told me before about the golden couple's ability to part fools from their money. 'Nothing too illegal,' she once said drily. 'They spin a tale about needing to get back to Australia to their dying mother, and not having the fare. Usually good for a few guineas.'

They are all getting on with their business and I have that invisible feeling that I have always relished. Though my main reason for being here is my friend Miss Abigail, I enjoy my life in this raffish company, with its dusty glamour and its relaxed take on right and wrong, its obsession with itself and the life of its members. But I have always needed to get away from them, to be on my own, either in my head or out on the streets. So tonight I let myself out of the saloon on to the deck, where the cutting breeze buffets me about like a plaything. I have to brace myself out here, but the brisk air is refreshing after the saloon, with its fog of pipe- and cigar-smoke lying on top of the perfumed reek of the sweaty bodies crowded in the limited space.

I tie my scarf firmly over my hat, hug my cloak closely to me and set off for my walk, skittering sideways across the scrubbed boards every time the ship chooses to take a tip one way or the other.

The engines in the belly of the ship throb like a deep pulse. We're travelling forward, ever forward, across the Channel. I'm relishing the thought of the sight of the English coastline. I know this so well from my mother's tattered textbooks. The White Cliffs of Dover, for instance, are very familiar to me. As well as this I know the names of England's towns and rivers. I can chant them like a poem.

> Fal, Fowy, Tamar, Plym,
> Avon, Dart, Teign, Exe,
> Otter, Frame, Stour, Axe,
> Test, Itchen, Arun, Ouse.

All these flow into the English Channel over which our boat now sails.

I know the way Britain sits off the coast of Europe like a prim lady withholding her skirts from any insalubrious passers-by. Such haughtiness pleases me, as more and more I relish my Englishness. And am I not finally on my journey – not to find my mother, as dear Miss Abigail imagines, but to discover who I really am? And if in that process I find my father, well, I'll not complain. To be honest, the thought gives me much pleasure. I knew my mother, and despite the dance she led me with the deceptions and her smoky ambiguity, I learned so much from her. The way she was herself has made me the way I am myself. I am *Pippa* and she made me. But there is another side to me, wrought not by seeing her every day, learning from her, imitating her, laughing and crying with her, hating her, mistrusting her, loving her. That other side of *Pippa* was wrought with a single act, such as I had witnessed so many times that it left me without curiosity. But now there is a chance, a rare chance to find the second actor in that single act, to find the other side of *Pippa*.

So I am excited as I make my way to the stern and lean over the rail to watch as the white wake gathers, disposes of the froth that swishes on to the boat and then retreats. Just think, the waves that carry that froth will not cease rolling until they travel all the way back to the coast of France. Departing with those waves is every part of that Pippa who was once hungry, who once sweated with bloody fingers in M. Carnet's workshop, who once hid in the pantry while my mother pursued her profession, who once held her grasping hand in the dingy hospital as she breathed her last.

On the other hand, there are good things that I choose to take with me to England: my mother's voice laced with laughter, her articulation, her wit, her dogged certainties, even her charm, though I'd never make use of that as she did. Most of all I'll take with me my mother's sense of the practical and the way things may be made to work.

I have to say it's my misfortune that I'll *not* take her good looks. I am not like her. When we were together she told me more than once that I resembled my father in my small stature, in my bright eyes, and my propensity for inventing new truths.

I'd deny to anyone that I'm on a quest to find that shadowy man who is my father, but that other hidden Pippa comes from him. Though perhaps my 'small stature, bright eyes and a propensity for lying' may not necessarily be a good start for me there. I do have one clue as to where he may be in England, but even now I don't know whether I really want to use it.

A deep, resonant voice startles me, cutting through the splash and rush of the sea. 'The wake of a ship. So significant, don't you think?'

With the edge of my eyes I make out a smallish man with a large cap. His voice made me expect a much taller man. He's standing so close to me I can smell pomade and tobacco and bitter wine. I don't answer him, but lean further to my left to increase the space between us.

A gust of wind tugs at my hat, teasing it from its moorings. I feel rather than see the man clamp his hand on his head to save his cap from flying. I turn now to see more clearly a mundane, crumpled figure in a long jacket. His eyes, almond-shaped like a cat's, pale and glittering in the growing gloom, hold me. They are not unkind. Rather they are curious and deep-lit.

I can't unclasp my gaze. I have to tell you that I've never

blushed. I've never in my life done this thing called blushing, this reddening of the face with embarrassment which we French call *rougir*. How could I, with the life I've been forced to live? But now in the dark I can feel the heat in my cheeks. At last I drag my eyes from his and return my close attention to the wake of the ship.

'You have had hard times but you show great determination, dear child.' The deep, liquid voice insinuates, the carefully enunciated words pour into my ear.

I turn away to stare hard at the fading, frothy wake and my thoughts are full of my mother in hospital, of her hand clasped tightly in mine. The ward is grey and bleak; the distant figure of a nun appears to be floating above the scrubbed stone slabs.

At last I feel a space beside me. The man has gone. I shiver and clutch my cloak even more closely to my chest. The sky has clouded over now and there is no light except the dull aura cast by the ship. The sea is black and even the wake has lost its charm. It has served its purpose for me.

I stay put there as long as I can, then go in search of Tesserina. She is in the same corner, now rocking slightly backwards and forwards, her face to the wall. I put my arm round her and whisper in her ear in English. I know she won't understand my words, but I'm sure my intention of comfort will be clear.

We do communicate, Tesserina and I. She has this great understanding of the tone of your voice. Her language is her silence and the grace of her body. The marvel is that she's still with us at all, has not been thrown out on her ear by the Palmers, who are no sentimentalists. But the cunning Miss Abigail has staged casual demonstrations of her graceful dancing and her unique sensitivity to music. Mrs Hermione

Palmer has begun to show some interest in this but Mr Palmer keeps saying that Tesserina's 'Not Ready For Performance'. Even so, he has consented to her travelling with the troupe. 'She may yet prove an asset,' he says airily from time to time. Still, I know Miss Abigail had to pay our fares as I have seen the tickets.

I glance around the saloon, seeking Miss Abigail, but there is only Mr Barrington sitting disconsolately on his own, a glass of port on the table in front of him. A dense over-articulated murmur draws my gaze to Mr Palmer's corner. The first thing I see is the large cap on the table. There, sitting at Mr Palmer's shoulder, is the man who spoke to me on deck. He is murmuring in the director's ear. He's not a commanding figure. The face that encloses those strange eyes is soft, pale and creased. At this distance he is not at all threatening.

My close attention must have drawn their gaze and they all look in my direction. Mrs Palmer holds up an arm in an imperious gesture to pull me into their circle. Some errand, no doubt. Mrs Palmer likes to send us lesser mortals on errands.

I'll not respond. I turn away, find a chair and drag it right into Tesserina's corner and sit close to her. She suddenly puts an arm round me and I rest my head on her soft shoulder. Despite the movement and sway of the boat, my eyes droop and I have an overwhelming desire to sleep, despite the cramps in my lower back, which are somewhat trying at present.

I have the Curse.

White Linen Strips

It fell to Miss Abigail to teach me all about the Curse. My observations from the pantry in my mother's apartment taught me many intriguing things but nothing of this matter.

I'd been with Palmer's Varieties only three weeks when this Curse – a new thing to me – started with an ache deep inside me, right at my very core. At first I thought I was dying of a wound from a sword that had slashed at me in a dream that was all too real. But when I babbled this out to Miss Abigail she comforted me, explaining that it was a woman's fate to bear the next generation. This was why women were more important than men and why men were cruel to women in revenge. Each month, she said, the body prepares itself to have a child. Then each month it weeps blood in lamentation that no child has come.

She went on to explain that this matter of the Curse was a secret, to be kept very private indeed. She showed me her own linen strips, embroidered with a lily of the valley at each end, which had served for more than thirty years to soak up her body's tears at not having a child. She had ten of these strips, five to be used each day, then soaked, washed and dried for use during the day after. She showed me her own narrow curse-bucket, which collapsed for convenience of travel. On tour during the time of her Curse she uses this contrivance to soak her strips of linen back to lily-white each day. No one but me knows about this.

I remembered then seeing such strips in my mother's apartment but, being a child, I gave them no further thought. They might be bandages perhaps, or some fixings for her elaborate undergarments. Periodically these strips would appear on the rail above our tiny fire. I realised that such days, though I didn't make the connection then, were also days when there were no men in the apartment and our time together was light-hearted and fine fun.

Tesserina already knew about the Curse when she came. You remember she brought nothing into our lives other than the small tapestry sack that she clung to on that first day. Inside that bag were a whole collection of ribbons; a tough linen jacket with pockets; a long coarsely knitted scarf; a man's cap and trousers, and a purple silk dress so fine you could crunch it – small as a child's ball – in your fingers. When I first saw her in the street she was wearing its twin, in green silk.

Seeing how little she had, Miss Abigail raided the property box to secure more adequate coverage for that beautiful body. She said the silk dresses were not decent for everyday life and the girl could hardly go around dressed as a man, even if such a ploy really had got her out of the madhouse.

So Miss Abigail kitted Tesserina out with a long woollen dress from *The Lady of Shalott*, a fine tweed man's jacket from *The Importance of Being Earnest*, and a small cloche hat from that same play. All this, added to her beribbonned hair, made for a strange appearance. However, her membership of Palmer's Varieties allowed her to enjoy a margin of eccentricity not usually tolerated in normal society.

As for the Curse, in her tapestry sack Tesserina had her own linen bands. These had scalloped ends, neatly finished in satin stitch. With a brilliant mime Tesserina showed us how, at the asylum, her monthly shows of blood were no private thing, but were measured and noted down by doctors in books. In some ways this was comical, with Tesserina being the frowning doctor with pince-nez, licking his invisible pen and writing in his invisible notebook. All this really shocked Miss Abigail, who said it was no better than being ravished in the worst way. She said to me that night, as she put out my lamp, 'The poor girl was there for three years. If she was not mad when she went in, it was enough to drive any person mad, truly.'

Tesserina's mimed stories were all so very strange that I wondered if, like me, she sometimes departed a little from the truth. Perhaps she'd never been in an asylum but was just plain mad. Then I would look into her fine eyes and find them clear and without artifice. Unlike me, she was no liar.

I sometimes reflected on this fact that I didn't quite tell the truth about my mother. Perhaps it came from her insistence that we spoke only English in our home, which had only English books and newspapers on the dresser. Outside that little room the babble of French around us was like the separation of truth from fantasy. Inside that little room I was encouraged to feel I *was* English. Outside, I pretended I was the daughter of a respectable *bourgeoise*, a bit above the common French people I met from day to day.

Buried at the centre of our lives together was my mother's absolute denial of her enforced profession. This was never mentioned between us, either in French or English. Neither did we speak of the English travellers who were her first customers, nor those genteel English soldiers smelling of soil. Relieved, I am sure, that she was different from other street whores, such men would sit at her table, drink tea and talk of London or their village in Somerset, before they led her to the bed. During the war some of them came back on every short leave until they were killed, or until the Armistice ended their war and they went back to their village wives. Such strange heroes in our life, who left English newspapers and mud-stained books for our growing collection.

In her own way Miss Abigail was as good a teacher as my mother. And despite being tuned to the inappropriate openness of life in the asylum, Tesserina soon came to join the secrecy of the collapsible bucket, and the use of 'soap shavings and three rinses' for perfect cleanliness of the strips. In this, and in many other matters in our lives together, the three of us settled into a pleasing rhythm: we lived together yet made space for each other's interior thoughts and private ways.

A New Act

Abigail had noticed the new fellow cosying up to the Palmers on the boat. It wasn't unusual for managers of companies to be approached in such a way. They had the power of patronage, after all. A company on the move was often short of an act, and many performers put high value on a solid company like Palmers, despite its modest status as a bread-and-butter company. And turns came and went. Hadn't they themselves lost that tenor in Bordeaux? Abigail was in on the secret that he was got rid of by Hermione Palmer, when she saw how peculiarly devoted the tenor was to AJ, who had a well-known weakness for beautiful men.

And now their French *bouffon* Clément had elected to stay in Paris with one of the Palmer dancers, cutting down adult dancing strength by a fifth. This was a loss, even though Hermione said they would be taking on a Madame Sophia Bunce and her Dancing Pixies in London. Abigail was uneasy about this. The misery and exploitation endemic in the employment of child performers reminded her too well of her own miserable introduction to the theatre.

Their own comic, the jealous Tom Merriman, had been delighted at the French clown's departure but there was no denying that there was now a gap in the programme. Abigail had her eye on that gap for Tesserina but it seemed to be closing quickly.

But now here was this Slater chap pitching for a position in the troupe with the aid of a full bottle of gin. The word was that he was a mesmerist. Abigail had seen many of these acts. They were mostly clever charlatans, using magic tricks to deceive and beguile audiences who longed to be shocked, amazed, terrified and delighted by tricks they themselves could not fathom. Josiah Barrington, watching one such with Abigail, had murmured, 'Canna see why they don't all gan to the church. Magic transformations there, regular, every Sunday.'

But in her time Abigail had seen one or two such performers – men who, while they used all the theatricality of performance, seemed to have some gift, some foresight, some insight that did not involve trickery or sleight of hand. The thing they had in common was that at the end of their turn, they were exhausted and grey, unlike the charlatans, who would get on then with their customary activity of flirting with the dancers or moaning about the management.

She hoped this fellow wasn't one of these. He looked harmless enough, slight and sandy-haired, with a head too big for his body and blue eyes just a bit large in his face. Abigail's informed instinct was that he might be all right. At least he did not look like a moaner.

Her glance passed on to Tesserina, hunched in the corner. These days nobody took any notice of Tesserina's strange actions. She had her own eccentric ways and people left her to it. It was not as though the other members of the troupe were above strange habits of their own. Cissie Barnard, in drink, had the tendency to take her clothes off. Lily Lambert, on travelling days, had a tendency to cry, tears falling unchecked down her face like a waterfall. Those Australian high-wire walkers were strange in their own way too. They played far too close with each other, even for brothers and sister. And Blaze and Marie played cruel practical tricks on their younger brother, Roy, who would go round with a stiff face for a couple of days until they bought him cake or made him laugh.

And then there was Tom Merriman, the comedian who had the audiences rolling in the aisles with his funny clown movements and lewd asides; offstage he could be as gloomy as a Scotch preacher and, even worse, told lies for the fun of it.

A theatre troupe could indeed be a madhouse. But unlike all the rest of them, Tesserina had actually spent some time in a madhouse. Or prison. Her mime of confinement was not hard to read. And worse things had happened to her than anyone here knew.

'A drink, Miss Wharton?'

Abigail's meandering thoughts were pulled back to the present by the mesmerist, who stood before her, a bottle of port in his hand.

'Mrs Palmer says that port's your preference?' Without invitation Slater slid into the seat opposite. He leaned over and filled up her glass, and after a moment's hesitation filled up the glass in front of Josiah Barrington. 'Mrs Palmer tells me you've worked with all the greats, Miss Wharton.'

She picked up her glass and sipped it. 'I've worked with those who thought they were great. But I was only ever in the chorus. Small fry, that's me.'

'Dan Leno? You worked with him? I saw him in Drury Lane as the Baroness in *Babes in the Wood*. And I've seen him in *Ali Baba*,' he said with an eagerness she thought might not be assumed. 'What kind of a fellow...?'

'Now Mr Leno, he was a great man. Never saw a better man as a woman. It was poor women he did the best. You would swear he was one of them, just off the street. He had their very walk. You could tell he felt for such people.'

'But, really, what kind of a fellow...?' he persisted, eyeing her closely.

She frowned and looked away, deliberately losing his gaze. 'Mr Leno was very driven,' she said. 'A great performer, but anxious, with great ambitions. Sometimes I used to think the man had too much energy inside him for his body or his soul. And sometimes he moved so quick, talked so quick you couldn't keep up with him. But on the stage it all slowed down. At his best, his timing was perfect.'

Slater nodded, eyes bright, brimming with delight at hearing of his hero so close at hand. 'And the great Miss Marie Lloyd? You worked with her?'

'So I did. When we were both quite young.'

'And...?'

'Whatever you may have heard is true. Miss Lloyd lights up the stage. She can be very vulgar and near the knuckle. But she's kind – kind to the poor folks at the stage door and kind to us poor lesser mortals in the wings. Big-hearted.'

'And what about Harry Randall – did you—'

Abigail opened her mouth but she felt a distinct kick on her ankle and closed it again. She looked at Josiah, whose eyebrows were raised into his thick black hair. He was right. What had made her start babbling on like this? Wasn't it a thing of honour with her that – unlike many music-hall people – she rarely indulged in gossip? This man, with his bright eager gaze, had pulled the babble out of her.

She smiled, lifted up her glass and drained it. 'Well, Mr Slater, here's to "the greats"! May they all prosper and not drown in alcoholic misfortune like so many of their predecessors.' She stood up. 'Now, my dears, I must find somewhere quiet to rest my weary head.'

Near the door she passed Tesserina, rocking backwards and forwards in the corner with her face to the wall. She glanced back at the table to see Josiah was now sitting on his own. Mr Slater had gone on, to cultivate people he saw as more important than the stage carpenter. He was working his way round the room, getting to know the troupe. He must be very keen to join Palmer's. Abigail was too tired to know whether this was a good or a bad thing. Good, probably. All change had its good side, in her experience. Why else would the life of a travelling player fit her like a glove?

London Town

From my wide, rather undirected reading in my mother's apartment I knew all about London Town and Old Father Thames and the Fire of London and the chimney boys who got burned cleaning chimneys, and those other boys who got into trouble picking the pockets of rich men.

So I was jumping with excitement when we were decanted from the boat train into the big cathedral-like station. Travellers of all kinds and colour burst from the boat train. Even at this time of day the station was bustling with travellers, luggage and uniformed porters pushing high-wheeled luggage carts. I examined one of these men closely: my first sight of an Englishman who wasn't a theatre gypsy or one of my mother's callers. He was young and had a neat moustache and his uniform was well brushed. You could say the same things about a porter in a French station, but in some way I could not yet define he was very different. Perhaps it was the smell.

'Pippa! Come on, will you?' Miss Abigail grabbed me by the arm.

NO REST FOR THE WICKED

A. J. Palmer was assembling us on the platform like a shepherd gathering his flock, with Mrs Palmer as his sheepdog, pulling in the stragglers. Miss Abigail, Tesserina and I stood near the back of the crowd. I stretched my neck to see the man with the large cap standing between Mr and Mrs Palmer.

'The new act,' Miss Abigail whispered in my ear. 'Mesmerist, so they say.' I glanced away from him, not wanting to meet the man's piercing gaze. He looked harmless enough in the daylight, standing there in his soft hat and long coat. But even now there was something about him that compelled your attention, that had to be resisted.

A. J. Palmer clambered up on to a barrow, steadied by a uniformed porter. Then he addressed us in his beautiful, penetrating voice, which rang through the decorated iron structure and resounded above the noise of engines gathering steam below. He instructed us to be sure that by six o'clock we were at the other great station, King's Cross. There we would all catch the night-train to the North of England where he had secured us a six-week season in some very fine theatres. Miss Abigail whispered in my ear that they were not all fine theatres. It was to be something of a bread-and-butter tour.

He went on, 'Mr Barrington here is deputed to supervise the transfer of the baggage and stage paraphernalia. Mrs Palmer and I have a meeting with Madame Sophia Bunce and her young dancers, who will join us on our English tour. You may wish to spend the day reacquainting yourself with our great capital. But whatever the temptations therein you are commanded to be at King's Cross Station at six precisely! Our train *North* leaves at six-thirty sharp. Anyone not there at that time is summarily dismissed. No excuses accepted!'

He said the word 'North' with the same note of satisfaction

as Miss Abigail, who originally came from those parts, and Mr Barrington, whose unique speech bears witness to the same heritage. I knew from Miss Abigail that her mother had a farm up there and that *the North* was her heart's home. *Wherever I wander there's no place like home.* She sang it to me sometimes, in her low contralto.

There had been much talk in recent weeks of this season in the North; no denying the mounting excitement among those familiar with its unique audiences, and the mounting curiosity of those like me who had no experience of it. As well as Miss Abigail and Mr Barrington, I learned that A. J. Palmer himself came from the port of Hartlepool, and Mrs Palmer came from Sunderland, where she started her performing life as a pianist in an orchestra in that town, at the Empire Theatre. We were to have a two-week engagement at that same theatre. I looked forward to that for my own personal reasons.

According to Miss Abigail, the Palmers actually met at that theatre when Mr Palmer was giving his Oberon in *A Midsummer Night's Dream*. In 1906 (the year I was born!) the two of them eventually raised the troupe in Sunderland, to be called Palmer's Varieties. And now they returned to *the North* for a season every year, except for the war years, when they performed in London and the South of England, to keep up the spirits of the troops who were massed there in great numbers. And they actually performed in France *during* the war, to keep up the soldiers' spirits on French soil. Miss Abigail would sigh when she told me of this and the great reception they always enjoyed there. 'Poor boys. Those poor boys,' she would murmur.

Miss Abigail told us Mr Palmer lost three musicians (one aged only fifteen), a comedian and a dog act to General

48

Kitchener. Of these men, three only were spat out again from the mouth of war and none of the survivors was in a fit state to perform on the stage again.

My chance to go to England came about only because, even after the war, it became a custom for Palmer's Varieties to include a season in France in their annual round. At first this was to entertain the troops still there after the Armistice. But then they kept going. It seemed that the Palmer blend of mime, acrobatics, tomfoolery and sentimental song went down well with us French. Even AJ's short, barking renditions of the classical roles in English tickled our French fancy!

Now, though, here we were in London Town, so familiar to me from my books. That being said, it was entirely unfamiliar, as strange as the surface of the moon. Perhaps I had romanticised it rather too much. There was much to take in, but it was so much larger, more crowded, dirtier and more threatening than I'd expected. Even Old Father Thames looked black and rather surly. The people *en masse* seemed dingier, and smelled of old potatoes, even those whose dress was quite fine.

But then we ventured on to London's broad highways, and its coiling, crowded roads, its bustling, energetic grandeur, blasted into your face like shot from a gun. Because it was so different from my taken-for-granted Paris, I looked at everything separately – the individual men and women and children clacking all kinds and sorts of English, the shop windows, the windowsills, the roof tiles, the ornate doorways, the street sellers and their stalls, the carriages and two-wheelers, the autobuses and the trams, the motor cars and the man-pushed carts. My eyes ached with looking.

Tesserina and I had spent some time gaping like country cousins at soaring, sooty, intricate buildings and the tangle of traffic charging by, when Miss Abigail took us each by the hand and led us to the *Metro*, where we caught an underground train and soon surfaced again into a large square. The English crowds in their drab clothes, umbrellaed against the persistent spring drizzle, stepped around us, glancing sideways at our finery as though we were some kind of circus.

We lingered in front of three great theatres before crossing a long boulevard to find a street called Bond Street. Umbrella up, Miss Abigail marched on ahead with confidence and we scuttled after her. There was no doubt at all that she knew this town as well as she knew her home village. She finally stopped at a smart millinery shop with '*Madame D*' etched in gold across the curved glass window.

The bell pinged as we went in. A smart woman, arranging a hat on a stand, turned towards us. She shrieked when she saw Miss Abigail, and fell into her arms as though she were a long-lost sister. Miss Abigail introduced her as Miss Dina Brooks, a friend from the old days on the London stage. Miss Brooks shook hands with us warmly and led us through to a small, elegantly furnished sitting room at the back. Here she brewed us tea on a shining brass spirit stove, talking all the time to Miss Abigail about these present times, old times and so many people of their mutual acquaintance.

'You never heard a better voice, Pippa,' Miss Abigail beamed at me. 'Dina here sang like a skylark.' She looked around. 'And now here she is, in charge of her own shop, her own life.'

'All thanks to our Mr Brown,' put it Dina with a wink.

'Thanks to our Mr Brown,' echoed Miss Abigail.

Then they both collapsed with laughter, just like girls half their age.

'Why don't you go and try on some hats?' Dina finally

gasped. 'Leave Abigail and me to go over old times. Not stuff for young ears!'

She followed us through and dropped the latch on the door, turned round the notice to 'CLOSED FOR LUNCHEON', then swept back in a wave of camellia scent to talk with her old friend.

Left in the jewel-box of a salon, Tesserina and I occupied ourselves trying on hats before the large cut-glass oval mirror. Tesserina tried on large old-fashioned hats with sweeping feathers and pranced around the small space like a duchess. I took off my beret and pulled on a small tight-fitting hat that was cut low on one side and had a single decoration of a small bunch of violets. When I looked into the mirror my eyes seemed suddenly very blue. Then Tesserina swept off her hat and started stomping round the room like a man, before coming to kneel at my feet in mock adoration. She put her hand on her heart then opened it out to me and, miming a ring going on to a finger, made a play of asking for my hand in marriage.

I roared with laughter at this and thumped her so hard on the shoulder that she fell on to the floor. In doing so, she pulled a hat stand down with her, and ended up covered with hats of all modes and styles. She laughed heartily up at me, making me laugh even more. In the end I had to put my hand over my mouth to stop my squeals penetrating the door to the back room.

In vain. The two women came through the door and looked askance at the mess. Miss Abigail frowned and immediately began righting the stand and rearranging the hats. 'I am so sorry about this, Dina. One of these girls is a lunatic and the other knows no better.'

Dina shook her head, trying to look fierce but failing.

'Don't worry about it, Abigail darling. Girls will be girls. Who knows that better than we do, dear? Haven't we tipped over many a hat stand in our time?' Her words gave me a sense, like a flash of lightning, of Miss Abigail's life: a youth spent on the London stage in the company of friends like Dina, enjoying the peculiar comradeship and freedom of the theatrical world, the patronage of great men. And young, so young.

As we left Miss Dina Brooks's shop, the milliner pushed a large brown paper package into Miss Abigail's hand. 'I got that stuff you wrote to me about, dear. Took some getting, I can tell you. As a matter of fact, you could have got it yourself. Came from Paris in the end.' Miss Abigail peered at the bill and handed over quite a few guineas from her purse to Dina.

I was very curious about this package and plied Miss Abigail with questions about it as we made our way back towards the railway station. But she shook her head and kept her own counsel as to its contents. Just what it contained only came to light much later, in our Waldron Street lodgings in a place called Bishop Auckland, where we were to have our first engagement. As a matter of fact the contents of that package were to be something of a signal in all our lives.

Old Friends

After cutting their teeth with Corrigan's Babes, Abigail, Hetty Palmer and Dina Brooks went their own ways in the theatre, only to find themselves years later dancing together in the chorus at Gatti's Music Hall at Charing Cross. The bill, which included Daisy May, the comedienne, was topped by the great Harry Champion. Abigail's particular favourite that season was a man who trained dogs, which were sleek and eerie off stage, but bouncy and intelligent when performing. In that, announced the young Dina Brooks with a flourish of her feather boa, those mutts were no different from a thousand other turns she'd encountered in the music hall. And none of *them* had the excuse of being a dog.

One night when the two of them were in the dressing room, changing between acts, Dina noticed some bruises on Abigail's back and advised her to slip off the chains tying her to this fellow she was shackled to, and go solo.

'Domestic bliss? Don't give me that, darling! The rascals sugar you to the altar, then make you work and milk you of your wages. Champagne and cockles all the way for them.

Then in their cups they bash the daylights out of you. Don't tell me! I've had it, me!'

This was so very near the truth for Abigail she kept silent. To be sure, Denis, her husband of six months, had been sleek and endearing at first. Something of a gent, he certainly hated to work or soil his hands. And he certainly liked his champagne. And for sure he was keen with his fists when he was drunk.

'Why don't you do it, darling?' demanded Dina, pursuing her favourite theme another night after the show. 'Why don't you throw the bastard out?'

Abigail looked at her through the deckled silver of the mirror. 'That'll make Denis even madder, Dina,' she said. 'He'll bash the living daylights out of me.'

Dina winked at her. The lines of black around her eyes and the bright rouge on her cheeks exaggerated the wink to a level of lewdness Abigail had only seen before in Marie Lloyd. 'Never mind about that, little chicken,' she said. 'There are these boyos I know now, in the boxing trade. Or that's what they say they're in. I don't ask for details. Those boyos of mine'll see him off.'

Which was how Abigail got rid of Denis Wanless and was free to follow Dina's advice to '. . . only deal with real toffs, chicken. They're usually ugly so they're grateful. They don't want to marry you and aren't after your money. They only want a jolly time and a dark joke. And you don't even have to go to bed with them if you play your cards right.'

Abigail played her cards right and, after Hetty left to work in America, went on dancing with Dina for sixteen years in shows at home and abroad. The two girls were usually in the chorus, though they were occasionally persuaded nearer to the spotlight before melting back into the chorus again. This suited them both as Abigail liked to dance but didn't want to be centre stage and Dina was no great dancer but liked the theatrical life and the after-hours attention from the men who paid them both such gratifying attention.

When Abigail was forced into retirement by her fall, Dina decided that it was time to retire herself. She allowed her current toff (a Mr Brown who dealt in Securities, whatever they were), to stake her in her Bond Street shop. The establishment enjoyed moderate success but the most important aspect of it was that Dina allowed herself to be persuaded to permit early evening visits from Mr Brown on Wednesdays and Fridays after his work in the city.

Before that time, through sixteen years, Dina had been closer to Abigail than any husband or lover: constantly there with her laughter and advice. She had encouraged Abigail to be herself. In Dina, Abigail found a companion more robust than herself, who rendered all the hardships of theatre life into one long joke.

When Abigail was in hospital after her accident Dina had visited her every day. And when Abigail returned from her convalescence in the North with Hetty, Dina had even subbed her rent until she started to earn money with theatrical sewing while waiting to take up the post of wardrobe mistress for A. J. Palmer, promised to her as a favour to his sister Hetty.

Abigail talked about all this on the train going north, adding that a person could never, not in a whole lifetime, have better friends than Dina Brooks and Hetty Palmer.

Ever Northwards

By the time we all got back to King's Cross Station, the other members of the company were already on the train. A. J. Palmer was marching in a military fashion along the crowded platform in the manner of his sketch about Napoleon at Austerlitz. (Miss Abigail had told me that this was remarkably similar to his performance for the English of Wellington at Waterloo, albeit with different demands on her wardrobe department.) His Napoleon speech was treated as comedy for his French audiences. I wondered if English audiences would give Mr Palmer's Wellington more respect.

AJ used his stick like a sword to direct his way towards us from the other side of the barrier. We could see him clearly through a crowd that was more workaday, less cosmopolitan than that at the other station. Here the air was filled to the ornate iron rafters with the shouts of paperboys, flower sellers, pie-men and porters. Families clustered round shabby mountains of luggage, men in dark coats marched along with briefcases and umbrellas. There were children and old soldiers politely begging at the very edges of the crowd.

AJ stopped at the barrier and called across, 'Hurry, hurry, ladies. You are late. Late! I fear the sleepers are all taken, Miss Wharton. We have Madame Bunce and her Pixies taking up a whole cabin, sleeping top to toe. And we have a new company member, a Mr Slater, a talented mesmerist who has consented to try out for our season in the North. I'm afraid he has taken your sleeper, Miss Wharton . . .'

The man from the boat. The man with the pale face and the rusty hair. And the watery blue eyes.

'. . . So unfortunately, Miss Wharton, I fear you will be obliged to take an ordinary carriage with your young ladies. That fellow there . . .' he indicated a man in uniform, hovering with our hand baggage on a barrow, '. . . has your hand luggage. He has instructions to deliver them to your carriage.' He waved his stick to the nether end of the train. 'Now, I must join Mrs Palmer in our carriage.' He tucked his stick back under his arm. 'She will be waiting!'

As we settled into our carriage I asked Miss Abigail about Madame Bunce and her Pixies, her child dancers. It seemed that in the past Madame was known as a great dance trainer. Miss Abigail said the woman started children at seven and never kept them after they were eleven. She never allowed the use of Christian names in her troupe: the children were always known as Pixie Smith, Pixie Jones and so on. Miss Abigail shuddered with distaste. 'A terrible life.' Even before I met her I did not like the sound of Madame Bunce.

For the first few hours of the journey I stood with my nose to the window. The sprawling city of London seemed to take hours to pass by, in great fields of stone, brick and mortar houses, valleys of lanes and black-water canals, and mountains of great factories and workshops, topped by ever-smoking chimneys. Although it was still daytime we looked out on a city that must never be fully light.

Eventually the buildings thinned out and we began to see snatches of field and tree. We puffed our way through the blackened seamy side of small towns, with their still busy stations. Then, a little before the real day darkened, I managed to catch a glimpse of intricate farmland peculiarly laced with hedges and trees, so unlike the familiar countryside of France.

'Miss Abigail! The horizon is so close!' I said. 'We could tip off the edge of the world here.'

'Ah,' said Miss Abigail. She glanced up over the spectacles clinging to the end of her nose, then peered down again at her knitting. 'So unlike the wide landscapes in France. I remember when I first travelled by train from Le Havre to Paris I thought the land went on for ever and ever. And I regret to say I found it colourless. I so missed the pure green of this old place.'

I nodded. 'I have been watching, Miss Abigail. This England which starts out as smoke and brick is very green when you get into the countryside. Like the green out of a paintbox, no?'

But soon it was dark and there was no green to be seen at all except where the light spilled grudgingly from the train on to the raw dry grass of the sidings. In the distance all I could see were stringed necklaces of light, which marked villages and towns. Miss Abigail explained to me that most towns were lit by gas and many towns, even small ones, were even beginning to use electricity to fend off the night.

After that there was little to see and Miss Abigail insisted that we pull down the blinds, despite my protest that I rather regretted losing that dark English exterior embedded with our own mirror images. I went back to take my seat between Tesserina (who had not taken a bit of notice of the journey and was now not only asleep but snoring) and Miss Abigail, who was still knitting furiously.

'Try to sleep, Pippa darling. It will be a long journey. We still have a very long way to go.'

I snuggled in beside her. 'Tell me about this where we are going, Miss Abigail. This place in the North. Tell me!'

She put down her knitting and wriggled her back against the plush of the seat. 'Well, my darling, we are going to three places. First the small town called Bishop Auckland, then the great town of Sunderland and finally the great city of Newcastle. They are all very different from each other.'

'Tell me.'

'Well, Bishop Auckland is a very old town. It has a castle where the Bishop of Durham stays. He has a cathedral in the city of Durham, seven or eight miles away, but he stays in Bishop Auckland. The town has a very fine straight high street that Josiah Barrington told me once was a Roman road. It's certainly very straight. There is a marvellous old market there every Thursday when all the farmers come in to buy cattle and sell their goods. Once, I was there in the autumn time with my mother and stepfather, and he hired a man and a boy at the market to work on his farm. They stood in a line, the farm boys and girls, standing around waiting to be picked for a whole year's work. The shepherds had shepherds' crooks and the milkmaids had stools. I suspect my own mother was once hired like that, although she would never admit it.'

I thought sleepily that here was another mother who didn't tell the truth. 'And is everyone a farmer in this town?'

She laughed. 'Not by a long chalk. There are coal mines and

coke ovens, workshops and manufactories all round. There have been times when it must have had the buzz of money, that town. Perhaps not recently. But there are fine houses there as well as grim hovels. And the theatre is quite good, has a bit of a reputation, perhaps better than the town deserves. I think that might be the view of the manager, who's a real old-style theatre man. His son's in America, in the moving pictures . . .'

Beneath us the wheels of the train had stopped clicking and lurching so violently and had settled to a creaking rhythm.

'The moving pictures . . .?' I yawned so widely that my jaw locked. I wanted to ask her about Sunderland but I was far too tired.

I have little consciousness of the rest of our journey north as I spent most of it asleep with my head in Tesserina's lap and my feet sprawled across Miss Abigail's knees. When I woke again my shoes were off and I was in my stockinged feet, so Miss Abigail must have removed them in the night.

At Darlington, in the early light, we scrambled on to another train for a shorter journey to Bishop Auckland, and our engagement at the Eden Theatre there: the first week of our northern season.

The town had a busy station with five lines and three platforms, each with its gaggle of expectant travellers. We climbed stiffly from our carriage and stood shivering on the platform. Tesserina was so cold that Miss Abigail took a shawl from her own valise and wrapped it round her. So this was the North. Cold. So cold and grey.

As we stood there in the drizzle, waiting for our orders from A. J. Palmer, I noticed a small engine slowing to stop on the platform opposite. A gaggle of men alighted, dressed in rough working clothes and big boots. The strange thing about these men was that their faces were all blackened, like the blacked-up minstrel acts that I'd enjoyed many times on the Paris stage.

'Pitmen.' Mr Barrington's voice in my ear. 'Up from the nightshift at some godforsaken pit or other. Coal miners,' he extended his explanation, nearer the French word *mineurs*. Now I understood. 'Nearly got sucked into that life myself, once. Close shave. Looking at them lads I'm pleased I escaped.'

I looked across in pity and my eye caught that of a less slouching, younger man. The coal that blackened his face sharpened the greyish blue of his eyes in the morning light. He scowled and shook his fist at me for staring, and I turned away, ashamed.

Outside the station there was a yellow and brown chara-banc waiting for us. The uniformed driver got down to help the Palmers into the back seat and wound up the canopy to protect them from the drizzle. Then he and Mr Barrington stacked the luggage and the prop and wardrobe boxes on the rest of the seats. There was no room for us.

Miss Abigail put up her umbrella. 'Come on!' she said. 'By the time the fellow has his chara cranked up we can be there.'

The wide straight street was already abustle with early workers and shop people putting out their goods on to the pavement and writing messages to their customers on the shop windows. This sense of opening up, of starting the day in a busy market town, reminded me of the early bustle in Carcassonne. But here the buildings were not dusty gold and faded yellow, but dingy grey-black. Here the air was chill and sharp-edged rather than warm and gold. And the smell of hot bread was missing. Then in my mind I was breathing that golden air, running through the narrow streets for the early-morning bread for my mother. And then I was not; I was merely scurrying down this wide grey street, sharing an umbrella with Miss Abigail. It was all so very foreign.

She was right. The chugging charabanc arrived at the theatre just as we came upon it. The Eden Theatre was quite a surprise. I had seen many theatres in my time, and while each one was different, each was the same, designed to entice and to pull in its patrons. Perhaps it was the early morning but this one seemed closed off and slightly forbidding. It wrapped itself round a whole corner leading off the high street. Its decorative arched corner frontage, ornate window glass and tall doors declared its difference from more common commercial neighbouring buildings. The large double doors, painted slick green, very fresh, were firmly closed.

But now those doors burst open and through them came the manager, an elderly, fussy man, immaculately dressed. He smiled wrily and put out a hand towards AJ.

'Mr Jefferson!' boomed AJ.

'A. J. Palmer! Well met!' He shook Mr Palmer heartily by the hand, then turned to Mrs Palmer and took her hand closely in his. 'You look well, Hermione! Blooming!' She was. Her lip and cheek rouge were immaculately placed and her hair swung glossily beneath her feathered cloche hat.

AJ looked up at the theatre. 'The old girl seems to have taken on something of a shine, eh, Jefferson? Somebody's been spending money, I see.'

This obviously pleased the manager. 'Not before time, AJ. Complete refurbishment this last year. I flatter myself I'm making a difference here. Although I sometimes think that attracting an audience in this town is the devil's own work. Look at the competition! The Hippodrome in Shildon a mile one way and the Cambridge in Spennymoor four miles the other. And now the Hippodrome in this town is putting on films. Moving pictures! Then there are all these dances here and the whist drives. Too many attractions here keeping people away. And then on the other hand we have strikes looming in the mines and the ironworks. Who'll pay for the cheap seats then?' His smooth face puckered as he chanted obviously well-rehearsed complaints.

Mr Palmer held up a hand to stem the flow. 'My dear fellow, look at me! I am all sympathy but, I assure you, *we'll* pull them in. We'll do our bit. Word gets round, with Palmer's Varieties. I promise you we'll have full houses by Wednesday. Full houses!' He took Mr Jefferson by the arm. 'Now, dear chap! Should we repair inside out of this dratted rain? I have in my bag a bottle of the finest French brandy to celebrate Palmer's Varieties' first engagement in the North this year.'

I looked up again at the fine building. It was a little dusty in the unforgiving morning light but there was that substantial frontage – much better than the fleapit in Paris – and when we went inside it was even grander, showing off its recent refurbishment to glittering effect. It had a fine proscenium arch, and rising ranks of seats and a large circle that must take some filling. Above the proscenium arch were carved words in gilded letters. 'One touch of nature makes the whole world kin.'

Mrs Palmer left her husband striding arm in arm with Mr Jefferson towards his office, and came across to us, a list flapping in her hand. 'Dear Mr Jefferson! Did you see him? He's been a very fine manager in his time but nowadays he can be such a gloom!' She consulted her list. 'Now then! Miss Wharton, you will stay with Mrs Jackson in Waldron Street as usual. I wired her that you have two young ladies with you and you will pay your own expenses. If you take your small luggage I will send the rest to you with Mr Barrington and a barrow. Now do go and settle in, but don't forget! Roll call at two this afternoon. The wardrobe will need checking. Today is Sunday, so no performance, thank the Lord. Apparently Mr Jefferson has a local choir booked. A sell-out. He was rather loath to speak of such success. Now then, we start proper tomorrow...' She turned to me. 'AJ and I have been discussing your need to pay your way, Pippa. You can't continue to sponge on Miss Wharton. He suggests that you might take on the number boards...'

Sponge! I have never heard that word but I can tell what it means.

'She pays her way already, Mrs Palmer,' interrupted Miss Abigail. 'She's my right-hand girl. Helps me all the time with wardrobes and costumes ... I need her backstage. She helps me fit the costumes and sews under my instructions. She helps Mr Barrington with practical things and stage management too. You know she earns her keep.'

Mrs Palmer held up a hand. 'We understand that, Miss Wharton. But nevertheless, the child needs other experiences.'

I can't say I was unhappy with her suggestion. When you work in a theatre company you soon learn that the only place that gets any credit is before the footlights. Miss Abigail had performed there with great distinction before she had her accident and this won her respect even now. How she must have loved those times! You could see from her delight at meeting Miss Dina Brooks that they had the best of times when they performed together.

But I myself was not devoted to the idea of performing. After all, I was here by chance: the chance of Miss Abigail finding me in M. Carnet's sweatshop; the chance of my then becoming so devoted to her; the chance of this great opportunity to come to England and find the other half of myself, perhaps even discover its embodiment in the person of my father. But by this very chance I became entranced with the life we all shared: the daily tension of performance and responses, the travelling about, the idea that every day was a new chance for any one of us to shine.

Mrs Dot Jackson, our landlady-to-be in Waldron Street, greeted Miss Abigail like a long-lost friend. We soon learned that she was the widow of a miner who had been killed underground. It seemed that after that disastrous event she had found her vocation keeping this boarding house, particularly because it was frequently used by theatricals. She also told us she was very popular with the travellers who supplied the huge variety of busy shops that lined the nearby high street, which, although very grey, was like a *boulevard*, broad and straight, with generous pavements shaded by awnings to protect the precious goods inside.

Mrs Jackson didn't know what to make of the silent, uncorseted Tesserina. She muttered in Miss Abigail's ear, 'What've you got me here, Abigail? I've dealt so much of me life with theatricals but this girl of yours is the queerest yet.'

Mrs Jackson acted as though she herself was a bit of a theatrical, like a pale imitation of Mrs Palmer: corseted like a pouting bird, her clothes very brightly coloured. Her hair – cut short and crimped on her head like a helmet – was a very suspicious shade of auburn. During our stay I discovered that in the evenings, in her drawing room downstairs, our landlady would accompany herself on the piano and sing for anyone who would listen. Her favourite songs were those made popular during the war. The real theatricals did their best to escape the honour of listening, but the travellers – many of whom had served in the war – seemed to relish her impromptu concerts.

The three rooms she allotted us were right at the top of the tall house: one room with a double bed for me and Tesserina, and a narrow slip of a room for Miss Abigail on her own. Alongside these bedrooms was a tiny sitting room with a fireplace in the corner, furnished with a couch and a chair. Janet, Mrs Jackson's maid, puffed up the stairs every day with a bucket of coal but announced we'd have to light the fire ourselves, her with ten bedrooms to sort. The fire had a little cast-iron arrangement above it so we could warm milk and make hot chocolate, or boil water for tea.

'It's all very fine here,' Miss Abigail beamed. 'Very fine. Good digs, Pippa. A haven!'

On our first night in the town, after the roll call and a quick technical rehearsal, we hurried back to the lodgings and, after a supper of potatoes, cabbage and overboiled meat, we withdrew to our little sitting room. Miss Abigail vanished into her room and returned with the battered parcel her friend Miss Dina Brooks had handed to her in the shop in Bond Street.

Miss Abigail clipped the hairy string with the tiny scissors that always hung from her belt and the brown paper fell apart, creating an explosion of fabric: yards and yards of silver-grey silk. At first glance it all seemed very crumpled but as Miss Abigail pulled out more and more, the sharp edges of the tiny pleats caught the lamplight and made the material leap and live.

Suddenly Tesserina was laughing out loud. We both turned to look at her. How rare it was that she laughed of her own accord. Up to now she had always reflected and mirrored our laughter, waiting for her cue.

She leaned over and pulled at all the fabric until it was free of its brown paper prison and then threw a handful over her shoulder like a Roman senator. Then she closed her eyes and started to dance, lifting and turning the cloth in her hands like angel wings, rippling it in the light, making it move like running water. Even in that constricted space it was a poem in movement.

I clapped my hands.

Miss Abigail chuckled. 'Sweet Tesserina has caught my idea. She has caught my idea before I have said a thing.'

She had said more than once that Tesserina needed her own fixed spot in the show. Only then would she be secure. One week she negotiated for her a little houri dance, which Tesserina performed in the background as Mr Merriman demonstrated some Egyptian magic. But the comedian did not really care for this. He could be very sour for a man whose job was to make his audience laugh. He'd come not to like Tesserina and me once he'd learned that his pinching our bottoms secured him no attention at all. I tell a lie. He did get attention one day from Tesserina. She boxed his ears. At least that made Miss Abigail and Mr Barrington laugh, although there was no more houri dancing.

Anyway, now at last, in our garret, Tesserina flopped down on to a stool, the pleated fabric in swirling pools around her.

Miss Abigail reached into her battered carpet bag and pulled out a folder, which she opened to show us photographs cut out of newspapers and magazines. The images showed this American performer called Loie Fuller, who wore vast gowns of this same pleated material, whirling it into fantastic patterns around her head with the aid of sticks to manipulate the yards of cloth. The way the camera portrayed the great arcs of silk as they caught the light was nothing less than a miracle.

'Like painting with cloth,' said Miss Abigail reverently. 'Loie Fuller is a true artist.'

Tesserina rummaged through the images and then chose some to examine one by one, holding them close to her face so that she could see them clearly. Then she took Miss Abigail's face in her hands and nodded. Carefully she stepped out of the material and vanished into our bedroom. In a second she was back with two wooden coat hangers. She stepped back into the pool of material and arranged the fabric along her arms, extended by the coat hangers. In a few powerful gestures in that tiny space she mimicked some of the dramatic shapes and swirls that we'd just been looking at in the photographs.

Miss Abigail gave a deep sigh of satisfaction and put her hand on mine. 'Now then, Pippa, it's your job and it's my job to sew this wondrous dress. Mr Barrington will find us sticks that will suit for extensions. Then Tesserina will have her place in Palmer's Varieties. Have no fear about that. She's safe now.'

'But what about the dance, Miss Abigail? What about the music? I still can't quite see how this will work.'

'I have it in hand. Tesserina is to try out. We've an appointment with Mrs Palmer at nine o'clock in the morning when the others are tucked up safely in their beds. We'll meet her there in the theatre. Hermione Palmer's a funny old stick but she didn't always pound away at those music-hall favourites, you know. She was playing in a classical quartet when Mr Palmer met her. Me, I can't see what the attraction was between those two.' Miss Abigail rooted around again in her bag. 'I have some music here. Chopin. She'll be familiar with it, I think.'

Tesserina wasn't listening to her. She was running the fabric through her hands, playing with it as though it were a magic fluid substance.

'So Mrs Palmer would really play for Tesserina?' I said.

'Ha! We'll know that by ten o'clock tomorrow! Perhaps we can tempt her. Perhaps Mrs Palmer is ready for a new adventure.' Miss Abigail pushed the dog-eared music sheets back in her bag. 'Now then, Pippa, you disentangle Tesserina from that stuff and get her to bed. You and me must stay up and burn the midnight oil and tack this dress together — just a temporary measure, so Tesserina can show off at her best and inspire Mrs Palmer to play her finest. Then we can get Mr Palmer to take Tesserina on proper and give her a wage. Then our sweet Tesserina really will be safe.'

Dancer of the Spheres

After I discovered just what the words meant I concurred with Miss Abigail when she said Mrs Hermione Palmer was 'a funny old stick'. AJ's wife was a strange mixture: half dame of the theatre, half small-town lady. Only an Englishwoman could be such a mixture. As well as pounding the piano for the troupe and leading the scratch orchestras provided for us at each place where we performed, she kept the Palmer's Varieties accounts and did the bookings for her husband, all the while making it seem that he was the master of all. On the Palmer letterhead she was the 'business and financial director' but in public she was careful to defer to him. Hermione Palmer was coolly steadfast for her husband even though she relished any attention from the colourful men who inevitably came her way. Look at the Italian tenor whom she threw off with such chill disdain! Didn't he go off with tears in his eyes?

The morning after we arrived in Bishop Auckland we entered the dusty theatre lobby and came upon a gaggle of men with stringy ties and a woman with meaty arms. They were lounging around smoking cigarettes, their violin and cello cases leaning against walls and chairs. No doubt this was the theatre orchestra waiting to go through their paces for Mrs Palmer. The heavy-armed woman was probably the pianist. If that were so, she was in for a hard time, as Mrs Palmer (no mean pianist herself), was always fiendishly hard on any resident pianist she came across. It was a matter of honour.

We made our way into the auditorium to find Mrs Palmer herself in the orchestra pit, standing at the piano, testing its tone. Even from the back of the stalls we could hear her '*Tchch! Tchch!*' as an ill-tuned note made her cringe. She was wearing a calf-length afternoon gown and full stage make-up. Her habit of parading in the streets like this tended to draw strange looks. But here in the theatre she always appeared the most consummate professional of us all. This impression was modified today by the black-rimmed spectacles she was using to peer into the belly of the grand piano. She never wore her spectacles in performance as (it was said) she had an almost perfect musical memory. But she did use her spectacles at other times, to 'give my eyes a bit of a rest'.

When she caught sight of us she stood up straight, pulled down her lace sleeves and looked enquiringly at Miss Abigail. From the very first time I met her I'd observed a strange contradiction in Mrs Palmer's attitude to my friend. On the one hand she often condescended to her, treating her as a menial, a mere wardrobe mistress. On the other hand from time to time she showed Miss Abigail wary, even fulsome respect. Her wardrobe mistress's reputation as an artiste in the early days was no secret and *she* had worked with people in the business who themselves would condescend to Mrs Palmer.

This seemed like one of the latter occasions. She was smiling sweetly at Miss Abigail. 'Abigail, this old thing is a monster, almost unplayable. However, Mr Jefferson has very kindly promised to hire a Steinway for me from Brotherton's, a music shop here in this town. They are musicians themselves, so at least they'll supply a good instrument.' Mrs Palmer sniffed. 'So, what's this surprise, Abigail? You have music for me?'

Miss Abigail pulled the music sheets from her bag and handed them over. Mrs Palmer riffled through them. Then she smiled, showing all her teeth (crooked, but her own). 'The Chopin? I know it well. Played it at the conservatoire as a test piece.' She turned to me. 'You know the Paris conservatoire, Pippa?'

We all knew.

Miss Abigail nodded. 'Of course. So you have said. I know you're really busy, Mrs Palmer, but I wondered whether you'd be good enough to play this now for Tesserina? Try her out. She's been experimenting with a new dance, a special kind of movement. She's making good progress but I thought it was only with you at the piano she could work on it properly, could perfect it.'

Mrs Palmer looked down at the music. 'Dancing? I don't think—'

'She's very promising, Mrs Palmer,' said Miss Abigail firmly. 'Original. Could be just the fresh touch the Varieties need. Something different. We need something to stop us going stale. Aren't you always saying that?'

Mrs Palmer had never said this, but the softening of her painted face showed that she thought perhaps she had.

Miss Abigail turned to me. 'Pippa, my darling! Go with Tesserina and help her into that gown. And do find a man to draw back the curtain. Our dancer will need space!'

The tentative tinkle of the piano followed us as we went backstage to 'find a man', and a dressing room so that I could get Tesserina into her voluminous gown. The man I found (slippers and braces, collar studs showing) said he was the stage manager and it was very early in the day for any of us to be about and he was just going to have his cup of tea. However, he thought it would be no problem at all to open the tabs for Mrs Palmer and he was happy to point us in the direction of the dressing rooms.

In the dressing room (a bit damp and flaky and smelling of old port, cats and peeled-off greasepaint: not as glamorous as the front of house . . .) Tesserina removed her hat, stripped down to her cotton shift, pulled the ribbons from her long hair and ran her fingers through it so that it floated around her head like a massive halo. She stood quietly while I climbed on to a stool and dropped the wondrous gown over her head. Of course, the enormous sleeves fell right to the floor. She moved this way and that before the mirror and smiled quietly at her reflection as the fabric rippled in the dim interior light.

You might think my friend was strangely placid, letting us do all this business about her. In the weeks she'd been with us I'd got used to her stillness even though it made me uneasy. She seemed mute but could speak: I remember the way she first thanked me when I rescued her. She might seem mad, but I no longer thought her so. I was haunted by this feeling that she was waiting. Clearly her queer stillness must have come from that shadowy time before she joined us. Now it seemed the shadows were lifting and I had the sense that she was nearer the point where she would retrieve her old self like a woman putting on a familiar dress. Then she would speak.

There was something alike between Tesserina and me. Here was I, trying to find a new self, and there was she, trying to find an old one. So there was a kind of balance between us and that's why we could still be friends, although she did not speak.

In the damp dressing room I showed Tesserina how Miss Abigail and I had cunningly attached the coat hangers to the sleeves so that she could hold them out to the side to take up the weight of the fabric and elongate her arms. She lifted them up and we wound the extra fabric around them until we got to the stage. Then I took up the excess fabric at the back of the dress so we could make our way down the narrow corridor and up the flight of steps towards the stage. The stage manager in his shirtsleeves stopped sweeping to watch us make our royal progress. He began to whistle 'It's a Long Way to Tipperary' under his breath.

In the auditorium Mrs Palmer's rippling chords were rising to the high, elaborately painted ceiling. She kept playing as I escorted Tesserina to the centre of the stage. Then the notes faded away as Tesserina held out her arms and I started to space the fabric along her arms and the coat hangers, and spread it in a great pool on the stage floor at her feet. She and her dress seemed to fill the stage.

'Well, I never!' said Mrs Palmer. 'How very strange.'

Miss Abigail climbed up the steps on to the stage with some difficulty, then went to stand before Tesserina. She pointed at Mrs Palmer and mimed the piano playing, then she held out her own arms wide and started to move from the waist only, demonstrating a ghost of the grace that must have brought her applause in her earlier years. Tesserina nodded vigorously. Of course she knew what to do. Miss Abigail clambered back down the steps to stand at Mrs

Palmer's shoulder. 'Start when you will, Mrs Palmer,' she said. 'Tesserina will follow.'

Mrs Palmer started to play, softly at first, then louder, anticipating the rhythms and the mounting dramas of the music. Tesserina raised her extended arms to lift the fabric which, though very light, still had some weight because of its sheer volume. She held up her head and closed her eyes, just as she had in the street when I first saw her. Then she began to move just as she had on that first day. This time, though, it was not necessary for the movement to come from some wild music in her head. Today she had Mrs Palmer's accomplished playing and the powerful measures of Chopin to guide her dance. Soon the rippling notes from the piano were mirrored in the rise and fall of the fabric in Tesserina's hands: the sinewy notes of the darker passages were reflected in the occasional drooped head, the sensual thrust of Tesserina's body, which punctuated the shimmering movement. The dance was very free, entirely improvised in response to the liquid urgency of the notes. When the music quickened to its climax, Tesserina's movements quickened. The easy flow of fabric became a blur. Then, when the music finally slowed, she paused and the silken pleats slowed to a shimmer, and finally settled on the floor as Mrs Palmer quietly fingered the last chord.

I was so happy that there were tears in my eyes.

From the back of the hall came shouts and applause. I turned to see the musicians making their way down the aisle. The woman pianist at the back of the line called, '*Brava!*'

Mrs Palmer was nodding, her rouged cheeks taking on a deeper hue. 'Very fresh! I have never seen anything like it. I am driven to agree with you, Abigail. I shall speak to AJ about her. Of course I'd have to play for her myself. One wouldn't want a ham-fisted provincial tackling this music.' She looked blandly into the eyes of the heavy-armed woman who was just level with her. 'Would we?'

'Pippa, darling!' Miss Abigail said sharply. 'Go and see to Tesserina!'

My friend was still standing there in the centre of the stage, her arms quite still by her sides. But her eyes were open and alive and she didn't have the dazed lunatic-look she'd had on that first day.

I kissed her on the cheek. 'That was wonderful, Tesserina, a fine poem in movement! See! Mrs Palmer loved to play for you.'

Tesserina held up her arms so I could rewind the fabric around the coat hangers. She looked down at me, the glimmer of a smile in her eyes.

In the end Tesserina went on the programme at Number Six as 'Miss Tesserina – Dancer of the Spheres'. Mrs Palmer thought up the name and was very pleased with herself. AJ made a fuss about changing the programmes but Mr Jefferson said, if Mr Palmer would foot the bill, he would harass the printer to make him a new programme in time for tonight's performance.

Miss Abigail and I were very pleased with ourselves. With Mrs Palmer as her *patronne*, Tesserina was indeed safe.

Zambra's

After the rehearsal, Tesserina, Miss Abigail and I came out of the theatre blinking like owls in the light of day. We were buzzing with extra energy, drunk on the heady delight in Tesserina's success with Mrs Palmer. We were pleased with ourselves, but didn't quite know what to do to deal with that pleasure.

We looked up and down the wide main street, which was thronging with traffic. As far as the eye could see, people in pairs and clusters were going about the business of a working day. The canopies were drawn down over the shops and vehicles from donkey carts to charabancs were making their way up and down the street. The sun was shining, breaking the edge of the cold. I pointed out the sharp shadow that ran down the centre of the street.

'An odd thing,' Miss Abigail nodded. 'I told you it was a Roman road,' she whispered. 'North–south. So one side of the road is east, the other side west.'

Directly across from the theatre was a double-fronted café with the name *Zambra* etched in gold on the window above a deep frill of white lace.

'We should celebrate,' I said. 'In the café?'

Miss Abigail nodded vigorously. 'Sustenance! We need sustenance after our labours!' She led the way across the road, nearly colliding with an immaculate horse-drawn van with the legend 'Bishop Auckland Co-operative Society' painted in black letters on its side. The driver, who'd been forced to pull in his horses too quickly, watched us process across the wide street. He removed his pipe from the corner of his mouth. 'Theatricals, are yeh? Shoulda known!' he shouted.

Only four of the ten tables that crowded the café were occupied. Miss Abigail led us to an empty table by the window. I looked around to find some space on the floor for the bulky parcel that contained Tesserina's costume.

'I will take it, *signorina*.' The bag was removed from my hands by a narrow-faced, white-aproned man. The hands that grasped the bag were long-fingered and lithe. He placed my bag behind the counter and came back with a small notebook. His large brown eyes slid across to Tesserina, magnificent again in her ribbons, then he addressed Miss Abigail. '*Signora?* You would like coffee?'

She put her head on one side. 'I had thought tea?'

He smiled down at her. 'We have all the wonderful English teas, *signora*, and I will serve any one of them to you. But you are from the theatre? Eh?' The waiter looked at us again, from one to the other. I noticed he had very thick, very fair eyelashes. He seemed quite old. Perhaps even thirty.

'That's so,' said Miss Abigail, very composed. 'We are at the theatre for this week.'

'Well, *signora*, the theatre people always love our coffee. They are wild for it. They have even been known to drink it instead of whisky. Perhaps you will love it too?'

Miss Abigail laughed – quite coquettishly for her – and

waved her hand. 'Go on then, *signor*. We'll try your precious coffee.' She looked up at him. 'This will be your café, *signor*? It's new in this town, I think. I was here two years ago and—'

He shook his head mournfully. 'Alas, not mine, *signora*. It is the café of my friend Joe Zambra, who comes from Newcastle. Old Mr Zambra, his uncle, who was a watchmaker in that city, acquired this café from a fellow countryman last year. My own family has ice-cream parlours in that city and I came here to show old Mr Zambra the tricks of the trade, as he no longer had the hands for the making of the watches. Then, alas, he died and now my friend Joe Zambra is the patron. The story told!' The waiter bowed slightly from the waist. 'Now I will make you the best coffee in the North of England!'

He bustled away just as the ornate clock on the wall struck twelve. At that moment, as if obeying a rallying call, the café began to fill up with all manner of people, from men in clerkish clothes to men wearing workmen's gear. So after the waiter had delivered our coffee with a flourish, he was lost to us, being very busy serving people, shouting in Italian to the woman behind the counter, who conveyed his instructions, also in Italian, to someone behind a hatch at the back.

Tesserina, sitting beside me, started to hum under her breath. I glanced at her and she stopped.

The coffee was indeed wonderful, lighter and frothier than the sour ink they serve in France and much more palatable. When we had drunk it and were ready to go, the thickset woman behind the counter took our payment, Abigail retrieved the costume, and we squeezed between the crowded tables to the door, passing our waiter, who was busy charming a group of men in serge suits at the corner table.

'Right, ladies!' said Miss Abigail. 'Two o'clock band call, so we have an hour to put our feet up before then.' With her injured legs it was *she* who needed a rest rather than we. But we went along with her suggestion. She had this way about her that made you do as you were told.

As we made our way down the high street I noticed that despite their decorative frontages, some of the shops were dark and understocked. Others were closed.

Miss Abigail, dragging along a bit with her arm through mine, caught my thought. 'Not so grand, is it? These are hard times and getting harder for the people around here. You should have seen this street before the war! Quite elegant. Like bits of Bond Street, in places.' She sighed. 'Now it's not quite the "land fit for heroes" our boys were promised.'

Almost laughably on cue we came upon a man playing the mouth organ. He was wearing soiled battledress with one empty sleeve pinned back to the shoulder. The tune was the same as the backstage man had whistled – 'It's a Long Way to Tipperary'. I'd seen such men in Paris on many street corners, although, of course, the uniform was different. My *maman* used to say, 'Everywhere visions of ridiculous sacrifice!' And then she would cry uncontrollably. Sometimes the singer Lily Lambert, with her tendency to tears, reminded me of my mother.

Miss Abigail dropped a whole sixpence in the man's army cap. He nodded his thanks, although he kept on with his vigorous playing of the mouth organ. He didn't miss a beat.

At least Miss Abigail didn't cry.

Rehearsal

This afternoon at rehearsal the meticulous AJ puts us through our paces. He leaves nothing to chance. He tells me I must watch my deportment, even in the simple business of the placing of the number boards for each act.

'Every single element, *mam'selle*,' he booms, 'is an expression of Palmer's Varieties. The parts make the whole! If someone even in your lowly position is unkempt or in disarray then this is what our audience will remember. They will talk about it in the bars and taverns of this town.'

In this theatre, as always, AJ and Mrs Palmer share the star dressing room, and as usual Mrs Palmer adorns it with shawls and lamps, a poster of AJ as Hamlet, and old first-night telegrams, to make her feel at home. Her first task always is to set out their make-up boxes – hers in fitted mahogany and his in figured leather – side by side beneath the mirror: his on the left, hers on the right.

As usual Tom Merriman has the next most important dressing room. People avoid sharing with him because of his bad temper, and drinking habits that can render him violent.

In two nights his room will be virtually uninhabitable, littered with tubes of greasepaint tipped out of their tin box, muddled up on his dressing shelf with empty glasses and bottles and half-eaten food.

On this tour Madame Bunce gets the next dressing room, which in fact is so small that she makes the Pixies sit cross-legged on the floor once she has got their make-up right. Then come the Divines, who, like Merriman, could be so unpleasant at close quarters that no one would share with them. The rest of us share the last two rooms – men in one, women in the other – quite amicably. The costumes are sorted in the wardrobe, where there is just room for Miss Abigail, but she usually stations herself with the women and sews where the light is best.

I've become very accustomed to the order of the Palmer's Varieties programme. Tom Merriman (who is billed as 'the Stitch' as, it is said in English, 'He has you in stitches'), is Number One. He gets the audience comfortable and chuckling in their seats. (He comes back later in the programme as a Spaniard who, no matter how hard he tries, can't complete a Spanish dance.) Then comes Cissie Barnard, at her best an accomplished *seriocomique*, with a heartfelt monologue telling the tale of a mother's mourning for her son who has lied about his age to volunteer on the first day of war and dies on the day of Armistice. (She'll come back later with a rousing, very naughty version of 'Little Miss Muffet'.) We are always grateful if she turns up sober and completes her act without removing any item of clothing. The thing is, if she manages this she is wonderful and very popular, and can evoke sadness or happiness in the audience at the click of her fingers.

After Cissie, to gladden our hearts comes Lily Lambert

(the Somerset Song Thrush) singing the chirpy song called 'So her Sister Says!'. You could never tell from her jolly demeanour that each day she cries a bucket of tears.

Then comes AJ with one of his theatrical extracts. He does this in front of the tabs to give Mr Barrington and the theatre's own stage manager time to lower to sight level the high wire for Roy, Blaze and Marie, the Three Divines, so they can go through their breathtaking routine. For me this is the highlight of the show. Even in rehearsal it brings gasps of fear and the relief of great applause from whoever happens to be there. The Divines are truly golden people – tall and muscular and unashamed of their bodies in a way that, according to Miss Abigail, has brought police and press attention to the Varieties more than once. Mr Palmer is always full of apologies and reassurances with whichever policeman is sent to enquire, but is well aware that such attention always fills the house the next day.

The thing that causes the problem with the police is not their teetering and tumbling (Number Four: *The Three Divines: High Wire Frolics*). It is their artistic poses (Number Seven: *The Divine Glories of Greece*).

For this item the stage is dressed with three giant gilded picture frames, made specially by Mr Barrington and occasionally regilded by him with my help. The frames are veiled by a golden curtain and seven layers of gauze. These are lifted, one by one, to leave a single tantalising filmy gauze pulled taut to reveal the still figures of Roy, Blaze and Marie, apparently naked, in classic Greek poses. At this point the audience always lets out a soft *a-ah* of appreciation, except for an occasional malcontent, who walks out, or who throws the odd cabbage or carrot on the stage. During the act the golden curtain and the seven layers of gauze are lifted five times, so giving five new revelations of the art of naked posing for the delectation of the public.

Of course, from backstage you can see that the Divines are not entirely naked. But you can't deny how very beautiful their bodies are: muscular and soft at the same time, shining with the gold lacquer that they paint on themselves. Roy, the least standoffish of the Divines, usually pinches my cheek as they come off stage. He is always very kind to me.

This first rehearsal is merely about the mechanism of the veils. The Three Divines just sketch their poses dressed in their acrobatic uniform of tights and waistcoat, with Marie in her more modest wraparound skirt. This is all done in a very matter-of-fact manner, as though they're rather bored with the necessity of going through these motions. But, like all good performers, they are meticulous in their attention to detail and make what they do look effortless.

At the end there is a buzz of interest as most of the company gather to assess the new acts. This is the convention at Palmer's. The company can be cruel judges. Roy Divine does not join his brother and sister in the stalls, but lingers to the side of the stage, along with me and Mr Barrington.

First we have our introduction to Madame Sophia Bunce's Dancing Pixies. With wide smiles enamelled on their faces, these little girls are like painted dolls, jerky and cute and as well drilled as any army platoon. The fact that Madame Bunce stands ramrod straight at the side of the stage with a major's cane under her arm, might have something to do with their military efficiency. The night before, Miss Abigail explained to me that the English have a taste for these painted children. She herself started out as one. 'It's very hard, darling. I wouldn't recommend it,' she said, a look of distaste on her face.

How hard it can be is illustrated by the scene in the wings

when they come off, when Madame Sophia Bunce uses her major's cane to tap the legs of the Pixie who stumbled during their second number. The child's eyes fill with tears and her pointed hat falls off. 'Do that again, Molloy, and you'll get a good strapping.'

'No need for that, Madame Bunce,' says Roy Divine, standing beside me in the wings, looking on. 'The kid tried her best?' There is always a kind of questioning lilt in his voice.

She freezes him with a glance and sweeps the child away.

Tesserina is next to try her act. After her will come the mesmerist, Stan Slater, whose stage name is apparently Stefane.

Behind the closed curtain I make sure Tesserina is centre stage with her dress properly spread out in her starting position. Through the spy-hole in the curtain I can see Mrs Palmer as she sits down at the piano with a flourish and spreads out the music on the stand before her. Then she lifts her chin – our signal for the opening of the tabs. They swish aside to show Tesserina in her rippling dress, illuminated by the single spotlight set up by Mr Barrington.

I scuttle to the side of the stage and stand beside Roy Divine, who nods and smiles at me.

Then the space is filled with sound as Mrs Palmer appears to draw streams of notes from the piano with her fingers. Tesserina lifts her enormous sleeves and begins to turn and move in response to the music. The single rehearsal light shines on her pale unpainted face and picks up threads of gold in her fair hair. Pianist and dancer work together: sometimes Mrs Palmer leads Tesserina's movement, sometimes she follows it. Between them they evoke pure emotion, welding movement with music, music with movement. At times the outline of her body is clear within the rippling fabric; at times her body is lost in a swirl of pleated silk. My cheeks are hot and Roy is gripping my shoulders. Tesserina's performance has something of eternity about it even though it lasts only seven or eight minutes.

The movement, then the music, come to an end. After a moment of silence the theatre prickles with cheers and enthusiastic applause from the company. Some people even stamp their feet. I can see Miss Abigail beaming. Mrs Palmer sits back, smiling and bowing from the waist, acknowledging the applause as though she had performed the dance as well as played the piano. Tesserina has her head up and is smiling faintly. I clap till my hands are sore. Roy Divine puts his arm round me and hugs me. He smells faintly of carbolic soap. 'Great work, Pippa. You and your friend Miss Wharton have done a good job there.'

The curtains close and I pull myself from his grasp to go to help Tesserina with her dress. 'They loved you, Tesserina. You were wonderful. You have your place. Did you see Mr Palmer's face? He was nodding, even smiling.'

She stands quite still while I wind the sleeves round the coat hangers. When I've done this and gathered the back of her dress over my arm she leans sideways to put her cheek against mine, her eyes very bright. She has enjoyed the applause. I know it.

How I wish she could talk to me properly, tell me about herself. She is still a mystery to me, the way she only ever lives in the present moment. And it's quite clear she doesn't want to talk to anyone, in her own language or anyone else's. Not even me. Not yet.

The Mesmerist

I don't know what the man called Slater thought of the comradely explosion of applause that followed Tesserina's dance, but when the curtains pulled back to reveal the mesmerist on the stage, he looked a different man. For one thing, with his opera hat and cloak, his tail coat and high black boots, he looked a foot taller. Stage make-up gave colour to his pale face, and kohl outlines sharpened his eyes to a penetrating steel blue.

He removed his hat and cloak with a flourish and laid them on a chair before bowing in response to the polite patter of applause from the company. Then he opened his arms wide as if to embrace us all. 'Ladies and gentlemen!' The voice that resonated through the nearly empty theatre was just as powerful as Mr Palmer's, but had a softer, more insinuating tone that made you lean forward and listen.

'In recent years,' he said, 'science has shown to us the deep mysteries of the mind! In order to grasp this, ladies and gentlemen, you must imagine the mind as a universe. Imagine the sky above you on a clear, cloudless night and observe the

87

millions of stars! I am here today to tell you that the human mind is no less filled with the brightest of mysteries! A million thoughts, desires, memories and fears.' He took a step forward and his voice dropped to an intimate, although no less resonant tone. 'I am here to show you those mysteries. My own science, ladies and gentlemen, the science of mesmerism, can give you access to those mysteries.'

An expectant pause. Slater looked down at Mr Palmer and changed to his everyday voice, which was rather nasal in tone. 'At this point, sir, I'll pick people from the audience and tell them some of their own deepest secrets, their own inner concerns.'

Mr Palmer removed the cigar from his mouth. 'And you can do this thing, Slater? I've heard of it but can't say I've ever seen it, if I'm to be honest.'

The mesmerist nodded. 'Oh, yes, Mr Palmer, I *can* do it! As I have told you here, it's a matter of science. This first stage – when you are getting an audience's confidence – is merely a matter of understanding the principle of universals. As well as this you need to know the secret of how people reveal their own truths through their bodies.' He looked round at the company, gathered in the first three rows of the stalls. 'Unfortunately this is only demonstrable with a proper audience, who have come open-minded to this experience. At these times the audience adds its own energy to mine. It gives me great insight. This is what makes the magic.'

A murmur of disappointment stirred through the company. AJ flourished his cigar, dispersing smoke far and wide. 'We might understand this, of course, Slater. But how, sir, are we supposed to believe in these . . . er . . . scientific powers? How do you expect me to put you on my stage without seeing some demonstration of these phenomena?'

'Well, Mr Palmer, perhaps I can give you a sample – a mere sample. For this I will need two volunteers for one demonstration which is amusing and enlivening, and a single volunteer for a further demonstration which is more of the mind.'

AJ turned round to scan the row behind him. For the first pair of 'volunteers' he selected Cameron Lake and Mr Harrap, the resident stage manager who whistled 'Tipperary'. Then, to my horror, Mr Palmer nodded at me. 'And you, young Pippa! You can be the third one.'

My blood froze but I could no more say 'No!' to Mr Palmer, than I could to Miss Abigail. So I hovered anxiously at the side of the stage while Slater proceeded with a demonstration on his first 'volunteers'. Roy Divine, still in his tights, stayed there beside me and looked on with keen interest.

Assuming his mellifluous stage voice once more, Slater called the two men to him and made them sit side by side in the centre of the stage. Then he moved to stand directly in front of each of them in turn and held his gaze, before gently placing his thumb right in the middle of that volunteer's forehead. Within a minute their heads sagged to one side and they were both fast asleep.

A slight murmur of appreciation rippled through the small audience. Slater turned to them. 'In a moment, ladies and gentlemen, I will wake our friends. But before then, into the universe of their minds, I shall place certain suggestions, proposals that will lie there dormant. But on specific triggers these suggestions will evoke certain responses. You will understand this is an experiment, a humorous illustration of the power of the mind.' He leaned down and whispered first in Mr Harrap's ear, then in Mr Lake's ear. Then he stood before each of them and snapped his finger and thumb – a loud *crack!* that resonated round the theatre.

The two men stirred, blinked and woke up. Mr Lake looked across at AJ and shrugged. I could see that he thought that nothing had happened to him. He made as though to stand up, but Mr Slater pushed him down again. 'You must sit quietly, gentlemen, so I may tell a story to this patient audience.'

The mesmerist then proceeded to tell us a story about how he had once been in London, walking by the Serpentine, enjoying the birdsong in the trees, when he saw a friend with a troublesome dog. How he then walked on and noticed the sunlight dancing on the water before he came upon two children fighting over an ice cream.

In the telling, pandemonium! When Slater mentioned 'birdsong', the two men started whistling and cavorting around the stage, flapping their arms, only stopping when Slater clicked his fingers. When he mentioned 'the dog', both men got down on all fours and barked and howled. He clicked his fingers again and they stopped. At the words 'sunlight dancing on the water', the two stiff, ungainly men started to dance, houri-like, running their hands up and down their well-clothed bodies as though they were naked. This time Slater was very quick to click his fingers. Then, at last, at the cue 'ice cream', these two grown men began to fight like infants over an illusory ice cream. At last Slater clicked his fingers twice and they calmed down and returned to their seats in the middle of the stage. The mesmerist made a great show of thanking them, and escorted them, rather bewildered at the continuing laughter, off the stage.

His demonstration was obviously a great success. Some members of the company were laughing so much they had to hold their sides. I looked across at Miss Abigail but she was clearly not quite so amused.

Then Slater made a sweeping gesture and the auditorium quietened down again. 'Ladies and gentlemen! I must have silence. I need great concentration for the next, perhaps more interesting, demonstration.'

I looked down at Miss Abigail and shook my head.

'Mr Palmer!' She tapped him on the shoulder. 'I expect Mr Slater's not going to make the child bark like a dog!'

Slater smiled calmly at her and at me. 'Be sure, dear lady, this is much more in the way of a scientific demonstration. No dogs will bark.'

'I expect not, Mr Slater.' Miss Abigail looked up at me and nodded reassuringly. Roy Divine squeezed my shoulder encouragingly. Mr Slater led me now to the centre of the stage and sat me in one of the two seats, removing the other with a flourish. He looked at me with those black-lined, steel-blue eyes. I noticed a bead of sweat on his upper lip. Then he put his thumb on my forehead. 'Miss Pippa . . .'

I am at the tall window of my mother's apartment. My mother is behind me, her chin resting on the top of my head. I can smell her special perfume of lemons and roses, I can feel the pressure of her slender fingers on my shoulders. We are peering down from the window at a man in uniform who is making his way, boots clattering, across the courtyard towards the archway into the Rue de la Tour and out of our lives. Before he vanishes he looks up at our window, doffs his army cap, and waves.

'Who is he, Maman? Who is that man?'

'Your father, Pippa.' Her voice is in my ear. 'Voilà ton papa!'

Now I'm angry with her. This man has just been here in our apartment. I heard his voice – just as I hear the voice of her other callers – from my perch in the little pantry. And, as with them, I ignored the voice, too keen to read another of my English novels.

Suddenly I wrest myself from my mother's grip, turn and punch her in the stomach, then run out of the apartment down the stone steps after this man. I run the length of the street to catch up with him. I touch his arm. 'Papa . . .' He turns round, but it is not him: the face is wrong. 'Je m'excuse . . .' I run on. Another man in khaki with big boots. This one turns. 'Papa . . .' Again it's the wrong face. Now the street is full of men in British khaki but not one of them has the right face. Not one. So I sit down there in the street and howl like a dog.

'Miss Pippa . . .' Slater's hand was gripping my shoulder. Roy Divine pushed him to one side and lifted me up from the floor. He stood me straight, brushing down my dress. His voice was low, earnest. 'It's all right, sweetheart. You're all right!'

I looked down into the auditorium. Miss Abigail was on her feet. The seat beside her, where Tesserina had been sitting, was empty. Miss Abigail rushed up the aisle towards me as fast as her poor legs could carry her. Mr and Mrs Palmer and the rest of them were looking up in some consternation. There was no merriment now, like that which greeted the awakening of the men who battled over the illusory ice cream.

Miss Abigail reached me at last, put her arm round me, pushing Roy Divine out of the way.

'What did I do?' I asked. 'Was it not funny?'

Miss Abigail cast a withering look at Slater. 'No, no, love. You did nothing wrong. It *might* have been funny but how would we know? It was all in a gale of French and you seemed very upset. It was very unpleasant.'

Mr Slater turned away to talk quickly to AJ. 'Of course, sir, this was just by way of a demonstration. And some chord was plucked in the child over which I had no control. It does show the impact of what I do, but in the normal turn of events, when I tell a subject to go back to being ten years old I have them do nursery rhymes, sing childish songs. The audience usually loves it.'

Mr Palmer stared at him a long few seconds, then shrugged. 'You certainly raised a reaction, Slater.' He turned round to survey the company, then looked down at his wife. 'We'll try them, Hermione. Pixies after Lily Lambert, Mr Slater will finish the first part and Miss Tesserina will begin the second. The audience will be the judge.' Even in my distress I remember thinking then that it must be nice to know that your word is law.

Then Miss Abigail led me away to make me some cocoa in her slip of a room by the wardrobe. I could feel anger in the way she gripped my hand, but I knew the anger wasn't directed against me.

Responsibility

Abigail was thinking that she shouldn't have trusted young Pippa to that Slater fellow. She'd seen such people before – mesmerists, illusionists, tricksters. Of course, audiences liked them, turned out in droves to see them. After all, each Sunday didn't they turn out in droves to see wine being turned into blood, bread to flesh? Why should they not believe that a man is transformed into a dog or his ten-year-old self? She knew that many of these people were charlatans little removed from fairground tricksters and fortune-tellers. But she also knew, she could not deny, that some of them had a certain skill, a flair, and this Slater might just be one of them.

She had once seen a woman conjure a whole figure out of thin air. At the time she was certain it was a true thing – that it truly happened – but later reckoned it was some kind of trickery.

Of course, the world was full of trickery. Didn't they in the theatre trade on illusion, the suspension of disbelief? Flounces and glitter in front of the footlights. Faces painted to mimic youth and people made to fly on wings above the gods. And

94

as a reward for this trade in illusion, didn't commonplace men and women, made rich by adulation, drive round in sleek motor cars and carriages, entertain kings and princes, and drink champagne for breakfast before going home to grand houses in town?

Of course, there was the darker side to the illusion: innocent children like the Pixies, drilled to perform, who lost their childhood in hard work, their innocence corrupted by a life without boundaries; comics dead twenty years before their time from overwork and whisky by the gallon; beauty drowned in champagne and gin, falling into prostitution.

She often wondered why they all tolerated it. But she knew it was made tolerable by things that were not illusions, things that had truth in them: moments like today when the company saw Tesserina perform and applauded and stamped. There was no greater feeling than that warmth, that feeling of community between the performer and her diverse audience. Mr Jefferson had it painted on the proscenium arch. 'One touch of nature makes the whole world kin.' That was no illusion. That was the essence of theatre.

But today Abigail's delighted recognition of Tesserina as a creator of this genuine magic was marred by this débâcle with Pippa. Slater must have touched a chord in the child that made her a different, unhappy creature, screaming and struggling like some small trapped animal. Abigail had not been able to get to her fast enough. The girl was obviously very shaken. As she clambered up those steps to her, Abigail had been angry with herself that she'd failed in her private vow to look after Pippa and protect her as no one had protected Abigail herself. Somehow in doing this for Pippa she was showing kindness to the child she herself had been: a child who had gone on from a carelessly cruel Madame

Corrigan, numbly to endure rough treatment from Denis Wanless until Dina Brooks brought her to her senses, and made her realise she need not suffer in this way.

But Pippa was hard to protect. On the one hand she was quick, cheerful, willing, good with a needle even though not so good on stage. Josiah Barrington thought the world of her and that meant something. On the other hand there was this whole world inside her that no one really knew about. She was secretive and did not always tell the truth. Take the language. Her English was quaint when Abigail found her, but was damn near perfect now. But what had happened to all that French inside her? And those stories about her mother – there was more than one version – rang strange, like a cracked glass when you flicked it with your fingernail. Strange also that now the girl was here in England, there was no talk of any search for her mother, nor yet her father who was, if one believed one version of the story, English.

Abigail had long decided that the best thing was just to let Pippa be, not to examine her like a magistrate to get the truth out of her. Nevertheless, this explosion of rage and fear today showed that Pippa was not content with herself, not as calm as she appeared on the surface. They would need to talk about it. Abigail was not quite sure how she would go about that. She'd never been one for unnecessary confidences, which could get you into deep trouble in the theatre. But she'd have to think of something.

So, what about this drama today? As well as Pippa, Slater's antics seemed to have upset Tesserina. As soon as he started the thing with Pippa, Tesserina had shot up from her chair like a rabbit out of a hole and had vanished, Abigail knew not where.

Despite her own poor French, Abigail knew Pippa had

been raving about her mother. Her '*maman*'. Mothers! On this trip north, Abigail had thought she might go and see her own mother up in Weardale. But, as always, as she got near her mother she felt disinclined. She and her mother had so little in common now. Her youngest brother was turning into a dour twin for her stepfather and the farmhouse was peculiarly haunted by her other two brothers, who had died in the war. The farm was not a pleasant place.

In any case, watching Madame Bunce in action brought to the surface her resentment against her mother for giving her up to the Corrigans for her 'apprenticeship'. How could she have done that? Selling her own daughter to such slavery? Look at those poor scraps now under Madame Bunce's lash. Abigail herself could never have done that to Pippa.

Abigail knew Pippa's mother, or her memory, was important to the girl, but she had not referred to her recently, certainly not since Tesserina had joined them. Abigail wondered whether, now that Pippa had found someone to nurture, her mother had faded somewhat in her mind. But she had shouted for her on the stage. And what was this outpouring about the father? Something had evoked those screams and the panic. What had happened to young Pippa? She was a deep one, that one. Troubled. Intelligent.

Not like Tesserina. Despite her strange life's journey, she was a simpler creature altogether, dumb or not dumb. No bad thing. Perhaps it made for a better dancer.

Escape

For Tesserina this was not like the last time she ran away. No men's clothes or cap this time. No looking behind for *gendarmes* or warders. No men in frock coats admonishing her. No sense of leaving evil behind her. But this man on the stage made little Pippa cry just as she herself had once cried at nightmares only found in waking sleep. It made Tesserina sad to see Pippa like this, especially after her own wonderful dance had pleased everyone so much. And Tesserina liked to please people; the doctors knew that and had, in the end, driven her away in their eagerness to use her.

She didn't run far. There across the road was Zambra's, where they made the wonderful coffee and spoke a proper language. The window glittered in the afternoon sun, asking her to come, to taste the coffee again and listen to the crystal-clear words. She waited for the traffic to pass, then ran across the road. She raced to the counter. The stocky woman stood there in a flowered apron. Tesserina caught her eye. She looked away. She caught her eye again. The woman frowned and lifted her cloth and fluttered it at her as though she were shooing chickens. She tried to attract the attention of the waiter. Clearly she thought she recognised some madness in Tesserina. That was no change. She was used to that.

Then Tesserina spoke. '*Signora? Possiamo parlare?*'

The woman's heavy shoulders relaxed. A smile blossomed in her lined face. '*Sì. Sì!*' she said in the language they shared. 'You have come here from home? From home?'

'*Sì.* I come from *home*. I need to speak. I am lost. I have been lost for a long time. I was here this morning. I came here with my friends from the theatre. I am a dancer,' she said proudly.

'*E! Aldo!*' she shouted loudly to the waiter. 'This one is from home. I take care of her.' She opened the counter flap. 'Come in! Come in! This is our home.' She pulled Tesserina through a door, then pushed her before her up a narrow staircase, through another door into a large room decorated at one end like any Italian salon. At the other end it was stacked to the ceiling with goods: piles and piles of stuff for the shop. In a chair in the corner lounged a boy in a white shirt, a newspaper in his hands.

'Here is Angelo, my son. Angelo Zambra,' said the woman. The boy stood up and bowed very slightly in Tesserina's direction.

She nodded her head in return. 'I am Tesserina,' she said. 'I am a dancer.'

Mrs Zambra sent Angelo down to get Tesserina some coffee. Then she sat Tesserina beside her in the window seat. She asked so many questions. Who was she? Where had she been? Where was she from, in their own country?

'I am lost in Paris, *signora*. Then I am saved by a little girl called Pippa, who is my great friend. I come from a village on the shores of the lake. There are boats that ply between the shores and the islands. And castles on the water.'

The woman shook her head and said she was from the South and didn't know this great lake in the North of their country.

Tesserina's voice felt rusty, but the warm tones of this stocky woman unlocked her tongue at last. 'In my village the sun makes the water sparkle in the morning, *signora*. Baveno – do you know it? The mountain looms out of the mist on the opposite shore. The boats pass, taking people right into Switzerland. People from the cities come to my village to rest and refresh themselves. I used to dance for these visitors in the square each night, for pennies, just as the light was fading. Then a dance master came and bought me from my father with gold coins, so I could go and dance for him in the city.' Her voice faltered. She could not say the rest. She'd come to the end of the beginning of her story. That was enough for now. If she told this respectable woman what had happened next she might push her away from her like spoiled meat. 'Many bad things happened,' she sighed. 'I forgot how to speak because I could understand no one around me. They spoke with the prattle of parrots. Then I was saved by Pippa and her friend and they spoke kindly to me. But still I could not speak. Then this morning in the café I heard Aldo and you, and my tongue ached in my mouth.' She beamed. 'So I came back!'

The boy came back with a tray. He was followed by an older man in a chef's apron. This one was fierce-faced, much darker than the waiter. The man's eyes were deeper set and lighter than the boy's. He reminded Tesserina of the baker in Baveno. Her heart lurched and she clutched her throat to save herself from choking.

He looked down at her. 'You are from the theatre?' he said. 'Aldo tells me you're from the theatre.'

Then willingly she began again to tell her story about being saved by Pippa in Paris, and taken in by Miss Abigail. She was eager to make this man like her. She told him about the dance and the shining dress. And how much she loved to dance. 'I have become a dancer and this makes me happy,' she said.

'They pay you well?' said Mrs Zambra. She certainly sounded like a woman of business.

'There is no talk of pay, *signora*.'

'Slavery!' said Joe Zambra. 'No one should work except for money. All the rest is slavery.'

'To dance is to be free,' Tesserina defied him. 'I need no pay.'

They were all looking at her curiously. She'd been used to such bald curiosity from people at the hospital. But she couldn't tell them about the hospital. She couldn't tell Mrs Zambra about that. And she couldn't tell this man and this boy here. How far away they were from those learned men and the tough keepers at the hospital. The people in this room had the perfume of Italy about them: the smell of olives and kindness; the scent of the warm South. Even this boy Angelo had that sweet smell and he spoke their shared language with a foreign, guttural accent.

Tesserina smiled from one to the other so broadly that her jaw ached. Now the vice was off her head, the lock was off her tongue. At last she was in the dance, lifting the fine cloth to make stars and diamonds with the flow of the music. Inside her was the creak of change, like the noise an old door makes when it is finally opened.

Missing

As I crouched on the seat backstage, my head began to emerge from the fog of shouting and fear. 'What did I do? What happened to me?'

Miss Abigail patted my shoulder. 'Nothing, nothing, my darling. You must have fainted. So much excitement after that long journey.'

But I know I must have said – or shouted – something while I sat on that chair and looked into Mr Slater's eyes. Despite Miss Abigail's reassurances I know I must have done something strange or why did Mr Palmer and the others look shocked? Why were they so quiet? Why was Mr Slater mopping his brow with his handkerchief? I looked round. And where was Tesserina? Had I shouted at her?

Roy Divine was still hovering around. 'She'll be all right, Miss Abigail?' He seemed quite anxious. I was puzzled at his interest. I stared up at him, my brain still in a fog. Why was he still here when most of the company had left? Away from the others he always seemed a bit lost, cut off from a brother and sister who were inseparable in their own creepy fashion.

Those two always held hands, which is a bit strange for a brother and sister. It seemed to me that Roy was the odd one out. Though his body was as beautiful as theirs, his face was rather homely, with its slightly knobbly nose and curved cheeks. Roy lacked their chiselled bone structure, truly classical in its appeal. He was different. He might not have been their brother at all.

'Pippa, wake up!' came Miss Abigail's voice.

'Pippa?' Roy said now. 'You're all right?' Really, he seemed concerned, kind.

I must have been staring at him. 'I'm fine,' I said. I looked round the theatre. 'Where's Tesserina? She's run away. I know she's run away.'

'I'll help you,' said Roy eagerly.

Miss Abigail took charge. 'Not necessary, Roy dear. Tesserina, I think, was overwhelmed by her success with her dance. She will have gone back to our digs to have a rest. You can be sure of it.' She held out my coat and threaded my arms through the sleeves. 'We'll go straight back there too. No doubt Pippa here could also do with a rest after her travails.' She buttoned up my coat as though I were ten, not sixteen years old, then tied her own scarf round her neck. 'But thank you for your help, Roy. I'm sure Pippa is very grateful for it.'

On our way back to Waldron Street we looked anxiously into the busy shopping crowds but there was no sign of Tesserina. No sign of her at the house either.

'Not a hide nor hair of her, Abigail.' Mrs Jackson looked sharply across at me. 'Is there a problem?'

The image of Tesserina dancing madly in the backstreets of Paris rose before my eyes. Perhaps she was doing just that, in the backstreets of Bishop Auckland, causing her own kind of havoc.

Miss Abigail shook her head. 'No. Everything's fine. We just seem to have mislaid her somehow.'

I turned back towards the door. 'I'll go to find her.'

Miss Abigail made as though to come with me.

'No!' I said. 'You stay here.' I glanced at Mrs Jackson's earnest, painted face. 'She might panic if she comes back and you aren't here. She'll probably come back at any minute. And you'll need to be here.'

To my amazement Miss Abigail did as I suggested. For the first time since we met, it seemed she wasn't quite in charge. Perhaps she thought my search might take my mind off the afternoon's dramas. Perhaps she thought Tesserina was really my responsibility. Which she was, of course. Or perhaps I had puzzled her with whatever silly things I'd done under Slater's eye. It must have been strange for her, to let me have my own way so easily.

I walked up the long, busy high street in the sunshine up one side and in the shadow down the other, but there was no sign of Tesserina. I walked all around the marketplace and in the little street behind the town hall, but she wasn't there. I walked up a narrow road that led off from the market. This street was crowded with bustling people and raw with the smell of fresh beer and the rotting, gamey produce-smell of a nearby vegetable stall. Somewhere in the haze of my mind it seemed as though I'd done this before, walking, walking through streets looking for someone who wasn't there.

He's not here. So many soldiers' faces and not one of them is his. A gang of soldiers comes round the corner and one of them picks me up and throws me in the air. Then they all form a circle and throw me between them as though I am a ball. Their hands are grasping. One has a dagger in his belt and as he catches me it scrapes my thigh. I twist out of the grasping hands and run on through the streets back to my mother. She'll call me 'méchante' and smack my face, but I am sure I'll not tell her of this. None of it.

I don't know how I got there but I found myself in a warren of Bishop Auckland streets where barefoot children played, and men and woman hovered by their doors, talking to passers-by. On one corner I had to skirt around a fight between two men, watched by appreciative onlookers. This so much reminded me of the mob that pursued Tesserina that I had tears in my eyes.

Then, as though she had spoken to me, I knew where she was.

The café was crowded. I had to fight my way through the queue to get inside. The Three Divines were in the corner drinking coffee. Roy stood up and beckoned me towards him. 'Here, Pippa! Are you all right now? Come and join us. Have some of this wonderful coffee.'

I shook my head.

He came towards me. His sister and brother lifted their beautiful heads and watched with blank eyes.

'I can't. I'm still looking for Tesserina.' I looked around. 'Has she been in here?'

'Not while we've been here,' he said. He took my arm. 'Look, Pip, come and sit with us! You look all in.'

I shook off his hand. 'I'm all right.' I went to the counter. Roy drifted back to his seat.

'You're looking for your friend?' The waiter from this morning, passing with a full tray, paused in his onward rush. He grinned in a friendly fashion.

I looked round. 'Is she here?' I could see that she wasn't, of course.

'Not now. Not here. She's upstairs with my friend and his mother.' He lifted the counter flap and gestured me through. 'Through that door, past the first turn on the stairs and the door is in front of you.'

The stairs were scrubbed clean but uncarpeted, and the walls were painted with a dull green distemper. The staircase and landing were impregnated with the smells of coffee and spices.

I knocked on the door and, hearing a welcoming murmur, went in.

Tesserina was there all right. She was sitting on a long settle under the window, hand in hand with the stout little woman from behind the counter. On the other side of her sat a stocky handsome man in a chef's apron.

When she saw me Tesserina leaped to her feet and came towards me laughing and talking rapidly in what must be Italian. She gestured towards the pair on the settle and laughed. Talking! Tesserina!

I shook my head. 'I don't know what you're saying, Tesserina. I don't understand.' Then she turned back towards the others and they all started to talk together. The man laughed and glanced from her to me.

That was when I experienced just how Tesserina had felt when everyone around her talked incessantly in a language she couldn't understand. No wonder she had chosen not to speak. I was newly sorry for her and very sorry for myself.

'Shut up, will you? Can't you see the lass doesn't under-stand?' The voice came from a tall chair to my left that was out of my eyeline. The boy sitting in the chair was not much older than me. Nineteen, perhaps. He was wearing a snowy

106

white shirt, canvas trousers and had clean, bare feet. He had a head of riotously curly black hair and eyes the colour of the sea that had brought me here to England. He was quite the most beautiful creature I'd ever seen. My heart stopped at the sight of him.

But he was not looking at me. He was glaring at Joe Zambra, who must be his brother. 'You shouldn't jabber away like that. How would the lass know what you're saying?'

His voice wasn't like that of Aldo the waiter. It was much more like that of Mr Barrington, with that soft growl in the throat. A voice of these parts. I liked it from the first.

Joe Zambra, nearly as handsome as his younger brother, laughed again and stood up. 'This is so, Angelo. But isn't this what happened to Tesserina here? Struck dumb because she cannot understand.' His voice is much more like Aldo's. No mistaking the Italian undertones, the slightest of lisps. 'So you're the heroic Pippa! I thought you must be ten feet tall and have an angel's halo. You are Tesserina's rescuer! She tells me all about it.' He took my hand and bowed over it. 'I am honoured. I am Joe Zambra. This is my mother, Mrs Zambra. And that young cockerel,' he nodded at the boy in the chair, 'he is my young brother, Angelo. Get on your feet, *An-gel*.' He said *An-hell*.

The boy got up reluctantly and shook my hand, grasping it very hard with a hand that was not a cook's or a waiter's, but a horny workman's hand with black dirt in the quick of his fingers. Now I could look at him openly and relish his beauty.

'My little brother, Angelo,' supplied Joe, 'is too good to work with us lesser mortals in my mother's café, so he chooses to work in the entrance to Hades, shovelling coal to make some other person rich instead of adding to the fortunes of his own family.'

The boy pulled his hand away and looked at me. 'I've seen you before,' he growled. 'And her.' He nodded towards Tesserina. 'On the station. You looked at me and my friends like we was dirt. Bad enough doing an extra Saturday shift. But to be gawped at!'

The miners. The miners on the other platform. He was the shorter one who'd shaken his fist at me. I remembered the sea-grey eyes. At this moment they were very cold. I dragged my eyes away from him and looked again at the smiling Tesserina.

'Come on, Tesserina,' I urged. 'We must get back. Why did you run away? Miss Abigail is at Waldron Street. She's so worried about you.'

Joe Zambra began to translate, but I stopped him. 'She understands me well enough. She has for all the time we have been together.'

Still she turned to him and spoke very rapidly.

He looked at me. 'She says I must tell you that that thing that happened to you on the stage with the hypnotist happened to her in the hospital in Paris and was the start of many bad things for her. She begs that you will not let that man do it to you again.'

I shook my head. 'No fear of that.' I went over and took her arm. 'Come on!'

Very gently, with an adult kindness, she took her arm away from mine and turned back to kiss Mrs Zambra on both cheeks, and to shake Joe and Angelo by the hand, before coming back to take my arm. Then it was she who led me down the stairs, through the crowded café and out into the street.

I noticed Roy Divine, alone now at the corner table. He raised a hand but before I could respond, Tesserina had swept me out of the place.

As we swung our way back to Waldron Street, Tesserina was humming quietly to herself, the occasional Italian word slipping out. So, for me, nothing about today was right; nothing about her was really usual. Nothing at all. I felt she had gone from me.

Suddenly I had my father on my mind.

Into the Light

For Tesserina, listening to the streams of talk from Signora Zambra and Joe had been like coming into the light, into the bright sunlight of a true day. In this blackish town the sky was so very grey: grey with the smoke from the dark houses and grey with heavy sacks of cloud. But now she felt she could let her heart imagine that blue, that bright southern blue again.

In these years since she last saw that blue sky above Baveno, since she lost the language of her homeland and her will to speak, her body had been an unhealed bruise. She would wake up with an ache, and go to bed with a weary heart. Then, since Pippa saved her life and she came to be with Miss Abigail, her heart had become lighter. And today when she danced with the music, all was forgotten except the throb of the music coursing through her to her fingertips and toes.

And then she'd been dragged down again by the man with the eyes. Those sharp pale eyes. There had been another man, with eyes just like that, eyes like daggers. He was the one who had taken away her will and made her perform. It was he who made her refuse to speak. There was a nurse in that place in Paris, a Signorina Lessi, who knew Italian. It was she who wrote down what was going on in the mind of the mesmerised Tesserina, the words that tumbled from her. Then she translated for the doctors, while they wrote in their notebooks, their pens scratching.

Later, in the quiet of her cell, Signorina Lessi told Tesserina that in speaking as she did she had exposed her own shame, that no man would do the things she described to any girl so she must indeed be mad, with such an evil imagination. No wonder the poor man who had been her dance master had been driven to bring her to the asylum. What decent man could cope with such ravings? Signorina Lessi told Tesserina she was to speak no more. She told the girl this in private, with no one watching.

Mr Slater today had brought all this back, making her flee from the theatre. She had to get out of that closed space that brought to mind the theatre where the doctor made her an exhibition, where she danced the dramas of hysteria so desired by the learned and curious men who gathered there at the foot of the master. She would no longer speak for them but she had to dance. If she were a good girl and did this, then she earned her pretty ribbons and her silk dresses and her soft bed. This was the way she earned their trust, so that one day she could walk out of that place dressed as a man.

But the habit of silence had bitten deep. Even with Pippa and Miss Abigail, no words would form on Tesserina's tongue. Not French, not English, not even Italian. They understood her and she understood them, but words had never been part of it.

Not until now.

Opening Night

On that first night the theatre was only half full. I overheard the manager, Mr Jefferson, sigh again to AJ about the hard times in the district. What with the shortage of work and the imminent coal strike, no one had money for theatre tickets. The theatre barely covered its costs these days. Hardly worth opening, in his view.

But at least tonight there was a buzz in the crowd. They seemed to be prepared to have a good time and would give Palmer's Varieties every chance. I was pleased AJ had given me the role of what he called 'the number wallah'. My job was to put out the board announcing each act, beside an electric board with the numbers on it.

Not a very taxing task, but it gave me a good chance to get the sense of the audience, to feel their temper. I certainly looked good. Miss Abigail had dipped into her wardrobe and cut down a Robin Hood outfit for me to carry the boards on in style. Although my outfit was green rather than gold, it was not unlike what the Divines wore for their high-wire act. I liked wearing it, as well as – or especially – the distinctive stage make-up that went with it. Out there before the lights, with this disguise, I felt I could do anything. I was no longer the 'child' they were always calling me.

The best thing on that night's programme – Tesserina's dance – brought forth gasps of delight, small flurries of applause and an ovation at the end. The impact of the dance was so great that it bubbled over into the next act, creating a buzz of pleasure punctuated by shouts of laughter. The excitement and goodwill brought about by her performance made the theatre feel nearly full rather than half empty.

So the mood of the audience, when they settled down to enjoy the mesmerist, was benevolent. They gasped in appreciation when he made people in the audience stand up in a spotlight and told them things about themselves that their best friends didn't know, when he gave them messages from the dead. They howled with laughter when he hypnotised men into thinking they were dogs or parrots or bullfrogs.

From the wings I watched very closely as two women volunteered to come on to the stage together for the next demonstration. Once they had sagged lifelessly in their chairs under his influence, he told them they were now ten years old. They were at a school concert and they must say their poetry for the school, including the headmaster, who was very strict and would smack them very soundly if they got their verses wrong.

They then proceeded to lisp – some verses singly and some in unison – Wordsworth's poem about daffodils and 'The Lady of Shalott'. At one point Slater stopped them and told them to shout louder as the headmaster couldn't hear. This they did, their squeaky childlike voices shouting out the words into the void of the auditorium. I noticed that one woman had tears flowing down her cheeks and realised I too was sobbing under my breath.

A hand grabbed mine. 'Don't worry, Pippa,' breathed Roy Divine in my ear. 'It's only an act. Fellow's a charlatan.'

After a final singing rendition of 'The Owl and the Pussycat' to much laughter and great applause, Slater sat the women down again and in turn put a thumb on each forehead. His voice rang out. 'When I snap my fingers you will wake and feel very happy and remember nothing of this.'

He snapped his fingers and the women sat up straight and looked around smiling and bewildered. They made their way down past the orchestra into their seats in the stalls to further applause. The orchestra struck up *Danse Macabre* and Slater threw on his wide cloak and placed his tall hat at a jaunty angle on his head, raising enthusiastic applause from the auditorium. The curtains swished to the centre and he came to the side of the stage, sweeping past Roy and me without a glance. He was sweating and looked pale and exhausted under his make-up.

The audience settled to an expectant murmur and Roy gave me a little push in the back. Behind him loomed the overlarge figure of Cameron Lake on his way to take his place, centre stage, behind the front curtain.

'You're on, Pippa,' said Roy. His hand was on my waist, pushing me.

I picked up the board Number Seven. *Cameron Lake: Baritone*, walked steadily on to the side of the stage and stood it carefully in its allotted space by the lighted number. I bowed to the audience and went back to join Roy. I pulled him further into the wings. The orchestra played the introductory chords, the curtain swished back and there was a ripple of anticipatory applause for Mr Lake.

I whispered to Roy, 'Did I do that? Did I sing songs like a baby?'

'No, I have to say not,' he whispered, his mouth close to my ear, his hand back on my waist. 'You started gabbling in French, then screaming and crying. Slater was very put out. Worried, I would say.'

'Did he tell me to be happy when I came out of the trance?'

'No. He didn't get the chance. Miss Wharton was down the aisle and at him like the goddess of vengeance.'

'Roy!' a cross voice grated behind us. Marie Divine was standing there, glaring at us, her beauty marred by an ugly scowl. 'Will you drag yourself away from that child and come and help Blaze set up? We're two down in the running order and the veils need checking. And you need to strip off so I can gold you up.' Her voice had a metallic edge that was anything but golden. She looked him up and down. 'Git a move on, will you?'

He dropped my hand and grinned down at me. 'Duty calls! Don't you worry about old Slater, Pippa. He's good but he's still a charlatan. Anyone can learn those tricks.'

I stared after him. It was all right for him to call Slater a charlatan, but what did he know? I saw what he did to those men and women tonight. They weren't pretending. I was sure of that.

I went across to my boards. Only four left: *Spanish Dance by Tom Merriman, Mr Palmer's Rendition of Wellington at Waterloo* and *The Divine Glories of Greece featuring The Three Divines*. After that we were all on stage for the *Finale*. Nearly the end.

The audience loved us. It had been a good night for Mr Palmer, despite the short audience. Tomorrow would be better. What did AJ always say? 'Word gets round. If the show's good, word gets round!'

Miss Abigail said that he wanted a good turn-out here in Bishop, not least because we were going on to Sunderland next week – for a two-week engagement this time – in a bigger, grander theatre. It was imperative to pull out a good performance here. As he said, word gets round.

Me, I just wanted to get this sticky make-up off my face, get out of these tights and go back to Waldron Street for cocoa with Miss Abigail and Tesserina. There were those dramas early in the day. Then there was the boil-up to the performance that left you both too excited and too tired to care. I wanted this day finished. I wanted to be tucked in beside Tesserina in our double bed, thinking of the beautiful boy in the white shirt.

Losing Tesserina

My mother brings in the bright morning as well as fresh bread for our breakfast. In her basket is the promised treat: a jar of expensive preserve from Normandy. She opens the tall casement window and the slanting sun streams on to our little table, with its fresh white cloth. She eats the jam from a spoon, tears off a piece of bread and pops it into her mouth. I copy her, and the jam in my mouth is so sweet that my jaws ache.

Then there is a man in the doorway, a dusty Belgian with narrow eyes. He grasps my face in his hands and is saying something about the morning dew. She drags me from him and hauls me outside on to the landing where she slaps my face and tells me to go to the dressmaker, Madame Augustine. 'She has work for you there, Pippa. You spend too long in that cupboard with your nose in those books.' She speaks in English to keep our affairs private from her Belgian client. Then her face inflates like a balloon and she starts to shout. But try as I may, I can't quite hear what she's saying.

There would be no cocoa in Waldron Street just yet. I'd stayed back at the theatre to return my boards to their slots and to give Mr Barrington a hand checking props. When at last I got to the narrow corridor leading to our dressing room, I came upon Roy Divine, wearing a long cloak covering his still golden body. He was leaning against the wall outside the women's dressing room. 'Are you coming with the others, Pippa?' he said, smiling. The gold paint had leaked to the inside of his eyes, making him look like one of the holy icons on Madame Augustine's wall.

I frowned. 'Where? Where are the others going?'

'Zambra's. All except the Pixies, who have just been dragged home by their dragon. The rest of us are resisting the theatre bar and going for coffee. Joe Zambra was in the theatre tonight with his mother? He said they'd stay open for all of us after the show? Free coffee and cakes? No theatrical would turn down free food?' Roy's voice goes up at the end of the sentence. The other Divines are the same. Every sentence is a question. Must be something about growing up upside down.

It was not unusual for us to go somewhere after the show. The company liked to find a place to unwind and pick over the best points in the evening. In a small town like this it would usually be in the theatre bar. Tom Merriman had been there for an hour before the performance. He calls his glass of whisky his Dutch courage.

At Zambra's tonight our after-show get-together would be oiled not with whisky but with the aid of fine Italian coffee. In France our rendezvous was usually some little café with meat and bread and lots of wine.

AJ and Cameron Lake always carried a flask in their pockets to 'pep up' (as they say) the dullest beverage. I've even seen Cameron Lake tip gin into tea! AJ once teased him that gin is for women: drinkable perfume. That time Mr Lake tossed his head and wondered out loud if AJ had ever heard of Cossack warriors. AJ said he must be thinking about vodka, not gin.

'Pippa?' Roy placed his fingertip on my temple and started to rub it. 'Anyone there? Aren't you the real daydreamer?'

I pulled away from his hand in case he'd left a smear of gold on my skin. 'Zambra's? I shouldn't think so. Miss Abigail doesn't usually like—'

'Miss Abigail's going tonight. She said so. And the gorgeous Tess. Wasn't she very fine tonight? Miss Abigail has already asked us if we were going for this coffee.'

I put my hand on the doorknob. 'Well, I suppose . . .'

'See you there.' A swirl of the cape and a glimpse of golden torso, and he was gone.

I paused with my hand on the dressing-room door and thought about Roy. Despite the gilding and the muscular body, and being the youngest Divine, he wasn't all that young. I'd always thought of the Divines as very glamorous, ageless in their exquisite self-presentation. I'd hardly seen them as separate people, not until Roy peeled himself off from the trio and started to pay me some attention. To be paid attention at all was quite appealing. It was quite nice not to have to play up to the soubriquet 'child' for once. Now they had some real children in the show perhaps they would show me some respect.

Miss Abigail must still have been checking in the costumes backstage as the only person left in our dressing room was Tesserina. She had creamed off her greasepaint and her face was naked under the bare bulb. She was wearing the purple silk dress she'd brought with her in her carpet bag and her hair was tamed, tied with seven purple bows. She smiled up at me, the customary shadow on her face almost gone. She had changed. She was so happy there in Zambra's today, and tonight she danced with a freedom, an abandon I've never seen before.

She watched me as I stripped off my Robin Hood outfit, pulled on my shift and sat before the mirror to take off the greasepaint with a liberal application of cold cream from our mutual pot. Then she stood behind me, took up a brush and started to stroke it through my hair, not an easy job with all the tangled curls, despite its being short. She took a purple ribbon out of her own hair, pulled a handful of curls on top of my head and tied them in a bow. There, before my eyes, my face became narrower, my cheekbones sharper. No one in their right minds would call me 'child' now.

Tesserina stood behind me, put her hands on my shoulders and kissed the top of my head. '*Bell-lla, Pippa!*' she beamed. A memory stirred somewhere in my head like a wisp of vanishing smoke.

I pulled on my skirt and jacket, bought second-hand but (with the help of Miss Abigail), a perfect fit. 'Zambra's?' I said.

'Zambra's!' she beamed.

Later, as I took Tesserina's arm to follow Miss Abigail across the high street to the café, it occurred to me that my world had shifted a little on its axis. Back in the changing room, Tesserina had looked after me, had brushed my hair, had acted the mother. Wasn't this what I had been doing for her all these months? A shred of sadness stirred in me. In all these months I'd never made her look that alive, that happy. It seemed only the thought of Zambra's did that. The wild talk from her own land.

The café was crowded with theatre folk: not just the performers, but the back-stage people too. Mr Barrington had kept a place for Miss Abigail. AJ sat with Mr Jefferson, the theatre manager, at his side and Mrs Palmer was talking earnestly to the first violin, a whiskery man in a black serge suit. The box-office girl was hanging on to Mr Cameron Lake's every word and the 'Tipperary' man was drinking what looked like whisky from a bottle supplied by Tom Merriman. Or vice versa. Mr Merriman was not that generous.

Stan Slater was sitting in another corner with Cissie Barnard and Lily Lambert. His large cap hung over the back of his chair and, his watery blue eyes gleaming, he was showing the two women an elaborate card trick with a pack of cards that had a royal coat of arms on the back. Lily clapped her hands at his cleverness, then started to cry and had to mop her tears, smiling as she did so. The tears were easily turned on – any story, happy or sad, would bring them to her eyes. And here she was crying at a well-turned card trick. But I always liked Lily. In France, during the early days, she would bring me sweets and make me feel welcome among all these strangers.

The Divines had two rather smart older men at their table: men with dark suits and gold watch chains. One of these was leaning towards Marie Divine, holding her in conversation. She leaned back in her chair, accepting this adulation as of right. Roy Divine, sitting slightly to one side, was surveying his fingernails. He looked up and saw us in the doorway. He stood up to greet us but Marie left off her conversation and pulled him back down beside her.

Aldo and Joe Zambra were weaving between the tables, placing cups of coffee beside the plates of small cakes already at the centre of each table. Mrs Zambra was behind the counter, passing coffee through the shining machine. I looked around for her sulky younger son, the one who was so beautiful, but he was nowhere to be seen.

Joe disposed of his last coffee and came across. 'Tesserina!' Astonishingly he kissed her on both cheeks and turned to do the same to me. He bowed over Miss Abigail's hand. 'We have saved you a table, *signora*.' He led the way to a table that had six chairs tipped inwards to prevent anyone taking them. He righted the chairs, got us all seated, then went to find our coffee and cakes. I glanced across at Tesserina. She was staring after him, a slight smile playing about her lips. I looked at Miss Abigail, who smiled and shrugged her shoulders.

In minutes Joe and Aldo were back with our coffee. They brought their own coffee cups and sat down at our table. They addressed us all at first, saying how wonderful the performance was, how much they had enjoyed it. Then Joe turned and said something to Tesserina that made her laugh and she answered him in quick liquid Italian. Here, she was fully alive again.

You'd think I'd be happy at this but I was not. I was suddenly in such a rage at these men for moving in and taking my friend from me. Oh, our own Tesserina would come back to be with us in our digs, or be up there on the stage, dancing. But the woman drinking coffee, her eyes smiling up at Joe, a gale of language bursting from her like water released from a dam, was not my Tesserina, my silent and beloved friend who had needed me so much. Here was a new woman who was nothing to do with me.

I looked across at Miss Abigail to see if she had caught my feeling of losing Tesserina. But she was leaning back in her chair, talking across the room to Mr Barrington.

I stood up. 'I'm going,' I said, 'back to the lodgings.'

The room quietened down. Everyone was looking at me.

'I'm tired,' I said, making myself droop like a child. 'It's been a long day. I'll go back to Mrs Jackson's.'

Miss Abigail reached down for her bag. 'I'll come . . .'

I glared at her. 'No. I want to go on my own. You stay.'

She dropped her bag back to the floor. 'Very well. Straight back to Mrs Jackson's, now!'

I made my way through the café and the talk rose again, closing in behind me like the tide. At the door I glanced back at Tesserina but she was deep in conversation with Joe. She was not conscious of me; it was as though I was not in the room.

Beyond the straying lights of the café the high street was dark, almost deserted, even though you could tell from the rumble of noise from the public houses and the lighted chinks in drawn curtains that not everyone had gone home to their beds. This street had a buzzing undertone as though it held some old secret. Tonight I knew that secret. However many people you have around you, you are always alone.

'Pippa?' Roy Divine caught up with me and took my arm. The gold in his hair glinted in the blue glow of the streetlight. 'Slow down, will you?'

I stopped in the middle of the pavement and looked up at him. 'Leave me alone. Who asked you to come?'

'Miss Abigail. She called me across and asked me to walk you back to your lodgings.'

'Did she?' That didn't sound like her. 'Well, I walked alone in the back alleys of Bordeaux before I met her. It's a bit late to worry now.' I turned away and walked on.

He lengthened his stride and caught up with me. 'The alleys of Bordeaux? Did no one take advantage of you?'

'Take advantage? What does that mean?'

'Like this.' He pulled me into a dark entry and, pressing me against the wall with one hand, ran his other hand down my body. Then his body was hard against mine and his full mouth closed on mine. I could taste spearmint and coffee. I wrenched my face away.

'No!'

Suddenly Roy was hauled away from me and now it was he who was on the ground, yelping like a kicked dog. Strong hands lifted me away from the wall, over Roy Divine's prone body and into the comparative light of the main street. I looked up into the pale sea-grey eyes of Angelo Zambra, the boy in the white shirt.

'Thank you.' My voice was hoarse.

'You keep very bad company,' he growled, flexing the knuckles of his right hand. 'Get yourself killed keeping company with folks like that.'

I straightened my skirt and began to walk on, saying angrily, 'I was not keeping him company. He invited himself.'

Then Angelo was walking alongside me, light on his feet, despite his big boots. 'Still, you want to be careful.'

I decided against explaining to him about the back alleys of Bordeaux. Look where that had got me a moment ago. 'How d'you happen to be here, then?' I challenged. 'Were you lurking around?'

He sniffed. 'If you want to know, I was coming back from the Hippodrome. They do films there, you know. Much better than the theatre. This one was called *Birth of a Nation*. About America. You can learn a lot about the world from films.'

I found myself staring at him in the light of the streetlamp. His face, his eyes, his shock of hair, all added up to a beauty I had never seen before in a man or a woman. 'I remember we passed that cinema on our way to the theatre yesterday. Miss

Abigail pointed it out to us.' I was desperate to keep things normal, ordinary.

'Well, I was coming down from there, saw you rushing out of the café and decided to follow you, to see you were safe, like.'

Why would he do that? He hardly knew me. 'I can keep myself safe, thank you. I'm tired of people who think they can keep me safe!' I shouted the words into his face and hurried on.

He quickened his steps, took me by the arm and stopped me. 'Anyway, that yellow-haired fellow was in front of me and I saw him pick up with you. I didn't like the look of him.'

'None of your business.' I was torn between delight at his attention and the desire to show my maturity.

'So you were happy letting that feller rough you up?'

There was no answering that. 'I was fighting him back,' I muttered, hurrying on. 'I'd have got away.'

'Anyhow,' Angelo said, walking alongside me now, 'what made you run out of the café like a scalded cat?'

I slowed down. 'Well, they're all in there, happy as kings because it's been a good night in the theatre. Mr Jefferson, who's a sour old puss usually, is very cheerful. He thinks it'll be a better house tomorrow night. And there was my friend Tesserina, whose life I saved and whom I've known for weeks, and has never said more than two words to me in any language. Till now. Well, she's sitting there in the café talking up a gale with your brother and Aldo Malteni. She's a changed person and no longer my friend. Me, I can't understand a word any of them are saying . . .' I'm mortified to say that tears were now flowing down my cheeks, a lump was blocking my throat and I could say no more. I remember thinking I was as bad as Lily Lambert.

Angelo dipped a hand in the pocket of his long coat and brought out a clean folded handkerchief. 'Here, blot your face and let's get you home. I'm losing time myself, here.'

I scrubbed my face hard. I was offended. 'Sorry that I have lost you time, sir,' I sniffed.

He shook his head. 'No bother, pet. But I have to get to bed so I can get up at two tomorrow for my early shift.'

This shocked me into life and the tears dried up. I set off again to walk and he strolled along beside me.

'So why do you work in the mine?' I asked, sniffing back the last of my tears. 'Do you really not want to work in your brother's café? Anything must be better than getting up at that time of day to go into the bowels of the earth.'

Shoulder to shoulder we turned the corner on to Waldron Street.

'I'll tell you why,' he said slowly. 'It's all about the men I work with.'

'What? What men are these?'

'These fellers do the hardest work in the world and they're their own men. They know who they are. When I met these pitmen – fathers of my friends from school – I admired them, like. Real men, they were. I wanted to be like them. The café, with its soft ways and working with your mother behind the counter, might be all right for our Joe and Aldo but it's not for me.'

By now we had reached Mrs Jackson's gate. It must have been her hand that pulled back the curtain, making a beam of light splash across the narrow front garden.

I turned to him. 'Thank you, Angelo Zambra. That was a good thing you did for me.' I handed him his handkerchief.

His pale eyes gleamed in the half-light. 'Feller's an idiot,' he said.

We were looking at each other. Into each other's eyes. My head was whirling. I was drowning in those sea-grey eyes. I had to speak. 'Will you tell me something?' I asked.

'What d'you want to know?'

'What does *pipistrello* mean? Tesserina called me that, once.'

He laughed. 'It means "bat". She called you a bat.'

'A bat?'

Now we laughed together, which was a great relief. We stared at each other. 'Do you like fishing?' he said.

'Fishing? How would I like fishing? I'm a town girl.'

'I'll take you fishing. Tomorrow when I come off shift.' It was not a question.

'Pippa? Pippa Valois? Is that you?' Mrs Jackson's voice floated towards us from the shadowy doorway. 'Is Miss Wharton there with you?'

'Coming, Mrs Jackson.' I nodded at Angelo, relieved to turn away. 'I'm coming. Miss Abigail's not here yet. I came on first.'

Later that night – in fact, the early hours of the following morning – I was disturbed by Miss Abigail and Tesserina trying to be quiet as they made cocoa in the little sitting room. I joined them, yawning and rubbing my eyes. 'You two seem to have had a good time.'

'Good time, good company,' said Miss Abigail. 'Our Tesserina was the belle of the ball. Her and that Joe Zambra were singing songs together. Joe has a lovely voice. Light tenor. Plays the accordion.'

Tesserina smiled sleepily down at me, holding out a cup of cocoa.

I took it and wrapped my fingers round it. 'Miss Abigail, you know when I went off earlier?'

'Yes, dear.'

'Did you send Roy Divine after me, to take care of me?'

She laughed. 'You? Of course not. I know you can take care of yourself. You know the streets. Always have. Why do you ask?'

'No reason.'

Later, Tesserina turned off the lamp and joined me in our big double bed. She reached out to slip an arm over me and fitted herself round me like a spoon. Her heavy breath tickled my ear.

I thought about Angelo Zambra and saw again that fine strong face. And then I slept. To my surprise I slept very well, even though before I finally closed my eyes I reminded myself that in this life we're all alone, each one of us.

Gone Fishing

Watching through the casement I can see her coming home from the market, leaning slightly to one side to compensate for the weight of her basket. She's very smart with her little suit and her hat with the feather. A man in a black beret stops her, pushes her against the archway, making her drop her basket. I open the casement and scream down at her but my voice has no sound.

Now she's in her hospital, curled up like a shrunken leaf on the narrow bed. She has been muttering all day. 'Moi, monsieur? I am a teacher. Always in disguise. Always in disguise. Not good-looking like a whore.'

I whisper in her ear, 'Not a whore, Maman!' and she smacks my hand with her claw-like paw and reprimands me for my bad language.

The spider's–web thread of fishing line snaked over the water, hesitated a split second and then – pulled down by the fly – it dropped on to the water, creating a rippling ring of light in the bright afternoon sun. The sunshine today was not honey yellow as it was in Carcassonne; rather it was cool white, without much heat. Miss Abigail said at breakfast how welcome this was, though, after yesterday's drizzle. That was the first time I understood that English people like Miss Abigail were a sort of grudging optimists, seeing marginal good even in the hardest situation. Perhaps in time I would learn to be like this.

'Not much hope they'll bite,' said the beautiful Angelo Zambra, sitting back on the grassy bank. 'Too much sunshine.'

You may find it astonishing that I was here on the riverbank, lounging around with a boy I hardly knew. I worked out later that it was a matter of recognition. I was fascinated by Angelo's beauty and he – well – he recognised me instantly as someone who needed a friend. Perhaps he took to me just because I was a stranger.

'Then why do you come here to fish?' I slipped off my shoes and leaned back beside him, happy that he'd called at Mrs Jackson's for me and persuaded me to come fishing with him on this brilliant day. Miss Abigail was down at the theatre for an early meeting with the Palmers and Mr Jefferson.

Tesserina had left the house with Miss Abigail. After the meeting she was to have a rehearsal with Mrs Palmer, using different music. There was talk of a second spot in the show. She'd hugged me in the doorway on her way out. 'After the dancing I go see Mrs Zambra.' English now! How times were changing.

So here I was on the banks of the river, tucked down below the palace of the bishop which gave this town its name.

'Why do I come here?' said Angelo. 'Because this loop in the river is where an old miner brought me, one day, to teach me how to fish. And often I come here to fish straight after I've finished my shift, so I see that day and don't end up looking like a white lizard with all that working in the dark.'

He was not nearly as dark-skinned as Joe or Aldo, but his olive complexion glinted nicely golden in the bright afternoon sun.

'Do you catch them? Do you catch lots of fish?'

He shook his head. 'Not very often.'

'It can't make you very happy, though, not catching any fish.'

'It's better than sitting in a clattering café and being asked to set up the tables or go and buy flour.' He glanced sideways at me. His lashes were thick and long. 'So how come you speak such good English? Tesserina says you are French. You sound French, but your English is not bad at all.'

'Well, *merci beaucoup*!' I struck him on the shoulder in a friendly fashion. Then I told him the story I told Miss Abigail, omitting as always the truth of my mother's profession. '. . . So I've always spoken English, even when I was very little. But Miss Abigail has taught me how to bite my tongue and say "the" instead of "zuh".'

He frowned. 'So you're here to find your father?'

I stared at the water. 'Not at all!' I knew my denial was too strong. 'I came to be with the troupe. I know nothing of his life or where he may be. He might have died in the war. We heard nothing of him after 1916 when I was ten years old.'

'But you know where he came from?' Angelo wound in his empty line and cast his fly again.

'I would not say that, Angelo. But I do have this jug with a picture on it of a place called Sunderland. We're doing a show there next week. It's a very big theatre.'

'Right then. Gives yer a chance to look for him up in Sunderland.'

'I would not say that. This is only a coincidence. I tell you I don't know this man. I'm afraid . . .'

'Afraid? Of what? Of who?'

I dragged my gaze away from him and stared out at the water, focusing on the glassy reflection of the stark trees on the other side and the tall greyish grasses fighting for space in the rocks at the river's edge.

Angelo stood up, pulled his line out of the water. This time he cast far out in the middle of the stream. Still he talked. 'So what are you going to do about that feller with the gold in his hair?'

I'd woken early that morning thinking of Roy Divine and the way he pushed me against that wall. Then I lay there battling with more shades of half-perceived memory of my mother that had been bothering me lately, some things I can't quite remember. The sense of Roy pushing me against the wall stayed with me. I've fought off other men and boys – and one or two women – in my time close to the streets, but none of these people got so far as putting their lips on mine. My insides wrenched at the thought of that touch but I knew I would have to shrug it off. Living close to the streets makes you pragmatic about such things. Survival is all.

Now to Angelo I said, 'You gave him what Miss Abigail calls a "good hiding". That's enough.'

'He wants more than a good hiding. He wants putting out of his misery like a dog.'

'He's just a stupid man, Angelo.'

'Say that again?'

'What?'

'My name.'

'I won't.'

He put down his rod beside him, leaving the line trailing in the water. Then he placed his hand on mine. 'Go on. Say my name,' he said softly.

His palm was hard, a workman's hand.

'Do the miners call you "Angelo"? They must think it's very foreign.'

He laughed. 'They call me Sam. From Zambra, you know. The English – christened me as one of their own, with a name like theirs.'

'Don't you mind that?'

He shook his head. 'Not one bit. I become one of them. Like I'm in disguise when I'm with them. But I still like my own name. Specially when you say it.'

'Angelo. Angelo, Sam, Sam, Sam . . .' It was like a children's naming game.

He laughed, took his hand off mine and picked up his fishing rod again. My hand felt cold without his touch, but, now separate, the tension went out of us. After a friendly, absorbed silence we spoke of more general things. I told him about Miss Abigail and how I got to be with the troupe. I made him laugh at some of Tom Merriman's antics, even made light of Stan Slater's sly skill of making such a fool of people. I didn't mention that I was one of the foolish people. I entertained Angelo with the peculiarities of AJ and Mrs Palmer, who ruled their little kingdom and moved it from place to place with a kind of royal flourish.

'Palmer's Varieties is their glory,' I said. 'They're king and queen of their own disreputable country.'

'So they pack up in bags and boxes every week and ship to another town, another country? Very much a life in passing. A life with no reputation, if you ask me.'

'It's their chosen life and I admire them for it.' I spoke quite sharply.

'And it seems it'd be your chosen life, Pippa.'

'Well, I choose to be with Miss Abigail and Tesserina.

Where they are, I am. Like Ruth in the Holy Bible. *Whither thou goest I will go.* That's how I see it.'

'Tesserina? Now she's a strange girl, isn't she? She comes from the North of Italy. She has a funny accent. Even so, our Joe thinks she's the bee's knees. Poor lass has had a hard time, hasn't she?' There was another silence while he lifted the line from the water and cast it in a different place. Then without prompting he started telling me Tesserina's story. How she'd come to Paris with a children's singing and dancing troupe and had been attacked by the man who ran it. How he brought her back when she ran away. How she fought him and defied him so much he had her admitted to the asylum before scuttling back to Italy with his young troupe.

'In that hospital it seems she was something of a pet for the director, who used her as a model for his lectures. He used science to bring on all kinds of mad things in her, made her rave about the terrible things that happened to her. How she was stopped from speaking of this by an Italian woman in there. After that she never spoke. It was three years before she got out but get out she did,' he concluded. 'She told us that was when you took her under your wing.'

'Was it?' I was suddenly very cross. 'You don't know Tesserina. How do you know all this?'

'Joe told us. He's usually pretty stolid, our Joe. Never says much. But he's very taken with your friend. Aldo too. They like her. They said your friend's dancing was spectacular. They were there at the theatre last night, in the circle.'

'My friend?' I said miserably. 'How can she be my friend? I've lived with her for weeks and I know less about her than you do.' I stood up. 'I have to go, Angelo. Miss Abigail will be waiting for me at the theatre.'

The line twitched and his face lit up. He stood up, his rod balanced gently in his hand. 'I've caught one. A trout, I'll bet you.'

I shook the strands of dried grass off my skirt. 'I'll see you another time,' I said, already on the pathway.

He looked back at me. 'Don't go, Pippa.'

'I have to.' I wanted to. I ran along the muddy path and when I was a hundred yards away I looked back. But he wasn't watching me. He was concentrating on landing his catch. Later, as I toiled up the steep road into the town, I reflected on my swift attachment to Angelo Zambra. There was something between us now, like a butterfly that you hold in your cupped hands. I wondered briefly whether they had butterflies in this cold land.

But that Angelo Zambra! Not only was he as beautiful as the dawn, he had this detached quality. He was on the outside of things. He reminded me of myself.

Encounters

When I reached the marketplace I almost bumped into Stan Slater, deep in conversation with a man in a long coat, so I crossed the street to avoid him. This strategy was to no avail. I was just turning into the stage door when he shouldered his way in front of me and loomed before me, stopping me in my tracks.

He removed his cap from his head and I could see the white dent it had left on his brow. Without the benefit of greasepaint his skin was pale, almost translucent. 'And how is our Miss Pippa today?' he said with a show of friendliness.

'I'm well, Mr Slater,' I said, avoiding those pale eyes.

'No bad dreams?' he persisted.

I scowled at him. 'Not at all.' I couldn't tell him about these half-dreams, things like wisps of cloud in the wind that I can't quite remember.

He went on, 'I can tell something's worrying you, *mam'selle*. You're having visions.'

'No I'm not. Now, will you let me by?'

He put a hand on my arm. 'That business wasn't finished

yesterday, Miss Pippa. All that uproar on the stage – they pushed me to one side. The procedure you went through, it needs finishing. You must come to my digs on Princes Street. The procedure must be completed. Dangerous otherwise. That way means nightmares.'

I wrenched myself away from him.

He stood there on the pavement and called after me, 'Then I'll see Miss Abigail and come to your digs. It's quite, quite dangerous to leave these things undone.'

'No!'

People were standing back, staring at us.

As I charged through the stage door I was brought up short by the sight of Roy Divine leaning up against the signing-in board, surrounded by some of Sophia Bunce's Pixies, who were giggling at something he must have said. He saw me and shooed them away. He stood up straight and smiled at me, thick greasepaint covering his black eye and his bruised cheek. It was quite effective but there was still the shadow on his face.

'What do you want?' I growled. 'Go away, will you!'

'I've waited here to say I'm very sorry, Pippa,' he said easily. 'It was all a mistake. I got carried away last night. You looked so pretty in the half-dark.' That lilt in his voice had become so hateful to me.

He put out a hand towards me and I crashed it away with the back of my hand. 'You leave me alone. I'll tell Miss Abigail about what you did, and she'll tell Mr Palmer. And he'll . . . he'll do something about you.'

He laughed softly. 'Old AJ? That pansy? I have him round my little finger.' He held up his little finger in a rude gesture.

I thought suddenly about the tenor who had fled the company in Bordeaux. Now a strange fact dawned on me.

That tenor who fled had a crush on Mr Palmer, not his wife. 'What about Mrs Palmer, then? Have you got her wrapped round your little finger? She'd sack you in a second if I tell her what you've just told me.' I said this desperately, doubting my own words.

'You think the old bag doesn't know? Why d'you think the tenor fled for his life?' He stood away from the wall and smoothed down his cuffs. 'You need to keep your rag, little girl. What's a kiss between friends?' He put his hand in his pocket and pulled out a ten-shilling note. 'What is it? Does the little whore need paying?' He looked down at me with mocking eyes. I could see the thick residue of make-up gathering in the creases around them.

I curled my fist in a tight ball, drew back my arm and punched him hard in the stomach. He groaned and doubled up. I fled, only stopping when I reached the big dressing room, which was empty. I shut and bolted the door behind me and leaned on it, breathing hard.

Whore? How dare he call me whore? He was no better than that himself, showing off his body as he did to the lascivious gaze of men as well as women.

I suddenly felt tired. There was a little couch in the corner so I went to lie down on it. I felt so very tired.

There is a hammering on the door and I go to open it. The Belgian with the narrow eyes is filling the doorway. I tell him Maman is not here, that she's at the dressmaker's and the pâtissier's but he still bustles past me into the room. I'm surprised to see him today. We're in the middle of those few days in a month that Maman doesn't have visitors, when the linen bands are draped above our small fire. And today we are to have cakes. For some reason her absence makes the Belgian cross and he marches through the apartment, puffing and blowing, looking everywhere for her. Then he calms down a bit and sits in my mother's favourite chair.

'Come, child, come sit on your uncle's lap,' he says. 'Come!'

I drift across towards him and he sits me on his knee. His whiskers scratch as he nuzzles my neck and strokes my cheeks. He pinches my knees and says I must be eating all my dinners. Then he bounces me up and down. I can see the beads of sweat on his forehead and his upper lip. Then the door swings open and in comes my mother, shrieking like one of the furies. She is smashing into him with her umbrella and beating him out of the apartment and down the stairs. When she comes back the screaming continues and she smacks my face and my legs, calls me a little whore, then locks me in the pantry. This is no pain. This is my own sanctuary. I reach out and pick up my book. It's very good. It's an American story called Little Women.

Someone was banging hard on the dressing-room door. I opened it, and Lily Lambert and Cissie Barnard trotted in on their bobbin heels.

'Locking yourself in, darling child?' tinkled Cissie, throwing two beautifully wrapped parcels on to a chair. She sat on a stool, carefully removed her hat with its large feather and placed it on the hat stand on her dressing shelf between her tin box of greasepaint and her large atomiser. 'Why, darling, for a minute I thought you had a lover tucked in here!' She laughed heartily at the thought.

I looked at the stained wooden school clock on the wall. Evening performance. I must have slept quite a while.

'Make us some tea,' said Lily, 'there's a chick. I've walked the length of this street and back again. Bought two surprisingly good hats and the darlingest little fur tippet. Absolutely exhausted, darling! How I'll manage to sing tonight I don't know. Perhaps I should have had an early night. Don't know that I can sing tonight.' Tears began to well up in her eyes and she took out the snowy handkerchief she kept for these occasions.

'Wouldn't risk missing it, darling,' said Cissie, examining her face closely in the mirror. 'Mrs Palmer'll have your life if you don't. The last slacker she had she sacked out of hand. Will of iron, that woman.'

Lily blotted her eyes and sniffed. 'D'you hear those Divines? What an unholy row!'

Cissie laughed. 'Crash bang wallop! Darling! I swear one of them must have been thrashing seven bells out of the other.'

'That'll be the dreaded Marie. She keeps those brothers of hers on a tight leash,' said Lily, cheering up now. 'But they seem to like it.'

'Yes, men are funny creatures,' chuckled Cissie, stripping off her day dress in a cloud of scent and sweat. 'Can't do with them, can't do without them, that's the trouble, darling.'

I put the kettle on the little spirit stove and by the time the tea was ready, Miss Abigail and Tesserina had come through the door, talking – well, Miss Abigail was – about Tesserina's new number. She was to dance to some new music from the opera *Carmen*. Apparently the composer was a favourite of Mrs Palmer's. Now she was talking about finding a slot for this new dance at the top of the show, after the last Divine spot.

'Some wrinkles to iron out, though,' said Miss Abigail. 'We're not ready quite yet. But even so, there's a chance it can go on, on Friday night. Mrs Palmer says she'll get AJ to think about it.' She was almost purring with pleasure.

Tesserina placed herself before me. Her hair today was

smooth and quite free of ribbons, which made me sad. 'Good music, Pippa,' she said slowly. 'Dance well.'

I nodded and smiled and touched her arm, acting more kindly than I felt. It's true that one part of me was really glad for her and these changes in her. She was at the end of her particular tunnel and coming into the light. But it seemed that now she was regaining her whole self and her own voice, she didn't need me. She needed Miss Abigail, of course, and Mrs Palmer, but not me. And she probably needed the Zambras, who had reminded her of her first real self. I knew this return to her real self was to be celebrated but I was suddenly drenched in that dark sense of loss that I had felt when I raced from the hospital and left my mother and our life together behind me for good.

Still, that night I made myself play a part. I was jolly enough with Tesserina and she noticed no difference in me.

After rubbing in my greasepaint and changing into my Robin Hood outfit, I went out backstage to check my boards. AJ was there, deep in discussion with Mr Barrington, watched by two of Madame Bunce's Pixies playing Patience at a small prop table. AJ was talking about introducing the table and adding a candelabra to dress the stage screen to enhance Cissie Barnard's set.

'I know we have the standard lamp and the carved screen but the stage seemed bare last night, old boy. No atmosphere. Bleak!' he intoned.

Then he turned and noticed me. 'Ah, Miss Pippa. Sterling work with the boards!' he said. 'Mrs Palmer was just saying. At last you're acquiring quite a stage presence, *mam'selle*.'

Mr Barrington was rescuing the table from the Pixies, who laughed and squealed their objections and came across to stare at me and AJ.

I waited for AJ to march away, but he paused. 'Your friend Miss Tesserina is also turning up trumps for us. Quite a find. Mr Jefferson is rather keen. According to him, the bookings are up today. I did tell him that word gets round. He really liked her dance. "Stirring, yet genteel." That's what he said. He likes a bit of class, does our Mr Jefferson. Loves the classical music. Has no time for vulgarity. Vulgarisms! Abhors them. Apparently there was a comedian here last week who'd been a circus clown. According to Mr Jefferson he should have "stayed there in the circus with the other animals".' He laughed at Mr Jefferson's great wit, which was lost on me. AJ was a strange old man, living life always outside himself, always in demi-performance. One could not imagine him as a child, or even a younger man. Perhaps he was just born old, with a booming voice.

He marched away.

'Ain't he a funny old man?' The taller Pixie with rusty hair burst into my thoughts. 'Doncher think?'

'Only funny,' agreed the smaller, fairer Pixie.

The rusty one thrust her face towards me. 'Doncher think, miss?'

I shook my head. 'I can't say that. Neither can you.'

She grinned. 'I just did. So what d'they call you, miss? I seen you around with that old cripple woman.'

'I am Pippa Valois. And the lady is Miss Wharton.'

She nodded. 'And me, I'm Pixie Molloy. And this here wonder is Pixie Smith.' She put out a paw and shook my hand vigorously. 'How d'ya do? The Bunce said you're from France. My granny was, but me, I'm from Spitalfields in London Town. Me and Smithy here have been watching you. We like you but we couldn't decide whether you were girl or woman.'

This made me laugh. 'P'raps something in between, Miss Molloy.'

Then we all jumped as a screeching voice penetrated the auditorium. 'Molloy! Smith! Where are you? You're in trouble now. Big trouble.'

The two children clutched each other. 'The Bunce!' gasped Molloy. 'Now we're in for it, Smithy.' They scrambled off, away from the threatening voice.

My way back to our dressing room was barred by Marie Divine. Her short sculpted hair was already sprinkled with gold but she was wearing her acrobat's tights and waistcoat for her first turn. Her face was a painted mask. 'Just who d'you think you are, girl?' Her squeaky voice belied her physical beauty. 'What this company wants with a foreign brat like you and your crazy friend I *cain't* think.'

'Who do I think I am? Is that what you're asking?'

'You had my brother beaten up. It took me half an hour to cover those bruises.'

'Your brother got himself beaten, Miss Divine. He's . . . a . . . slimy snake. He got what he deserved. Creeping around like that in the dark.'

'He told me about your pert ways, miss—'

'Pert!' I pushed past her. 'I tell you, Roy held me against a wall. I could not move. I don't know what would have happened if . . .'

'Who? Who did that to him? We'll settle that bully!'

They probably could. Two brothers and a sister, all with muscles of steel. 'I can't remember,' I say vaguely. 'Some man who came by.'

She glared at me, the natural flush of anger glowing through her greasepaint. 'You keep your hands off my brother, you little trollop. I'm warning you.'

I held her gaze. 'P'raps you should keep your hands on him, Miss Divine. I hear that's what you like, isn't it? Keeping your hands on him? You do that, and keep your brother out of my way.'

At that I turned and fled.

Losing Time

Mr Jefferson and AJ Palmer were right about the better audience on the Tuesday night. The stalls were nearly full and the front row of the more expensive circle was quite crowded. Even so, some of the back rows were still empty.

Each act was well received: even Tom Merriman was treated to gales of laughter for his tired old performance. I wondered again at how he managed to lose his drunkenness when he stepped before the footlights. Madame Bunce's Pixies performed with military precision and painted smiles. Pixie Molloy winked at me as she ran off the stage at the end of their number. Tesserina's dance received rapturous applause and Stan Slater's mesmeric performance was greeted with laughter and an occasional stunned, appreciative silence. I cannot say that I liked the man, but the more I watched him the more I thought that his understanding of the people he brought up on to the stage was amazing, beyond any trick or artifice.

The high-wire spectacle performed by the Divines made people catch their breath and applaud with great enthusiasm.

Even now that I had cause to hate two of them, I had to agree with that. Blaze performed back flips actually on to the wire. As he landed he seemed about to fall, but saved himself. They stood on each other's shoulders – Roy on the bottom, Marie on the top – and walked across the wire. The audience loved them. They might be awful people but they were great acrobats.

Later in the programme the golden trio drew murmurs of more subdued delight with their 'Glories of Greece'. I noticed that tonight Roy faced the other way for his poses, hiding his battered face. Unlike Pixie Molloy, he didn't spare me a glance as he left the stage, which was a relief.

The Finale – with Lily Lambert singing 'Irish Eyes' before she was joined in the final chorus by Cissie Barnard and Cameron Lake and then by the rest of us – felt very good. As the tabs swished across and back, and the company took its bows, we could feel the warmth of a good night's theatre. For these few, fine hours the audience had forgotten its troubles, the company its differences. My time with Palmer's had taught me that this was the magic of theatre: the gift that we offered in every town we visited. Miss Abigail had described to me many times how this magic had been a true gift in times of war. It seemed to me now that it was equally needed in these hard times of peace.

When we came out of the theatre I wasn't at all surprised to see Joe Zambra and Aldo already at the stage door, waiting to escort Tesserina and Miss Abigail across to the café. Tonight, without the benefit of Zambra's offer of free coffee and cakes, most of the company had made their way down to the theatre bar to drink beer and spirits to celebrate a good night.

As for me, I was feeling very odd; seething inside. Not

wanting to follow the chattering Tesserina like a pet lamb, I was at a loss as to what to do. She called to me in Italian, but I pulled back, excluding myself from her and Miss Abigail's company.

Then Angelo Zambra emerged from the dark shadow behind the open theatre door. We stared at each other.

'I saw you on the stage,' he said, smiling widely. 'I was there.'

My heart was in my mouth. Though wrapped up in a scarf and a long coat, Angelo was still beautiful. Even now, I can't say what I felt then was love. It was more the adoration you feel when you see something new and perfect. Perhaps it was a crush, like the tenor felt for AJ, although AJ is no object of beauty.

I took some very deep breaths. So he'd been in the audience. No cinema for him tonight.

'Pippa?' he said, frowning.

'Just putting out the boards,' I said. 'It's nothing much.'

'Still, must be hard to go up there in front of all those people.'

'You get used to it. Me, I think it must take courage to go down into the bowels of the earth.' I was trying to feel comfortable with him but with this crush or whatever it was, it felt such a long time since the simplicity of our fishing trip that morning.

He stared at me. 'Anyway,' he said, rejecting my implied compliment, 'are you coming across to the café for coffee?'

I looked at Tesserina, who was way ahead of me now. She and Miss Abigail were linking arms with Joe and Aldo. She was talking twenty to the dozen, turning first at one of them, then the other.

He caught my uncertainty. 'What if you and me went for a walk?'

'Where to? It's dark!'

'Down by the river. There's a bridge down there. It's blinkin' wonderful down by the river at night. You look up and you can see all the lights of the town.'

'Sounds nice.' I was pleased that he'd asked me. There would be no trailing behind others now. Of course, I'd have to face Miss Abigail's catechism when I got back to the digs.

Angelo read my mind. 'Just wait here,' he said, and darted across the road, his long coat flapping. In a minute he was back. 'She made me promise to see you safely back,' he said. 'She can be fierce, your old friend.'

At the Theatre Corner we bumped into Stan Slater, who glared at Angelo and pushed past us. 'Don't you forget, Miss Pippa,' he growled in my direction, 'we've unfinished business.' And he vanished into the dark.

'What was that about?' asked Angelo.

'Nothing,' I said. 'Take no notice of him.'

'That's the mesmerist feller, isn't it? He looks kind of smaller out in the street. Mind you, that stunt of his tonight was not bad, not bad at all.'

Angelo led the way, weaving up through the town towards the marketplace, and then down a narrow road still ticking over with men returning home from a night out spent in one of the many public houses that peppered the town.

He was right about the river. It lay still and black under the bridge, and then curved away under a much higher bridge, where a train was even now chuffing away towards the west, its lighted windows twinkling against the dark night sky. Up to our right the lights of the town on its rising hill glittered against the night sky. The dinginess of its streets vanished beneath the comforting blanket of the dark. He took off his scarf, looped it round my neck and used it to pull me towards him. I could smell the clean-soap, olive-oil, gritty-coal scent of him. I could feel the soft-silk touch of his lips on mine. Then nothing.

Nothing except a grey muzzy gap, a yawning space in time: a void within and a void all around. And now there I was, fully clothed, lying on my bed at Mrs Jackson's. No Tesserina beside me. Our rooms at the top of the tall house were silent, but I could hear the distant tinkle of Mrs Jackson's piano and her sprightly contralto voice. The black outside the uncurtained window told me it must be night, not day. Was it yesterday I was on the bridge with Angelo? No, that must have been tonight. So where had I been? I had a nasty taste in my mouth and felt slightly sick. I poured myself some water from the night glass, my head whirling. The others couldn't be back from the café. I rubbed my head hard to get rid of the fog that seemed to be lodged in there. Where had I been? I remembered being on the bridge, thinking about the beauty of the town and shivering a bit with a kind of delight because Angelo was there. And Angelo's soft lips.

But then? Nothing. I couldn't remember. I knocked my brow hard with my fist but there was nothing in there. Nothing. It was too, too hard to think. So, dressed as I was, I crawled under the covers and slept again without dreaming at all.

Madness

The next morning I sat for a long time in the dressing room watching Miss Abigail making some alterations to Tesserina's dress. I looked at her, thinking surely she must realise I was mad. But apart from telling me that last night I had been so dead asleep that Tesserina had been obliged to undress me and get me back to bed when they came in from the café, she didn't seem to notice anything was amiss with me.

She'd found a favourite spot in the corner of our dressing room that had a scrap of natural light. This searching for natural light was an old habit of hers, but here we were lucky, as there was electric light even in this tiny space. 'In the end, who knows? Perhaps the natural light is not so important!' she said placidly.

In the last few days I could not help noticing how much Miss Abigail was focusing on Tesserina, how intense was her concentration. When I found her by the window I thought I might try to talk to her about how I'd lost some time in my life last night. And while I was doing this I might tell her about these dreams that were not dreams. And how I think I might be mad. But the words that came out of my mouth were about Tesserina. How different Tesserina had become now all that Italian was tumbling from her, how she'd lost her stillness, how it seemed to me that the sense of pain that made her movement so compelling was leeching away.

At this Miss Abigail stopped sewing and examined my face, from my hairline to my chin, over her spectacles. 'Pain? What wise words from one so young. So why should this be a cause for worry, child?'

'Well, her dancing to the music's good but it's not so good as the dancing she did in the street when I first saw her.' I searched desperately for words to say what I meant. 'Perhaps the dance is beautiful now, but she seems encumbered by the dress, by the deliberateness of it all.'

A rare frown marked Miss Abigail's smooth brow. 'Perhaps you don't understand, Pippa. The change you're talking of is the change between being a wild thing and being an artist. It's true that we experience great beauty in seeing birds in flight, in the onward rush of the waves and the tide. But isn't art about being conscious, being deliberate and disciplined in what you do? What you saw in Tesserina was the beauty of a bird in flight who blinds us all with its natural beauty. Do you want her to stay like that? A dumb creature tied to your charity or to mine? This discipline makes her better, not worse.' She put a hand towards me but I stepped back to avoid her touch, my lips trembling. 'What is it, my darling girl?' she murmured.

'Tesserina's forgotten me, even though I was the one who found her. And you're the same. You're all for her. The dress. All this talk to Mrs Palmer about how . . .' I was afraid to say the miserable words and they came out in a whisper.

'I'm not "all for her", Pippa. I have this great interest in her. In her gift for the dance, which once was my own precious gift. And she's not forgotten you. Not at all.' Miss Abigail laughed out loud.

'No, my darling, she's just preoccupied in remembering herself. Young Aldo and Joe are helping her. They know her country, they can help her inhabit her own memories, to live inside them. And I suppose I'm helping her in another way, to properly inhabit the present, by introducing her to the deliberate disciplines of the dance. None of this could have happened had you not rescued her.'

'What about me? I am left behind!' I muttered, half ashamed to say the miserable words. In my mind I was shouting – *who would help me inhabit my past, help me properly inhabit my present? Who would save me from feeling mad? Who would help me remember?*

'You? My darling, you're the one who saved her, liberated her from a dingy, dark world, and brought her intact into our real world. And now she is making it her own. Don't you see?'

Before I could say anything the door crashed open and in Mr Barrington bowled. 'Her ladyship wants you up top, Abigail,' he says. 'Something about new music for the Italian girl.' He sniffed. 'Down to an errand boy, now, me,' he said.

Miss Abigail stood up carefully and handed me the dress and the threaded needle. 'Can you do this, darling? See these narrow slots here? I'm sewing these to fit the wires Mr Barrington has kindly fashioned for us. So much better than the wooden rods. Just as firm but not so rigid. Like a butterfly's wing. So much more responsive to the way Tesserina moves, don't you think?' she beamed.

So I sat on there by the window, putting in tiny stitches to complete the slot, wondering if I was, as Miss Abigail implied, envious of Tesserina. Or indeed envious of Aldo and Joe, who had got so much closer to Tesserina than I had, by the simple act of speech.

I bit the cotton and held the needle up to the light to rethread it. Stitching away, I tried and failed to call up the image of Angelo's face. I could see Joe and Aldo, but Angelo's face eluded me.

Then, without bidding, the thought came to me that I should really look for my father while I was in these parts; search him out. Perhaps not talk to him, but just look at him and see if I too could, in Miss Abigail's wise words, inhabit my own memories.

'I know, I know, I know about you!'

I am beating my mother about the face and shoulders. Finally she manages to hold me away from her in a vicelike grip. Her eyes are bright and her glance is quite kind.

'What do you know, ma p'tite?'

'That you are a whore.'

'And what does that mean, that nasty word?'

'That you do horrible things with dirty men for money. Gerard le Blanc told me so, and his mother said yes he was right. He put his hand right up my dress and pushed his finger into me but his mother said I was a liar. She made me think, remember things. Things that happened here in our home.'

Maman's face is blank now, her eyes staring. I can hardly recognise her. She pulls a hand back and slaps me so hard on the face that I go reeling away into the corner.

Now she's leaning down beside me, lifting my head and kissing my brow, my cheeks. 'I am so sorry, ma p'tite, *so very sorry.'*

* * *

For no reason I can fathom, as I was sitting there stitching, Gerard le Blanc came into my mind. He and his mother had the apartment below us in the Rue de la Tour. They were usually quite kind to me. They gave me *bonbons* and patted my head when I passed them on the stairs. I think Madame le Blanc was quite intimidated by my *maman*. She called her 'madame' and asked her help with her son, who, although quite grown up, could not read. 'Teach him to read, madame! I beg you!' This service was, of course, to be a neighbourly act, without payment.

One day – I must have been about ten – Gerard le Blanc came to the apartment for his lesson but my mother wasn't in. He came in to wait and I showed him the book I was reading: a modern English novel. He betrayed great amazement. Not only was I reading, I was reading in a foreign language! I think I tossed my head then and – pride coming before a fall – I suddenly became the victim of Gerard's anger. I can't quite remember what happened next but I know he was very angry and when my mother came in I flew to the shelter of her arms.

It was not long after these events that we left for Toulouse. Sitting there by the theatre window my thoughts moved on from Gerard le Blanc to Angelo. Now I could see that perfect face. We were on that shadowy bridge with the twinkling lights above it. I remembered how the dark made me feel safe with Angelo, the two of us alone in a serene world. I remembered wondering if he would kiss me and what I'd feel if he did. I wondered if he would touch me in that intimate way I'd witnessed many times in my life. How would I feel if that happened? Then I felt it, the soft silken feeling of his lips on mine.

Then there came the blank: a yawning grey space in my

head between standing in the darkness on the bridge with Angelo and the time later when I lay in the wide bed, pondering the whereabouts of Miss Abigail and Tesserina. Everything between was a grey whispery wall of consciousness, like that time between sleeping and waking where you're trying desperately – and by that very effort failing – to remember your dream.

When I got up I had looked at my clothes but there was nothing to show that anything strange had happened. I looked at my arms, then at my face in the little mirror, but apart from a small reddening on the cheekbone, nothing looked amiss.

I was roused from my daydream by a persistent knocking sound. Then Blaze Divine popped his head round the door.

'Oh, yes. Miss Abigail said you'd be here,' he said. 'Have you seen Roy, Pippa?' I noticed then how much more handsome he was than his brother. His face was smooth and untroubled, and his eyes, though rather blank, were sapphire blue.

I shook my head. 'No. I haven't seen him. He was there talking to Madame Bunce's little dancers before the performance last night. After that, nothing.'

'You must know!' His sister appeared behind him and pushed him into the room, so the two of them filled it with their muscular presence. Her voice was shrill. 'You've been creeping after him for days . . .'

'We haven't seen him since last night, Pippa,' Blaze said smoothly, his voice tipping up in that Australian manner. 'He never came back to our digs. And we've a band call in half an hour.'

'How d'you entice him?' stormed his sister. 'Just what did you do to him?'

'I tell you, I've never seen him since the show.' I was angry myself now. 'Why would I want to see him? He's as old as Methuselah and as ugly as sin.'

'Ugly? My beautiful brother?' She looked me deep in the eyes and said slowly, 'You whore, you little whore . . .'

Now I was on to her, beating and scratching her like a cat. It took all Blaze's superior strength to pull us apart. At last he bundled Marie out of the door, then turned to me.

'Just let us know if you see him, Pippa,' he said blandly. 'As it is, we'll have to modify our act for tonight. I can't think that AJ'll be pleased by that!'

I sat down on Tesserina's stool, fighting against the desire to run across the road and find Angelo Zambra to ask him whether I did anything strange last night in that time I couldn't remember. Had he brought me home? Did I seem mad when I was with him? No, I couldn't do that – seek out Angelo. There was too much shame in it. Shame.

But what was that about? Why on earth should I think of that – about the shame?

Dealing with Anger

Blaze Divine was right. Neither AJ nor Mr Jefferson was pleased at Roy's absence. They were met with the news just as they came into the theatre, warmed and benevolent from Mr Palmer's talk to the Rotarians, which – though he said it himself – had gone down very well.

The dapper Mr Jefferson was just in the process of gloating that AJ's excellent talk would make a difference to tomorrow night's house, or even tonight's, when Mrs Palmer gave him the news.

I was at the side of the stage watching Mr Barrington repaint the board for the Divines – tonight they would not be the Three but the Two Divines – so I heard Mr Jefferson begin a well-rehearsed complaint about a very famous actress, a friend of Mr George Bernard Shaw, no less! She had reneged in her commitment to him and ruined his house for the week. 'I know this Divine feller is much less of a fish, but I see it as completely unprofessional, Mr Palmer. Completely! How do they expect us to compete with the picture houses if they have this attitude?' he puffed. 'There was a lot of interest in the Divines. Great applause last night. Very tasteful. Not vulgar.'

'Unfortunately, word of mouth will have done its work,' said AJ, unhelpfully. 'People will be expecting three Divines and will get—'

Mrs Palmer shot her husband a very severe glance. 'The two of them have adapted the act, Mr Jefferson,' she said firmly. 'I can assure you the audience will know no different.'

But she was talking to the theatre manager's back as he stalked away in the direction of his office in search of some solace, probably liquid. She looked at her husband. 'AJ! You're no help! No help at all in a crisis!' she said coldly before she too stalked off.

He caught my glance. 'What are you staring at?' he snarled in a very untheatrical voice, and hurried after his wife.

'There you are!' Mr Barrington held his artwork up to the light. 'They'll never tell the difference.'

I hastened off to get into my costume and to dress Tesserina, who loved the new wire extensions to the sleeves of her gown. She gave her pleated wings an experimental swish even in the small place of the dressing room. She'd been very busy today: an extra early rehearsal this morning with Mrs Palmer, who was trying to develop this new number with her. I heard Mrs Palmer say to Tesserina, 'We can't let them say you're a flash in the pan, my dear.' *Flash in the pan!* Despite my jealous protestations I found myself smiling at this, wondering how much of what Mrs Palmer said Tesserina could understand. Perhaps everything, the way things were now.

Tesserina was watching me in the mirror as I brushed her hair right out, so that it tumbled over her shoulders and mingled with the fine pleats of the dress. I reached for one of her ribbons and she shook her head. 'No ribbon, Pippa!' she said firmly. 'Not smart. Mrs Palmer say so.'

She was timid and silent no longer. She was not my creation. She was her own self.

'But I like your ribbons, Tesserina!' It came out as a childish wail.

She shook her head again. 'Tesserina no child, Pippa. Woman now. Grow up.'

I put the ribbon back in its box and closed the lid.

She turned on her stool to look at me, adjusting the voluminous skirt of her gown. She frowned. 'You angry, Pippa?'

In the distance I could hear the orchestra tuning up. I checked my own make-up in the mirror, pulled down my Robin Hood tunic and smoothed it over my thighs. 'I have to go,' I said. 'I need to be ready with the boards.'

And I left Tesserina sitting there, sandwiched between mirrored versions of herself in her pleated splendour. Suddenly I didn't feel so bad about her as I had when the day began. I couldn't think why. Perhaps it was my decision to go and find my father.

'Decision!' I said that word out loud as I lifted the first number board.

Fragments of a Dream

My mother is behind me, her hands on my shoulders, her chin resting on the top of my head. She smells of lemons. Down below us in the courtyard a man in uniform is clattering, across the courtyard towards the archway into the Rue de La Tour. I know he is going away. I can feel my mother's sadness even without seeing her eyes. He is going out of our lives. Then he looks up at our window, doffs his army cap, and waves before vanishing through the archway.

'Who is he, Maman? Who is that man?' Tears are dropping from my eyes on to my pinafore.

Her voice is in my ear. 'Voilà ton papa!'

I am so angry with her. He has been here. I have heard his voice from my perch in the little pantry. And, as with the others, I ignored this male voice, too keen to read about some mystery in an Engish mansion house.

Thankfully the audience that night did not seem to notice that they were entertained by Two rather than Three Divines. The theatre was three-quarters full, and Mr Jefferson spent the interval at the front of house with a faint smile on his face, bowing to ladies left and right, and shaking hands with men in suits with chains on their waistcoats and watches on their wrists.

The greatest applause that night went to the remaining Divines, the mesmerist, Stan Slater, and Tesserina. Two women fainted during Slater's presentation and had to be carried out. And Tesserina's new self-assurance showed in her dance. She seemed to engulf the stage with light and movement. She was both more relaxed and more precise, her movements complementing Mrs Palmer's virtuoso playing as though they'd been performing together for years. The audience held its breath a moment before showing its appreciation in loud applause.

The audience loved them both. At the end Mrs Palmer joined Tesserina in acknowledging the applause, standing with her under the proscenium arch and bowing regally to the left and to the right. AJ, in the wings, shouted, '*Brava!*' Cameron Lake, standing beside him, applauded with great generosity.

Tom Merrimen caused only a ripple of laughter, and Lily and Cissie were quite well appreciated but their applause was measured rather than rapturous. Cameron Lake's applause was merely polite. He was very upset but from the other side of the wings I saw AJ put a reassuring hand on his shoulder. I remember thinking what good friends they were.

That night the audience seemed reluctant to let us go and, much to their delight, Mr Palmer signalled an encore of our final song before they eventually emptied the theatre.

Miss Abigail cleared up and went off quite quickly to see Mr Barrington in the theatre bar.

Tesserina and I had just got into our street clothes when there was a loud knock on our dressing-room door. I hoped this wouldn't be a repeat of this morning's drama, with the angry Marie Divine calling me foul names. I felt bad enough today, without that.

Angelo

It was not Marie at our dressing-room door, but Joe Zambra. I stood back and looked towards the beaming Tesserina. He shook his head. 'It's you I want, Pippa.' He came close to me and looked me in the eyes. 'It's Angelo,' he said. 'He's in the hospital here in the town.'

'Has there been an accident? In the mine?'

He sat down on one of the narrow stools. Tesserina went to hold his hand. She spoke to him in Italian and, of course, when he answered I couldn't understand. In the end I went and put a hand on his shoulder and shouted, 'Tell me! Tell me! Was he hurt in the mine?'

'The pit? Why, no. He was never there for his early shift. We all thought he was there, like. He's never in the house when we get up. Always off away on his early shift. So we never thought. Then someone comes to the café and tells us our Angelo was at the hospital. A cart-man found him down on Skirlaw Bridge. He'd been badly beaten. And he was cold. Had been there all night. The doctor at the hospital says he's lucky to be alive. He was lying there, out cold.' Joe looked at

163

me intently. 'Did you see anything, Pippa? He came to the café to tell Miss Abigail he was going for a walk with you. Where d'you go?'

I shook my head numbly. 'I went down to the bridge with him. We were looking at the lights of the town.' I rubbed my forehead. 'But I can't remember what happened after. I just can't remember. I've been trying to think all day.'

'You must!' Joe took me by the shoulders and shook me. 'You must remember what happened to him! You were there.'

Tesserina pulled him away, talking rapidly to him in their language. She put her arm round me and we both faced him.

'Honestly, I can't remember,' I said miserably. 'I think I must be mad. I remember being on the bridge, then nothing.'

Tesserina put her hand on my sore cheek and spoke rapidly to him.

'Were you hurt? Did someone hit you?' he said.

I shook my head. 'I don't know,' I said. 'I just don't know.' I looked up at him. 'Will Angelo be all right? Can I see him?'

'He has cracked ribs and a badly bruised face and arms. And he's unconscious, so we don't know what happened. They won't let you in. They won't let none of us in. Not tonight.' He sighed. 'My mamma is sitting with her apron over her head. She's inconsolable. He is her *figlio del favorito*. Her favourite.' He turned to speak to Tesserina.

She moved to his side. Now her arm was round *his* shoulder. She was moving between us like a ball in a game.

I stood up. 'I'm tired, really tired. I can't remember.' I kept my voice steady, though I wanted to weep. 'I'm going back to Waldron Street. Will you go to the theatre bar, Joe, and tell Miss Abigail about Angelo, and that I've gone to the digs?'

Now Tesserina was by my side. She nodded to him. 'I go

with Pippa. I see Mamma in the morning,' she said to him in English.

Reluctantly he turned to go. Then he turned back. 'You think hard, Pippa. Think what happened. Try to remember. We must know what happened.' His voice was chilly, deadly serious. I wondered what terrible thing he was likely to do to the one who had done this to Angelo.

I must remember. I must remember. The words were drumming in my head. But the harder they drummed the more blank my mind became.

Tesserina held out my coat for me, as Miss Abigail often did. 'Come, Pippa. We will have cocoa. We go think about Angelo. I help.'

We were ready for bed and had drunk our cocoa when Miss Abigail got home, smelling of port and cigars. 'What awful news about young Angelo, darling! Joe says you can't remember what happened. How very odd that is.'

My head was low, almost on my chest. *'Je suis trés fatiguée.* I'm weary of all this, Miss Abigail. I can't remember. I've been trying and trying all day. There is nothing, nothing in my head between standing on the bridge with Angelo and being in bed here with Tesserina.'

Miss Abigail put her hand on my cheek. 'There's this bruise. Perhaps you were knocked out. You too were attacked and got away?'

Tesserina looked up from her cocoa. 'Slater,' she said.

'Slater? You think Slater did this?' demanded Miss Abigail.

Tesscrina shook her head. 'Pippa is no good since that, since she on stage with that man,' she said. 'Pippa still sleeping, eyes open.'

'Perhaps there's something in that,' said Miss Abigail.

'Did you see him tonight? He's very good. Perhaps he could help.'

I shook my head. 'I'm not letting him do anything else to me.'

'But how else will you remember? You can't *not* know something as important as this. You are walking in a dream.'

That did describe what I'd been feeling in these last days. It was not just today. What about those other blanks, fragments of dreams that I couldn't quite catch? Even so, I wasn't going to have anything to do with Slater. I stood up. 'I'm really tired, Miss Abigail. I'm going to bed.' And I left them to their cocoa.

From my bed I heard their voices murmuring in the room next door. I wondered that this was a conversation *in words*. Tesserina must have understood so much, learned so many English words when she wasn't talking. But then Miss Abigail had never had any problem communicating with Tesserina, right from the start.

Examination

The hospital ward smells of strong soap and blood. The wide skirts of the nun's habit swish around me as we walk down the ward towards the narrow bed in the corner. The nun strides like a man and her grasp on my hand is so tight that I have to trot to keep up with her. The patients in the beds are still, like soldiers lying to attention. As we make our progress down the long ward, I can hear stifled moans: pain bitten back out of the air.

My mother also lies straight as a soldier, her arms alongside her body over the coverlet, her hands loosely curled around an unfamiliar rosary of amber beads. (Her own rosary is made of cream ivory and jet and is rarely used.) She is muttering a prayer. Someone has brushed her lovely hair and braided it loosely into a plait, which lies like a snake on the pillow beside her. The face on the pillow is bony and white, and I can see the globe of her eyeball beneath the fine crepe of her eyelid. Still there is the breath of beauty about her.

The nun stands at the end of the bed and pushes me in the small of my back, allowing me to stand up close to my mother, to lean over her, to put my hot cheek on her icy one. 'Maman . . .'

My mother's eyes flash open and her hand grasps mine. 'Pippa,' she whispers. 'I dreamed you went to England. I thought you ran away from me. I want you to take it, take the jug.' Her hand flutters towards the familiar jug on the narrow shelf by her bed. I pick it up and turn it in my hands. There is a picture of a bridge on it underscribed with English words. I recognise it from her armoire. It's been there a long time, tucked in among the clutter of the flowers and porcelain perfume sprays.

When I turn back, my mother's face is waxy, all life drained from her, eyes blankly staring, on the pillow. I open my mouth to scream and am enveloped in the nun's habit, my one free hand flailing out against the voluminous cloth, the other clutching the jug. The nun is dragging me back down the ward and I am kicking her, catching her bare ankle beneath the habit. Now she has me by the back of my dress and I am choking. She is speaking in my ear, very softly.

'Your mother is gone, child. But do not worry. We have a very good house for children. It will be easy for you there. It cannot have been easy for you in the house of a whore.'

And I am running, running back to our little apartment, putting books and clothes into a cushion case, wrapping the jug in my second-best petticoat, tying my second-best shoes round my neck and pulling on my two coats, one on top of the other. And I am running, running . . .

The next morning a constable came to Waldron Street on a bicycle to ask me the same questions as Joe Zambra. First, I had to say and spell my name so he could get it into his notebook. He thought the spelling very comical and I had to tell him how to spell it three times.

Then I repeated to him how Angelo and I had gone down to Skirlaw Bridge after the theatre. The policeman then suggested that we retrace our steps. So I walked with him right back up to the theatre, then down through the warren of backstreets to the road that led down to the bridge.

'Retracing the steps,' he said proudly. 'Always a help.'

I walked alongside him as he wheeled his bicycle, and his heavy cloak, lifted by the wind, swished round me. Three times he stopped, leaned his bicycle against the wall, took out his little notebook and wrote down words that I'd said, identifying the streets down which I led him. 'Down Newgate Street . . . up Tenters' Street . . . threaded through some narrow back lanes . . . on to the hill down to the river.' I couldn't think why he needed to write all this down. After all, it was very straightforward. The way was not difficult to remember in such a small town. I thought perhaps he made such a fuss to make himself feel important.

The narrow streets seemed flush with people crouching in doorways, clustering on the corners. They looked at me with open curiosity. Clearly, for them, anyone being marched through the town by the police was something of a show.

We reached the bridge to find a narrow man wearing a large cap standing right in the middle of the roadway. Beside him, held firmly by a leading rein, was a patient pony shackled to a high-sided cart.

The constable introduced us. 'This is Mr Lynus, Miss . . . er . . . Valois.' He turned to me. 'This man found your friend Zambra all battered and bruised on the ground here.' He pointed to the side of the road and I could see blood, red at the centre and black at the edges, in the dust. I put a hand to my mouth to stop the desire to vomit.

Mr Lynus, a middle-aged man, slightly bug-eyed, with his cap low on his brow, looked me over from head to foot.

'You found Angelo, *monsieur*?' I said faintly.

'Aye. Right there beside where you're standing. Tell yeh

the truth, ah thowt it was a bundle of rags. Or a bit of matting. Never a man. You see many a queer old thing on this road.'

'Did he say anything?'

'Nay. Shivering wi' cold. Bletherin' on. Eyes rolled back. I seen it many a time.'

'Seen it?' said the constable sharply. 'Where's that then?'

'At Messines, and before that on the Somme. Night-time sorties to haul our own lads back from them bliddy shell holes.' He looked blandly up at the constable. 'Bit like what happened here, like, last night. Ah bundled the lad in the back of me cart, threw me coat ower him and got Goldie here to run hell for leather to the poliss, only for them to get me to take the lad down to the workhouse. Not the nicest place, that. Been there on me own behalf once, and not for any doctoring.'

'Did Zambra say anything? Nothing at all?'

Mr Lynus shrugged. 'He groaned plenty so I knew he wasna deed.'

'And you'd no sight of this young lady here?'

'No, sir.'

'No one else?'

'No. Not a soul. I tell a lie. I saw Raymond Golightly on his way to the pit. And a gadgie in railway clothes. Whether he was coming or going to the station there's no tellin'.'

Mr Lynus and I had to wait while the constable wrote all this carefully in his book and tucked it back in his pocket with a flourish. He looked at me. 'When you hear all this, nothing comes to mind, Miss . . . er . . . Valois?'

I looked over the parapet at the river, greenish grey in the April light, then up past the viaduct at the town, now no fairy-tale city but a jumble of blackened buildings climbing up a hill. 'We just stood here enjoying the view. The town looked so pretty.'

'Pretty?' I could see the constable resisted the impulse to get out his notebook and make a note of the strange word. 'Pretty? And what next?'

I sighed. 'Nothing. The next thing I knew I was in my room in Waldron Street.'

The constable scowled at me, licked his pencil and wrote down my words, which were evidently very important.

The cart-man climbed up on to his cart. His serge trousers were too short, and inside his heavy boots his feet were bare. 'I'll gerroff then, Marky,' he said to the constable. 'Things teh do, ye knaa.'

'You mind how you go, Doug.'

The cart-man kissed the air to urge the pony on. 'Oh aye, Marky. You know me.'

We watched him cross the bridge and whip his long-suffering pony to labour up the steep rise on the other side.

'Could that man not have hurt Angelo?' I wondered, almost to myself. 'What about him?'

The policeman set his bicycle upright. 'Doug? He's all right, is Doug. Fighting drunk on a Friday and Saturday. Always back in them shell holes. I've had him in the cells more times than you'd reckon. But he only ever hurts himself, setting himself up against bigger men. Rest of the time, meek as milk. Wouldn't hurt a fly.'

'I just wondered, perhaps . . .' I gave up. 'Can you tell me, please, where is the hospital?'

'I can tell you where it is, but they won't let you in. They'll let Joe Zambra in, and his ma. But not anyone else.'

'But I must, I must . . .' I wailed.

The constable stood astride his bicycle. 'From your talk you're another of these foreigners, then?'

'I come from France.'

'You foreigners! I was just saying that to that Joe Zambra. You foreigners!'

It was hard to know what to reply.

The constable was still not moving. 'Can't fault them like, those Eyeties. D'you know that Joe Zambra and his mate Aldo fought in France? Not the lad who's been hurt, like, cause he's too young. Those Eyeties were in the British Army, mind you! I was at France meself two years. Wipers. Canna tell yeh where else. So much mud.' He put one foot on the pedal and lifted his large bottom on to the bicycle seat. 'Well then, Miss . . . er . . . Valois. You remember anything, you come and tell me. And you gotta stay here, stay in this town until this matter is sorted out. Theatre people's worse than gypsies for vanishing. I've had this before. *Disreputable* types, fly-by-nights, if you don't mind us saying so. You have ter stay in the town and come and tell us if you remember anything about last night. The police station is just on the way into the town from here. You can't miss it. It says "Police Station" on the outside. D'you read English?'

I stood up very straight, proving I wasn't a questionable type. 'I read it very well, sir, very well indeed.'

My borrowed theatrical dignity must have had its effect because he touched his helmet in some kind of salute. Then the wheels of his bicycle ground into the dust and he set off on his stately way, to do more pressing police work than investigate an attack on some foreigner.

As I walked through the market-day crowds on my way back to Newgate Street I passed two board-men: walking advertisements for the Eden Theatre, Bishop Auckland.

NO REST FOR THE WICKED

Emblazoned on one side was 'Tesserina, Exotic Dancer of the Spheres!' The other side, in tall letters, proclaimed 'Professor Stefane Slater, Teller of Secrets!'

Red Bandages

The café, when I reached it, was full of neatly dressed people taking a rest from scouring the Thursday market for bargains. Aldo glanced at me over his laden tray. 'Like a bear market in here today. We're short-handed. Joe's mother's at the hospital and Joe's serving up as well as cooking.'

'I want to know about Angelo.'

He nodded at the counter flap. 'Go through. He'll have to cook and talk at the same time.'

I lifted the counter flap: a strange privilege, like going into a priest's sanctum in church. To be honest, I don't really know so much about that church thing. I was christened well enough, but have been inside church very little since, if you except the time I accompanied my mother to light candles before she went into hospital. Perhaps she wanted to make her confession, although she didn't. I think now that the priests, disgusted by rumours of my mother's profession, had withdrawn the sacrament years before. The only time I remember her saying her prayers was when she was dying, fingering a rosary that was not her own.

As for me, I've never taken Communion, which puts me quite beyond the pale.

Joe was wrapped in a large white apron and his face was shining with sweat in the heat of the kitchen. He was arranging slabs of meat, mountains of potato and hillocks of green cabbage on big white plates. He caught my look and smiled slightly. 'They have simple tastes, these people.' He pushed the tray through the wide hatch and clicked it shut.

He turned to me. 'Now then, little one, what about my brother? What about *An-gel*? What happened?' His voice was kind but his eyes were hard, questioning. 'Have you remembered?'

'How is he?'

He shrugged. 'My mother is with him at the hospital. Today we are only pleased that my brother is alive at all.' He sat on a narrow bench and leaned up against an old dresser. He looked up at me. The thought came to me from nowhere that he was old enough to be my father. His eyes were smaller, sharper, colder than Angelo's. 'What happened?'

'I don't know. Honestly, I said it to you and I've been saying it to the policeman. I was down there with him. It was dark. After that I remember nothing.' I put my hand to my cheek. 'I don't know. As I say, I can't remember. I would if I could.'

'An-gel was badly beaten.'

'So the policeman says. He also says that I may not go and see him in the hospital. I thought if I went to see him perhaps I will remember.' I swallowed hard to lose the tears that were gathering behind my throat. 'It might help me.'

The fastener on the hatch jumped and rattled and we could hear Aldo's voice shouting. Joe stood up and turned out a light under a great pan of potatoes. He looked straight at me then nodded, as though someone had said something in his ear. 'Tell them you're his sister. You're dark enough.'

As I made my way to the café door two men, black-faced and pit-clothed, came through it. The café hushed at the sight of these underworld men. The taller one looked across at Aldo. 'We're marrers of young Sam. Wasn't on shift today. Never misses. We were wondrin' about him. They say he's had a brayin'.'

Aldo shook his head. 'He's at the hospital. He'll be all right. Tough little nut.'

'Aye, that's the lad. Tough little nut,' said the man. 'Anyway, tell him his marrers William and Tegger is askin' after him.'

Aldo bowed his head politely. 'Yes. We'll do that. And thank you . . .' The café door had already shut behind the dark intruders and the place buzzed up into life again.

As I walked to the hospital I pondered on Angelo's decision to join the world of those dark men rather than the clean, genteel world of the café and its clientele. How little I knew about him and how much I wanted to learn more.

The hospital was even dingier and meaner than the hospital where my mother died. And here there were no immaculate nuns in voluminous black gowns. The nurses were dressed like maids or waitresses and had very visible sturdy ankles.

The nurse led me to a ward lined with beds, only four of them occupied. She nodded towards a bed in the corner shrouded by a screen of taut linen. Behind the screen Signora Zambra crouched on a stool staring intently at Angelo's sleeping face. Her big capable hand clutched his where it lay on the threadbare blanket. His head was bound in a bloody bandage and one side of his face was lumpy with bruises still red and angry. Poor Angelo. His beautiful face.

To my relief Mrs Zambra looked up and nodded first at

me, then at the nurse. Her weary eyes had a welcome in them. There was no denial here that I was the patient's sister. I turned to the nurse. 'How is he?'

The woman's bulky shoulders moved slightly. 'No telling, love. The lad's taken a big beating. Doctor says it might take days for him to come round. But come round they do. I've seen it before.'

'Do they always come round?' I felt as if someone had punched me in the stomach.

Her glance slid to her patient. 'Wouldn't worry about this one, honey. He's young and fit. Well fed. We get some in here that don't fight their illness 'cause they've not had a decent meal for years. There's nowt on 'em to fight it.'

I looked down at Angelo. The uninjured side of his face was still beautiful, his cheekbone sharp, his blue eye glittering blindly under his thick half-drooped lashes.

I could feel the impatience of the nurse standing behind me. 'You gotta go, miss. Both of you. No point in staying just now. Against the rules.' Her voice sharpened. 'Will you tell your mother, young lady? She doesn't understand a blind word that I say. Foreigner, like. I've been trying to get her to go for half an hour. Doesn't understand a blind word I say.'

Good News

My mother is holding me from behind and I turn and punch her in the stomach and wriggle out of her grip. Then I run down shallow stone steps in pursuit of someone. I am under a high arch in a narrow street with tall tenements either side. In the distance there is someone in khaki. I run and run until I'm level with him and say, 'Papa . . .' but it's not him: it's the wrong face. I gasp an excuse, run on and bump into another man in khaki whose boots have been striking sparks off the cobbles. 'Papa . . .' But again the face is strange. He lifts me up and kisses my cheek, laughing a deep northern laugh. But it's no one I know. He puts me down and says something to the other soldiers. They all laugh indulgently, so many mouths laughing. Just mouths. Then they stroll on down the street and suddenly vanish. My legs have no strength and I sit down there in the street against the wall of a big church.

Having delivered Mrs Zambra back to the café and an anxious Joe, I finally tracked down Miss Abigail in the theatre, where she fell on my neck and asked me, Where in Heaven's Name had I been? She'd actually been to the police station to see if

I was in the cells and then had given up, trusting that I'd come back when I was ready. She smiled then. 'Which you have. Ever sensible!' I told her about my morning and described to her this problem I had, in remembering, but she just shook her head. 'Poor boy. And the hospital sounds too dreadful. Mr Barrington tells me it's the workhouse as well.'

I asked her what this was, this *workhouse*. 'Is it a house of work? A manufactory?'

'Not quite. It's where the poor go when they have no home and no money. Where children go when they have no mother or father. A lot of old people end up there when they are no use to anyone.' She shuddered. 'Horrible places.'

Perhaps it's like the place the nun would have taken me, if I'd not run away from her. 'The hospital seemed very bare but there were no old women or young children.'

'A different part of the building, perhaps,' she said vaguely. 'Now then, tell me more about the boy. How is he?'

I told her how Angelo had looked and what the nurse had told me about him.

'Poor boy,' she said again. 'Weeks, you say? And poor you. The company'll have to up traps on Sunday and you'll have to leave him behind. Sunderland next week, remember.'

Sunderland. The place with the bridge. The picture on my jug. But how could I go there?

'I must stay,' I said. 'I can't leave Angelo.'

Miss Abigail frowned. 'The boy has a family, my darling. They will take care of him. After all, you've only known him a few days.'

'But—'

Tesserina crashed into the dressing room, sparking pleasure as only she could. 'Mrs Palmer say I dance twice tonight.' She beamed. Her glance dropped to me. '*An-gel?*' She said his name the same way as Joe. I shook my head.

She frowned. '*Morto*? Has died?'

I shook my head. 'No, very ill. *Il est blessé*,' I said desperately. 'Wounded.'

She stared at me, then collapsed into a seat and we all sat in silence for a while.

After a few minutes Miss Abigail stood up and brushed her hands down her skirt as though she were brushing trouble away. 'Well, my dears, work is the best thing for worry.' She looked at Tesserina. 'I'd better talk with Mrs Palmer to see what she means about "one halfway and one at the top".' She glanced at me. 'Tesserina will need dressing twice a performance,' she said.

'Two dresses?'

'How can we do that? There's only one dress. No. Your job is to keep Tesserina calm and trim between her turns. Blot off the perspiration. A touch more make-up.' In the doorway she turned. 'But two dresses would be good. We'll have to get Dina Brooks to order more fabric in a different colour.' She beamed at Tesserina. 'I think you're on your way, my dear.' She turned to me. 'We're very pleased about that, aren't we, Pippa?' Her tone was firm, insistent.

'Yes,' I said miserably. What was all this talk of dresses with Angelo at death's door? 'We're very pleased.'

Full House

At the six o'clock on Thursday night AJ called us all together to inform us that tonight the grand circle, and the not so grand 'gods', would be full: the circle because of his stirring speech to the Rotarians, and the gods because tonight the unemployed and the people from the workhouse had been promised free seats. This was to be a treat paid for by the parish. There were mutters of protest at the thought of such hordes of the poor.

Madame Sophia Bunce sniffed. 'They smell so. I cannot stand the smell of the poor.'

'Smell!' The Pixies, in a row beside her, chorused their agreement. Pixie Molloy, at the end of the row, managed to nip her nose and wink at me at the same time.

AJ scowled at Madame Bunce.

Then Mr Cameron Lake said, quite loudly, 'Oh, I say, AJ . . .' in tones of disgust.

AJ shook his head. 'You may groan, dear friends, but these people are our bread and butter, they are our audiences of tomorrow. A pauper today, a prince tomorrow! These are

Modern Times, my dears. Raise your eyes and look above you.'

We looked up at the elaborately decorated arch above the stage.

'Read those words for our fine friends, *mam'selle*.'

I had to stretch backwards to read the carved gilded letters. ' "One touch of nature makes the whole world kin." '

'*Troilus and Cressida*,' said Mr Palmer. 'Act Three, Scene Three.' He stood up very straight in Shakespearean mode, filled his lungs with air and declaimed:

'For beauty, wit,
High birth, vigour of bone, desert in service,
Love, friendship, charity, are subjects all
To envious and calumniating time.
One touch of nature makes the whole world kin.'

He looked around us all, taking in every face. 'A touch of nature, my dears! When we look a pauper in the face we see ourselves in hard times. When we see an old man dithering along with a stick we see ourselves in twenty years. When we see someone bearing an injury. . .'

Beside me Miss Abigail folded her hands in her lap.

'. . . we must think: there, barring accidents, go I.' He relaxed a little then and spoke softly. 'When tonight those poor people are cheered by our performance and applaud us to the roof, we should remind ourselves that this is what we're here for. Make no mistake about it, friends. These people are our kin.'

This made me think about the miners who were so concerned about Angelo. So I clapped my hands and shouted '*Bravo!*' and the others joined in. For a few minutes you could have warmed your hands on the feeling down there in the auditorium. It was not always so in the troupe, but on that night many were chastened by AJ's words. It was easy then to understand why he was the leader and we – even Mrs Hermione Palmer – were all mere followers.

As we made our way to the dressing room Miss Abigail said, 'Dear AJ can be a bit of a stuffed shirt at times, but there are other times when he just cuts through the fog.'

That night we had the most enthusiastic audience we'd had in many months. Each act was applauded to the roof. Some people even whistled. It is the English way. Tom Merriman, off stage so dour, was a riot. As well as his sleight-of-hand tricks and his comic dancing, he told one or two stories that I didn't quite understand but that brought roars of laughter from the stalls, circle and gods in equal measure. He was almost smiling as he came off.

I worried that the air might be bubbling so much with laughter that the people wouldn't be quiet enough for Tesserina's dance. But they were. Perhaps it was Mrs Palmer's spot-lit, upright figure at the piano. She turned to them and waited, and they settled down. She played her soft introduction, then the curtains parted to show Tesserina in her dramatic starting pose. There were appreciative gasps all over the house as people caught their breaths. Then as Tesserina started to dance they breathed out and relaxed, sharing in the magic. At the end there was such applause! Some people in the gods stamped their feet.

Later they cheered loudly when I put out the board to say she was dancing again. When she'd finished that dance they applauded so much that Mrs Palmer, with a glance at her husband, initiated a reprise of the same dance.

I clapped my hands till they were sore and Tesserina

nodded towards me and glowed with satisfaction. In my mind's eye I could see her doing this many more times in other towns and cities. I had to admit that while she was not the same as she was in that street in Paris, she was so much better. The combination of her own instincts, Miss Abigail's choreography and Mrs Palmer's music had turned her into a star.

This audience was a pushover for Mr Slater. He sensed their goodwill and wound up his act to a higher level than ever before. At one point he had five men on the stage acting like different kinds of horse while the audience rocked with laughter. He called two women up, but once on stage they lost courage and fled, to mocking laughter. Then he had two young men up who swore they couldn't dance but had them waltzing together round the stage like professional dancers. It was all quite good-humoured and responded to the robust sentiments of this crowd.

At the very end of the act the light dimmed and the stage was in darkness except for the single spot, which made Slater's face gleam whitely in the dark.

'I have something for someone,' he said. 'Something here for someone . . .' He frowned and cast his head on one side as though he were listening. Then he nodded. 'There is someone here who has been looking in vain for . . . her father.'

My blood froze.

In the audience several women stood up.

'A name beginning with a P . . . Pauline . . . Patricia . . .'

All except one of the women sat down. The one that was left called in a clear voice, 'Me. I am Pauline. Pauline Tressell.'

Slater looked across at me. 'We will help you to get up here on stage, Mrs Tressell.'

I went to the bottom of the steps and helped the woman

184

up. She was wearing a hat and, it seemed, several coats. She was quite stout but no older, I think, than Tesserina.

Slater shook her by the hand and sat her down on a chair facing the audience. He then proceeded to pluck facts about her from the air. How she had lost a brother and sister in childhood and she herself had lost a baby. Her answers and assents were in whispers but he relayed them to the audience in his clear voice, pausing now and then to emphasise the amazing truth of his findings. He told Mrs Tressell that her father had been lost in the last weeks of the war at St-Quentin in France.

She nodded vigorously. 'Yes. Just before the end. Six weeks from the Armistice.'

But, he said, she was to stop fretting and searching, as her father had gone over to The Other Side out there in France, and was happy to have done his duty for King and Country, and was now quite content. She was to Get On With Her Life. She must Look Forwards Not Back. Through Mr Slater the woman's father reminded her of times when she was 'a bairn' and they had played ball and gone fishing together. He said she was to remember those times and not dwell on the fact that he was no longer with her in the flesh. She was to Be Happy. He was in a Better Place with his comrades around him.

There were patters of applause as each revelation emerged.

The woman, now in tears, was nodding and sniffing so much that she could not get a single word out. She grasped Slater's hand and kissed it and he glanced across at me so I could shepherd her off the stage.

He then turned to the audience and delivered a little homily about how we must not fear the unknown, how we must go forward and grasp our lives for they are fragile things and must be treasured. Then, with a flourish, he picked up his top hat and cloak and bowed deeply to great applause. Mr Palmer stood on the other side of the stage nodding his approval. Slater was matching Tesserina in terms of audience appeal. A battle was certainly afoot. Very good for the company.

Standing at the side, I entertained the traitorous thought that Mr Slater was the better performer than Tesserina, as each night he created something new from the human material of the audience. What he did was perpetually risky, whereas all she had to do was dance to higher and higher levels of perfection, which depended only on herself.

Mr Slater, sweating and exhausted, nodded as he passed me in the wings and to my surprise I found myself nodding back at him quite kindly.

The evening had had only one slightly sour moment. When Marie and Blaze Divine were doing their still Greek poses, some idiot in the gods shouted, 'Lift up that last curtain, will yeh?' There were lots of *shshs* but the delicacy of the moment was spoiled. Marie was furious when she stalked off the stage, almost pushing me over in her keenness to get back to her dressing room.

After the show Slater stopped me in the corridor on my way through to the back of the theatre bar. I moved to one side and he did the same. He put a hand on my shoulder and I stood quiet. The touch of his hand was quite light. His blue eyes bored into mine. 'How are you feeling, Pippa?'

'I feel very well, Mr Slater.' I managed to keep my voice steady.

'You look bad, *mam'selle*. You've shadows under those pretty eyes. Have you had no problems, no dreams, no lapses of memory?'

186

How could he know? 'No.' I said. 'None of that.'

'You should come to see me and we can take those dreams away.' His grip tightened. 'Come now. We will find a space.'

I wriggled but couldn't loosen his grip. 'No!' I couldn't believe how weak I was. Normally I would have kicked or punched someone who came this close without invitation. I kept my eyes away from his. At least I managed to say 'No!' and stand my ground.

At that moment the light from the end of the passage dimmed as Tesserina blocked it. She came up behind him then stepped between us, breaking his hold on me. She kept her back to him and looked into my eyes. 'Come, Pippa. Miss Abigail waits.' I turned, then, within the arc of her arm and we left Slater behind us. His soft voice followed us. 'But you should tell Abigail Wharton that she's to bring you to me. Otherwise it will all go on. All of it. It is dangerous. There is unfinished business.'

The lights of the town are dancing, melting into each other, into the liquid dark. Hands are pushing me into the stone. A leg jams itself between mine. A thigh thrusts itself against my thigh, a wide mouth, half open, is spreading itself over mine, stopping the very breath of me. I manage to bring up my fist and it rams into the throat of the man who is doing this, eliciting a grunt of pain. Then there is a sweet smell, like my mother's hospital and I cannot . . .

Aldo and Joe had saved a table for us in the theatre bar tonight. Miss Abigail was at the next table with Lily Lambert and Mr Merriman. Her large handbag was sitting on the seat beside her – she was obviously saving it for Mr Barrington. I longed to go and sit beside her and whisper something about Mr Slater, but Tesserina pulled me down beside her. Joe, tired-eyed, asked me again about Angelo, making me repeat word for word all I told him when I took his mother back to the café. He asked me again about the bridge too, but I couldn't tell him anything. Then I was forced to sit there while they chattered on in Italian, leaving me out in the cold.

I closed my eyes and I was in my mother's apartment, half hearing my mother joke with her visitors as I sat there at my English books. I was there but invisible. It was the same here, in the theatre bar. Inside my head, there was an undertow of misery, pulling me down into some kind of interior dark. I kept hearing Mr Slater's voice. Not the words, just the soft dark tones of his voice rising and falling like a spell. Miss Abigail caught my eye and made Mr Barrington pull another chair up to their table. 'Sit here, my darling. I think we need a word.'

Gratefully I went and sat down and allowed my shoulder to lean against her. I could smell her faint scent of violets. At last I could tell her about Mr Slater and what he said in the passageway. Then, instead of laughing at him she looked at me thoughtfully. 'Of course he might have something. He's a bit of a weird one, but he might have something. There's no doubt there's something wrong with you. Look at those weary eyes. That business on the bridge has taken it out of you . . . you look like death warmed up.'

I drew a very deep breath and nodded. Then I leaned my head on her shoulder and closed my eyes and tried to think of Angelo's beautiful face. But all I could see was that poor battered face with the bloody bandage, lying back on the drab hospital pillow.

I am in the apartment again. My mother is out again. The Belgian is pulling me on to his knee, putting a hand on my cheek, then into the neck of my dress. He is bouncing me up and down on his knee. I am very uncomfortable. My hand reaches out, out, and I find the copper lamp my mother keeps at the centre of our breakfast table, the light she does her sewing by. Somehow I get the neck of the lamp and lift it, bring it across and crash it into his cheek. I am rolling, rolling off his knee, watching the blood drop off his cheek and my mother is coming through the door shrieking.

Seance

Mrs Jackson had lit a big fire for us in her drawing room. Stripped of people, this big room was as hollow as an unsung song. The closed piano was like some kind of reproach.

Tesserina bravely stayed in the room with us. I think she thought she could protect me. But she sat by the window with her back to the room. She could never look Mr Slater in the eye. Miss Abigail and I sat side by side on the settle, her hand over mine. At ten o'clock sharp Mrs Jackson showed Slater into the parlour with a theatrical flourish. He looked quite dapper in a new-looking three-piece suit and a homburg hat that he laid on the cluttered sideboard.

Mrs Jackson, obviously impressed, announced, 'Here's *the professor* to see you.' She hovered and would, I think, have stayed.

But Miss Abigail smiled and said, 'Thank you, Mrs Jackson!' in a brightly dismissive tone.

Mr Slater was at his most effusive, clasping both of Miss Abigail's hands in his, then taking both mine in his and squeezing them. This time I could not avoid his gaze. He glanced across at Tesserina in the window seat, but she was ignoring everything that was happening in the room, her back rigid. 'Now, ladies,' he said, rubbing his hands together, 'to business!'

Miss Abigail looked at him grimly. 'You watch your step, Mr Slater. This is a precious child and it seems you have brought her to trouble.'

He shook his head. 'That was an accident of the drama, Miss Wharton. Her extreme reaction at the time gainsaid any immediate repair. She has been floating in a dangerous place. That's why I have been so concerned.' He glanced over at Tesserina's back. 'In that place lies madness, and some would say genius. It grieves me to admit fault, Miss Wharton, but even I know that this needs mending. Thank God you have been sensible. I've approached Miss Valois several times but she looks at me as though I am the devil incarnate.' He sighed. 'I am no demon, Miss Wharton. My misfortune is that occasionally I bring out the true demons in others. And that must be mended.'

He pulled a chair to the centre of the floor and looked at me. 'If you sit down, Miss Pippa Valois, we will finish what we started on Monday.'

Miss Abigail clutched my hand reassuringly and led me to the chair. 'I want to hear everything you say to her!' she commanded. 'No whispering!'

His steely blue eyes bored into mine. I felt his thumb on the point between my brows. I heard his voice. 'Now, Miss Valois, you are ten years old. You have been remembering that time in your life. And you have gone on recalling and recasting things from that time and this has disturbed you. And somehow it has spilled into the present time. Now. . .' His voice deepened, 'you're to put those things away. Some

191

of it is real but some of it is a false amalgam of many things. You'll not forget the events or your memory of them, but now they must go back to their resting places deep inside you, where they belong. All else is a game.' He put his thumb on my forehead again. 'Such things as I do are for entertainment, perhaps even guidance. They are not to frighten you. You'll not be dragged down by these things again. Have no fear.'

I heard everything he said, as clear as a bell.

Then he snapped his fingers and I blinked. I felt no different from before. No better, no worse.

'Right!' he said briskly, turning to Miss Abigail. 'Nothing else to do here. Business finished.'

She looked at me and I shrugged. I'd no idea whether anything had happened to me or not. She stood up and leaned over the table to dig about in her bag. I heard the chink of coins and saw the glitter of gold. Then I heard the murmur of his voice.

As the door clicked shut, Tesserina's shoulders relaxed and she turned to look at us.

'You paid him?' I said to Miss Abigail.

She sniffed. 'I thought if I paid him it might help us to resist the spell. Then we'd be under no obligation to him. But he refused, said it was unfinished business. So we are under his spell.'

'Spell? I wouldn't have thought . . .'

She was smiling at me. 'Well, dear? How do you feel now?'

'I can't tell.'

'Well then, it's time that will tell.' She was still standing. 'What now? Tesserina has her rehearsal with Hermione Palmer and I've my sewing box to restock from the haberdasher's. You . . .?'

'I'd like to go up to the hospital to see Angelo Zambra.'

'Such a bad business.' She frowned. 'Can you really still remember nothing more about all that?'

I remembered something. 'I had this dream – last night, I think – about being on a bridge. But I don't know whether it was about Skirlaw Bridge. And I didn't think it was happening to me. I thought it was happening to my mother. What Mr Slater called recasting.' I looked at the watching Tesserina, then back at Miss Abigail. Then I took a very deep breath. 'I have something to tell you. And afterwards you will not like me and may not want me near you.'

Miss Abigail laughed heartily at this. 'Impossible, my darling. You and I are a team.'

I looked at her with love. I would really, really follow her to the ends of the earth. I swallowed. 'I have to tell you a terrible thing. I have to admit to you that my mother – my dear *maman* – sold herself for money.' I breathed out very slowly and looked away from her. Then the words burst out of me in a stream. 'There's a word for it in English *and* in French, but I will not use either of these words. I did not realise just what she did for a very long time. She . . . managed things, and I was blind. Then when I worked out what happened in that room she was so very angry. With me! For knowing. So then even so young I understood that I must pretend. I must forget.' I turned my gaze back to Miss Abigail. 'And now, just recently, since Angelo was hurt, has come a memory. Of me hitting one of her . . . clients . . . with a brass lamp. I know then we had to move again. We moved from Carcassonne, to Toulouse, to Paris . . .'

Miss Abigail came and led me to Mrs Jackson's overstuffed sofa and pulled me down beside her. 'Your mother?' she said softly. 'Your own mother?'

'I must tell you, Miss Abigail, my mother did not look – like one of those women you see in Montmartre. You would not have known. She was clever, and very elegant. If you saw her on the *boulevard* you would not know her profession. Not at all. But this way she could keep me and have our nice apartment. Although she never said, I know this was so.'

I could still feel Mr Slater in the room.

'Then when I was thirteen she died. The church had rejected her but do you know a funny thing? She lit candles and wrote a plea to the saint in that church where I saved Tesserina. But it was still no use. It did not save her.' My lips felt like wooden logs with a dry husk of bark. I rubbed them to bring them to life again.

Miss Abigail held my hand tightly, examined me very carefully. She knew my words at last as the truth. And she still held my hand. I could have swooned with relief.

Then she said softly, 'Then who are you looking for here in England, my darling? If not your mother?'

The answer was obvious.

Truth and Lies

As I walked to the hospital I called up into my mind again that look on Miss Abigail's face as she let me know she'd noticed my earlier lie. I had supposed that in blurting out the thing about my mother I was letting her know I hadn't told her the truth before. But she already knew. She was a wise woman, opening up the lie between us. Hadn't she told me many times how theatre people were good at making up their own lives? How often did they rename themselves? Dina had been Beryl, Stefane Slater had been Stan. Tom Merriman was really Bernard Gomersall. The Divines had not been born Divine. It was all invention. People peeled off their past like an old coat. It was an ideal situation for deception. The constant moving about meant there was no one to say yea or nay about this or that fact.

Miss Abigail had her own interpretation of this loose acquaintance with the truth. She said because theatre people travelled on Sundays, there was no time for Sunday schools and such places where you were stuffed with thoughts of hellfire and damnation for the telling of an untruth. And acting and performing were the resorts of invention. Actors and performers abandoned the truth in their working lives so that others could find some real truth in their own lives. It was a kind of alchemy. For Miss Abigail that meant that although performers in the music halls might have a tinge of wickedness about them, they were true innocents, like Adam and Eve before the Fall. And like Adam and Eve they had to learn how to act in an invented world. Their innocence was their sacrifice.

But then, she would also say, it was that tinge of wickedness, that craving for excitement, for virtuous deception, that kept theatricals on the move. 'No rest for the wicked!' she would say calmly. 'It's our fate.'

But I was quite aware that *she* was different from this. She was as upright as a plane tree. She had been named Abigail Wharton and would always be that. Any story she told about herself was true. You just knew it. In this Tesserina was so very like her. There was no lie, no deception in her dance. And until the advent of the Italians she had not even had the sophistry of language, which might have supported untruth.

In fact it now turned out that Miss Abigail and Tesserina had similar stories. Weren't they both snatched as children so that someone else could peddle their talent on the stage? Like the dreadful Madame Bunce's Pixies. The outcome, of course, was very different for each of them. Although Miss Abigail was stricken eventually by the tragedy of her accident, she loved her life in the theatre. But Tesserina had the infinitely worse tragedy of meeting a truly evil man. But the nub, the beginnings of their stories as child performers, was the same. Perhaps that was why they had communicated from the first.

As I made my way through the town I thought of the first time I saw Miss Abigail in the dusty light of M. Carnet's sweatshop. Her still, grey-haired beauty struck me like a thunderbolt and I knew in that first moment that the feeling was mutual, that we would know each other. It was the same when I saw the barefoot, white-shirted Angelo in the chair in his mother's parlour. Instant recognition. What did I know of him? He was no slavish son, having rejected the easy life of the café. He was brave, like those other men who worked down below in the dark, who showed him so much respect. He was loved, by his mother and his brother. And by me now, even on so brief an acquaintance. How strange. How true.

These thoughts were piling one on top of the other in my mind as I made my way to the hospital. Then, as I walked over the railway bridge, I thought of Miss Abigail's comment and finally allowed my father to come to the front of my mind. I started to do some sums. How old would he be, that day I saw his back through the archway? I was ten years old then. And now there are these restored threads of memory: about seeing him through the arch; about chasing down the street looking for him. Didn't men turn round and weren't the faces all wrong? He was just one of many men in khaki in Paris at that time.

The faces I did recall were not very old. Perhaps no older than Joe Zambra and Aldo were now. When I was ten my father could have been thirty, the same age as my mother. He might be only forty now. Younger than Tom Merriman, than Josiah Barrington and all the others! A *frisson* ran right through me, from head to toe. Young!

Then my thoughts moved to Roy Divine, who was still missing. Just where was he? So where had he gone? Running away from the gorgon Marie? Hadn't they been fighting in the dressing room? At that point something came into my mind with the blind force of a gale and I stood stock-still.

Two women with laden shopping baskets bumped into me. I turned to say sorry but they were very ungracious and just hurried on.

I leaned against the wall, trembling. Mr Slater's intercession had stripped away another veil. That dream about the bridge had been no dream. It wasn't something that had happened to my mother, as I'd surmised with Miss Abigail. It was something that had happened to *me* on Skirlaw Bridge. It was *me* who was being pushed against the parapet. The face looming over me was Roy Divine's. Angelo was curled up in agony on the ground and Roy was grasping me, saying, 'Please, child, please!' I was struggling for my life and he seemed to be drawing back his hand to punch me. And then that smell, the choking, the swirling light.

(There in the street I put my hand to my cheek and pressed the bruise to make it hurt more.)

Then my memory failed me again and I could remember no further. I kept pressing the bruise, feeling the pain, so guilty that I had abandoned Angelo there to be beaten and left for dead by Roy Divine.

I set off again, hurrying on to the hospital. I would find Angelo awake so I could say sorry, sorry, Angelo for running away. I must have run, but I could not remember.

The dingy door to the ward was locked and I could find no one to let me in. I banged on the door but for many minutes there was no response. Finally a key ground in the lock and the door opened. A nurse in a shawl emerged, an empty shopping basket in her hand.

'Oh!' she put her head on one side. 'It's the little Italian girl.'

I didn't protest my nationality.

'You're too late, honey. Your big brothers have come with

their cart and got the lad. He's awake now, and wincing. But Doctor says a bit of his mother's tender care's all the lad needs now. Must have a head as hard as Gateshead, your brother. Doctor said there were signs somebody had bashed him against a stone wall or sommat.'

I stood back to let her past. 'Right!' I said. Then I set off back down the high street at a run.

The Patient

'How is he?'

The café was busy. Aldo lifted the counter flap to let me through. Mrs Zambra was counting money at the ornate till and I could hear Joe clattering behind the hatch.

'Angelo's upstairs in his chair,' said Aldo, smiling slightly. 'He don't want anybody fussing. But mebbes you'll put a smile on his face.'

I leaped the stairs three at a time. In the cluttered room Angelo was on a couch, trussed up like a turkey, heaped with blankets and shawls. Still, when he saw me a smile lit up his bandaged face.

'Well, now. Pippa!' he said. His voice was reedy and not very steady.

I sat down beside him and took his hand. He winced, so I laid it carefully again on the arm of the couch. 'I won't ask how you are,' I said. 'I can see.'

The fine clock on the wall ticked, and downstairs the door clashed as the last of the lunchtime crowd made their way into the café.

Angelo lifted his hand towards my cheek. 'Are you all right?'

I touched the bruise, so familiar now. 'Yes. Thanks to you. If you'd not pulled him off me . . .'

He frowned. 'Off you . . .? I can't quite remember.'

'Roy Divine.'

He nodded. 'That one? Feller shouldn't have touched you,' he stated. 'But he felled me when I . . . winded me so I couldn't help.'

'But you pulled him off?'

'He was a madman. Pervert.' The thin voice deepened to a growl. 'Didn't you see that?'

'He didn't seem anything – not horrible like that, before. He was just a brother of those acrobats. Never bothered about me. Not in Paris. Never before. Just in these last days.'

'You can never tell what people are underneath. Except the ones you . . . love. People lie, even to themselves.'

Lying to myself. I'd been doing this. This is what I'd been thinking about as I walked to the hospital. I wondered now what stories those three Divines told, to conceal who they really were, what they'd done before.

'I never noticed Roy at all, until the mesmerist started his tricks.'

'But mebbe he'd noticed you for a long time. And mebbe this was the moment he decided to pounce.'

'Did you tell your Joe about it – that it was Roy who did this?'

Angelo shook his head. 'At first, when I woke up, everything was a bit fuzzy. And it hurt, them manhandling me on to the cart and trundling me through the town. Now you coming here, saying this . . .'

'Even so, you could have said . . .?'

Angelo moved his head slightly and winced at the pain. 'Our Joe'd find him and kill him. Be sure of that. Get himself hanged. And then I'd have to say why and I'd have to say. . .'

'About me? About what he was doing to me?'

'I thought I'd need to ask you first. I couldn't quite . . . I told you I woke up a bit fuzzy.'

'I'll tell him. And when I go from here I'll tell that policeman. I tried to talk to him about it but I couldn't remember. Now I'm remembering.'

His one visible eye examined me. 'What did you remember?'

'For a while all I could remember was being down there on the bridge and you . . . and me . . .' I could feel myself blushing.

He reached out and put a finger on my cheek. 'You have these very soft lips.'

'Then it seemed I was in my bed and it was the next morning. I had no idea what happened.' I paused. 'Then just when I was walking here today I saw it in the eye of my mind. I saw you hurt in the road. And Roy coming towards me with something in his hand. He pushed me against the parapet.' I put my hand over my mouth. 'A cloth. Then nothing.'

The single eye narrowed. 'Were you hurt?'

I knew what he meant. I shook my head. 'He did not even kiss me. I know he didn't. Something must have happened. But I can't remember.'

He grinned and winced at the same time. 'Strange pair, we are. Remembering in bits.' He closed his eye and put his head sideways on his cushion. 'So what will you do?'

'There was this policeman, a strange man. So very slow at everything. But he did say to go back to tell him if I remembered.'

'So what will you tell him? The way the Divine feller got on to you?'

I dropped my glance to the rough counterpane so I didn't have to meet the glare of the single uncovered eye. 'I don't see that I need say anything about that. I'll say he knocked you to the floor and then attacked me, you rescued me and I ran. No more need be said. That policeman will need to come to see you. He takes such a long time to do everything.' I smiled into his eye. 'He calls you and Joe "Eyeties".'

'They call French people Froggies, you know. They like to get you into their own lingo, one way or another. Like then they own you, can understand you. They have you in their slot.'

'Like your friends who call you Sam?'

'Something like that. Anyway, if you tell your story, that policeman'll go and arrest Roy Divine for sure. Put him in the lock-up.'

'He might if he could. But Roy Divine's vanished. Run away. Nowhere to be seen. His family was very cross. They had to do the act without him last night. But now they'll know. I wonder . . .'

But Angelo's body was sagging and his single eye was closed.

I put a hand on his shoulder. 'Shouldn't you rest now, Angelo? Lie down properly?'

'I'm sore with lying down. Dead sore.' His single eye was still closed. 'But then I'm dead tired.'

I stood up to leave. Then I remembered something. 'Your friends from the pit came into the café, Angelo. The ones called William and Tegger. They asked about you. They were so very concerned. Said you never missed a shift before. They came straight from the pit.'

His eye opened and the edge of his mouth crinkled into a smile. 'They came in their black?'

'In their black!'

'Trust them!' he said. 'Real men, Pippa. True men.' He closed his good eye and his head dropped back against the cushion.

'I'll go. You're tired.'

He lifted a hand and sighed a very deep sigh. 'What more can a man want? A new friend like you, a brother like Joe and marrers like my friends from the pit. I'm truly blessed.' His head dropped sideways and he was fast asleep.

I looked down at him, my head, heart and muscles raging with regret and sorrow. If Palmer's had not come to town, if Tesserina and Miss Abigail and I had not dropped in at Zambra's for coffee on Monday, I would never have met him and he would be safe and well now, digging his coal, teasing his brother, eating his mother's pasta. If he had not met me.

I didn't know it then, but that was the last time I'd ever see Angelo alive. I did see him once more, still and handsome in his satin-lined coffin. But that day in his mother's parlour, when we talked about his marrers, was the very last time we saw each other in the living flesh. There is an English phrase – 'a crying shame'. Those words say it.

After I left the café I went straight to the police station to tell the policeman my tale. Of course, I was obliged to wait patiently while he wrote it all down. Then he told me he'd go and talk with the young Eyetie and then go and talk to the acrobats whose brother had gone missing. That was as much as he could do, he said wearily. 'But you never know!'

I had no time that day to go back to see Angelo. Miss Abigail was waiting for me with a needle and thread as we were sewing a new costume, in midnight-blue silk figured with lines of swansdown, for Tesserina's second performance. 'I've sent to Dina Brooks to get me more of the pleated cloth in midnight blue. But I found this fabric in a store here so in the meantime we'll improvise. Necessity is the mother of invention, Pippa. A good rule in our trade.'

That day we even ate our lunch at our work table, sewing away like elves. Mrs Jackson had offered us the use of her Singer sewing machine but Miss Abigail turned her down, saying the heavy action would snag the fine fabric.

Tragedy

That night there was a very full house at the theatre. Word had 'got around' that Palmer's was a good show. There was standing room only at the back. I actually saw Mr Jefferson rubbing his hands together, smiling slightly. It was good, even for a Friday night. Tesserina's second turn went down very well, although her more revealing silk dress drew whistles rather than respectful silence. The applause was very prolonged. She had something that the audience – that any audience – would want. She was sensual as a cat, but unknowing. The quiet, almost passive person we knew was replaced by this gorgeous colourful butterfly who could intoxicate strangers with her movement and passion.

Tonight there were gasps from some parts of the audience. From my place in the wings I heard Mr Jefferson humming the music as she danced.

Miss Abigail told me later there was a Mr Ward in the front stalls, visiting from the Empire Theatre, Sunderland, which was our next date. Mr Barrington had told her that Mr Ward was very impressed. Said that the show would be 'just the ticket' for Sunderland. In fact he was so pleased that he allowed Mrs Palmer to negotiate the Sunderland contract to sixty per cent of the take, rather than fifty per cent. AJ was highly delighted. Mrs Palmer was especially pleased, convinced the success of Tesserina's act was all her doing and that her virtuoso piano playing had done the trick.

After the performance Miss Abigail stayed in the theatre bar with the others, but Tesserina and I made our way straight across the road. Zambra's was closed but there was a dim light by the door. We peered through the window to see Aldo sitting at a table, reading a spread-out newspaper by the light of a single lamp. The rest of the café was in darkness.

We rattled on the window and he came to unlock the door. His face was dark and scowling.

'None of you came to the performance,' I began. 'You should have seen Tesserina—' I was stopped by the urgent pressure of Tesserina's hand on mine. 'What is it, Aldo? What is it?'

He ushered us in. 'The boy's back in the hospital. The doctor took him in his car. Joe and the old woman too. We couldn't wake him up. Something very wrong, according to the doctor.'

I turned to the door, 'I'll go and see him . . .'

He grabbed my arm. 'They'll not let you, Pippa. Come, sit here and keep me company.'

We stayed there with him for nearly two hours, drinking cup after cup of his exquisite coffee. Before long Miss Abigail and Josiah Barrington arrived and, grave-faced, joined us in our vigil. More than once I was made to tell my tale of what had happened on the bridge. The dreadful nature of that, and its consequences for Angelo, settled round us like a dark cloak. I tried to express my regret that I was the cause of all this, but both Aldo and Miss Abigail murmured reassuringly. Tesserina put her hand in mine. In the end our voices faded and the last cups of coffee stayed undrunk. An exhausted Tesserina spread herself across three seats and went to sleep. Miss Abigail put on her glasses, brought out some crocheting from her bag and began to work with neat precision. Josiah smoked his pipe and Aldo went through cigarette after cigarette.

It was two o'clock in the morning when the door rattled and Joe and his mother swept through the front door, bringing the chill night air in with them. Tesserina sat up blinking, and shook herself awake like a wolfhound. Mrs Zambra walked blindly past us all to the door behind the counter and clattered upstairs. Tesserina stood up and followed her. Joe threw off his coat and flung himself on to one of the café chairs. Silently Aldo stood up, took a bottle from under the counter and poured out a large glass of brandy. He placed this gently before his friend.

'What?' he said simply.

'He died,' said Joe miserably. 'Something wrong with his head that they hadn't noticed. I asked them if moving him in the cart made it happen but they said no. Nothing could have made a difference.' He struck his own chest with his fist. 'Jesus!' he said.

'Did your mother get him a priest?' said Aldo suddenly.

Joe blinked. 'What do you think? Of course she did.'

'Well, that's something,' said Aldo. 'Gone to a better place. A true innocent. A hero. A good boy, our Angelo.'

'He died?' I whispered. 'Angelo died?' Miss Abigail clutched at my hand.

The others all turned to look at me.

'I'm sorry, Pippa. *An-gel* liked you,' said Joe miserably. He

208

pushed the brandy glass across towards me. 'Have some of this. You're as white as a ghost.'

It was Miss Abigail who put the glass to my lips. The liquor burned all the way down my throat.

Josiah Barrington knocked out his pipe and stood up. 'We'll be getting away, Aldo. No place for outsiders. You need to be with your own.'

I stood up as well, pushing the brandy glass back in front of Joe, who was still slumped at the table. My movements were wooden, like those of a puppet, and my eyes refused to cry.

Aldo jumped up. 'I'll go and get Tesserina, then you can all get yourselves home . . . well, to the place where you stay.'

As he opened the door to the back all we could hear was Mrs Zambra's voice, high-pitched and wailing, funnelling down the stairs into the café.

Aldo came back alone. 'Tesserina says she'll stay with Mrs Zambra. She'll see you in the morning.'

Still Miss Abigail hesitated.

'She said you would understand, Miss Abigail,' said Aldo. 'Mrs Zambra needs her. There are no daughters here, you know.'

That night at Waldron Street Miss Abigail crept in beside me in the bed I usually shared with Tesserina. She held me in her stiff arms while I wept wildly for Angelo, a boy I barely knew. I wept on for my dead mother and my shadowy father. But I wept mostly for myself.

I had truly loved four people in my life. My mother, Miss Abigail, Tesserina and Angelo. My mother and Angelo were gone now to a Heaven they both believed in, although it meant nothing to me. Now only Tesserina and Miss Abigail were left. And already Tesserina was being enfolded in the arms of the Italians and working her strange magic in the theatre where surely she would be famous. That left Miss Abigail. And she would move on, as all theatre people do, whether I was at her side or not. The theatre was her vocation as surely as God was the vocation of the nun who dragged me away from my mother's body.

And Angelo! Truly the most beautiful creature I'd ever seen. His God must be a jealous God to take him away from me. This week Angelo and I were just on the edge of something special. We both knew it. He was in no hurry. There were no furtive grabs. He made sure he knew me. He showed me his beloved, grubby town made beautiful by night. I knew he liked me from the moment he saw me, and that made me pleased to wait for him, for us. Surely our lives were mapped before us? We would have taken a year or so to become acquainted. We would have been married, maybe even in a church. We'd have a little house. Some little children who would wear dresses made by me. I would wear dresses made by Miss Abigail and sent from Eastbourne or London or Paris, wherever she was working. Angelo would come home 'in his black' and wash himself all over and change into a beautiful white shirt. Then he'd take one of our children on his knee and sit opposite me at our table. He'd smile at me with those sparkling grey eyes and tell me he loved me.

And so I cried as I remembered my future and my life – the one with Angelo Zambra – that was now over before it began.

At last, in the early hours, Miss Abigail patted my shoulder. 'Sleep, child,' she said. 'You will feel better in the morning.'

Loss

Although she didn't show it, Abigail was profoundly disturbed by the turn of events. So the beautiful boy who had taken such a brief shine to her little Pippa was dead! What a terrible thing was the death of the young. Abigail thought of two subalterns she'd met on embarkation leave before the Boer War: two of many stage-door Johnnies who were more than just that. They were souls jubilant with thoughts of fighting for their country and their own future glory. But underneath, with their dawning awareness of the transitory nature of things, those boys, like her own friends, were at once strong and youthful, fragile and needy. It was not surprising that they craved the irresponsible, butterfly touch of stage creatures – much more than the worrying, homely touch of their women at home.

If not handsome, these boys were fresh and bright, at the height of their young manhood, and so very irresistible. In that bright distilled time offered by war, Abigail, a beautiful dancer of twenty-five, had come very close to two of these embryonic heroes. One had died of enteric fever somewhere in Africa. The other died of wounds in a hospital ship on the way home.

And that, Abigail reflected, was a mere rehearsal for the loss of young life in the Great War. By the time that war came round Abigail was no longer in the Front Line of the chorus, she was Behind the Lines in the wardrobe, consoling Josiah Barrington, who had lost his two sons (whom he had brought up entirely alone) in the first weeks of the war.

On the day after Angelo Zambra died, the Saturday night performance – a sellout – went like clockwork. The comedian made the audience laugh, the singers made them weep with one breath and sing with the other, and Mr Palmer's speech at Waterloo was heard in respectful silence. Mr Slater pulled out all the stops and had a respectable Bishop Auckland businessman attempting clumsy cartwheels around the stage. The Two Divines worked mechanically. Even so, their routine was so well honed that, although it lacked sparkle, their turn was professional and the audience noticed nothing amiss.

Abigail was proud to note that Tesserina was again the star of the show. Her passionate, sensual style went down a treat, causing a change of heart in Mr Jefferson, who had now abandoned worries that it might be vulgar, and replaced them with thoughts that such elegant physical pattern-making might be above the heads of this pedestrian, provincial audience. He even confided to Mr Palmer that Tesserina might just go down well in The Capital, where the audiences were more sophisticated.

Despite such a successful night, the death of young Angelo Zambra had cast a shadow among the company. Hadn't they all enjoyed fine coffee in his mother's café on that first night? Few members of the company had any heart for their usual end-of-engagement party with the manager and other local favourites. Even those who didn't know the Zambras reflected on drinking their coffee and the welcome received in the little café.

The Palmers would never have gone so far as to cancel the show – there was a deep superstition about that. But AJ had moved audiences to tears with dramatic evocations of death in battle and he knew the respect due to that fact of life in reality. He told the company he had sent his condolences to Mrs Zambra and out of respect they would desist merry-making, despite the very successful engagement. He and Mrs Palmer made do with glasses of fine whisky in Mr Jefferson's office and the rest of the company went their own way.

Vigil

Miss Abigail and I stayed behind to pack up the wardrobe ready for the railway van to collect the next morning. We worked efficiently, managing very well without Tesserina, who sat on a trunk, watching.

I was used to this passivity but tonight I was angry with her. I finally burst out. 'Do you never want to help, Tesserina? To do something for yourself?'

She frowned, puzzled by my angry tone. 'Pippa?' she said, then glanced at Miss Abigail.

Miss Abigail said quietly, 'We have our routine, Pippa. You know she would get in our way.'

I found myself scowling at her too.

'It's Tesserina's job to dance, Pippa. That's what she does. We do the wardrobe. Horses for courses.'

Horses for courses. Another stupid English phrase.

Miss Abigail pulled on her hat and stood at the mirror, pushing her wild grey hair away under it. Her gaze met mine through the mirror. 'Perhaps we should call on Mrs Zambra? Perhaps it's not too late to pay our respects.'

We let ourselves into the darkened café, where the tables had been piled in the corners; the chairs had been lined inside them in a circle. In the space in the centre two tables had been pushed together and laid with white cloths. There Angelo lay in his open coffin, watched over by his mother, whose fingers moved constantly through her rosary beads. Beside her, bleak-eyed, sat Joe and his friend Aldo. They all looked up. Grief rose in the air like smoke.

For a second everyone remained quite still. Then Miss Abigail went to Mrs Zambra and put a hand on her shoulder, and Tesserina went to Joe and – taller than he – put her arms around him, hugged him, then kissed him hard on the lips. Aldo stood up and took a step towards me but I avoided him and went straight to Angelo. He was dressed in an unfamiliar suit, a little bit puckered at the collar. Someone had wrapped a white linen cloth around his head so he looked like a young sultan, with only one or two of his dark curls escaping. You could see both his closed eyes now, although the right one was slightly strange where they had laid on some fleshy paste to cover his bruise. From a distant part of my mind came the thought that they must use something like greasepaint for this. Flesh tint No. 2?

I leaned down, laid my cheek against his, then recoiled swiftly from its icy touch. This was marble; it was as though it had never been flesh. *My mother white and cold on her bed and the nun's claw-like hand on mine, pulling me away, making me leave my mother.* Now Angelo was just as surely dead. I started to shake.

'Pippa, dear,' said Miss Abigail quietly. 'Enough, I think.'

I could feel Aldo's arm around me, warm and fleshy. 'Sit down, Pippa. Here, sit down on my chair.'

I wriggled from his grasp and stayed where I was.

'We should go,' said Miss Abigail. 'Leave Mrs Zambra and Joe to—'

'I'm staying,' I interrupted. I was dragged away from my mother. I would not leave Angelo. 'So little time.' I could feel them looking blankly, resentfully at me. I looked across at Tesserina. 'Tell them I'm staying, Tesserina. I have to stay. How can I leave him now?'

Tesserina nodded and talked swiftly to Joe and then Mrs Zambra, who responded with a few weary words.

Then Joe spoke. 'He's not been here with us long. There's to be a coroner's inquest. That'll be on Monday. Talk about it being no accident. Him being killed by someone. They mentioned this Divine feller, but the police say he'll be the other end of the country now.' He sounded exhausted, resigned rather than vengeful, which surprised me.

Mrs Zambra looked up from her rosary and said something.

Joe said, 'My mother says you can stay, Pippa. Says at least you put a sparkle into his eye,' he said. 'Like he put a sparkle into our life. That's what she says. And like you say, there's not much time left for any of us. The priest'll be here in the morning to sort out the funeral.'

Miss Abigail frowned. 'Oh, Joe, I'm sorry, but we won't get to the funeral. We'll be miles away by then. We have our train to catch tomorrow. Opening in Sunderland on Monday.' She looked at me. 'We have the train to catch tomorrow,' she repeated.

Tesserina came across to join arms with Aldo, creating a circle round me. 'I go with Miss Abigail, Pippa,' she whispered in my ear. 'I will go to Sunderland. I will dance for Angelo. Like Miss Abigail says, that is what I do. You must stay with Joe and Mamma. Watch Angelo. Not much time.'

Miss Abigail nodded slowly. 'We can manage for a little

while, I suppose, without you, although it will not be easy. You know that. I'll come here to see you tomorrow before we go for the train.' She kissed me on one cheek and Tesserina bent to kiss me on the other. She paused at the door and watched me drag Aldo's chair nearer the coffin and sit there, holding on to the carved mahogany edge like a drowning woman clutching a boat.

As Miss Abigail closed the café door behind her, the carved clock in the café tinkled out eleven notes, one chime after another. Then Aldo brought another chair and pulled it close beside me and Joe went and sat again by his mother.

So, with his mother, his brother and his friend, I watched over Angelo all through the night. And then, in the numb pain of this vigil for a boy I barely knew, I found myself for the first time properly mourning the loss of my own *maman*. So that long night, in a way, was for her as well as for the beautiful Angelo Zambra.

Staying On

In the end, I stayed on three more days at Mrs Jackson's so I could be at the funeral. During the day I lay on the plump bed I'd shared with Tesserina and only went downstairs at lunchtime. Mrs Jackson, bored by one-word answers, gave up trying to make conversation.

On Monday I was called to give evidence at the inquest. The constable read to them all his careful notes, including my account from Angelo that his attacker had been Roy Divine. (According to the constable, 'One of the theatricals in the town, now departed in a very suspicious way.') I was called to ask if the details the constable had read out were a true account of my statement. The coroner asked me if I myself had seen Roy Divine at the scene and I had to say that I could not clearly remember that. I touched my bruised cheek. 'I find it hard to remember properly. He might have been. The memory comes and goes. I think he might have been there.'

The coroner frowned and made a note. Then asked if I had any notion why the man called Divine would so savagely

218

attack Mr Zambra. I looked him in the eye and said I had no idea. They barely knew each other, after all.

In the end the verdict was what they call 'Open', which, Joe told me, meant they had no idea how it happened.

That afternoon I called at the darkened café but everyone there seemed distracted. The coffin was now closed and I could only bear to stay for a short while. Joe was very brusque with me and made me feel very awkward. The comradeship of our joint vigil had dissipated and I suppose the inquest had reminded him of my role in Angelo's death.

They obviously did not want me there so I had to go back to Waldron Street and endure Mrs Jackson banging on my door asking, was everything all right, and was poor Mrs Zambra bearing up?

I lay there in misery. I missed Miss Abigail and Tesserina like part of myself. I felt their absence like physical pain. I was sick twice in the commode. Then on Wednesday morning, like a spark of light, there was a postcard in Miss Abigail's ornate hand, postmarked Sunderland: 'Darling Pippa, you are in our thoughts. Monday night surpassed our expectations, Tesserina the queen of the show. Come to us very soon. All love, A. Wharton (and Tesserina).'

Angelo's funeral finally took place on Tuesday afternoon. I stood at the back of the crowded church, which smelled of dust and old incense. A distracted part of my brain picked up the rise and fall of the priest's voice as he chanted in vaguely familiar Latin. In front of me were rows of men in neat coats and women in long skirts and black hats. I was surprised at how many children were there, some of them chuckling and squeaking like little animals – voices of hope at a time of death.

Aldo had told me some Italians had travelled to the funeral

from all around the North, even as far away as Newcastle. Origonis, Alonzis, Gabrieles, Rossis, Pochinis, Bianchis, Lazzaris – he rhymed the names off like so much sunshine. Aldo said they barely knew Angelo but Mr Zambra, his late father, was much respected by these Italian families. At one time they, like me, must have been strangers in this chilly northern place. Now here, unto the third generation, they were part of its fabric. I wondered what it must feel like, to live for ever in a cold, foreign place. But that had happened to the Zambras and there was Angelo, proud to be part of this place and to be one of its people.

Proof of this was in the row in front of me, which was filled with men in creased black jackets, smelling faintly of mothballs. Some of them wore white silk scarves tucked into their uncollared shirts. One man clutched his cap on his knee, the quick of his nails ingrained with pit dust: like Angelo's, even in death. I recognised Angelo's 'marrer', the man called Tegger. Coming from another religious tradition, these men did not murmur with the service like the rest of us, but stood stiff and awkward in the dusty perfumed atmosphere of St Wilfred's. I knew from Aldo that Joe and Mrs Zambra had arranged the funeral for the afternoon rather than the morning, so that Angelo's friends from his shift at the mine could attend.

Half-listening to the voices murmuring into the rafters, my thoughts returned yet again to my *maman*. Of course, I couldn't go to *her* funeral. I didn't even know if they had one for her. Didn't I run away? If I'd gone to her funeral the large nun would have captured me for her school. But I knew my mother was certainly dead. Didn't I kiss her on her icy brow?

I don't know where my mother is buried. But I *do* know where Angelo is buried. It is on a slope above a river, paths winding among trees, its many graves kept fresh and clean. Angelo is buried beside his father. *Joseph Gianni Zambra, beloved husband and father. 1870–1919.* There are other Italian graves close by. Mr Zambra's grave, like some of the others, has a photograph mounted behind a glass panel set in the marble. His face, though much more closely lined and carved, reminds me of Joe.

Joe was coolly polite with me. I knew he was thinking that without me his brother would still be alive. I didn't blame him. I thought so myself. I said as much to Aldo, who mocked my self-absorption and told me I was not the centre of the universe. I asked him why *he* should bother with me, when his friend Joe was (rightly) so offhand. He said that this was what Angelo would have wanted and, anyway, everyone knew the only one to blame was the acrobat feller who would get his dues when the police caught him. If they caught him, that was. They seemed in no hurry.

Angelo's beautiful coffin, like the elaborate funeral carriage that brought it to the cemetery, was the best that could be had in the town. Two of his miner friends helped Joe and Aldo carry it from the carriage to the graveside. As they carefully lowered the coffin into the hole in the ground I thought of all the work and care that had gone into the making of it, so that for this brief time of the burial it might be seen to mark respect and love for Angelo. Such a short time. Like a short life. Nineteen years is less than a blink in God's eye. And the few days I had known him was a millionth part of that.

But I comforted myself with thoughts that what I had felt with Angelo was love in a tiny fragment. We shared a love that had a whole story of its own, a whole present and past, a missing future. Like one of AJ's ten-minute dramas. He, in his grand way, might have said that for me they only played the overture. Acts One, Two and Three remain unperformed, in a future only dreamed of.

I knew it was special when I first turned in the upstairs room and saw Angelo sitting there in his crisp white shirt. I knew it even more that night as he took my hand and we looked up at the twinkling lights of this town.

You might wonder, was I fit to recognise this love, having lived only in the house of a whore and out on the streets, with strangers poking and hitting at me as though they owned me? But my apprenticeship had been sure and true. My mother truly loved me, nurturing my English side with a steady hand; keeping me safe from the depredations of her own necessary profession; running for hot bread on rare mornings when the house was free of callers; brushing my hair and showing me how to turn it round on the top of my head in exact imitation of hers.

Angelo's dying made me see all this. Now perhaps I could put it alongside the recent dreams I'd had of my mother. Now I understood that the clutch of her hands on my shoulders, as we watched the soldier walk away, meant she loved the man: my father. She had spoken to me in my dreams of her love for him. Had she sent me to find him now, to complete some kind of circle started that day when they met in Carcassonne?

In my heart, that day I buried my mother alongside Angelo on that tree-lined slope. And with them I buried a childhood that I could now see from a safe distance. For ever in the future, when I thought of her, I would think of him. And vice versa.

Such wild romantic thoughts were floating through my mind as Angelo's coffin, ropes creaking, was at last lodged in the bottom of the grave. The priest started to speak and a brief scurry of wind made me look up, turn right round and stare through the trees that lined the path behind us. Just beside a tall elm stood the unmistakable figure of Roy Divine. With his long coat and the cap pulled down around his ears, he could have been anyone. But I knew it was him. He caught my look and turned to walk swiftly away. I walked towards him and he started to run. I speeded up, chasing him through the graves and the trees down a long greensward between two rows of houses and out on to the busy high street.

He soon outstripped me. After all, his legs were twice as long as mine. I looked up and down the long straight street. He was nowhere in sight.

'You're a quick runner for such a little person!' a voice gasped beside me. 'Where d'you think you're going?'

I looked up at Aldo. 'I saw Roy Divine. Behind there in the trees.'

He frowned. 'That feller? He's long gone. The policemen said so. They say he got a train. They're searching, but not straining themselves. Like I said, we mean nothing to them.'

I shook my head. 'He was there.'

'Why would he come here? He'd be a fool to do that.'

'I tell you, I saw him.'

'Mebbe he wanted to see you. He thinks you'll let him in, with the police.'

I clutched my bag to my chest. 'No.'

'We should tell the policemen. They're not making enough fuss about this. Out of sight, out of mind. D'you hear what the coroner said? *Open verdict*. Even if they think it's something to do with Roy Divine they think he's long gone. Someone else's problem.'

We were standing outside the shrouded café. 'Will you come in?' said Aldo. 'I'm sure Signora Zambra, Joe . . .'

'. . . never want to see me again.' I shook my head. 'No. I'm all packed up. I'm going.'

'Where?'

'To Sunderland, of course. Miss Abigail's expecting me. She sent me a card. They'll be halfway through the first week there. I can't think how Tesserina is managing without me.' I couldn't say to Aldo Malteni that I had nowhere else to go. Back to Paris? To Carcassonne? No. To me now, home was not a place but people. First Miss Abigail, then Tesserina, but as well as these there was Mr Barrington, even Mrs Palmer: people who recognised you, who had watched you grow. Even though you merely worked with them and they paid you for it, they knew who you were. Perhaps it was not much of a family but it was all I had.

Of course, Roy Divine could very well be waiting there in Sunderland. *His* family were there as well. Perhaps it would be safer for me to turn my face south and make my way back to London Town. I'd risen from the streets once, and could rise again there. What stopped me doing just that was the jug carefully wrapped at the bottom of my carpet bag: the one with the elaborate imprint of a bridge in Sunderland, the one *Maman* told me to take, that last day in hospital.

I'd seen Angelo buried and put my feelings for him in a precious inner casket that would always be with me. And somehow with him I'd finally managed to bury my mother, allowed her to be free of my own lies and uncertainties. Perhaps now, if I could find this man who was my father, then I could lodge him in the past where he belonged and get on with my own life. I felt so much older now. I knew more about the past and felt more responsible for my own future.

Oh dear. The habit of lying, even to yourself, is very deep. To be honest I felt impelled to go to Sunderland. I was quite desperate now to meet my father.

If only I could peel out of my mind the sensation of Roy Divine pushing me hard against the parapet of the bridge. If only. I shook that thought away. I needed to get to Sunderland to be with Miss Abigail and Tesserina. And to find this place where they made jugs. And to find my father. I had things to do.

A New Stage

From the moment he had swept through the doors of the imposing Empire Theatre in Sunderland, AJ had been on hot coals, pulling together the troupe for this much bigger, more impressive theatre. The troupe took possession of their dressing rooms, exclaiming how much better, more convenient they were than those in Bishop Auckland. To their noisy delight the Pixies had the second chorus room, which furnished them with a seat each before the long mirror. Madame Bunce, of course, quickly took control of the single easy chair lodged in one corner. Abigail Wharton moved quickly to secure a separate dressing room for herself with Tesserina and Pippa. It was a sign of Tesserina's improving status that Hermione agreed quite readily to this arrangement.

Hermione was visibly happy to be here in Sunderland, the big, rangy industrial town where she had grown up: a great industrial place, clustered round a river lined with wharfs and shipyards, where hundreds of ships were built each year, and goods ranging from coal to silk had been exported and imported from all parts of the world since the Middle Ages.

On that first, Sunday night AJ and Hermione Palmer were sitting at a plush corner banquette in the circle waiting rooms, talking to friends old and new, clearly relishing their own territory. Hermione was deep in conversation with Jacob Smith, the theatre pianist, who was also a friend from her childhood and had once carried her music case to their piano lessons.

At the other side of the table Mr Weaverson, the assistant manager, who was sitting beside AJ, called across a tall young man who was hovering by the door. 'This is my second cousin, Mr Palmer. Louis Hernfield. Right clever lad, this one. He works at printing but is by way of being a writer. He's written plays here for the amateurs that've been well received. But he's better than that.'

The young man smiled broadly and shook AJ by the hand. 'A pleasure to meet you, sir. I've heard so much about you and Palmer's. You have a good reputation here in Sunderland.'

AJ lit a cigar. 'Palmer's has a good reputation everywhere, dear boy. Now then, what's this?' His cigar pointed to the cardboard folder clutched in Louis' hand.

'It's a short drama, sir, called *Death by Night*. It's a drama of life, of politics.'

'Then it has much to overcome. Read it to me, boy. Read it!' His imperative tone made Hermione look up from her conversation.

The young man stood up and opened his folder, took a breath and then gave a very affecting reading for them there and then in a fine, supple voice. The drama told of two men caught burgling a house when one of them is shot dead. The central set piece of the play was a long speech by the surviving burglar bemoaning his fate and the loss of virtue: how he was driven by poverty to rob, despite having fought with valour in the Great War.

In the end, all within hearing stopped talking and listened. Hermione, recognising the popular themes, loved it. She urged AJ to give it a try. '*You* could make such a *thing* of that central speech, my darling.'

'We-ell,' said AJ. 'Fresh idea, fresh blood. The way forward. We'll try it! Come and see me nine a.m. sharp.'

Louis Hernfield laughed out loud. 'Thank you, sir, thank you!' He thanked Hermione for her support, shook hands with every single person around the table before he gathered up his papers and marched off, his boots striking the tiles on the mezzanine.

By Monday afternoon AJ had met with Louis Hernfield and cast his play, he had rehearsed four new dancers, seen a snake and rabbit act and watched an engaging set of Swedish tumblers, just off the boat at North Shields. In private he reflected to Hermione that he felt the Divines had become somewhat wooden since Roy did his bunk. With just two of them, the acrobatics were somewhat limited and the Greek poses would not be so impressive in such a very large auditorium.

'I have always liked them, d'you know,' he confided in Hermione. 'Very sensual. Ideal for France, even for smaller theatres here in England. But perhaps their act is designed for a more intimate venue, don't you think, my dear?'

Everyone was working to keep their place in the company on this important engagement. By Monday afternoon, as well as assessing Tom Merriman's new insert – an energetic and ultimately sad song called 'Up in a Balloon' – and a new comic song for Cissie Barnard called 'In My Fust Husband's

Time', he had looked at an extra routine by Sophia Bunce's Pixies that might be a good filler.

He was also rehearsing the drama by Louis Hernfield. Of course, this new inclusion would cost the company extra money. As well as paying him for his sketch, they were obliged to employ the writer himself to act the dead burglar. AJ roped in Josiah Barrington as a very effective wooden policeman and Sophia Bunce as an hysterical housewife. Madame Bunce was no actress but she was only obliged to scream 'Burglars! We've been burgled!' so it was not a demanding part. AJ himself, of course, would take the affecting role of the flawed war hero. It was this moving speech that had attracted him to the play in the first place.

As always, Abigail Wharton was asked, with selected members of the company, to review the first read-through. When asked her opinion, she said she thought it very affecting. 'Should go down very well in this town, AJ. You've got all those big houses sat cheek by jowl with dark tenements. Burglars must be very tempted.'

'Things're slowing down here like everywhere,' put in Josiah. 'Some ships are still here, but only for mend, not for build. Mebbe the warehouses are stuffed with fine things from the East. But I went down there this morning – favourite view of mine, Ayres Dock first thing in the morning. My own grandfather worked there.'

AJ nodded sagely. 'And my own grandfather worked on the Hartlepool docks. Always boom or bust, that was his favourite saying. The old boy once told me even acting was not so chancy.'

'I see today some of the wharfs are empty and the old dockmen are desperate for work.'

AJ glanced at the rest of the company.

'It's very affecting, AJ,' repeated Abigail.

'I have to say that your rendering of the big speech was very moving, AJ, the local intonation coming through just right,' said Cameron Lake helpfully. 'So full of feeling.' He touched AJ on the arm to emphasise his point.

Hermione looked at him sharply. Of course, the baritone was aware that changes were afoot in the company. You couldn't blame him for taking care of his own position in it. He knew very well that AJ's Achilles heel was his weakness for charming men. Who could blame him? Theirs was a hard world.

She said, 'The real experience of ordinary men is the little spark of grit at the centre of the shining oyster of performance, Mr Lake. AJ has a feeling for such a spark. Always has. This is a moving drama. But to do it justice on this huge stage I just think we need to consider impact and scale.' She looked up into the huge cavern of the auditorium. 'We're not playing for yokels here, you know! Vesta Tilley, Hetty King, Marie Lloyd, G. H. Elliot, Gertie Gitana – they've all played here. This place'll take some filling, and this audience'll take some entertaining. They're no fools.'

But the company agreed that Louis Hernfield's drama was worth a shot. The young man was delighted and again insisted on shaking hands with everyone he could reach. His fair good looks, his bright self-assurance and optimism reminded Abigail of one of her young Boer War subalterns. She held on to his hand, looked up at him and smiled. 'A good start, Mr Hernfield.'

He kissed her cheek. 'The best, Miss Wharton. The very best.'

In the end AJ, prodded by Hermione, also decided that they would make space for the Swedes, drop those final

Greek Poses and leave the Divines with the single spot: their more dramatic high-wire act before the interval. Louis Hernfield's drama would take the place of the Poses, and they would finish with Tesserina's second dance. Then, of course, the Finale, with the whole party singing a wartime medley to send the audience home happy.

'Send'm home happy,' AJ said. 'That's the ticket.'

Of course, this meant that the Divines' wages were halved and – despite Marie Divine's furious protest – AJ made it clear that his word was law. He told Marie very mildly that perhaps she should not forget he had good acts queuing up at the stage door at this very minute. 'Lots of talent in the North, my dear! Teeming with it,' he said gently. He did give her the obvious choice of dropping out of the show altogether, and finding a place more suited to the fine talents of herself and her brother. She swiftly turned this offer down, switching on a wide smile for him.

'We'll show you, AJ. We'll be even better and you'll want a second spot from us.'

Then, her sharp chin still up, she went down the corridor and swept into the wardrobe, where Abigail Wharton was sitting finishing the hem of a skirt for one of the new dancers. Tesserina was lying on the floor beside her, fast asleep on a rug.

Marie pointed a finger at Abigail. 'See what you've done, you harridan! Bringing that wicked child into this company. Ruined me and my brothers.'

Abigail went on stitching. 'Wickedness? I suppose you'd know about that, Miss Divine. You and your brothers can ruin yourselves without any help from me.'

Marie stared down at her. 'You! You picked the kid up off the streets in that godforsaken hole of a town. And she worms her way in here even though she has no talent for anything. She just casts those sly eyes on all and sundry, beguiling them and acting all innocent. Then she brings in the lunatic and suddenly the lunatic's the belle of the ball, over the head of people who've worked long and hard to get where they are.'

On the floor, Tesserina started to stir. Then she stood up with the rug around her shoulders like a cloak of an Amazon queen. Her head nearly reached the ceiling in the low room. She took a step towards Marie but Abigail shook her head.

'So, Miss Divine,' she said blandly, 'is there any news of your brother? I hear the police are very anxious to speak to him about the poor Italian boy.' She bit off the end of the thread with her sharp teeth.

Marie glared at her. 'I warned Roy, warned him about that French brat of yours. But she drives him off with her insinuations. Got him running scared.'

'I can't think what my Pippa has to do with your brother beating a boy half his size to a pulp. Has he always had such a bad temper?' Abigail peered through her glasses to focus on the needle she was threading. 'Of course he has. It's a family thing, isn't it? We've all heard you at it behind closed doors in every place we've set down. Mrs Palmer has been very concerned . . .' She made her first stitch. 'Of course, you're famous for it, keeping *it* in the family. In my view you must be rather jealous of Pippa, catching your brother's attention like that.'

Marie took a step towards Abigail, but Tesserina moved in front of her. Marie was strong but she knew better than to take on a woman twice her size. And a madwoman at that. She turned and left the room, slamming the door behind her with a bang.

Tesserina turned back towards Abigail. 'Pippa come here soon?' she said. 'I miss Pippa.'

Abigail attended to her sewing. 'It's poor Angelo's funeral tomorrow, Tessa. I think she will come after that. I left her money for the rail fare.'

'Perhaps Pippa will stay with Joe and Aldo,' murmured Tesserina, sitting on a low stool at Abigail's side and leaning against her legs.

'I don't think so, my dear. Now if young Angelo had still been there she might have stayed. There was something about him and her together. A blind man could see that, even on so short an acquaintance. That would have been something to keep her there, you see? I have seen it happen. People join and drop away from a travelling troupe like seasonal birds.' She sighed. 'I have lost some good friends that way. But I'm sure Pippa will come back to us now. She's not ready to fly alone just yet. And we need her.'

'Is it a good thing that Angelo die?' said Tesserina, her face serious.

'No!' Abigail shuddered and nudged Tesserina hard with the toe of her shoe. She thought she understood the girl but now and then her naïve amorality made her catch her breath. 'How could you think such a thing? Sometimes I forget the barbarian years you spent in that hospital.'

'Barbarian?' Tesserina frowned.

'Never mind.' Abigail decided to change tack. 'What about that Joe Zambra? I reckon you took a fancy to him.'

'Joe?' Tesserina smiled happily. 'Joe said he would come here Saturday to see me dance.'

Abigail put down her sewing. 'Now how do you reckon that, dear?'

'He told me. Told me when we come to train.'

'I wouldn't set your heart on it, dear. Promises are like pie-crusts. Easily broken in transit.'

Tesserina frowned. 'Transit?'

'Don't set your heart on him coming.'

Tesserina shrugged. 'Joe will come.'

Abigail restarted her sewing. 'Well, dear, I'll just settle for my darling Pippa. She's left a hollow space at my side since we set out for this place. I miss her too.'

At that point Josiah Barrington came bowling through the door, to tell Tesserina that Mrs Palmer was waiting for her on the stage, as her dance needed blocking into the larger space. Tesserina leaped up gracefully from her stool and drifted past him and out of the door without a word.

'Queer lass, that.' Josiah sat down on the stool. He took out a handkerchief and mopped his brow. 'Phew! AJ's got us all with our skates on.' He nodded at the closed door. 'That Tesserina gets no better. Swept by us without so much as a by-your-leave.'

'Give her a chance, Josiah. She's just got out of some vale of tears. She'll never be just ordinary. Just when she should have been learning right from wrong they were using her like some puppet. How would she learn to think and feel for anyone else in a place like that?'

'How long d'you make excuses for a person, Abigail?' He took out a small cigar and lit it. The fruity smell was a relief in the air of the dressing room, which smelled of clean soap, dust, mothballs, and deceased moths. He breathed out the smoke and his words came with it. 'These folks come and they go, don't they, Abi? I tell you what, girl, you and me should tie the knot. A sign that no matter whether anyone else comes and goes, it's not us.'

She shook the hem of the garment at him as though she

was shooing a chicken away from a doorstep. 'Go away, Josiah. You'll set fire to my lovely costumes with that filthy cigar.' She put her head on one side. 'I think I can hear AJ calling your name. You'd better run, my boy!'

He grinned, stood up and made for the door. 'I'm serious, you know, Abi. Never more so. I'm serious.'

She watched the door close behind him. It was easy for Josiah to talk about marriage. He did this quite often. She knew he wasn't eager to marry simply for the comfort of her body. He'd always enjoyed that once in a while when she was in the mood, and always would. But he was younger than she was. Surely he would get impatient as she got older and her poor legs rusted up altogether. Their present ad hoc approach in their friendship had worked well for her. And if one day she ended up in a Bath chair – well, sufficient unto that day may that evil be! She would be responsible for herself as she always had been.

In the meantime she had the grieving Pippa to see to and the mad, unfeeling Tesserina to direct. Surely her hands were full enough, without thinking of getting married again at her age?

She laughed out loud, picked up the next dancer's skirt and surveyed it closely for any damage. Those girls could be so very careless!

Betrayal

The station waiting room at Bishop Auckland was nearly empty, its only inhabitants being a pigtailed woman with a square basket on one side of her and a small child on the other. The room was comfortable, with clean painted high walls, polished benches and a bright fire.

I'd walked to the station alone with my bags and baggage, dragging the heavier bag along the ground. No one had offered me any help. Suddenly the friendly people of this town were strangers – as they might well be in any small town in England or in France. In such places some alchemy renders us – outsiders by our garb and our demeanour – invisible to more respectable and established citizens.

I'd thought Aldo might turn out to see me, but I passed the café and noted it was open; the business of food was in full swing. No doubt Aldo was needed in there. And Joe wouldn't have bothered about me anyway. I'd felt the shadow of his dislike since Angelo's tragedy. Who would blame him for this?

The pigtailed woman stood up and left the waiting room.

I was alone for a second, then the door behind me opened again. Someone else had entered the room. I could sense them standing in the doorway. The stillness of this presence made me turn round to face the lumpy-handsome face and the slender-strong figure of Roy Divine.

'Well, Pippa?' he said, his voice light and natural. 'Here we are again?'

I glanced through the waiting-room window at the busy platform but didn't move from my chair. 'I thought you'd gone. That you'd run off, away from this place, in shame for what you'd done.'

He shook his head. 'I've waited for some time to talk to you but there were too many people around you. Too much interference.'

'Your sister was angry, really angry, Roy. Did you talk to her?'

'I left her a note. Told her not to worry.'

'She was fuming – so hot she might catch fire. She was angry at me, you, everyone around her. But then that is no change.'

He shrugged and sat down on the chair just inside the door. 'She's always fuming. That's my sister. A fellow needs to get out away from her from time to time.'

'You must have known the policeman is looking for you.'

'I got wind of that, so I went to ground. But in truth there's no reason why any policeman should be looking for me.' His voice was easy, relaxed. 'So, Pippa, what am I supposed to have done?'

'You beat Angelo Zambra and now he's dead. You know that. I saw you at the funeral. Angelo's dead.'

'That's very unfortunate. But nothing to do with me.'

'You were there on the bridge. He told me. I kind of remember.'

'Kind of?' He laughed. 'Right. I was there on the bridge. But I did him no injury. It was you. I pulled him off you.'

'No! No. It was you.'

'I have told you, Pippa, I pulled him off you. Then he turned and aimed a punch at me and it landed on you, not me. Then you hightailed it up the hill like a jack rabbit. Then he jumped right on me and I threw him away from me and he crashed against the parapet and he was still. Then it was my turn to hightail it.'

Suddenly I was a jelly of uncertainty, haunted again by all my dreams and half-dreams. Lies layered over truth. Truth on lies. I couldn't actually remember what happened on the bridge, any more than I can remember truly those things about my mother. They were like stories someone else has told me. I'd had to rely on what Angelo said to me. And he was dead. Then I did remember something. 'You said, "Please, child." That was you, I'm sure. I remember that. Why did you say that? Why did you pull him away?'

His head hunched deeper into his shoulders. 'I have to admit, I'd followed the two of you and I was jealous of how easy you were with him. I didn't like how familiar he was with you.'

'But the night before! You did that horrible thing.'

'That was the trouble, Pippa. Don't you see? I felt guilty about that, and then there you were, holding hands with him.'

I looked at his keen, creased face, almost invisible under the shadow of his peaked cap. 'What are you saying, Roy? You're old. Old enough to be my father. Old enough to be Angelo's father.'

He closed his eyes for a second. Then he opened them. 'Do you have brothers or sisters, Pippa?'

I shook my head. 'Only my mother and myself. Then just me.'

'My brother and sister and I were orphaned when I was fifteen and since then we have, if you like, infested each other. You could not tell where one ended and the other began. You might say it came out very well. We were not alone. We had each other. We perfected our act, we laughed, cried, quarrelled, drank, ate. As though the three were one?' Again, that questioning tone without the questions. He glanced out of the window.

'Your brother and sister . . .?' I said helpfully.

'Well, Marie has always been the boss, keeping us on a tight leash, keeping us practising, rehearsing. She has always kept us both on our toes. Made a pet of Blaze one month, a favourite of me another. But when we were in Paris it began to change. Since then she's been interested only in him. Those two have been tight as a drum, with me on the outside.'

'Shut out,' I said. 'I can see that.'

'Yes,' he said eagerly. 'Shut out.'

'I'm sorry for you.' I was.

'That was when I noticed you. Suddenly, after Paris, I seemed to see you everywhere. That was when I realised that I need not be shut out. That it wasn't all about Marie. I could be close to you and you could be my friend. It seemed so simple.'

'But don't you see how strange it is? You're not fifteen years old now. You're—'

'Old enough to be your pa. I know that. But Marie, she's been so much . . . well . . . the boss. Kept Blaze, and me at just fifteen, I suppose, hanging on to her skirts. It must seem strange but that's how it's been. Then it dawned on me that making a friend of you would show Marie something. To be truthful, after all those years as her pet puppy I hardly knew what was right or wrong, in the way a person goes about things.'

'Like Tesserina,' I said. 'She has never learned. Not really.'

He frowned again. 'How's that?'

'She was shut away in a prison asylum for years. When she came out she didn't know that the "normal" way she acted frightened people; made them call her lunatic. She frightened them, and you certainly frightened me.'

He nodded, his eyes on mine. 'I see this now, Pippa. I know the way we went on was not the way we should. You know, Marie . . .?' His voice trailed off.

The big clock on the waiting-room wall ticked away. Outside on the platform a train began to chuff up steam.

At last I found the strength to stand up. I wanted to get rid of him. In spite of his protestations he still made me feel uneasy. It was a simple thing to blame Marie. Too easy. 'You have mixed me up. I don't know what I remember. I have to go. My train will be here soon.'

'Wait! Wait!' He stood before me, blocking my way to the door. 'I want you to do something, Pippa. I want you to come with me to the police station and tell them what I've just told you. Tell them that it was a mix-up. That it wasn't my fault. I can't leave here with a blotted copybook. I'll never work again.' His hands came down on my shoulders, his grip far too strong. His eyes were boring into mine. I started to struggle.

'Come, Pippa! Just come with me and tell them it wasn't my fault. That there was a mistake and I thought the lad was attacking you? My idea was to save you *from* him? Not the other way round?'

I was overwhelmed with the thought that I would never

get away from him, never get away from this place. So I stood up and let him usher me out of the waiting room. I don't know whether at that moment I finally thought there was something of the truth in what he was saying. Whether I had dreamed up some other version of those events. Or perhaps it was just those pale eyes of his boring into me, mesmerising me as Stan Slater had done. Or perhaps . . .

He hustled me to the stationmaster's office to leave my luggage. Then I went with him to see the policeman. I told the constable Roy's side of the story and said that I was confused. I didn't really know which version was true. I said it might be true, that I was confused from the blow I'd received and had no idea what had really happened. I did say I found it hard to think that Angelo Zambra may have landed the punch that knocked me out. I said I could not remember being knocked out, but then I wouldn't, would I?

I can't say why I was so compliant over this. I could have run away from Roy in the crowded station. I could have denied the tale he told the police in his smooth voice. But I just stood there watching, as the policeman wrote down my new statement with a careful hand. 'I'll pass this on to the magistrates. The waters is very muddy now.' There was doubt in his voice. 'Could have been one of those Eyeties themselves, mebbe. It's not unknown for that lot to make war among themselves.' He turned to the clerk at the desk and said as though we weren't there, 'Show-people and foreigners! Troublemakers all. Best shot of them, in my view.' He then turned to me, his face bland. 'You'll be getting on your way then, Miss Valois?'

'I was on my way. I was at the station when Mr Divine spoke to me . . .'

'Well, miss, we'll just get on and get this other statement

written out here for Mr . . . er . . . Divine. So you can run along now.' The three men looked at me then with blank eyes. I was dismissed. I fled, happy at least to be away from the stuffy police station and those watching men.

I didn't go straight back to the railway station. Instead I went up to the cemetery to say sorry to Angelo for this new betrayal. This last week had been such a whirl of events and dreams that I wasn't sure any more just what I really knew. Hadn't I had dreams then, when the opposite happened to what I first thought? Had I beaten the Belgian in my mother's apartment or was it *Maman* who was beaten and pressed against the wall? Or who beat me? And what were those soldiers doing when they passed me from hand to hand? And was that a dream or was it real?

Any sense of certainty was slipping away again.

Slowly I made my way through the trees to the flowery mound that was Angelo's grave. As I stood there, I became steady again inside. Whatever Roy said, I knew that Angelo was not my aggressor, that he was as pure as the white shirt he changed into when he came in from the mine. It was not he who attacked me. I knew that without remembering it. I couldn't be so certain about Roy. In fact, I *knew* the opposite. Hadn't he engulfed me there in the street the night before? Hadn't Roy just admitted to me at the railway station that he was looking for someone to replace Marie in his warped affections? Weren't the Divines famous for attacking each other?

I licked my lips, remembering the bad taste when I woke. Perhaps he had put something on my mouth, had made me unconscious and somehow got me back to Waldron Street. Or, half conscious, had I run away and got myself to Waldron Street? Amid all the uncertainties I knew for certain that it was not Angelo who had hurt me.

I stood for a long time, staring at the mound of flowers. 'I'm sorry, Angelo. I ran away once from my dear *maman* and I'm running away again. I'm sorry.' I whispered the words. Ugly lumpy tears were flowing down my cheeks. 'I'm sorry, Angelo.'

A hand gripped my arm and I looked around to see the white, strained face of Mrs Zambra enclosed in a tight black silk scarf. She began to pat my arm comfortingly with one hand. With the other hand she touched her own cheek, which was also wet with tears. I longed to tell her of my bad day's work but I couldn't. And she just patted my arm and said in English, 'My Angelo.'

I knew there was nothing now that could help either her or me, so I walked with her back into the town. I refused her gestured invitation that I should go into the café with her, then walked back to the railway station to catch the next train, whenever that might be.

Now, sitting again on the station seat, I'd managed to betray my own very first love. Never before – even when I was first destitute on the streets of Paris, or when I was labouring for the importunate M. Carnet in Toulouse – *never* had I felt as alone as I did now in that polished waiting room with its low fire. Full of misery, I tried to conjure up inside me an image of Angelo's handsome face, his bright eyes. But I couldn't. I could see the faces of Joe and Aldo. The white face of Mrs Zambra. Without doubt I could bring to mind the narrow, bitter face of Roy Divine. But for me Angelo's face was a grey blank above a glistening white shirt.

This, I could see now, must be my punishment for betraying him. I was not a good person and probably never would be.

Louis Hernfield

In the end I caught a train to Durham and ended up sleeping overnight in the waiting room there. Then at dawn I obtained a seat on a rattling milk train that took me to the busy sprawling town of Sunderland. A cart-man out early at the station gave me a lift with my baggage to the theatre, ornate with a rather grand corner entrance, not so blackened as other buildings in the street. The door was locked. I settled on the steps until a man in braces and rolled-up sleeves unlocked the door, and, hearing my business, let me in.

The deserted theatre had the hollow feeling and the smell of a dead place. Used-up lives. I made my way through to a long plush foyer where I sat down at a table, took off my beret, put my head down on my hands and slept; at least for now I had no further to go. Miss Abigail would find me.

But the hand that woke me was not hers. I looked up into the face of a man with a shock of hair that stood straight up from his brow, above oversleepy, knowing eyes. He was staring straight at me.

'So who have we here, washed up on this far shore?' he

drawled. His voice was soft and deep. 'Just off the boat, perhaps?'

I shook off his hand and blinked to force my brain into action. 'I'm waiting for my friend. She's expecting me to be here.'

He performed this funny mime of looking round the deserted foyer, into the gilded niches and under the elaborate tables. Then he came to stand before me. 'No friend here, I fear, miss. But I could be your friend.' He put out his hand and grasped mine. 'I am Louis Hernfield. I'm a printer and lithographer by trade, but my greatest wish is to write plays for the theatre.' He said his name Louis in the French way, not *Lew-is* as the English have it.

I pulled my hand out of his. 'My name is Barbara Philippe Valois. They call me Pippa.'

His face brightened and he took my hand again. 'Ah! It's the French girl. I have heard of you from your friend Miss Wharton, a wise and perceptive woman. But I didn't recognise you, seein' as you have no wings and halo.' His voice was not stagy. It had the sea in it. He clearly came from these parts.

I pulled my hand away from his a second time as the very subject of our conversation scurried towards me with her awkward gait and flung her arms round me. 'Darling girl! I was beginning to think you must have run away from me.' Still holding me, she turned to the man called Hernfield. 'And you've met our clever Mr Hernfield, who's written a brilliant drama for AJ, which the people here love. I've met quite a few dramatists in my time but he's by far the most handsome, don't you think?'

This made me blink a little. Miss Abigail was seldom so effusive, so coquettish. She must like this man.

Mr Hernfield, formerly so bold with me, now blushed up

to his ears. 'Miss Wharton is too kind to me. I really earn my daily bread in printing, Miss Valois. But have always been involved in some amateur theatre round here. Then the assistant manager here – cousin to my mother – recommended my play to AJ. So, here I am. You are looking at a lucky man, Pippa.'

Then Miss Abigail started to grill me about my lateness and I told her about sleeping in Durham Station and getting the milk train. Louis Hernfield, listening to all this, glanced at me. 'Seems you've not even broken your fast, Miss Valois. I'll go and find bread and milk. You're a growing girl. You must be very hungry.'

I was furious. 'I'm fully grown, thank you.' I glanced at Miss Abigail.

But she ignored my fury and beamed and ferreted around in her bag. 'What a good idea. I'll go and brew tea on my little stove.' She gave Louis Hernfield a shilling. 'Dear Louis, you may go out and get bread and cakes, and we'll break our fasts like queens.' She hauled me to my feet, keeping her hand on me as though she were afraid I'd run off.

Louis Hernfield winked at me, pushed his hand through his hair – making it stand up even more – and then vanished through the ornate doors.

Breakfast

Abigail was very relieved to see her dear Pippa again. She had really begun to think her young friend might have run away, driven by those dramas at Bishop Auckland. When they first met, the girl had been so used to running, was so much her own woman, that Abigail had always felt honoured that she stayed. She flattered herself that the girl must have stayed with her because she chose to, not because of some misguided gratitude or sense of duty.

Both happy to be together again, they ate their first meal in Sunderland in their theatre dressing room. Pippa sat munching her cake while Louis Hernfield and Abigail talked of the theatre in Sunderland.

It seemed that all the prominent people in variety, and even the straight theatre, had performed there. Louis seemed to have met and talked to them all. But he asked Abigail urgent questions about the London theatre, which was his obsession despite the fact that he'd never been to London. True, he had aunts and cousins involved in the amateur theatre in this town. But Abigail and Pippa learned that he was aching to dip his toe in professional waters.

Encouraged by his bright eyes and intense interest, Abigail talked rather more than usual. She was also encouraged by the presence of her dear Pippa, who – eyes peering over a rather large iced bun – seemed to be taking in every word.

Catechism

The voices of Miss Abigail and Louis Hernfield dimmed to a murmuring chorus as I allowed myself to be flooded by strong, sure relief. Sitting there, my guilt at my betrayal of Angelo, my uncertainty and self-deceit over Roy Divine — all these began to fall from me like a sloughed skin.

I was at home again, within the kindly aura of Miss Abigail, watching her laugh and talk with a man who (even while he did this) was gazing at me with the satisfaction of a fisherman who has caught a particularly delightful catch.

At one point he actually addressed me. 'Have you been in this town before, Pippa? There's sommat about you . . . sommat familiar.'

I thought of my father, but shook my head. 'I've been in England a little less than a fortnight. I have not been here, though.'

'Anyone could tell you're foreign from your talk but . . . well, you speak better than many a person round here. We've Scotch and Irish round here that talk so thick a brogue you can't make out a word.'

'My mother was a teacher of English. I've a suspicion her own grandmother was English but I'll never be sure.' I think I made that up, the bit about my grandmother. I was not ready yet to tell Louis Hernfield about my father.

'She's cleverer than ten monkeys, this young woman,' said Miss Abigail. 'Reads more English books than you'll ever get a chance to. Talks like a book herself at times.'

Louis Hernfield shook his head. 'She can't have read more than me. I've a whole shelf of books and borrow from the library here and, like my dear pa, am a member of the Literary and Philosophical Society. We bring home books from there to read.'

This sounds a great deal for a mere printer.

Then he started on a catechism. 'Have you read Charles Dickens?'

'All except *Hard Times*.'

'Charlotte Bronte? *Jane Eyre*?'

'*Oui*. And I read her sister's novel about the wild boy on the moors.'

'Jane Austen?'

'Yes, but to be most honest she's a bit too plain and allusive for me.'

'Allusive, eh? What about Trollope?'

'Some. A bit stodgy and very English.'

'Thackeray?'

'Just *Vanity Fair*. That Becky Sharp is my most favourite. A *méchante*. A naughty girl.' I paused. 'All these books make me dream of England.'

He flicked his hands in the air. 'I give up. Could be you've even read more than me.'

A curious thing. While all this was happening, even while I was speaking, at the edge of my mind something else was happening. Like in those multiple mirrors you see at fairgrounds, I could see another scene – the scene in the upper room at Zambra's café when I turned and looked at Angelo for the first time. How different was this man, with his putty-coloured hair and his sleepy eyes, from the dark, golden-skinned Angelo. He was ten years older for a start, more fluid and sinewy and less handsome than the compact, muscular Angelo Zambra. They could not have been more different. But the feeling that surged inside me, the certainty, was the same: the certainty that I would know and like this person. The recognition. I had felt it for Angelo and here I was with this same certainty about Louis Hernfield.

But my realisation of this was only beginning on that first morning and I was soon distracted by Tesserina, who popped her head round the door, shrieked loudly, hauled me up from my stool and did a little jig with me in the confined space.

I blinked up at her. 'Your hair, Tess! What have they done to you?'

It was no longer a mop of long curls barely controlled by ragged ribbons. It was swept upward in a mass on her head; only a few curls escaped confinement and lay on her brow. Her cheeks and her lips were touched with rouge. She looked like a stranger.

Tesserina fingered her hair. 'Isn't it fine? Mrs Palmer's dresser did it for me.' She hugged me close, as if to assure me that beneath the lacquered surface was the real Tesserina, not this fine bird groomed in the style of Mrs Hermione Palmer.

She turned to Louis Hernfield. 'Now, Mr Hernfield! Now you meet my friend Pippa. *Pipistrello.*' She laughed her usual deep laugh at her own personal joke. 'The little bat who saved me from hell on earth.' She took the last of the iced bun from me and popped it into her own mouth.

'A true heroine!' He stood up and brushed the crumbs from his jerkin. He was not as tall as Tesserina, but was, like her, all in proportion. He fitted his own frame as well as she did hers. 'I should go, Miss Wharton. I've an appointment with Mr Palmer to show him another short drama I've written, about a keel-man of this town who was a great hero. I fear it'll be too long for his purposes. I was hoping he knew someone I could send it to. I've only these few days off from my job and I need to make the most of them.'

He vanished through the door, leaving me with a sinking feeling of disappointment: a wish that he had stayed.

Miss Abigail looked thoughtfully at the door as it clicked behind him. 'A clever young man, and ambitious. He's losing five days' pay to spend this time here with us and learn our ropes. I've never been questioned so closely. I suspect he won't be a printer all of his life.' Her tone was warm. She certainly liked Louis Hernfield.

Tesserina pushed me back on to my stool and kneeled beside me. 'You saw Joe before you came?' she demanded.

I shook my head. 'I am not Joe's favourite person,' I said. 'He blames me for what happened to Angelo. I blame myself, so this is no surprise.'

Tesserina smiled happily. 'Joe will come to see me dance. He told me so.'

Would Joe come? I felt certain that she was wrong. I hoped she was. I wanted to leave Joe and Aldo and the black thoughts of Angelo behind in Bishop Auckland, to start afresh. I'd just framed this thought when I felt a pang of guilt. Of course it was not all over. Angelo still sits in the hall of mirrors that is my memory, alongside the memories of my mother – false and true – perpetually reflecting back into my life.

I watched Tesserina rehearse at the band call. She went

through two dances on the larger stage, performing with the full orchestra. She was fabulous, dancing with assurance and style and distilled passion. To my perverse regret she was now far away from my wild dancer in the Paris street. Mrs Palmer played the piano for her, sitting side by side with the resident pianist who sometimes played the left hand for her. Miss Abigail whispered in my ear that these two had been friends in the old days, some say sweethearts, and Mr Palmer wasn't best pleased at what was turning into a duet.

The lyrical sweep of the string section, the articulation of the percussionist, all directed by Mrs Palmer from the piano, heightened the wild passion and marked the poignancy of Tesserina's dancing. Even at the rehearsal there was a clatter of applause from everyone in the auditorium. The orchestra, in their shirtsleeves, put down their instruments and stood up to clap. The cleaners near the door put down their mops to applaud.

I knew now for certain what I had recognised from the first. Mad as she appeared, Tesserina was entirely unique and would reach way beyond me. And I would lose her, that was for sure. For her own survival she had cultivated an entirely self-centred approach to life and now at the centre of that self was her dancing. As far as she was capable she loved me and Miss Abigail, but we were part of her journey, not her destination.

'Your friend is a genius. Charismatic.' Louis Hernfield's voice was in my ear. I didn't know how long he'd been standing there. I had one of my mirror images then, not of Angelo, but of Roy Divine standing behind me in the wings at Bishop Auckland. I shivered but Louis Hernfield didn't seem to notice. He persisted. 'How does she do that? It's much more than the dance.'

'I think she feels it in her heart and her muscles. She doesn't think.' I don't know where that thought came from but it made sense to me then.

I was relieved that AJ called him away then, so I didn't have to justify my strange theory.

It was sweet to spend the rest of that day amid the comforting certainties of the company. There was nothing really for me to do. AJ had changed the programme order but there were no boards to see to. In this theatre they just relied on the panel of electric numbers for the running order. So that night I was able to watch the whole programme, reordered with its new acts, from the wings.

I watched the Two Divines perform expertly on the high wire. Their act was much improved. They had changed it so that the wire was fixed up to go some way over the orchestra stalls and even the audience, who craned their necks and gasped at the daring acrobats. Much more spectacular.

Marie Divine had marched past me in the wings without a look. I didn't care about her but she made me think again about Roy. It was only a matter of time until he came back and sought out his sister and brother. And the image of me signing that account for him at the police station lay festering in my head. Ever since I arrived I'd been building up courage to tell Miss Abigail what Roy had made me do. But everyone was so busy. There was no quiet time.

Watching that Thursday night performance I noted that the routine was familiar but there were differences. There were more dancers, and a new juggling act, which involved a unicycle. Also some Swedish tumblers. Tom Merriman's jokes were broader, more saucy. The Pixies were even more sickeningly cute.

Pixie Molloy stopped by me as they ran off stage and asked

me where I'd been. 'I was finkin' you'd run away for good,' she gasped.

'No chance of that,' I grinned.

'Me, I'll run away for good, one day. All right! All right!' she said to Pixie Smith, who was pulling her on towards a shrieking Madame Bunce.

Louis Hernfield winked at me in the wings as he waited in his torn jacket and blackened burglar's face. I have to admit I watched closely as he made his appearance as the second burglar, who was shot accidentally by his fellow felon in the third minute of the play. He crumpled very effectively as his accomplice (AJ, also in rags) missed the policeman and shot him by mistake.

AJ's following oration, unlike his noble Wellington or his patrician Hamlet, was permeated with local northern tones. The audience listened intently to his evocation of the misery and disillusion of this former soldier forced to turn to crime by dire circumstances. It was an intense piece of drama but, for me, I think AJ rather overdid the rhetoric as the conscience-stricken burglar.

The audience obviously didn't agree with me. As he pleaded his case, there was a murmur of agreement from the audience. So many women here had lost their husbands, brothers and sons. So many men here had seen action in France. The thought struck me that my own father might be out there among them.

The applause, though not uproarious, was appreciative.

Mr Slater smiled faintly at me as he returned backstage after another virtuoso performance. The audience here had really taken to him. At one point he had a dozen men on the stage at once, creating a human mountain. Thirteen in all, they were balanced and graceful, even those who had earlier tottered on to the stage on bow legs. There was no doubt Mr Slater had this strange power over people. I had the sense now that in creating these bizarre spectacles to entertain this large audience he was using only a fraction of his skills. This audience was too large for him to display the more intimate magic of making people revisit their childhood or understand some truth about themselves. He contented himself with the less demanding but more spectacular magic of turning them into clowns.

The Bridge

It was my second morning in Sunderland before I got time to unpack my bags. I set about the job very carefully, shaking out each garment as I loosened the folds, saving and smoothing the tissue paper for the repacking. I had learned long ago to pack well, in the way Miss Abigail has taught me, to ensure that my clothes were least-creased at our destination. Being performers, she explained to me more than once, did not make us vagabonds.

In the bottom of the second bag, wrapped as always in my second-best petticoat, was the jug, safe and unbroken. I needed no light to see the design on the surface. 'Presented at the opening of the Alexandra Bridge, Sunderland 1909': a small, potbellied, rather undistinguished item.

'What are you doing, Pippa?' Tesserina's deep voice came from her side of the bed. 'You let in the naughty daylight, darling.'

I wrapped the jug in some of the tissue paper and tucked it into the small satchel I carried with me every day. 'Nothing,' I said. 'Nothing at all.'

Later that day at the theatre I was sitting in the deserted
back stalls with Louis Hernfield. On stage Mr Barrington
was working with the resident stage manager on a sequence
of colour gels in the spots. These were a new inspiration for
Tesserina's last dance. The idea was that the different
coloured lights would shine through the fabric of her dress
and create, according to Miss Abigail, the most wonderful
sensual effects.

'Your Miss Wharton has very clever ideas,' said Louis. 'A
true professional.'

'She has seen the effect before – light and silk and the
body. An American dancer in Paris was famous for it.'

'A wonderful idea, anyway. Very theatrical.'

I looked at him hard, then rooted in my bag, took out the
jug. I handed it to him. 'Will you please look at this for me?'

He held it up to catch what dim light there was in the
back of the stalls. He turned it this way and that. He held it
upside down, then the right way up, then ran his hands over
it. 'An old Sunderland jug, all right. A commemorative jug.
Where d'you get this?'

'In France. It was my mother's. She's always had it. Or
nearly always.'

'I'll be beggared. France! An old Sunderland jug.'

'Do you know this bridge, Mr Hernfield? The one drawn
here?'

'Call me Louis, Pippa. *Louis.* It's funny, hearin' you say my
name the French way. They still don't get it right here.'

'Do you know this bridge, Louis?' I was very patient with
him.

'Everyone knows this bridge – folks from Sunderland and
all over the world. It's a very famous piece of engineering.
The heaviest bridge in Britain then.'

'Is it far away? Will you take me to where it is? Show me the bridge?'

'It's not so far. And I most certainly will take you to see it. I warn you, though, Pippa, we might be very proud of it, but it's only an iron bridge.' He was looking at me with those sleepy eyes. I wasn't sure whether or not he mocked me. I had much to learn about Louis Hernfield.

I wrapped up the jug again and put it back in my satchel.

It took Mr Barrington and the theatre stage manager another hour to get the desired effects of the colour gels. I reflected rather sourly on all this trouble being taken for Tesserina, who never gave anything back but the abstraction of a fine public performance. She seemed to notice less and less what people did for her, to take it as her right.

Suddenly my heart clenched inside of me and I had a vision of Tesserina, step by step, dancing her way upwards, out of Palmer's Varieties, out of my life. She was destined for great things. I'd heard Miss Abigail say it. *Great things.* Such great things would take her – and perhaps Miss Abigail – away from me, for sure. And then I'd be alone again. I could not let that happen. I looked for Miss Abigail but she had gone to the shops with Tesserina. Something about shoes and shifts, according to Mrs Palmer.

Later that afternoon, when the theatre quietened down, Louis Hernfield offered to walk with me down through his town to see this famous Sunderland Bridge. Though the town was gaunt and grey it had a kind of grandeur, with its broad main thoroughfare and some stately buildings. But, like Paris, behind the fine façade were the narrow teeming courts and streets and workshops that make up the dirty heart of any great town. Like Paris too, Sunderland had a broad river flowing through its dark watery heart. On these wharfs, Louis told me, ships loaded and unloaded goods from as far away as Japan and America. In the best years, scores of ships would queue to wait their turn for unloading. They even still built ships in some of the docks along here; actually built them and sold them to merchants all over the world.

The pride Louis had in his town shone brightly from him. He pointed further along the dockside towards other industrial works and great warehouses, drawing my attention to the cone chimneys of a glass manufactory, then to the crowded roofs of a pottery. 'They make everything here, everything!'

At last he took me to a place where I could take a long view of the bridge. 'There!' he said. 'See?'

I held up the jug and compared it with its real-life original, a very fine structure arching over the dark oily canyon of the river, crawling with busy workmen and humming with life and commerce.

'It was the first of its kind. We could build it here because it's the same kind of thing they do when they build the ships. And they were always good at that,' Louis boasted. 'Do you know, once we were the greatest shipbuilders in the world. Before the Great War we were making as many as sixty ships a year. Less now, though. Unfortunately things are tailing off. Not so much work at all these days, to be honest – just repairs. And they say there's worse to come.'

'This is not quite the same view,' I said, holding up the jug at a slightly different angle.

He took it from me, peered up at the bridge, then said, 'Right!' and, jug in hand, led the way across the bridge and down to the docks on the other side to get the right perspective. 'Here, take a look.'

It was as though a nut and a bolt had clicked into place.

He handed the jug back to me. 'Tell me again. How did you come by it?'

'My mother bequeathed it to me.'

'And how might she have come by it?'

'A man gave it to her. I think it was a man from this town. He gave it to her as a present.'

'Is that why you're here?'

I shook my head. 'I came here because this was where Palmer's were booked.'

'Oh!' He sounded disappointed.

I tried to repair the fault. 'But it *is* one reason why I was pleased that Palmer's were coming to England. I didn't know we'd come to this town precisely, or that it had a great theatre also. So when I found out, I thought I might find the bridge and perhaps even the man.'

Louis smiled, obviously happier now. His face lit up when he smiled. 'So what was this man doing there, in France?' he asked.

'I don't know. Well, I do know he came to see her twice. The second time was during the war. So he was there to fight, I imagine. But I think there was another time, before. Before the war.'

'And now do you really want to find him?'

'I would just like to see him, once. To talk to him.'

'What was his name?'

'I don't know.'

'This is a very big town, Pippa.'

'I have eyes in my head.' I rewrapped my jug and tucked it away again. 'I can look for him.'

'But at least we do have the jug,' he said thoughtfully. 'There might be something . . . Is there anything else you know about him?'

'No. Nothing.'

'At least you know he was there in France. When was that?'

'I think it was the second time he was there, in 1916. He brought the jug for my mother then. I was ten. He was in uniform. I remember this belt with a shiny buckle, and a peaked cap. But I'm sure he'd been there before. He must have been. Years before. When he wasn't a soldier.'

He looked at me thoughtfully. 'So he was there before, then he came back?'

'I have no idea why he came back,' I lied. I did have an idea. Something about my mother. Something about me.

'But still you're keen to find this man?'

I did not deny it.

'Well, we'll find him. Maybe he was sommat to do with the pottery trade. What we have here is a set of clues!' He counted them out on his fingers. 'In France . . . er . . . some time *before* the war. Then in France *during* the war. Army officer – peaked cap, see? And this special keepsake from this town. And maybe even in the pottery trade. That would make it easier; reduce it to maybe a hundred or so men. Not impossible to sift through them.'

I relished his optimism but I started to worry that Louis Hernfield seemed too keen, too interested. 'We should get on,' I said as brightly as I could, although my voice cracked into the air like chipped ice. Distant. 'I can't be too long. Miss Abigail will be missing me.' In reality she was probably still preoccupied with Tesserina, but he wasn't to know that.

Louis caught my more sober mood. He kept his distance as we walked back across the bridge and down the docks on the other side. There was no question here of hands clashing and someone holding on to your arm to make walking together easier. But we did talk. Or rather he did, and as he did I forgot Tesserina and warmed towards him again, pleased to know more about him and his life.

He told me that Mr Palmer liked his second play very much and had advised him to send it to a certain agent in London. An influential man.

'And do you have another play now, Louis?'

He laughed: a hearty sound that seemed to come from very deep in his chest. 'Another one? I have seventeen more in a box in the corner at home.'

I found myself liking his voice, wondering whether, as time went on, someone would tempt him to act a more prominent role than the second burglar, as well as write for the stage. 'And where might "home" be?' I asked, just to keep him talking.

'I live just south of the town, off the Ryhope Road.'

Of course this meant nothing to me. I risked a further question: the crucial one. 'I suppose you have a family?'

There was a pause.

'Cards on the table, Pippa. I have a family.'

I felt breathless, as though someone had thrown cold water over me. 'And do you have many children?' I said brightly, drowning even further.

He laughed merrily at this. 'Not exactly. I have many sisters and brothers. It's my misfortune to be the last in a very long line of siblings. I am the last left at home who now must take care of his ancient parents. The fate of many youngest children, I fear.' He did not sound too troubled by it. 'My dear old ancients are the reason why I haven't yet scurried down to London clutching my box of plays in my hand, like Dick Whittington wanting to make my fortune.'

To commiserate with him would have been rude to his

'ancients', so I stayed quiet. Even so, I found myself very glad, glad that he didn't have a pretty wife and a brood of children tucked away 'off the Ryhope Road'.

'I'd invite you there for tea,' he went on. 'But it is a big, gloomy place and the dear ancients haunt it as though they were already ghosts.'

I tossed my head. 'I'd not thought to come to tea,' I said. 'But big gloomy places hold no terrors for me. I have been in many terrible places, places that would frighten even you.'

We walked on again in silence but when we reached the theatre it was wonderful that he was with me because there, leaning against the wall just inside the stage door, was Roy Divine.

He straightened up when he saw us. 'What ho, Pippa!' he said heartily. 'Another gallant friend, I see? You waste no time?'

I was forced to stand and watch while he introduced himself to Louis and wormed his name out of him. Then he turned to me. 'You haven't seen old Marie and my dear brother Blaze, have you, Pippa? I've been waiting here to see them but they have not yet appeared? They must have run away, I can't think why.' Then he winked at me and I knew that of course he'd served me false in Bishop Auckland, had made a fool of me, and really had hurt Angelo. This made me frightened again, for myself and even for Louis Hernfield.

I barged past him down the passageway and Louis came after me. 'So who might that be?' he said. 'Queer codger, with that brown skin and dyed hair.'

'No one. A monster. No one,' I mumbled, and fled towards the wardrobe, hoping Miss Abigail was there and had lots of work for me. She was standing ironing a dancer's skirts, with a pile more beside her.

I offered to do them for her so she could sit down and rest her feet. She finished the skirt and handed over the iron, then sat down and looked up eagerly. She was intrigued that Roy had returned, and wanted to talk about it. 'I thought he would be long gone. Weren't the police in hot pursuit?'

Keeping my head down over my ironing, I blurted out the tale of my self-betrayal. 'I am so stupid, Miss Abigail, but he was so sure and I was not so sure. Not until afterwards when I became certain that it wasn't a dream, it was a real thing that happened there on the bridge. That he had hurt Angelo.'

'And you?' said Miss Abigail quietly. 'He hurt you?'

'That I cannot remember. I can remember a sour taste or smell . . .' I shook the skirt out, hung it up and took down another one, still not meeting her eye. 'I think there was a cloth over my mouth . . .'

'Did he hurt you?' she repeated. 'Did he hurt your body, Pippa?'

I looked up at her. Her face was flushed and set hard. 'No,' I said. 'I just found myself in Waldron Street. I was all right. I must have got away somehow. Perhaps Angelo being so bad made him flee.'

'He is an evil man,' she said. 'And he'll get his just deserts. There's a balance in these things, believe me. Now!' she went on briskly, her colour back to normal. 'Iron! No need to mope over such a creature.'

I finished the next skirt, then asked about Tesserina. Miss Abigail said she'd gone off to have a rest on Mrs Palmer's couch, on Mrs Palmer's orders. 'She wants her protégée to be on top form tonight, and I must say our Tess is savouring the attention,' she said drily. I looked at her sharply. That dry tone was the nearest she came to being critical of those she normally liked.

I had just finished the fifth skirt when the corridor exploded in a noisy, vocal row in the Divines' dressing room. Miss Abigail opened the door slightly and stood there, so she could 'catch the drift'. When the row died down she said, 'Did you hear? Seems they're not taking him back. Seems he's not welcome, that Marie and Blaze are managing here very well, thank you. AJ is very pleased with their transformation and there are to be no more upsets. Roy is furious. They're throwing things.' There was a grim satisfaction in her voice. 'And Roy used to be such a dumb ox.'

Was it me, I wondered, who had changed him from that dumb ox? Or had he been like that all the time, a tiger disguised in the pelt of an ox? I shook out the dancer's wide skirt and put it on a hanger. 'I'm surprised at you, Miss Abigail. I thought you abhorred gossip.'

She began to unpack a parcel that had just arrived from Dina Brooks in London. She smiled contentedly. 'Sometimes, my dearest Pippa, gossip can be the breath of life in our narrow world.'

Then the silky fabric leaped out of the parcel and we were both exclaiming at its beauty. Miss Abigail told me that Mr Barrington's lighting sequence would make all the difference.

'Go and find Tesserina, Pippa. Drag her from Hermione Palmer's couch. Tell her to come and see this glorious cloth. We'll have our work cut out making up this one,' she said happily. 'What fun!'

On my way down the corridor I skirted round Roy Divine, who was now deep in conversation with Mr Slater. The mesmerist met my glance and blinked but Roy ignored me.

Tesserina was rather cross to be woken and it was only the mention of the new dress that encouraged her to follow me.

'Go, go!' said Mrs Palmer from her mirror where she was

laying on her first layer of skin tone. 'You look perfectly rested, darling, ready for the fray.'

Later that day Miss Abigail told me that Mr Slater had called in to tell her that he was considering taking a new assistant. Of course it should customarily be a woman, but Roy Divine, resplendent in his gold paint would, she had to admit it, add a touch of much-needed glamour to Stan's act. 'And,' she added, a glint in her eye, 'Marie Divine will be incandescent. Sweet revenge. That'll be a sight to see.'

'You told him it was a good idea? You said that to Mr Slater?' I was puzzled.

She smiled. 'We had a nice chat, Mr Slater and I. I said that at least it would stop Roy Divine rolling round here like a loose cannon ball.'

'But he would have gone!' I wailed. 'Gone away.'

She shook her head. 'He would not stray far from that sister of his. And now Mr Slater will keep an eye on him.'

'Miss Abigail . . .'

'Leave it alone, Pippa darling. Don't worry your head about it. Now then, this dress! We have a mountain of sewing and must start in the foothills.'

Electricity

Abigail was quietly pleased to have Pippa back at her side. She'd had some misgivings when her young friend didn't arrive as expected from Bishop Auckland. The business with the Zambra boy had made a dreadful impact on her. At first Abigail had thought it all very charming: a simple boy-girl romance, which was part of any girl's growing up, to be felt and lost like the freshness of water as one dipped one's hand in a passing stream. But Abigail knew the tragic event of the boy's death would have a more permanent effect on Pippa. There would always be a small dent of sadness in the child's heart, no matter how many times she fell in love.

And now here was this Louis Hernfield. Much more suitable, if one could say that, for someone like Pippa. Perhaps not so handsome and strange, but literate and — one had to say it — more like them in his love of the theatre. The two of them had a lot in common. The assistant manager, a relative of Louis, had told Abigail that he was a fine boy and promised well. So Abigail decided not to interfere. It would cheer the child up after the business with Angelo.

Louis was obviously intelligent. So energetic. Such a free spirit. The boy could certainly write, and – if acting a corpse counted as acting – perhaps he could act. There was no doubt at all that he loved the theatre. But would he relish the drudgery of travelling with a company like the Varieties? Perhaps he would rather pitch up in London and stay there. But London was full of young writers, hanging on to the coat-tails of the great and the good. And bad, of course . . . There was often a price to getting on in that dark intricate world.

Abigail's thoughts turned to herself. When she was young she had no thought or time for young men. In the early days she was too busy rehearsing every day with the Babes under the whiplash tongue of Madame Corrigan. And later, for a long time she was too exhausted to run about with chorus boys or take any notice of the inevitable leering older men. Then life seemed to ease out a little and she had some flirtations, even some offers of marriage. But the price of matrimony – to give up the theatre and dancing – was too high. Then along came the charming Denis, who was quite happy for her to keep on dancing to support the gentleman's life to which he aspired. So she had always had a living to make.

As she did now. This week there would be no money for Pippa, as she was not doing the boards and had been absent half of the week. There might be something for her to do next week here in Sunderland and the week after in Newcastle, but no doubt they had these same miraculous electrical boards there. Electric light and electric irons were a veritable revolution in the modern theatre. There were always things to be grateful for.

Perhaps she should persuade AJ to designate Pippa as the

official assistant wardrobe mistress with appropriate regular remuneration. But then the girl would be obliged to be in the theatre all the time and she could no longer be the will-o'-the-wisp she was and enjoy the last days of her childhood. Abigail, who had been denied her own childhood, would regret that.

Pippa had certainly been cut up by the reappearance of Roy Divine, who had cynically used the child to wriggle out of the bad business at Bishop Auckland. When pressed by Hermione Palmer, Marie Divine asserted – in Abigail's presence – that all that Bishop Auckland drama had been a Big Mistake and that Roy had been exonerated.

And yesterday Roy had inveigled Stan Slater into letting him join his act. The two men had spent all day closeted together, rehearsing. Hermione declared to Abigail that Slater would get no more money, despite his new golden assistant. But then Slater's act had achieved a good mention in the Sunderland paper, and as time went on he might get more. And the man had a peculiar talent. If he chose to share some of the mysteries with Roy Divine it was his business. Abigail had been surprised that Slater had shown her the courtesy of coming to talk about it. He had listened carefully to her opinion. Even so, he gave nothing away. He was a very enigmatic man.

Pippa was of the opinion that Roy would learn all the tricks of the trade from Slater and steal his act. Just this morning backstage she had seen Marie tap Roy on the shoulder and hustle him back to her dressing room. You could hear their voices right along the corridor. It seemed Marie didn't want him, but she didn't want anyone else to have him either, especially not Stan Slater. Abigail told Pippa she couldn't see what Marie Divine had to complain about.

Clearly she had booted Roy out of the act when he got here. She couldn't have her cake and eat it. The trouble was, confided Abigail, that Marie Divine thought she owned both her brothers body and soul. That seamy fact was there for anyone to see. Not healthy, in Abigail's view.

She said as much to Josiah Barrington, with whom she was spending more time these days. Pippa was off about her own affairs. And now it seemed Tesserina was very much in cahoots with Hermione Palmer. They had much in common, after all. Tesserina needed Hermione's music, and although Abigail had suggestions to offer and could make the fancy dresses, Tesserina's intuition about her dancing was so complete that it seemed to be generating its own development, even though she still depended on Hermione's piano playing. Her instinctive use of the wider space in the Empire Theatre was very exciting, almost masterly. And with the new lighting effects they would be using on tonight's performance there should be even more acclaim. The newspapers this week had been very complimentary. Just let them wait until this evening. Then they would have something to write about.

The new spotlight gels came about because Abigail had been telling Josiah about Loie Fuller, who had achieved such a marvellous effect with coloured lights glinting on and through her dress. Abigail omitted to mention that when Loie Fuller was lit from the back, she sometimes seemed momentarily naked. That would be far too lewd – not just for Sunderland but for Tesserina herself. Just now she was such a strange amalgam of savage experience and absolute innocence that to propose such an effect would be unthinkable.

But things were changing, thought Abigail. At first Tesserina had indeed been an innocent. But now that she was talking more each day and was privy to the sophisticated shards of wisdom falling from the mouth of Hermione Palmer, that pure innocence could not survive. It would drop off her like the ragged bows she used to wear in her hair. Abigail shivered at the thought of what might happen if and when Tesserina began to reveal the darker side of her own experience in the dance. Then the audience would devour her. They would take savage amusement from it. It could make Hermione's fortune. Of course that would never happen as long as Tesserina was with Abigail and Pippa. But she would go from them. Abigail knew from experience that the theatre engulfed the great and transformed them into glorious monsters. But how could she stop it? She could hardly take Tesserina and plant her back in the alley where Pippa had found her.

So with both Tesserina and Pippa preoccupied, Abigail had found herself spending more time again with Josiah. He'd renewed his pleas for her to join him in a loving, companionable marriage. As well as this, he had another idea, which came to him when he was in a shop replenishing his stock of nails and screws. Why shouldn't he open a little shop for tools and electrical things, right in the middle of Sunderland? He had savings and skills, and if he were honest with himself, he was beginning to tire of the travelling life.

Abigail told him that the possibility of tiring of this life was unthinkable to her, even though she could imagine him behind a counter dispensing his special kind of practical magic. But for the very life of her she couldn't imagine herself standing beside him in a canvas apron. Dina Brooks selling her fancy hats in Bond Street was one thing, but Abigail couldn't see herself dispensing valves and tacks. Ever.

But the determined Josiah had a sweeter idea. What about a little shop divided into two halves! Through the left door would be electrical and handy goods. To the right would be fine stuffs and cloths, with threads and items for those who loved plying the needle.

This idea Abigail did not reject out of hand. It might even be worth thinking about.

Comeback

Mr Ramsden, the Empire Theatre manager, expected a big house, perhaps even a sell-out on the Saturday night. The newspaper reviews had been good and Ramsden told AJ that he knew of people who had been to the theatre earlier in the week who had bought tickets for Saturday. 'A comeback, Mr Palmer,' he said to AJ over some expensive cigars. 'Always a good sign.'

The gels had now been perfected by Mr Barrington, so Tesserina's dramatically lit dance would be the evening's surprise. Another piece of added glamour was the gilded, half-naked Roy Divine, who was to have his spot as Stan Slater's assistant in his act. AJ gave the innovation his reluctant approval, which was heartily endorsed by Mr Ramsden.

'The folks here, AJ, may *tut-tut* at a little bit of decadence but, by God, they enjoy it. We always get comebacks for this kind of thing.' He sucked hard on his cigar. When he spoke, the dense air in his small office thickened even further. 'Just enough, of course. All within the bounds of good taste, if you see what I mean.'

NO REST FOR THE WICKED

Because Palmer's Varieties were in the town for a two-week engagement, the innovations and changes reported in the *Sunderland Echo* would ensure the magical 'comeback' that was Mr Ramsden's ideal. AJ was grateful that in his enthusiasm for the innovations the manager conveniently sidelined the fact that Cissie Barnard had been too drunk to perform more than one song in her second spot on Friday and had her skirt off before she got into the wings. Fortunately the audience had taken her staggering around the stage as a comedienne's tomfoolery but AJ knew better. He'd given her a severe warning and privately told Hermione that it was her very last. No more chances.

'The woman's a clever comedienne but is turning into a liability.'

'The audiences love her,' Hermione had said mildly. 'Don't forget that, dear.'

They'd been sitting up in bed at two o'clock in the morning, drinking cocoa prepared by Hermione. Her head was tied in rag curlers and bound in a silk turban. Her face was almost invisible beneath a thick coat of cold cream. She was buffing her nails with great energy.

AJ had removed his toupee but still looked rather smart in his silk pyjamas and cravat, even with his glasses at the end of his nose. He was filling in his journal with his careful, regular hand. In this book he recorded all the company's financial affairs, the hiring and firing of acts and his assessment of the quality of their performances. Sometimes he indulged himself by making more personal notes, which added some colour to his dry business report.

He closed his book. 'I see that Jacob Smith has been of great assistance to you,' he said drily.

'Dear Jacob!' Hermione said calmly. 'He hasn't changed a

bit since we played duets when we were fifteen. He's very talented. Wasted here as resident pianist. I told him so myself.'

'Seems fully occupied,' grunted AJ. 'Ain't this theatre at full blast?'

'London! London's the place. I told him so.'

'London! You tell everyone to go to London!' AJ removed his cravat, folded it and placed it on his bedside table. 'Far be it from me to criticise you, my darling,' he said evenly, 'but do you think perhaps that you tend to advise people rather in excess of their needs? Certainly of their talents.'

Hermione put away her mother-of-pearl nail buffer, reached out to pull the light cord and plunged the bedroom into darkness. Then he could feel her hand on his arm, her slightly greasy face beside his. 'But, my darling,' she murmured, 'how can you say that? Without my advice to you there would be no Palmer's Varieties and you would be toiling away, even today, at someone else's behest.'

He showed his gratitude by kissing her thoroughly and sliding down in the bed so they could make vigorous plunging love quickly and efficiently, as they had done most nights since the night they met. This was their custom wherever they found themselves, whether they were on the high seas or in a sleeper bunk on an interminable train journey. This close congress expressed the totality of their relationship. It saved AJ from the uneasy attraction he felt for the young men who drifted in and out of the company. It reassured him that Hermione loved him and needed him, even though she was the stronger person in the relationship and was the least needy person he knew.

When they had finished she put on the light again and reapplied her face cream while he repaired to the bathroom before slipping sleepily back into bed.

'I can see Roy Divine will certainly brighten up Stan's act,' she said, continuing an earlier conversation. 'Stan's good, even brilliant, but at times he does so look like a depressed loading clerk. No glamour. Roy will add the glamour.'

'Old Ramsden certainly thinks it's an improvement,' said AJ, yawning. 'Called it "a little bit of decadence".'

'Perceptive fellow,' said Hermione, putting her light off again and sliding down the bed beside him. 'Did you notice Roy making cow's eyes backstage with the little chorus girls? Practising his mesmerism? Not very nice, if you ask me. No wonder the dreaded Marie kept him under wraps.'

AJ put an arm out under the blanket, pinched her plump upper arm then stroked her long thigh. 'So to speak, darling.'

'You are dreadful, AJ,' she said sleepily. 'Now for goodness' sake will you go to sleep? Tomorrow is another day. We only have tomorrow night's performance and then it's Sunday. A day off and no travelling! How rare is that?'

Then just as they were both drifting away she'd murmured, 'We must do something about young Pippa. She's wandering around like a lost soul and needs something specific to do. What do you think?'

But AJ was asleep, gently snoring.

The Potter

Louis Hernfield proposed that we go down to the pottery works on Saturday morning to ask questions about my jug. We walked down there from the theatre in a dense chilly rain that I now recognised as peculiarly English. Louis had brought a large black umbrella, which was also peculiarly English. 'It was threatening rain when I walked up to town from Ryhope Road, so I borrowed the old boy's brolly, which, as you see, is rather like a bell tent.'

We had to walk closely to share the protection of the umbrella, which I quite enjoyed, even though our hands and arms didn't touch even once.

When we reached the pottery we found the sagging gate to the yard wedged open. We stepped through it to see a large, very old building with a steep roof that seemed to sit in a sea of wooden pallets, with packing straw still sticking to them after the rain.

We pushed a door open and wandered through one empty workshop into another, where a crouching man was throwing a big clay pot the colour of old leather. The wheel thrummed, driven by some kind of engine, allowing the man to concentrate on working on the pot itself. His face was rimed with a fine dust, and pearls of clay stuck to his beetling brows. The pot before him was already eighteen inches high. We watched as he pulled over the rim with a sure hand. On a long bench beside him were seven exactly similar pots.

We take so much for granted. Cups and saucers that we use every day are made in this way, starting off as the sloppy malleable stuff that still moves under the potter's hands. It occurred to me that children were just like that floppy clay, and the people around us were like this potter, moulding us to our permanent selves with the sure touch of their hand. And whose hands had been on me? My dear *maman*? The Belgian? Monsieur Carnet? Miss Abigail? Tesserina? Angelo? Now Louis Hernfield? At what point are we finally fired to the shape we will always have, the shape that is ourselves?

His pot finally complete, the potter attended to our query. He directed us past the great, tight-shut doors of the kiln, down a grimy corridor to a dusty office. We knocked and entered to find its occupant hurriedly pulling on a jacket to cover his braces.

The man introduced himself as Herbert Wilkes, and he took the jug from me. He turned it in his hands, this way, that way, upside down, right way up. 'Bridge jugs. Big event in the town, that, the Bridge. We made these jugs for years. They turned them out by the score and sent them across to the painting shop. The shelves were lined with them. We sent racks off into the shops in the town and much further afield. We did other commem. pieces, like, not just these. Some were made for events further afield. Mafeking. We were known for it. Mourning for the old Queen, Coronation of the King then mourning for him. Transfers mostly. Always some occasion . . .'

I stopped his nostalgia in full flow by holding up my hand. 'I know the date on here is much earlier, Mr Wilkes. But I am interested in a man who might have had one of these in 1916. That's what I'm trying to find out.'

'In France, who would have them in France?' supplied Louis Hernfield.

'France?' The manager scratched his head. 'Well, one time we certainly had a go at selling commem. designs for foreign towns. Seemed a queer thing to me. Not so bad doing it for Empire places, like the Delhi Durbar, for instance. India's ours, after all. But France?' He turned the jug upside down again and peered at it, frowning, as though an answer might be written on the bottom. Then his brow cleared. 'There were travellers,' he said triumphantly. 'We don't go in much for it now, sticking like we do to less fancy pots. Garden stuff mostly. But those days we did have these travellers, who went out to show our fancy wares, take designs there, and then send back orders. But these fellows were high-ups, men used to travelling, like. Mr Benedict – who owned the place then – would send only his cousins and nephews. I suppose he had to trust that the orders and designs they sent were genuine as their own inheritance depended on it. It has to be said that a lot of money would hang on those orders, after all.'

'So this man in France would be a Benedict?' I have to admit I was excited. Here was a name.

He shook his head. 'Couldn't say that for sure, miss. Who knows how a jug would get into someone's hands? But if the man who had this jug were the man who was travelling with it as a *sample*, then mebbe he was one of the Benedicts.' Mr

Wilkes wandered across to a corner of the office where dusty ledgers were standing shoulder to shoulder on a shelf.

'I'm looking for someone as well who was in the southern part of France, far south, nearly Spain, in 1905,' I said.

'And, perhaps,' said Louis, looking inspired now, 'in the British Army in Paris in 1916.'

'In Paris 1916.' I nodded my head. I was making the connection as well. 'That's when the jug turned up.'

Mr Wilkes took an age to select a volume, another age to place it on his table and put on his glasses, a further age to rifle through it to find the page he obviously wanted.

'Should I look?' Louis leaned forward. 'Perhaps I . . .'

The man waved him away, jealous of his territory.

'Ah!' he said at last. 'Mr Ambrose Benedict. Son of Mr Benedict's cousin. Let's see, 1906. He obtained orders from Bordeaux, Toulouse, Carcassonne. I remember now. He sent back drawings that he'd made himself. Even some photographs. There is a record of it here. It has a note "Vanity orders" beside it. See? They were only very small orders. My father, who was foreman here, said it was a mistake to go to such places. They make their own fine pots there. Coals to Newcastle, as you might say.'

I was flushed, my body was zinging with excitement. 'Was that Benedict there in 1916 also?' I held my breath.

He shook his head. 'No. Couldn't have been. He'd be in the army then, like the rest of us.'

'But if he was in the army he'd be in France?'

He smiled broadly then, showing that he had a tooth missing in the front. 'Yes, yes! That could be the case. Most of the fighting was there, after all.'

'Where is Benedict, then? Where is he now?' The words hurtled from my mouth.

Mr Wilkes' smile faded. 'Never came back, well, not here to the works. I've got a feeling he was wounded. I know his two cousins were killed. Old Mr Benedict sold this place and we moved to more workaday items. Garden pots. Business has not been good. We've had to lay off hands. Me, I was lucky. Promoted to under-manager. No men left, you see?' he said modestly. 'I'd never have got a job like this before the war. Not me. They lost the best.'

'And this Mr Ambrose Benedict . . .' I have to admit my voice was trembling, 'did he leave Sunderland?'

'Maybe he did. But maybe he didn't. If he were wounded he'd need his family, wouldn't he?'

'Do you know where he lived?' said Louis, giving me time to collect myself.

Mr Wilkes shook his head. 'I couldn't say as to that. But it wouldn't be down in the Hendon rows, would it? Not a family like that.' Then he struck the table with the flat of his hand. 'The papers! Wounded hero and all that. Try the newspapers.'

It had stopped raining when we got out but the air was still clenched in a kind of gritty damp. At his insistence, Louis and I walked back through the town by way of the docks, breathing in the salty scent of sea, gritty rope and burning metal. We picked our way through stockpiles of metal plate and racks of raw new Scandinavian pine. We were treated to some startled glances from the men up aloft on the half-made ships. One man leaned towards his mate and said something and they both laughed. Then the first man started to whistle 'It's a Long Way to Tipperary'. In our town clothes and smart demeanour we must have seemed as out of place here as birds in a bee colony.

It was easy to see that this place fascinated Louis Hernfield.

His eyes were everywhere. I could tell he was taking notes without a notebook. He had deliberately come this way – whether to educate me or follow his own interest I couldn't tell.

I nodded upwards towards the workmen. 'Poor souls,' I said. 'To have to do such work on such a cold day.'

'Poor souls? Not quite, Miss Pippa. You have there some of the most skilled men in the world. And sons and grandsons of skilled men. What they make will still be here in fifty years from now. Not many of us can say that.'

Such respect. I suddenly thought of Angelo and his beloved miners. 'Couldn't you say the same? With your plays? Won't they be here in fifty years' time?'

'You should talk to the ancients. They see my plays as pure bits of fluff, flotsam and jetsam on the tide of life. Folly. Fond amusements. A young man's flights of fancy. More paper boats that a child might push than great ships of the line.'

I walked along, my head buzzing with the discovery of Ambrose Benedict, happy to let Louis talk. A piece of flotsam myself, I was fascinated to talk to someone so rooted in his own beloved place. I liked Louis Hernfield. I liked how clever he was, the way he seemed so certain of what he was about, so secure in his talent. He was not beautiful like Angelo but I liked the way his hair shot straight up from his brow and loved the sparkle in those sleepy, knowing eyes. Even so, I was not at all certain whether he liked me, despite the attention he was paying me. He did love the theatre. Perhaps my being a protégée of Miss Abigail (that great woman of the theatre) did cut some ice with him, as the English say.

Talk of London

Her crying seeps through cracks in the doorway of my pantry and bleeds across the pages of the book, obscuring the words, making them scatter and lose sense. I close the book, place it carefully on the shelf with the others and open the door. She has her head on her hands and her shoulders are shaking. Before her on the table are the pieces of the lamp, some of which still have the Belgian's blood on them. I stand beside her for a while and she says the Belgian wanted to marry her. He would have married her and we would have had a bigger apartment and I would never again have to hide in the pantry. I ask if he's dead. No, no, Pippa. You saved us from him. It would have been no life. She sits up and puts a hand on mine. Perhaps I will have to work a little longer, she says.

During the Saturday show I spent most of my time in the wardrobe room sewing Tesserina's new dress. Miss Abigail had tacked the seams and I was sitting under the light, sewing tiny stitches, my mind wandering back to the dockland pottery and this man called Ambrose Benedict, the man who might just be my father. Was he tall? Was he short? What made my mother fall for him and then, in a peculiar way, stay faithful to him and never marry? Was he as beautiful as Angelo or as clever as Louis Hernfield? Or was it just that he, like me in this place, was a foreigner, and therefore interesting?

I did not see Louis Hernfield for the rest of the day. He spent it very much under the wing of AJ, who had apparently had a postcard from a London man who was in the region, who might turn up tonight and might even read Louis's plays.

Miss Abigail was in and out of the room, fitting the chorus with their new wide dance skirts and administering first aid to Cameron Lake, who had split the back seam of his dress jacket.

She only came back to sit down when Cissie Barnard was in the middle of her first spot. She stood there, smiling. 'Hear that laughter? She has the touch, does Cissie. She slips now and then but she's a real professional. If she didn't have her little problem she'd be permanently on the London stage. You mark my words.' She stretched out her crooked legs and wriggled her feet, wincing a little.

'Where's Tesserina?' I asked. 'I thought she might wait down here with us till her call.' Thing were changing so much with Tesserina. For months she had never left me. And now, like some love-lorn swain, I had to ask for her.

'Hermione's got her glued to her side. Says this is her big night and she needs to be calm. Fellow from London will be in the audience, according to Hermione.'

I tried to swallow back the bad feeling I had about this. It was a side of Tesserina I had not understood till now. Tesserina was about her own survival. In the first place that had kept her close to me, and to Miss Abigail, which made me feel not just important, but loved. Now this new Tessa, this dancer-

Tessa, did not need us any more. But Mrs Palmer had something to offer her. So she stuck to her like glue.

'Pippa?' Miss Abigail was staring at me.

I lifted up the fabric, which glittered in the air then settled round me like a cloud. 'Pity this wasn't ready, I suppose. She'd make an even better impression.'

Miss Abigail shrugged. 'No matter. If she's good enough, she's good enough. And she is. Those new lights might help a bit. But even without them she is wonderful. A phenomenon. You and I both know this, darling,' she finished gently. 'She was always bound to get that attention.'

'I do so miss her, Miss Abigail. She was always with us, and now sometimes I feel that she has already gone from us; that she's thrown us off like an old coat.' It was only when I said the words that I realised it was true. Of course, tonight she would come back with us to our lodgings and she would snuggle down beside me in bed. But now she spent most of her time with Mrs Palmer, fetching and carrying for her and drinking in every word she said. And her Engish was improving all the time, only marred by her occasionally mimicking Mrs Palmer's sharp, stagy tones. This was so irritating that I had to fight back the desire to shout at her, to stop her being so silly.

'Do we know if Joe Zambra will be here tonight?' said Miss Abigail suddenly. 'Wasn't he supposed to come this Saturday to see her dance?'

My heart lurched. What a long week this had been. This town; these new people; Louis Hernfield; the dockland and the pottery; the thrilling-frightening thoughts of Ambrose Benedict: all these events had stretched this week into an enormous space in my mind, making the dramatic events of Bishop Auckland distant and unreal. It occurred to me that to lose sight of such a thing as Angelo's death even for a moment might seem quite wicked and heartless. Yet Miss Abigail had taught me that this was what theatre people do all the time. The only permanent thing in their lives was the notion of the company as a kind of abstract. The only reality was within its daily and transitory routines; the only permanence was its programme. Events and people came and went but the company was our home territory. It was who we were.

Now Miss Abigail had brought all that back by reminding me that Joe Zambra might turn up and bring to life again the pain and difficulty of the events I'd been forgetting.

'Go and see if he's there in the audience,' said Miss Abigail suddenly. 'Look through the curtain. Tesserina needs to know.'

I went to peep through the hole, but of course I couldn't see beyond the first two rows where the people were cracking their sides laughing at the witticisms and innuendo embedded in Cissie's last song.

It was only as she was sweeping off to great applause that I realised that Stan Slater and Roy Divine were standing there waiting for AJ to announce them. In the rosy stage lights Roy looked handsome, a golden Apollo there to do Mr Slater's bidding. Mr Slater glanced at me gravely, but Roy winked at me and I felt the colour in my cheeks. But I did not flee. I waited to watch them make their entrance, Slater strolling on first, and Roy carrying his master's cloak and a carved chair. There was a ripple of interest in the audience when Slater called out and introduced Roy as his new assistant, adding some reference to 'the Sorcerer's Apprentice'. 'And you will have to watch him, ladies and gentlemen! He is already mastering his mesmerism studies and who knows where he will go then?'

I took one glance at the smirking, bowing Roy Divine and at last turned to flee, almost falling over Pixie Molloy, fully enamelled and in costume, who was watching him closely.

'Ain't he wonderful?' she said breathlessly. 'Ain't that Roy Divine the most beautiful, wonderful man?'

I grimaced. 'He's really horrible, Pixie Molloy. How could you say that?'

She shook her head. 'Excuse me, miss, but you don't know him. He's really, really kind. Don't you know that?'

I looked down at her enamelled, eager face, into her bright eyes, and felt very tired. 'No I don't,' I said, and swept past her.

'No luck,' I said to Miss Abigail when I got back. 'No chance of ever seeing anyone past the first two rows, so many people out there.' I flopped down on to my stool and picked up my sewing. 'I nearly fell over one of the little dancers making cow's eyes at Roy Divine.'

Miss Abigail nodded. 'Pixie Molloy! Hermione mentioned it – he encourages them all but Molloy is following him round like a kitten. Hermione has talked to Sophia Bunce about it and she said she'd give the child a thrashing. Foul woman. Not a lot you can do about it, really. It's no new thing, of course. You'll always get men gawping at youngsters. Fresh innocence can be very intoxicating. I know that first-hand.' She looked at me over her glasses. 'He paid more attention to you than he should have, didn't he? He's a troublemaker. Look where that led to.' She paused. 'Best to give such people a clear headway.'

I sewed on in silence and Miss Abigail sat on her stool, her eyes half closed in her normal resting pose. Funnelled through from the stage we could hear the roars of applause: Slater and Divine were making their impact.

I wanted to ask her about this, whether we should take Molloy under our wing, to save her from him. I had just formed the words in my mind and opened my mouth when she stood up, brushed her hands down her skirts and said briskly, 'That's Slater's final applause, I think. I reckon we should go and see that Tesserina's dress is right, then watch the new lighting from the side. The effect will not be so good from that angle, but at least we'll see the reaction of the audience.'

When we got to the wings Tom Merriman was standing in front of the drawn curtain, raising a titter with his jokes, and Tesserina was behind the curtain settling into her dance, in her starting pose. Her eyes lit up when she saw us, but it was Mrs Palmer who was attending to her, seeing that her dress was right. She glanced at us and nodded. And then she hurried down, her high heels clicking, to her place beside Mr Smith at the piano.

Tesserina looked across at me. 'I'm ready,' she whispered hoarsely to us, beaming. 'Mrs Palmer is very good. Now you see how these lights work, Pippa? Mrs Palmer says they are "wonderfully effective".'

And they were. The audience gasped with appreciation as she swirled and moved and the lights flickered through their changes. At the end of the dance, those many hundreds of people roared their approval as though they were one creature. The lights did change the dance. Where usually the billowing and swirling dress, with its larger-than-life shapes, had given the dance its character, now the lights seemed to emphasise the curves and hollows of the body underneath, to make it express passion and danger. The dance now was very much more sensual, even slightly *risqué*.

It was a great success.

The great success of Tesserina's dance did not at first make up for Joe's failure to materialise. She waited backstage after the Finale, listening with us to the familiar sequence of sounds as the theatre emptied: the hollow call of distant voices, the crack of seats as they flew up and the rasp of brushes about their business.

She sent me – 'Go, Pippa! Go and find Joe!' – to scour the auditorium but there was no one there. I went outside and looked up and down the emptying streets but all I saw were Sunderland people going about their late evening business. I came back empty-handed, and Tesserina – quiet, dreamy Tesserina – stamped her feet like a spoiled child, then dissolved into a storm of tears and tore her hair down from the edifice so carefully constructed by Mrs Palmer's dresser. Miss Abigail and I stood by, entirely helpless, as she completed the destruction.

Then, as quickly as it had swirled up, the Tesserina-storm receded. She sniffed back the last of the tears and shrugged. Then she leaned towards the mirror and started to fix her hair. 'Well. No Joe is no Joe. So I will go to London with Hermione.'

Hermione. Not even Miss Abigail called Mrs Palmer that. Not in front of us.

Miss Abigail looked up at her. 'London? *Mrs Palmer* didn't say anything to me about this, Tesserina.'

Tesserina pinned back the last curl. 'Hermione said there was a man in the audience twice this week. A Mr Terrance from London. He tell Hermione. She and Mr Jacob Smith and me. We must go to London and he will find a theatre for us. She told me this.'

Miss Abigail glanced at me, frowning, her face unusually grave. It was all there in that single glance: how I had found

Tesserina in the street; how between us she and I had brought Tesserina into the sane world; how we'd taught her our language – or rather Miss Abigail's language; how Miss Abigail had taught her to tame her dance and bring it into an explosive form that she could share with the world; how we had all eaten together and slept together like a family for so many weeks.

Now Tesserina finally caught our tension and looked at us, one to another. 'You and Pippa come as well, Miss Abigail,' she said. 'Come to London with Hermione and me.'

Miss Abigail was already shaking her head. 'No, dear. AJ will be bereft without Mrs Palmer. I wonder that she could bear to go. I will be needed here with the company.' She turned to me, keeping her glance neutral. 'But perhaps Pippa . . .'

I thought of Louis and my search for the fugitive Ambrose Benedict. And I thought of Miss Abigail, my dear old friend. I was already shaking my head. 'No. I can't go to London, Tesserina. I am obliged to stay here.'

Tesserina frowned. 'But, Pippa, you must come with me. How can I go to sleep without you?'

The sheer selfishness of it almost made me laugh. Tesserina, as always, remained at the centre of her own world. This was how she survived in the dark days in the asylum. This was how she had flowered in our protection. Now she had chosen Hermione Palmer as her protector. I thought in a sudden flash that in her life there would be other protectors and in the centre of all this protection Tesserina would flourish, on her own.

There was nothing further to say. But we all stood there, very still. It was as though if anyone moved or spoke that would be the end of the three of us as a family. Not one of us

– not even the insensitive Tesserina – wanted to do this.

Louis relieved the situation. He came crashing through the door and stopped, cap in hand, looking at each of us in turn. He was in his street clothes but had been careless about his make-up and had not removed the black lines round his eyes. He looked so very glamorous. 'I'm sorry, am I interrupting something?'

We all relaxed.

'No. Nothing,' said Miss Abigail with a kind of forced gaiety. 'We were just chatting.'

'I came to tell you the London man liked my plays.' He glanced across at me. 'And I came to ask Pippa if she'd come to tea tomorrow, with the ancients. My parents, that is.' He turned to Miss Abigail. 'If that's all right with you, Miss Wharton.'

She relaxed and smiled. 'That's fine, Louis.'

He hesitated. 'Perhaps you would care to come too?'

She shook her head. 'Mr Barrington has persuaded me to go to the Baptist chapel with him. He declares that he went there as a boy and there is fine singing to be heard.'

He turned to Tesserina. 'Would you come to tea?'

'No. I will have tea with Mr and Mrs Palmer at their hotel. Hermione says we must talk business.' She beamed. 'We talk about going to London.'

It was hard to remember that just minutes before she had been tearing her hair out with grief because Joe Zambra had not turned up.

The Ancients

The next day, Sunday, was our day off. I had arranged to meet Louis outside the theatre. He had washed off his glamorous eye-lines but still looked very elegant in a waistcoat and a smart tie, and he was clutching that peculiar English hat they call a bowler. I too had made a special effort. I wore a slender two-piece suit that Miss Abigail had cut down to fit me, finished with a little fur tippet from the property box. I felt quite elegant. Louis complimented me on the scrap of a hat that Miss Abigail had concocted for me just that morning.

'You look quite the fine English lady,' he said, offering his arm. 'I hardly recognised you.'

I spoiled the whole effect by laughing out loud. 'You mean instead of a French *gamine* in her Basque beret?' I said, taking his arm. 'Perhaps your parents would not let her through the door?'

He shook his head. 'They would hardly notice. Poor Ma can hardly see, except at the edges of her vision and Pa is very unworldly and would not know a French beret from a cloche hat, or even this bowler.'

The town, as we walked through it, buzzed with that air of *fête* that the Sunday holiday may bring in any working town. I knew it in Carcassonne: people in their best clothes promenading in family groups, on their way to pastimes denied them during the week. As we walked Louis pointed out a fine glass building he called the Winter Gardens, as well as a very beautiful, very green park that teemed with families walking and bowling and playing, determined to make use of this rare fine day.

As we walked on, the crowds on the pavements began to thin and the houses grew larger and more separate. Then at last we came to a square of houses, with large windows and fine doors, which faced inwards over a green garden that had three great trees at its centre and green plants at its edge. Louis led me half the way round the square, then up a short path of black and red tiles to a green door whose windows were decorated with deep blue irises set in lead.

Louis rang the bell, then instantly turned the knob and opened the unlocked door.

'The bell is just a signal,' he explained, 'for the ancients to wake up from their snooze. Ma would hate you to come on her with her cap awry.'

Breakfast for Two

'We can't afford to do it, my darling,' announced AJ, buttoning a snowy napkin on to his top waistcoat button and eyeing his grilled herrings with some anticipation. 'Not only would I miss you for very obvious reasons, but who would keep our wayward troupe in order? Who would do my books? Who would scold people for me?'

'My darling,' Hermione put a plump hand on his, 'the books are in perfect order. Haven't I worked on them with Cameron for some weeks? He is a dab hand at them. He's very nice, Cameron.' She looked into AJ's eyes. 'He does so like to work with you, darling. Practically has you on a pedestal. And so loyal.'

'It's true, he's a sound feller,' muttered AJ, taking a forkful of herring and chewing it slowly before he spoke again. 'But what about the troupe, Hermione? Those damned fighting acrobats and all that bother with the Italian back in Bishop? Me, I would have sacked them. Sorely tempted. Same with Cissie. Woman's a drunkard. Couldn't have managed that without you.'

'Darling AJ, you underestimate your own brilliance. Me? I am a mere cipher. You've always been so good with our people. They'd lay down their lives for you just as your soldiers did in Africa.' Hermione was not averse to a small lie when it got her what she wanted.

He changed tack. 'Can't think why you want to go haring off to London with that mad dancer. She has a cold look in her eye. She'd put a knife in you while you are sleeping. You mark my words, Hermione. She is not to be trusted.' He chewed glumly on some more herring as though, far from being succulent, it tasted like sawdust. He wanted to ask her how she thought he would manage without the other intimate things: the private world they had shared so long. But he couldn't.

She chuckled. 'My darling. Now I know you're clutching at straws. Tesserina is eccentric, I grant you. But she is as mild as milk. Abigail has got her trained. And you heard what that Mr Terrance said about her. "Star quality." Another Loie Fuller or he'll eat his hat. A future on the stages of Paris and New York as well as London.'

'Feller's a crackpot,' muttered AJ. 'Doesn't know his arse from his elbow. Never trust an agent.'

'Arthur! No need to be crude.' Hermione paused and tried again. 'My dear, you know full well old Terrance is a decent enough chap and could bring the girl on. Make her fortune. Make *our* fortune, what's more.'

'So let the feller take her. Bad enough losing one of my best acts, but losing *you* is damned unthinkable, Hermione.'

Hermione stared at him. A month ago she would never have dreamed of leaving AJ on his own. She'd have been too worried about Cameron, for a start. But here in Sunderland, the place where she had grown up, something had changed inside her. Perhaps she had been affected by the abandon of Tesserina's dancing. Perhaps the applause they achieved between the two of them gave her the longing again to be herself, to perform in her own right. It could be that playing alongside Jacob Smith had made her think that another life was possible; that she could finish with babying AJ through his adventures and have a few of her own. This realisation had come to her early one morning when she had woken up before the dawn light and had looked down at AJ's balding wrinkled head, vulnerable and starkly naked without its protective toupée. At that moment, instead of the usual warm protective feeling, a wave of revulsion had swept through her. She knew then that things had changed. She and AJ would never be the same together. She would not hurt his feelings. Never. But she had changed. There was no question of that.

Now she shook her head. 'Tesserina can't go on her own, AJ. She depends on my music. She would be disturbed if any other person played for her.'

'Just as I said. She would knife a person in the back.'

'Don't be silly.'

'And why does she need this Jacob Smith feller as well? You played for the girl from the start. Why does she suddenly need him?'

Hermione decided to tell another lie. 'I'm afraid Jacob has decided not to go. His sister is ill and he feels this is not the time to make the move.' She paused. 'I had thought that he could come with us and learn the ropes; then after a time I could leave Tesserina in his hands and come back to you at the earliest moment.'

AJ put down his knife and fork. 'Is his sister very ill?' he said. 'Perhaps you should put some pressure on him. Feller shouldn't cling to his sister's apron strings, too timid to leave the nest. Get on to him.'

Pleased at having won the argument, Hermione folded her napkin and smoothed it on the white damask tablecloth. 'I'll make an enquiry, AJ. It would be so convenient, don't you think, to have him as my understudy? And so important, my darling, to strike while the iron's hot. Mr Terrance wants us to travel down with him tomorrow.'

'*Tomorrow?*' AJ pulled off his napkin, bringing a button with it, and threw it to the floor. 'Really, Hermione! What has happened to you? You have no thought for the company at all. A gap in the programme halfway through the run! I can't allow it.'

'Give Stan Slater and the glamorous Roy more time. The audience went wild about them last night. Didn't Stan come to you with that idea of making a drama of training Roy Divine? Asking the audience to test him? That would be such fun!'

At last he waved his hand at her. 'Do it! Do it! Don't you always do what you wish? I am nothing to you, nothing!'

Hermione flounced around the table and he could hear her stays creak as she bent down to put her arms round his rigid shoulders and kissed him soundly on the mouth. 'You are a dear, AJ. I promise I will send you a letter – well, perhaps a postcard – every day. And as soon as Jacob Smith is up to it I'll be back by your side. It's a promise.'

He shook himself free. 'So much for the mad dancer making *our* fortune.' He sat there, scowling. 'To leave halfway through an engagement. Really, Hermione. It's too bad.'

Then she sighed. 'I suppose I could wire Mr Terrance and say we could go down when the Sunderland engagement finishes. That would give you . . . us . . . time . . .'

'I am not happy about this. Not happy at all.'

She stood away from him. 'Well, AJ?' she said coldly. 'What do you want? A fortune in your old age, or me perpetually by your side? You can't have both!'

He avoided her gaze and looked towards the dining-room door. 'I wonder if they have any more of those herrings? They are excellent. Better than I've had in years.'

Winter Gardens

Over late Sunday lunch at their digs, Abigail tried to persuade Tesserina not to rush off to London with Hermione at the whim of a single agent. She suggested that perhaps Tesserina needed a little more real dance experience on the stage before taking such a step.

Tesserina frowned. 'What does it matter, Miss Abigail?' she said. 'I dance here. I dance there. Hermione say many people in London will like my dance. Thousands of people.'

'What about Pippa and me? We will miss you. Pippa especially.'

Tesserina looked at her blankly.

'Your new dress,' said Abigail desperately. 'We haven't finished your new dress.'

Tesserina beamed. 'You give it to the postman. Send me a parcel.'

At that, Abigail gave up. When they'd finished eating she proposed to Josiah and Tesserina that they should all take a short walk to blow away the cobwebs and see a little more of this great town. The breeze was getting up but the day was still bright. When Josiah demurred Abigail reminded him that she *had* agreed to go to chapel with him that evening. The least he could do was to show her the courtesy of accompanying her on a brisk walk now in the watery sunshine. Josiah was too kind to mention that, with her ankles, the briskness of a brisk walk would be questionable. He stood up and reached for his coat.

She buttoned up Tesserina's coat herself and the three of them battled through the town to the Winter Gardens, where they sat for a while and admired the glamorous building and the distinctive green plants, some of which reached their fronds up to the vaulted roof. On the way back to the digs, Josiah took charge and led them through some streets where, in his opinion, their little shop might be located – just between the smart shops and the more everyday shops used by all and sundry. He spoke quickly, full of enthusiasm. Abigail smiled and nodded at his fervour but kept her own counsel.

Then they turned the corner and found themselves in the street where the theatre stood in its shrouded Sunday state, apart from a flapping, hand-written poster announcing that on this Sunday evening four local amateur choirs would offer a performance of the *Messiah*.

A man was standing outside.

Tesserina yelped with delight and started to run. Leaning on one of the columns, looking very smart in a two-piece suit and sporting a gold watch chain, was Joe Zambra. Beside him was a small case and a larger, more bulbous case that Abigail knew contained his accordion.

Tesserina ran to greet him and – taller than he was – engulfed him with a warm embrace, laughing into his face and talking away in a torrent of Italian.

When Abigail and Josiah finally reached them, Joe disentangled himself sufficiently to greet them and shake their hands, which was somewhat difficult as Tesserina was still hanging on to him.

'We thought – well, Tesserina thought – you were coming here last night,' said Abigail at last.

'Boiler blew up,' said Joe. 'Had the fire brigade and everything.' He looked at Abigail and then nodded at Tesserina. 'What's this she's saying about London?'

'She's firm about going. An agent was here. He recommended it to Mrs Palmer. It seems this man thinks she's very good.' Abigail nodded slightly. 'He is not mistaken.' She explained about the agent and Mrs Palmer, and their proposal to leave on Monday.

Joe frowned.

'Signor Terrance said I'm very good,' put in Tesserina. 'A great dancer, he said.'

'Are you going too?' Joe looked at Abigail.

She shook her head. 'I'm not asked, to be honest. But if I were, I still wouldn't go. I have my life here, with the company. I have Pippa to take care of.' She glanced sideways at Josiah. 'There are other things to think of.'

'She canna go there on her own – even with the Palmer woman. How can she?' said Joe. 'She'll get upset. No one to talk to.'

Abigail shrugged. 'I'm inclined to agree with you but she's happy about it.'

He looked round. 'Where's the French girl?'

'She's off on an errand of her own.'

'I bet she is,' he said sourly.

'That's quite enough of that,' said Abigail tartly. 'You may resent Pippa because of Angelo but that was clearly not her fault. And you may remember it was young Pippa who rescued Tesserina from terrible things in Paris.'

Tesserina nodded vigorously. 'Pippa is a good girl.'

'Then why,' Joe muttered through his teeth, 'can't Pippa go to London and take care of Tesserina?'

Abigail was very patient. 'Because, like me, Pippa has her own life to live and will not live it on the petticoat tails of anyone, not even this Tesserina whom she loves like a sister. Mrs Palmer has taken charge of Tesserina now. And she's a sensible woman.'

'Won't do,' said Joe stubbornly. 'The woman sees Tesserina as a dancing puppet. Likely somebody who'll make her fortune.'

Abigail did not protest against this view. It had seeds of truth in it.

'I'll go,' he said suddenly. 'I'll go with Tesserina. I've brought my accordion with me. I'll play in cafés. There are hundreds of cafés in London.'

Tesserina yelped with pleasure and clapped her hands.

'But what about your mother?' said Abigail.

'What about the café?' said the practical Josiah, getting a word in at last.

Joe Zambra shrugged. 'The café is closed for some days now because of the fire. Aldo will look after it. After that we'll see. Aldo can hire a new cook. Labour's cheap these days.'

'And then?' said Abigail.

He shrugged again. 'We'll see. See what happens in London. If Tesserina needs me I'll let Aldo and my mother get on with the business.' He disentangled his arm from Tesserina's hand and put it around her. 'Me and Tesserina'll not part. Angelo's gone now and I'll not lose her. No other girl I'll ever meet'll touch Tesserina. You know that.'

Looking at Joe and Tesserina standing there, Abigail felt a rare twinge of envy. What would she have given if once, just once, someone had thought that much about her?

Then she felt the warmth of Josiah's hand in the crook of her arm. 'What say we get to the digs and have a cup of tea, Abi? That easterly off the river can be quite cutting. Or am I getting old?'

Cakes and Wine

Louis was right about his mother's cap. An old-fashioned muslin cap trimmed in handmade lace, it was set against the side of her head at a precarious angle. Louis's father also wore a cap, a little round one. It was quite straight, anchored by thin elastic to the crown of his head. The old ones were both overjoyed to see their son, greeting him as though they'd not seen him for a week, rather than this morning at breakfast.

'Hello, ancients!' With gentle hands Louis set his mother's cap straight and then shook hands heartily with his father, a diminutive man who came up only to his shoulder. 'And see! I have brought my friend Mademoiselle Pippa Valois to meet you,' he announced.

He introduced me first to his mother, who stood up and pulled me gently into the centre of her vision before she shook my hand. Then she turned her head sideways so she could sweep me from head to toe with her one-sided gaze.

'French, I hear,' she murmured in a voice not louder than a bird's, as she shook my hand with a hand no more solid than a bird's claw. '*Französisch!* How very exciting.' She felt behind her then sat down on her chair.

'And, Pa! Here is Mademoiselle Pippa Valois.'

The old man took my hand in a hand that had the consistency of dry paper and bent his head over it, half kissing it. I could feel the feathery touch of his beard. '*Enchanté, mademoiselle. Je suis enchanté de faire votre connaissance.*'

I found myself bobbing a little curtsy. '*Merci, monsieur. Vous parlez français?*'

He shrugged. 'Just schoolboy French, *mademoiselle*,' he said in English and smiled a gap-toothed smile. 'But then I have schoolboy Russian and Latin, not to speak of German and Yiddish. So I am a very clever chap, don't you think!'

Just beside me I could hear Louis chuckle.

The old woman piped up from her chair. 'Have you come to marry our son, Mam'selle Pippa? Louis is a stubborn boy. We have quite given up thoughts of him having a nice girl of the faith, so now anyone will do so we can go to our rest in peace.' Like her husband she had a lisping accent that was not quite English. Like mine, I suppose.

I could feel myself flushing from my collar to my fringe.

'Ma, that is just too bad!' protested Louis mildly. 'Must you always be on the prowl? Pippa and I have just met and we are getting to know each other. Becoming very good friends.' His eyelid flickered in my direction in the barest wink. 'I'll go and get the tray, Mother.'

So he left me under the eye of these very strange old birds. I sneaked a glance at the room: slightly dusty with too many mirrors, which glimmered rather than shone.

'Our son Louis is very clever,' announced the old man. 'He was the cleverest boy in his school. Like his grandfather, my own dear father, he can learn anything.'

The old woman nodded vigorously and her cap started to move on her thin locks. 'My Louis can learn anything: physics, astronomy . . .'

'My friend Miss Wharton, who knows all about the theatre, says that Louis writes good plays,' I said, determined to have some kind of say in this pantomime of praise.

The old woman threw up her hands. 'No good, no good! Child's play. Flotsam. Not of the brain. The boy must use his brain.'

'Do you act in his plays, *mam'selle*?' said the old man suddenly. 'If you think them so good?'

I shook my head. 'No, but I have seen one. It's very good.'

'Do you dance?' said the grandmother. 'We must be worrying if you are a dancer.'

'No,' I said firmly. 'But my very best friend is a dancer. She is a very beautiful dancer. She will be famous one day.'

'Well, what *do* you *do*?' rasped the old man suddenly. 'Do you do nothing in this troupe of yours?'

I can hardly say that I am cared for by a very kind hardworking woman who supports me in my folly. 'I sew,' I said carefully. 'I sew costumes for the performers at the theatre.'

'Sew?' said the old woman. 'Now *that* is a good thing.'

At this point, to my great relief the door was kicked open and Louis came in, weighed down by a big mahogany tray on which stood a bottle, small glasses and a silver salver of small shining cakes. 'Now for a little of old Vienna,' he said. 'The wine is strawberry wine from Bohemia, the cakes are a speciality from some Viennese ancestor of mine and have been made in my family by generations of servants who had never been nearer to Vienna than Lowestoft.'

I suddenly knew that this ceremony – the pouring of the wine into the small crystal glasses, the handing round of the cakes on small china plates held in snowy napkins – echoed thousands of other scenes played out in this family for hundreds of years.

The old man embarked then on a tale of a journey he once made across the Danube to Bratislava as a boy. Louis nodded and listened with respect. The old woman closed her eyes.

Then, as I bit into the blindingly sweet cake, tears started to fill my eyes, then drip down my cheeks, over my hands and on to the cake.

The old woman's eyes snapped open and she caught me. 'Mam'selle Pippa appears to be crying,' she said drily.

The men glanced up and to my mortification I started to sob in earnest. In a second Louis was at my side, mopping my face, blotting up the tears with his napkin. 'It's all right, Pippa. What is it?'

'It's beautiful. It's all so beautiful,' I muttered wildly through the embarrassing tears. 'All this.'

As quick as they had started, the tears stopped. 'I'm sorry,' I said, sniffing. They were looking at me anxiously, the three of them curiously alike, despite the difference in their ages. One part of me registered that Louis's mother must have been sixty when he was born. Surely that was impossible. I took another bite of the cake to reassure them that I had stopped crying and they all relaxed.

The old woman sat back against her cushion, dislodging her cap even further. 'You are a nice girl, *mam'selle*,' she announced. 'It is rare to see true emotion. The English are so frozen. Their pain comes out in chips of ice.' Then she closed her eyes and appeared to be asleep.

We stayed until all the cakes had been eaten and all the wine drunk. By the time we left the room the old man was quite tipsy and giggly and the old woman was snoring.

Louis asked me to help him with the tray and I followed him down the corridor to the cavernous kitchen, all laid out for the next day's cooking. I looked round. 'Does someone help in here?'

He nodded. 'Janey Doby and her daughter Flo. But they are Baptists and don't work on Sundays.' He laughed. 'They'll be up in their attic reading their Holy Book as we speak.'

'I think rather they'll be up there sitting with their feet up, pleased to do no work. This is a very big house to clean.'

He glanced round the kitchen. 'How very caring of you,' he said, then led me through to the narrow scullery and put the tray on the draining board of a large warped wooden sink, which looked stained and unclean. I looked towards the white porcelain sink on the wall opposite. He shook his head. '*Glass-and-porcelain-in-the-wooden-sink*,' he chanted. 'I learned that from Janey many years ago when I was quite small.' He turned on the tap, then took off his jacket and rolled up his sleeves. He vanished and came back with a pristine glass cloth. 'You dry. I wash,' he said. 'Then we can make our escape.'

I was very conscious of his body in that small, scrubbed space: how his hair curled down over his starched collar; how his shoulder was muscular under the soft fabric of his shirt; how he smelled faintly of tobacco and strawberry wine. I noticed too how slender and deft his hands were as they dealt with the glasses and plates. From the side I could see his straight nose – less aquiline than his father's – the generous curve of his lips and the downward slant of his eyes. Angelo came to my mind and those dratted tears started again. I blinked them away and dried the glasses with great concentration.

Louis didn't appear to notice. He was very jolly and practical, almost cool. Perhaps I had frightened him with my floods of tears in the drawing room. Perhaps part of him was thinking I might be as crazy as my friend Tesserina, to break down over a tray of cakes and wine.

Later, as we made our escape down the pathway and round the fine central garden, he took my arm and I relaxed.

'Well? What do you think?' he demanded.

'What do I think of what?'

'The ancients.'

'It is more what they think of me, perhaps?'

'I know what they think of you.'

'Do you? I would think they think me a cry-baby.'

'They think you are charming and have true sentiment and a warm character.'

'Did they tell you?'

'They didn't need to tell me. So, what do you think?'

'I can't say.'

'Say!'

'Well. I thought they were charming and warm characters, too. And interesting. They made me curious about them.'

'And . . .?'

I kept my eyes straight ahead. 'I couldn't do the sums.'

'What does that mean?'

'It's hard to think they're your parents. At their age.'

'Well, they're not. I will tell you the truth. Though they have not told me, I suspect they are really my grandparents and that my mother was their middle daughter who vanished into the depths of America in 1898, the year of my birth. However, no one ever speaks of it.'

'I'm so sorry.' I was bright red, embarrassed at his disclosure and feeling cursed at my own long anger at losing my mother.

He hugged my arm to his side. 'No need to be sorry, dear Pippa. The ancients have adored me all of my life and have been the best parents a man could wish for. But you see why I could never go galloping off to London or anywhere else at the behest of my playwriting? This is why I plod on here at my printing and take an occasional holiday to imagine myself an actor or a writer of plays for others to act.'

We walked on a little and I waited a while before the question that had been burning in my head burst from me. 'Why do you tell me all this, Louis? Why take me to see your ancients?'

He stopped and pulled me round to face him. A family – mother, father and a flush of children – flowed past us like a stream making its way round a rock. 'As I said to the ancients, you and I have just met. And if you were any other girl, Pippa, I could take months over it. I would cook up chances to meet you accidentally. Create false excuses so that we may meet. I would talk to you casually at first, then with more intensity. But you are here a week and we have to waddle on very fast, like Charlie Chaplin in a film, before you get on the train with your bag and baggage and go to another town and break another man's heart.'

Heart? I wrenched my arm away from him. 'Who have you been talking to? Roy Divine? Marie Divine? You think me a whore . . .'

I ran away from him, leaving him there in the street, the Sunday crowd flowing round him. I heard his voice and the curses of the people I kept bumping into. But inside my head I was back in the little pantry in my mother's apartment, hearing her open the door and greet her callers warmly and with interest and then, with her own particular grace and style, go about her business.

I turned a corner and cracked into a woman who was all furs and perfume. It took me a moment to realise that it was Mrs Palmer, arm in arm with Mr Smith, who played piano with her. She held me fast.

'Pippa, what is it, my darling? Why are you blubbing like this? Not like you.'

But now I couldn't stop. She drew me into a locked shop doorway. Mr Smith raised his hat and walked on discreetly. Mrs Palmer took out a tiny lace handkerchief and dabbed at my eyes. Her presence, and the ridiculous handkerchief, brought me to my senses.

'I'm sorry, Mrs Palmer,' I sniffed. The tears stopped. 'I am *folle*. So silly.'

'I know, darling. You're sad because your dear friend Tesserina is off to London. No need, my dear. You may write to her – oh, she doesn't read, I forget – no, write to me and I will read your letters to her.' Then her voice lost its absolute certainty. 'Of course, you could come with us . . .' Her voice tailed off. She didn't mean that at all. That was the last thing she wanted.

'I couldn't leave Miss Abigail. Ever.'

She patted my shoulder. 'Of course you couldn't. Dear Abigail has been more like a mother to you. More than a mother, if one judges what one sees.'

I gulped back more tears. 'I'm all right, Mrs Palmer. Really I am.'

'You'll get over it, darling. Think how good it will be for your friend. She'll be famous. No doubt about it.'

I moved to get away from her grasp. 'I'm all right. Really I am.'

'But you're not!' she said. 'Any fool can see. What is the matter, Pippa?'

312

Mr Smith sauntered back and hovered by the doorway.

'My mother died, Mrs Palmer. My *maman*,' I hiccoughed. 'I remembered that my mother died. And Angelo my friend. He died too.'

Mr Smith coughed.

Mrs Palmer frowned. 'Your mother? Was there a letter? A wire? Abigail didn't say . . .'

'She died four years ago.' Now I really sounded *folle*.

Her hands dropped from me. Then she pulled up my collar and rearranged my tippet. 'Oh dear, Pippa. Pull yourself together, there's a dear. That was a long time ago. I think you should hurry along and find Miss Abigail. She will be a comfort to you.'

Then she hurried off, arm in arm with Mr Smith. The sight of them together dried all my tears. There was something so comical about them: she so tall, stout and highly painted and he so small and dapper with his neat moustache. I smiled after them in a watery fashion and made my way back to my digs.

As I hastened along, it dawned on me that Louis Hernfield must now think me quite a washout. A veritable waterworks. No doubt that would put him off and he wouldn't need to worry about me being here only a week. He would be glad to get rid of me. If I were Louis I would be glad to get rid of me.

When I got back to our rooms, what a surprise! Tesserina was toasting her toes beside the crackling fire with Joe Zambra. So Joe had come. Tesserina announced that Miss Abigail and Mr Barrington were out at 'the chapelle' singing holy songs.

Joe scrambled to his feet and shook hands. 'Hello, Pippa,' he said gravely. I searched his gaze for the hurt and blame that

I saw in them last week. But his look was open and enquiring. 'How're you today? My mother told me she saw you at Angelo's grave.' He rubbed his cheek thoughtfully. 'And she gave me a roasting about you. And now I've had a roasting from Miss Wharton for being . . . I came to think they are right. Mebbe you were more sinned against than sinning.'

It was a long speech, but counted as an apology and I was grateful for that.

'So you got here?' I said, glancing at Tesserina.

She smiled up from her place on the couch. 'And Joe, he will come to London now with Hermione, with me. He brings his *acc-or-dion*.' She smiled again, that wonderful smile: all blind innocence and pure survival-selfishness.

'Good!' I said. 'Now there is no need for us to worry about you.'

Unlike Tesserina, Joe recognised the irony. 'Well, at least I'll be able to write to you for her. She can tell, I can translate.' He looked down at her fondly. 'Though how I'll keep up with her I can't think. She talks twenty to the dozen, doesn't she?'

I excused myself to go to my bedroom but they barely noticed me. As I brushed my hair before the cracked mirror my thoughts switched strangely from Joe to Ambrose Benedict, who I now badly wanted to find, and to Louis Hernfield, who would probably now have nothing to do with me after my ridiculous impression of a waterfall. For a second the face in the mirror, staring back at me, was the face of a stranger. I wondered if somewhere inside me I wanted to make Louis run away from me. Then he'd escape the risk that I'd brought to my mother and to Angelo. He would be safe.

Miss Abigail came in then, to say good night. She announced that Joe Zambra was still there in our sitting room although he would have to be expelled very soon as it was nearly nine thirty. She also announced that she'd met Mrs Palmer on her way back from the chapel. 'She asked about *you*! I assured her you were in fine fettle, and keen to have a permanent place with us. She herself was in good spirits although it now seems they won't go to London for another week. It seems AJ has prevailed.' She smiled slightly. 'I think Hermione was all for running off with Tesserina and that pianist of hers. Of course, as AJ is quite aware, it could have broken up the company. I'm surprised at Hermione, to tell you the truth. All this talk of London and fame has befogged her native common sense.' She was so preoccupied that she forgot to call Hermione Mrs Palmer for my young ears.

I jumped into bed and Miss Abigail absently pulled up the covers and tucked them in all around me. This was not her custom and it brought my mother to mind and – this being the day for tears – my eyes filled up. Miss Abigail, kneeling on the threadbare hearthrug to rake down the bedroom fire, did not seem to notice.

I blotted my tears on the sheet and said, 'So how was this chapel? Was it very nice? Was there good singing?'

'Some very fine singing, Pippa, but such blatant faith! Verging on the vulgar. I must be honest with you, Pippa. I'm afraid I am too much of a pagan to relish any church or chapel.'

I thought of the nun who dragged me away from my dead mother. 'Me too,' I said. 'Me too.'

She glanced at me. 'I have only just discovered that Josiah is quite keen on all that kind of thing. A revelation to me. Quite another side to him. You can know a person for many years and still not know it all. Perhaps this is a good thing. I've

315

seen him visit chapels in towns where the company happened to land, but if I were to be honest I have not thought much of it.'

'Mr Barrington is a good man,' I said. 'Do you love him? You have known him for such a long time.' Such things had begun to interest me: in Louis's ancients, who have been together for more than sixty years; in my own mother and father, who knew each other so fleetingly, perhaps not much longer than Angelo and me. Then there was Louis himself. And me.

'He is a good man, and I feel tenderness for him. I am tempted. But could you live with someone who espoused such a fervent belief?'

I thought about it. 'No,' I said, realising that something had happened between her and Mr Barrington. 'But I don't have to, Miss Abigail, and neither do you.'

'You're right,' she said. She eased herself on to her feet and looked down at me. 'I never quite know what goes on in your head, Pippa. Sometimes I think you can play catch-as-catch-can with the truth. At other times I think you see things with a very clear eye. You *are* a strange girl.' She turned down the lamp and made for the door.

Now was the time to tell her about Roy. 'Miss Abigail . . .?'

She turned. 'What is it, Pippa?'

'Nothing.' I snuggled down in bed, careful as always to leave room for Tesserina. 'Nothing at all.'

Quest

The next morning at ten o'clock Louis Hernfield, let in by our landlady, was at our sitting-room door. I was thankful to see him after that débâcle yesterday. To my relief he was smiling the self-deprecating, almost mischievous smile that had become so dear to me. At least I'd not frightened him off.

'Come on!' He held out a hand.

I touched his hand, then glanced back into the room, where Tesserina and Miss Abigail were having breakfast still in their dressing gowns, and pulled the door to behind me. I'd been up since eight o'clock. Miss Abigail sometimes commented that I was not built for theatrical hours. 'More an early bird than a late owl, my darling.'

'Where?' I asked Louis Hernfield. 'Where are we going?'

'We're going to the newspaper office to hunt down the homecoming hero of 1916.'

Miss Abigail looked up briefly when I told her I was off on an errand with Louis. I pulled on my jacket and clapped my beret on my head.

Tesserina took a bite of toast. 'Louis is a very clever man,' she said with her mouth full. I should have been pleased with her praising him, but I knew now she was not really interested in him, or me for that matter.

In the street I turned to him. 'I thought that after yesterday you'd want nothing to do with me.'

He laughed. 'I thought that after yesterday you'd want nothing to do with *me*. I thought you'd slam the door in my face. I thought you'd not want to spend time with someone who made you feel so sad.'

'Don't take any notice of me,' I said. 'Miss Abigail takes no notice of my strange ways and we get on famously.'

'Wise Miss Wharton,' he said. And he took my arm. I felt very comfortable, walking along with him in the keen spring sunshine.

He'd obviously already been to the newspaper office because we were shown instantly into a small dusty room with a big table stacked with vast leather folders holding newspapers in date order. In there somewhere would be my father. I was certain of it. When I sat down my hands were trembling.

The folder open on the table was labelled 1916. We sat shoulder to shoulder for a long time, turning the pages. It was fascinating. The articles and illustrations reflected the prime concerns of this great town in that year: its preoccupation with the war; its booming industrial enterprises connected with the war; its personal stories of adventure and loss. So many deaths, so many wounds, so many changed lives distilled here in formal lists of names. We came across a Gerald Hernfield who was Louis's cousin. Louis told me that three members of his family had been lost in the war. It would have been tempting to linger but we raced on, waiting for the name Ambrose Benedict to leap out at us.

And it did, in the edition of November 1916.

Wounded Hero Returns!

Captain Ambrose Philip Benedict has returned to his home from hospital, having survived the horrors of the first day of the Battle of the Somme. His family, of 43 Laurel Avenue in Sunderland, were there to welcome home their hero. On the field of battle in France he acquitted himself with such courage that he has been awarded the Military Cross. Captain Benedict has been in hospital in Surrey recovering from his wounds and is now deemed well enough to complete his convalescence at home. It is through bravery such as this that the tide of battle is turning and the British Army in the end will prevail over the enemy, bringing a just victory within our sights.

Louis made a note of the address and turned to me. 'Pippa, I think when we met you told me your name was Barbara Philippe Valois? This is where the Pippa comes from?'

I nodded. 'Yes.'

'And this man's name is Philip? Surely he must be the one.'

My heart was in my mouth. 'I don't know. My mother told me nothing about him, but I have these memories, like visions. Sometimes I don't know whether they're memories or dreams. But then there is the jug. That's not a dream. Captain Ambrose Philip Benedict,' I paused, lingering over the name. 'Whoever this man is, I think that he *is* perhaps a last link to my mother. Perhaps no more than that. Perhaps he just knew her then, before she became what she became. When she was her real self. That's all.'

Louis frowned. 'What did she become, Pippa?'

'You must understand that she was a very fine woman, beautiful, well educated . . .'

'I thought no less because I know her daughter.'

'. . . but she had me, and was driven . . .' it was hard to say, '. . . to be another kind of woman to survive. So, the accident of meeting him and having me pulled her life in a certain direction . . .' I couldn't say any more. I hardly knew what I wanted to say.

'Well.' Louis closed the leather folder with a slap. He held up the piece of paper. 'We have an address here. We'll go and see him and you can ask . . .'

I snatched the paper from him. 'No. Not yet. I need to think about this. And we must get back to the theatre. It'll be band call soon and Miss Abigail will be looking for me.' I frowned at him. 'But how do you manage to be here? You said last week that you had a few days off. Here we are. It is the second week. You should be back at your printing works.'

'Well, dear Pippa, I have you to thank for that.'

'Me? I have nothing to do with you.' I put another foot of space between us.

'Well, the ancients were so tickled by you that Pa said he would fund me for a year to see if this ridiculous thing with the plays might work.'

'Why me?' I was perplexed.

He shrugged. 'Perhaps because you are foreign as they are. Perhaps because they admired your sensibility.' He paused. 'Perhaps because they fell in love with you, as seems to be happening to me. Pa said you reminded him of Mater, when he first met her in Vienna. That she wore a hat with a little feather, just like you.'

He said all this very casually but I felt as though someone

had struck me a blow. I almost staggered. The only way I could deal with his casual declaration was to ignore it.

'Really, I've got to get back,' I mumbled, and I fled in the direction of the theatre.

New Deal

Abigail turned up at the theatre to find that backstage the air of tension was worse than usual. Mr and Mrs Palmer and Sophia Bunce were clustered together just inside the stage door.

AJ called Abigail over. 'Crisis, Abigail! Crisis!'

'Pixie Molloy has not turned up for rehearsal,' said Hermione.

'That bad girl has vanished from the lodging house. Run away,' blustered Madame Bunce, two purplish-red patches the only sign of the volcanic rage within. 'The reprobate, never liked her.'

'It's too bad,' growled AJ.

'Pray don't worry, AJ,' said Madame Bunce. 'I'll rehearse the others all day so you won't miss her. And we can import a new dancer tomorrow.'

'I'll help you with that,' said Hermione.

A fat smile. 'You are so kind, Mrs Palmer. I always say Mrs Palmer is so kind.'

'But where is she?' said Abigail urgently. Privately she

thought that Bunce must have thrashed the child too hard. 'A girl cannot just vanish into thin air. We must find her. She's only a child.'

Sophia Bunce threw up her hands. 'These girls, you work your fingers to the bone for them and they get a better offer and – *pouf!* – they're gone.' She sighed heavily. 'They think they're women of the world, those girls. You give them your all, then blink once and they're off. Not a scrap of loyalty.'

'But the child cannot be more than eleven,' persisted Abigail. The woman treated her dancers like marionettes. What was this romance of loyalty in a situation like this?

'Well,' said AJ gloomily, 'have we a choice? You'd better get on, Madame Bunce. I need your troupe fully *au fait* by curtain up.'

'I'll do it, AJ. Rely on me.' Madame Bunce rose to her feet. 'The show will go on.'

'Should we inform the authorities?' ventured Abigail. 'The police, perhaps?'

Madame Bunce sniffed. 'And have the girl turn up and make fools of us? The miscreant will certainly turn up. I've had my runaways before. This one's London Irish. Always wanting to return to the bog.'

The three of them watched her sweep to the door, then relaxed. 'Terrible woman,' said Abigail, grimacing. 'I'd be the first to run if I were under her whip.'

Hermione sighed. 'A disciplinarian, it's true. But you know, Abigail, that's the only way to get these girls up to scratch. We've been there, you and I. I started playing on stage when I was eleven.'

'So we have.' Abigail stood up and steadied herself on her feet. 'But we don't have to think it's right, do we? It wasn't right then and it isn't right now.'

'At least we know they'll be ready for tonight.' AJ's tone was brisk. He brushed one hand against the other, as though brushing away the problem of the terrible woman and her Pixies. 'Now then, Abigail, we have a proposal, don't we, darling?'

Hermione explained what Abigail already knew: about her decamping to London as chaperone to Tesserina for a short but unspecified time. Jacob Smith was not mentioned.

AJ coughed. 'And, dear Miss Wharton, we'd like to propose that you should deputise for Hermione in her absence. You know the ropes at Palmer's, and we consider yours a safe pair of hands.'

Abigail was silent, thinking of Josiah Barrington and his little shop. How tempting that seemed at the moment: to escape the cruel vagaries of people like Madame Bunce, and the self-serving pragmatism of the Palmers. Just herself and Josiah and beautiful bales of cloth and glittering needles and razor-sharp scissors. The two of them working side by side, building up their worldly wealth by their own endeavours . . .

AJ broke into her thoughts. 'There would be appropriate remuneration, of course, Miss Wharton. And it might only be a matter of weeks.'

Abigail wondered what it would be like to get up every morning and do the same thing, and to go to chapel every Sunday and sing faith from the heart. She had a choice to make. 'There would be more responsibility,' she said thoughtfully. 'There would be great demands on my time.'

'Of course,' he said smoothly. 'We anticipated that.'

'Well,' said Abigail, 'in that case I have a condition. I feel you should give young Pippa a proper job, AJ. Call her assistant wardrobe, if you like, but it should be a proper job, with remuneration.' She held her breath. She knew that if they said yes, then she herself had chosen Pippa over Josiah. If not, then Josiah's proposal should be considered further.

AJ stared at her, his eyes bulging slightly. 'There's logic in it, I suppose.'

'Go on, AJ!' urged Hermione. 'Isn't it overdue anyway? I have to say that the girl is very handy. And she's trained by Abigail.'

'Well, if you think so, Hermione . . .'

'Five pounds a week for me,' said Abigail firmly. 'And two for Pippa.'

AJ laughed. 'You have me in your grasp, Abigail. Agreed.' Here was some acknowledgement of her status. Although they had worked together for many years, he rarely called her by her given name.

Hermione clapped her hands, smiling. 'There. It's all settled. Now I can go to London with an easy conscience. Fair exchange, Abigail. You'll take care of darling AJ and I'll take care of your dancer. Isn't that nice?'

A Job of Work

When I got back to the theatre Miss Abigail was buzzing with good news for me. I had a role; I had work. I would even have some money at the end of the week. This would be an improvement on relying on change from Miss Abigail's purse. I felt inches taller as I walked around backstage.

She showed me her workbook with her list of weekly tasks: checklists, tasks to do, mends, makes and acquisitions. We went through this and listed things I could start to do this week and things she would continue to do. 'Just for training,' she said. 'Next week, when Hermione goes, you'll have to take on more.' She paused. 'Our priority this week is to complete Tesserina's new costume before she goes away.' She smiled her own sweet smile. 'But that, of course, will be a labour of love.'

My mind began to race at the implications of the news. 'This will mean I cannot come and go as I usually do, Miss Abigail?' The paper with the address on it was burning a hole in my pocket.

'Well, this week perhaps you can go on your wanders once

326

the jobs are properly done. But while Hermione's away I'll need someone down here to keep their eye on things. Why do you ask?' she said shrewdly. 'What special mischief are you up to now?'

'Louis and I have . . . something we have planned to do.'

She raised her brows. 'Louis, is it? I forgot to ask you – how did you find that visit to his home?'

'It was a big house,' I said.

'And his parents?'

'They seemed very old. But *charmants*.'

'How nice.' She paused. 'Well, if you and Louis have errands to run I suppose you'd better run them this week. Next week it'll be all hands on deck. But by then we'll have left Louis behind so I suppose you'll have more time on your hands to do the work.'

I thought it best not to mention that Louis now had a year's grace from his parents. He might go to London, as everybody else seemed to be doing, or not. Who could tell? I tried not to think of him going away. I tried not to wish he would come on with us to Newcastle. For the moment I concentrated on the paper in my pocket, and the address he had scrawled on it.

When he arrived at the theatre, Louis did not mention my running off again. I cornered him about the address, asking him exactly where this Laurel Avenue was.

He nodded. 'You know where we walked to my house? It is a turning off that road.'

'Right.'

'But no need to worry. I know the way. We can go together. I have a session now with AJ about my play, but will be finished by two. We can go then.'

I left it there but I had no intention of going to Laurel

Avenue with him. This was something I would do on my own. Ambrose Benedict was — or was not — *my* father, after all. There had been too much lately of doing things with other people. Even Louis. There was a time when I relished doing everything on my own. A lot had happened to me since I came to England but I had not changed that much.

Laurel Avenue

I found it easily enough. But where was number 43? I walked along twice, carefully counting the numbers, but even the second time the numbering finished at 39. I walked up and down the road a third time, checking each house carefully. I passed a woman with a perambulator, a man with a dog and two children with hoops. They spared me a glance, but that was all.

I considered knocking on a door but the doors – solid, four-panelled and in dark wood – looked forbidding in the grey noon light. I did manage to make my way up one short path but at the door my courage failed me. One part of my failure was the thought of what I might meet behind the door. A father? Not a father? Incomprehension? Rejection? Even worse, perhaps – recognition and welcome. I was suddenly not clear what I wanted myself.

I fled.

Later that day I had tea with Miss Abigail, Louis, Tesserina and Joe. Joe had taken Tesserina to Joplings and bought her a new dark green coat – long and slender, in fine wool with lace-trimmed velvet panels inset in the front. 'Good for London,' she said. She paraded it for us and we all clapped and laughed. She put a hand on Joe's shoulder and said, 'Joe told me he loves me. He will take care of me always.'

'Tesserina!' He laughed, and took her hand awkwardly. But he didn't deny he loved her. I could feel Louis's gaze on me but I ignored it. Hadn't he said that same thing to me? That the ancients 'fell in love with you, as seems to be happening to me'. What a fearsome thing to say to another unsuspecting human being. Like throwing a net over them. Miss Abigail and I had never said that to each other. Nor had I said it to Tesserina. Even though it was a most powerful truth.

Louis took me to one side. 'We'll make some time to go and check that address,' he said quietly.

'I went,' I said. 'There was no house with that number.'

I could tell from the flicker in his eyes that he was hurt but he merely said, 'Pity, that.'

Of course I felt bad about it. 'I was going to knock on a door, but my courage failed me.'

He stayed silent.

Now I was desperate to make up for my slight. 'Perhaps if we both went it would be easier to knock on a door?'

He smiled then and, as the English say, let me off the hook. 'Why not?' he said. 'Tomorrow, perhaps?'

I nodded. 'Maybe . . .'

Then I was called away by Miss Abigail to mend a skirt that Cissie Barnard had ripped as she fell off the stage, and to hem a silk square sent to Lily Lambert from an admirer in Morocco. The singer had been in floods of tears over the kindness of a man who had only seen her perform once in Paris. Then, of course, there was Tesserina's new costume. It was a relief to sit there stitching and forget about her new distance, her desertion to Joe and to London. Then I could allow thoughts of Louis and his ancients, and the mystery of Laurel Avenue to flow through me.

Mesmerism

That night's performance went like clockwork. The remaining Pixies filled the stage with their rechoreographed dance. It was perfect, as though the missing Pixie had never existed. Lily Lambert brought the house down with a new song about a nightingale; Cissie Barnard managed not to fall down and Tesserina was cheered to the rafters. But that night the turn of the evening was Stan Slater and Roy Divine. AJ had given them more scope, anticipating the gap that would be left by Tesserina. His gamble paid off.

Central to the act now was some new business, quite comic, about Stan teaching Roy to be a mesmerist. At first when Stan showed Roy how to do it he scratched his head, disturbing his immaculate golden curls, raising a titter of laughter. Stan encouraged him to try it on a man he led up from the audience. The man chuckled into his face, refusing to be mesmerised. Then Roy went down into the audience himself and led back a middle-aged woman who wore her clothes like the plumage of a dusty town bird. She told him her name was Mrs Miles and she came from

Monkwearmouth. He went through the motions Stan Slater had shown him, then carefully placed the edge of his thumb on her forehead. He whispered something in her ear and then slowly she began to dance like a houri dancer, in a sad echo of Tesserina's swirling and dipping movements. Then in a loud voice Roy told her she was on Roker beach and all around her there were seagulls who didn't see her as a woman but as a tasty morsel of fish thrown down by a fisherman. She flinched in terror, and began desperately to fight off savage clouds of imaginary seagulls, finally sinking to the floor in terror. Then he pulled her to her feet and handed her a feather duster. 'And this, Mrs Miles, is your baby, your long-lost baby who was stolen from her pram one day when you left her to take the sun on the pavement outside your house.' She took the feather duster from him and cradled it in her arms, crooning and muttering to it. There were real tears in her eyes.

The applause for this feat was full of such a strange glee that I shuddered as I sat in the wings with my sewing box. Milking the applause, Roy bowed to all parts of the house and Stan awarded him with a golden scroll and a golden academic cap. It was entirely clever to make the audience arbiters in this process. I wondered who had thought this one up. Had Roy mesmerised Mr Slater into making him the star centre of his turn? Or was Mr Slater so clever that he could make even wooden Roy into something special? I noticed AJ hovering in the wings opposite, watching closely. Although he didn't laugh or nod himself, it was clear that he was impressed.

'So, what d'you think of that?' Louis was perched on a large basket against the wall. 'Strange magic, d'you think?'

I shook my head. 'I thought it was horrible.'

'You don't like him, do you?'

'Who? Mr Slater or Mr Divine?'

'Either.'

'I don't like Roy. Mr Slater is more of a puzzle. But still I think what they do is cruel to people.'

He laughed. 'You have a tender heart, Pippa.'

I shook my head. 'Mr Slater once did that to me and I wasn't my real self for days. It gave me bad dreams.'

I didn't want to go on about it, even though I longed to stay there and fence words with Louis. But now I had work to do: Tesserina's turn to attend to. I had to help Miss Abigail arrange her dress and sticks, and set her in her beginning pose. Then the opening chords from Mrs Palmer banished us to the wings as the air was filled with the fluid sweep of bows across strings, and the curtains opened to warm applause.

When I got back to the wings Louis had gone. That was very frustrating. I'd made up my mind to ask him to come with me tomorrow to Laurel Avenue, to find out about the missing house number. No matter. I would find him later. My mind was made up.

Choices

Sophia Bunce had been prevailed upon by hysterical pressure from the other five Pixies to do something about the absence of their comrade Pixie Molloy. She brought this up again with Abigail. Dancers were always running away, she complained. 'Ungrateful wretches. You feed them, you water them, you train them. What more can they want?'

Abigail thought that you might pay them more than pocket money, and desist from beating them, but she let that thought pass. 'The girls say she has not run away of her own accord?'

'According to them she loved Palmer's and the dancing. A bit wooden, if you ask me, but they say she loved it and would never leave. They are very close, this crew, never had a lot like them in thirty years.'

'Will you go to the police station?'

'I suppose so. I don't suppose you'd care to come with me, Miss Wharton?' She barely glanced down at Abigail's legs. 'We could always get a cab, of course.'

Irritated though she was with Sophia Bunce, Abigail was happy to go with her because today she was avoiding Josiah

Barrington. Ever since they'd been to chapel together he had been different with her: more familiar and more implicitly demanding. He had started to talk about '*when* we get our little shop' and asking her when she would tell the Palmers their news.

Despite her genuine affection for him, as far as she was concerned there was no news about her and Josiah. The changes this week, with all these new developments about Tesserina and Hermione, would give her and Pippa a new role in the company. Abigail was very fond of Josiah. He was a stalwart in her life but when she really thought about him she couldn't contemplate life with him away from the business of Palmer's Varieties. In her mind he was bound up with the moving and lifting from place to place, the improvisation of sets, the late-night drinking and the gossip implicit in a moving company. Without all that, she felt now that Josiah would just be a shopkeeper obsessed with nuts and bolts and hammers and nails. That wouldn't do. It wouldn't do at all.

Josiah was there backstage when she and Madame Bunce came back from the police station, where the sergeant had listened to their tale of a lost Pixie with barely concealed boredom before entering the details in a big ledger. As they bustled through the stage door, Josiah smiled his sweet smile and Abigail felt the familiar weakness. If only he would stay and not flee to his shop. He was such a comfort to her.

'Another row among the Divines,' he reported to Abigail, handing her a cup of tea. 'Marie thinks Roy has upstaged her and will soon oust old Slater and take top spot. She's furious.'

'She's overestimating him, I'm afraid. Slater is the master there.' Abigail eased off her shoes and spread her aching feet flat on the floor. 'Maybe she regrets that she opted for the wrong brother as her partner. Love him or hate him, Josiah,

Roy has more about him than that wet fish of a brother who asks Marie's permission to breathe.' She looked across at her old friend and wondered how she would manage without him when their ways parted, as they surely would.

He smiled at her. 'I've been to see this shop, Abi, in a row down by Fawcett Street—'

She put up a hand to stop his flow. 'Stop, stop, Josie. I have something to say. I have thought very hard about this. My darling, I can't do this, can't settle in a little shop and serve needles and threads to all and sundry.' She made a broad sweep with her arm, encompassing the cluttered backstage cubicle and the whole theatre, invisible around them. 'This is my life, Josie. It has been my life since I was nine, when I was dancing for a leader much fiercer than floppy old Sophia Bunce. I couldn't leave Palmer's Varieties, Josie. AJ needs me more than ever now that Hermione's jumping ship. Then there's Pippa . . .'

His face fell. 'But, Abi—'

'No, Josiah! No. My mind's made up.'

With dramatic and extreme care he put his cup down on the floor beside him and stalked from the room. He left the door open, allowing a cold draught from the chilly corridor to seep into the narrow space.

Abigail shivered and pulled her shawl closer around her.

Photographs

The next morning as I ran through the town I could hear a clock strike eight. Even so, I still had no thought that the Hernfield household would not be up. I rang the bell and waited while it pinged its way through the house. Then I rang it again and jumped when the door was instantly opened by a tall thin woman with an apron over her black dress. She had skin like washed porcelain and her iron-grey hair was pulled into a high knot on her head.

'Yes?' Her voice was even: neither too hostile nor too welcoming.

'I wish to speak to Mr Hernfield. Mr Louis Hernfield.'

The woman's glance swept over me like the touch of a hand: from the old beret on my head to the mended shoes on my feet. It occurred to me that in my street coat I was not as smart as in the one I wore the last time I visited the house off Ryhope Road.

'Ah'm afraid he's at his breakfast,' the woman said. 'A bit early, this, for visitors. The old'ns are not even up.'

I was suddenly aware that it was early to call on anyone. I'd crept out of our silent lodgings and raced through the town, urgent as always when I wanted to do something. Louis had gone home early from the theatre last night so I couldn't plan with him this final sortie to solve the problem of Ambrose Philip Benedict.

Last night Tesserina had been late into the bed we shared. There was no doubt now that things had changed between us. She was as carelessly warm and affectionate as ever with me, but entirely distracted by the rehearsals with Mrs Palmer, and her preoccupation with Joe. She was not fazed at all by the thought of life without me or Miss Abigail. We were concerned but she was not. This made me angry with her but there was no way to express that because she really didn't care. At the beginning of our friendship I had been hurt when people called her mad. But I had to admit now that her madness did not lie in her dancing or her demeanour; it came from her complete self-absorption, a childish quality I think she must have cultivated in the asylum to survive at all. And I worked out that although I was hurt by her lack of care, I still could not blame her. If I cried and railed at her she would just be confused. The most loving thing I could do was to let her be. She didn't need me. She would always find someone to take care of her. Hadn't she already shown this?

She and Joe spent a lot of the time chattering and giggling in Italian. Joe played his accordion for her, and even in our little sitting room she would improvise a dance to his lilting music, charming him just as she had charmed me.

I was certainly third on her list now: behind Joe and Mrs Palmer. This was made worse by the fact that Joe was still wary with me. Despite his earlier protestations, he rarely addressed me directly and avoided looking me in the face. No wonder really. Every time he looked at me he must be reminded of his brother. Of course, every time I looked at him *I* was reminded of Angelo. But this was made worse by the fact that, try as I would, I could not bring Angelo's face to mind. All I could see was Joe's face imposed on a smaller, tougher body in a very white shirt. Angelo himself was fading fast from me.

Now, in Laurel Avenue, I looked the woman hard in the eye. 'My name is Pippa Valois. Will you tell him I'm here?'

'Yeh're that French lass, ehn't yeh?'

I must have looked surprised.

The woman laughed, her smooth face suddenly very merry. 'Mrs Hernfield told us. Nee secrets atween Mrs Hernfield and me.'

I relaxed and smiled back at her. 'And you must be Janey Doby!' I said. 'I've heard about you also.'

'Then wor evens,' she said. 'Now mebbe you should come in and I'll go and seek our Louis for yeh.'

I shook my head. 'No. I'll wait out here and sit on that little wall. If Louis is too busy with his breakfast would you be kind enough to come and tell me? Then I'll get on my way.'

She left the door ajar and I went to sit on the wall. It was still damp from the overnight rain, so I stood up again and tied my scarf more tightly round my neck to fend myself against the morning chill. Strange that it was so cold in April. I wondered how cold summer in England must be, if this was the spring.

When he came outside Louis was pulling on his long top coat with one hand, clasping the giant umbrella in the other. 'And here you are!' he said, grinning. 'Like the early morning post.'

'I disturbed your breakfast? Are you just awake?'

He shook his head. 'No. This is late for me. Normally I'm at the works by seven thirty. But I went down there yesterday to finish some pending jobs. So today I am free for the whole year. I was just having my breakfast in the kitchen with Janey and Flo when the bell rang. Twice! Janey called it a "ready-money" ring.'

'I thought it must be Janey, that woman who opened the door.'

'She asked me what I'd said about her, what lies I'd been putting out about her.'

We turned off the pathway on to the wider road.

'She also said you looked like a street urchin,' he went on. 'No lady.'

'Did she? She must think you're far too good for a street urchin like me.'

'Not at all. She said you must be some kind of girl, to put up with me.'

'Does she then not like you?'

'Janey? She loves me,' he said complacently. 'When I was a baby she was my foster mother and her daughter Flo was my playmate, and between them they've kept me in order ever since.'

'She has remarkable skin. Like porcelain.'

'You must never tell her that. She has forsworn vanity. She sticks by her Bible. "Vanity of vanities; all is vanity." She'll give you chapter and verse on that.'

'Many women would pay her for her secret.'

'I once pestered her to tell me how she did it. Told her that I would make a fortune out of it. The papers are full of beauty secrets. Guess what she said?'

'I can't.'

'That you couldn't put a price on it. She said it was The

Good Life. A life without sin, and reading the Bible every day.'

'The price would be too great for most women. Did she read the Bible to you, then?'

'She was only allowed by my mother to read the Old Testament. But there are wonderful stories in that great book; a thousand plays, if you think about it.'

'How nice it must be to have two mothers,' I murmured.

'Three, if you count the invisible one over the water.'

My sadness made him uneasy. 'But Miss Wharton's a mother to you, in her own way, Pippa, and a great one at that.' He put his arm through mine. 'So. Where to?'

'Laurel Avenue. In search of Ambrose Philip Benedict.'

'Right. Shall we ring his bell and raise him from his breakfast table?'

But it was after eight thirty when we reached Laurel Avenue and the street was busy with the setting out and sorting out, which is everyone's morning routine in a street like this. One woman was shaking a doormat, cracking it against a low wall, raising clouds of dust; another was perched on wooden steps, cleaning windows; another was polishing a brass door-plate.

We stopped beside the window cleaner. She had on a drab overall and a flowered cloth cap covering her hair. It was hard to tell whether she was mistress or maid. She paused in her labours and looked down at us. 'Do you want sommat?' she said.

Louis glanced down at me, forcing me to speak. 'We wondered whether the houses always had these numbers? We're looking for number forty-three but they only go as far as thirty-nine,' I said.

She nodded, came down the steps and dropped her chamois

leather into a zinc bucket, making the water slop out on to the pavement. 'Well, that's because the folk in those houses – the ones with the front gardens down the far end – started to fancy themselves and changed to Laurel Gardens. Too good for numbers, folks down that end. Names, they have now. Number forty-three they called Carcassonne. Queer name, if you ask me.'

My heart flipped at the fractured way that name came out of the woman's mouth. In Carcassonne the spring is warm and full of the promise of a hot summer, and if Ambrose Philip Benedict had called his house Carcassonne then he must certainly be my father.

'That will be it,' I said. 'Thank you.'

The woman leaned down to wring out her chamois leather in the steaming water. 'Don't mention it,' she said. 'Now I'll just get on, if you don't mind. I have people coming.'

So this must be her own house. Perhaps in the afternoons she took off the flowered cap and the drab overall and became the mistress, not the maid.

The wall in front of Carcassonne was slightly higher than its neighbours and was topped by railings like linked spears. It had a high green hedge surrounding a garden of rocks and low plants. The open front door disclosed a square vestibule where a glazed inner door guarded the rest of the house.

The rain, which had been threatening all morning, now began to fall in earnest, and Louis unfurled his umbrella.

My blood was racing. I needed no encouragement to go and ring a doorbell for the second time that morning. This ring was answered quickly by a young woman in a green dress who wore her hair short, just touching her ears. 'Yes?' she said.

'I . . . I . . . Good morning, *mademoiselle*,' I said, consciously retrieving my French accent. 'My fr-riend and I were just walking in this road and I saw the name of your house. Carrcassonne. This is the name of the town where I was born. I know this town. It is warm there, and very beautiful. I know it very well. I was surprised to see such a name on a house in this town.'

To my relief she was smiling. 'How terribly interesting,' she said. She waited.

'We wondered,' put in Louis, peering out from under the dripping umbrella, 'how this name came to be used here in Sunderland.'

The girl glanced at the green hedge now being spattered and splashed by heavy drops of rain. 'You'd better come inside or you'll be drowned.'

The vestibule broadened out into a square tiled hall with doors leading off and a staircase going up on the right. The girl kept us there. She was obviously not prepared to invite strangers further into her house. My eye fixed on a large oil painting on the wall opposite the staircase.

'There!' I said. 'There is the bastion of Carcassonne above the Pont Vieux. How many times have I climbed up to the old town there with my mother when I was small. Who painted this picture, *mademoiselle*? Did the painter make this picture in Carcassonne?'

I knew one thing. Whoever the painter was, he had never been to that town. The picture of the great crusader castle above the twisting streets had been well drawn; the architecture was well conceived. But the colour, he had missed the butter-yellow light, the inky green shade, seeing it with a cold English eye that must see light in shades of white and shadow in cold shades of blue and black.

The girl was already shaking her head. 'I'm sure not. The painter was never there in the town itself. My father paid an artist here in Sunderland to paint it from one of his photographs . . .' She stopped. 'I am forgetting my manners. I am Philippa Benedict.' She shook our hands in a firm grasp and we told her who we were. She looked at Louis. 'But you're not from Carcassonne, I think?'

He smiled. 'Like you, I'm from Sunderland, Miss Benedict. But my friend Mademoiselle Valois, like she says, is from Carcassonne in France. She's at the theatre, with a group appearing at the Empire.' He paused. 'I have a play being performed by her group. I said I'd show her round Sunderland.'

'And you ended up in this road? How very intriguing.'

I peered up again at the painting. The artist had painted the bastion under dour northern skies, like those above Sunderland. It was an odd effect. Of course, the black-and-white photograph he worked from would not show the hard bright blue of the true South. 'You say you have photographs, *mademoiselle*?'

She stared at me then and I wondered whether I'd overstepped some English sensibility. Then she laughed. 'Wait here,' she said.

A door clicked behind her and Louis said in my ear, 'So this is the Benedict house. You never mentioned Carcassonne.'

'It was not significant to me until I heard that woman say the name of the house. I was born in Carcassonne, then my mother and I went to Toulouse, then Paris, then I went back south to Toulouse before I joined Palmer's.'

'And now the delights of Sunderland!' said Louis, with a broad sweep of his hand around the hallway, and we both laughed.

We were still laughing when the girl came back into the hall with the small leather folder. 'It took a little finding. I knew my father had it tucked away on his bookshelves somewhere, but there are so many books.'

My heart jumped. 'Your father?' I said, glancing round.

She stared at me and I waited for her to say he was dead. 'Oh, he's not here today, or I'm certain he would have liked to talk to you about Carcassonne. He speaks of it sometimes, as a place of mystery and delight.'

'So he's away now, *mademoiselle*?'

'Well, if you count the city of York as "away", yes. He got the early train this morning.'

I waited for her to tell me more but of course she didn't. Who was I, after all, but some stranger taking shelter from the rain? I found myself wondering how old she was. *Philippa*. My name also. Barbara Philippe Valois. At first I thought this girl was much older than me but now decided not. She must be about twenty; not much older than me. And her name. So like mine. A peculiar thing. A wave of disappointment and despair flooded through me.

She spread out the photographs on a dusty *armoire* that filled one wall in the hallway. 'There you are. He has some good views of the bastion. Here, I'll put on the light.' The hall flooded with blinding light from an elaborate electric chandelier.

I looked at the small square photographs one by one. There were some good views of the alleyways and squares of the old town; several views that had obviously inspired the painting, of the bastion from the Pont Vieux; there was one of the old mill by the swirling river where my mother and I picnicked. 'There was some talk, apparently, of Benedict's making pots decorated with this view. But that was abandoned,' said Miss Benedict.

Then I came upon a photograph taken through a familiar stone arch. It showed a high interior window with a woman standing inside, her face in shadow and her white blouse like a flag against the grey stone of the tall casement. My pulse was throbbing. And there, floating somewhere near her elbow was the smudgy, indistinct face of a child. It took an age to drag myself away from this photo to the next one, which was an image of a soldier. Here was a man in officer's uniform with a shining belt and a peaked cap: a man in his late thirties whose eyes peered heroically out of the photograph. I put my finger on the face: sharp-eyed and not too handsome, not unlike the face I saw every day in the mirror.

'Is this Ambrose Benedict?' I said.

She looked at me sharply. 'Yes. That's my father. I didn't tell you his name.'

'Didn't you?' I made my voice vague. Then I pointed to the leather wallet. 'I noticed the names on there. Etched in black.'

Her brow cleared. 'So they are.'

There were three more photographs: two of them of Ambrose Benedict with a group of soldiers, not all officers. I turned these over and each man was identified in a neat, tight hand. Then in pencil beside three of the names someone had later written in pencil: 'died 17 October, St-Quentin'.

'It's all very sad,' said the girl. 'Every one a comrade. That was what he always says.'

I picked up the last photograph. It showed a woman leaning up against the Pont Vieux with the bastion in the background. I turned it over. On the back he had written 'Barbara 1916'.

'I've asked him many times about the woman,' said the girl. 'But he will only say she was very kind to him. That the soldiers depended on the kindness of the French people when they were on leave from the front. He must have been on leave when he took these. Carcassonne, so far south, is a long way from the trenches. My father was interested in the Crusades against the Cathars and said this was a chance to see a great site. He had a short leave and took the opportunity.' She smiled slightly. 'How my mother used to tease him about that picture.'

I was too stunned to speak but Louis grasped that nettle. 'So your mother . . .?' He looked round the hall.

'No,' she said. 'She's not with us any more. We lost her two years ago. A complication after influenza.'

'I'm sorry . . .' I began.

She shrugged. 'It has to be borne. My father was very cut up. They had been childhood sweethearts, you see. Married just out of school. Family straight after. I'm the last of them.'

No you're not, I thought.

Miss Benedict blinked away her thoughts and looked blankly at us for a moment. I imagine she was wondering just why she was confiding in strangers in her own hallway. 'Well, I . . .'

Louis put a hand out to shake, a bright smile on his face. 'Thank you, Miss Benedict, for being so kind to two passers-by. We must go. There are things we've to do at the theatre.'

I shook her hand. 'Thank you, Mademoiselle Benedict, for showing me your pictures of my beloved Carcassonne. It all makes me – how do you say? – quite homesick.'

She smiled. 'My dear father loved France, even though it robbed him of his health. He's been back there twice since the war but I don't think he'll go again. He was very tired when he came back last time. He'll have to make do with his photographs. I'll tell him of your interest in the name of our house. He'll be tickled pink at the coincidence.'

Tickled pink? This language continued to amaze me.

It was still raining when we got outside. I grasped Louis's elbow and hustled him down Laurel Avenue to the Ryhope Road before he had time to put up his umbrella.

He forced me to stop. 'Whoa! Whoa! We'll be soaked through.' He put up the umbrella and pulled me round to face him. 'I can see that was a big thing for you in there, but take a breath, will you? Do you want to talk about it? We can go to my house and talk perhaps.'

'No. I want to get back to the theatre. Miss Abigail has jobs for me.'

'She won't be there. She's rarely there before twelve.'

'Well,' I said, 'I don't want to go anywhere or talk about anything.'

Suddenly it stopped raining. He pulled the umbrella to one side and shook the rain off it before he collapsed it. 'Well then,' he said, 'we'll walk back by way of the docks and we'll get to the theatre at twelve. Does that suit you?'

I nodded and he took my arm and we set out to make our way towards the river. I couldn't think of anything to say to Louis. He didn't bother me with any pleasantries and for this I was grateful. Inside me, as we walked along, elation battled with despair. I had found my father, but finding Ambrose Benedict had not been a solution to my problem; it had presented me with another problem. I had thought my father would be special, different. But he was just like my mother's other callers: a married man a long way from home. So the only answer to this problem was to do nothing. Nothing at all.

A Pow-Wow

It was nearly noon when Abigail bumped into Josiah Barrington at the stage door. He nodded glumly and stood back politely to let her go ahead of him, but once in the narrow passage she stopped, so that he had to speak to her.

'Now then, Josiah,' she said. 'Don't you think we should sort this out? We can't go on bumping into each other like blind men at noon. Come on and talk to me.' She led the way to her cubbyhole, not waiting for his refusal.

Once there she turned to face him. 'Now what is it? What is it now that makes you treat me like a leper, turning back when you see me, avoiding my eye when we're in the same room?'

'You know why,' he said stubbornly.

'Because I wouldn't stay here and play shopkeepers with you?'

He stood there, staring at her. 'Aye. Make a joke of it.'

'Because I wouldn't marry you?' She smiled slightly.

'*You* can smile!' he said sourly. 'You and me were all right before. If we'd 'a gone on like we went on before, we'd have been married by now. Mebbe had the shop already. Or some shop, somewhere.'

'Before? Before what?'

'Before Pippa Valois. Before the dancer.' He crumbled slightly at her look. 'Don't get me wrong, Abi. I do like young Pippa, even though I can't make head nor tail of the dancer, who's as strange as a fish with legs. But we were all right before they came, you and me. Now look where we are! Having words. We've never had words in all the time we've known each other. In all these years. I've loved you and in your own way you've loved me.'

'Words? We're only having words because I won't agree to leave Palmer's and settle for an early old age. Let's put Pippa and Tesserina aside, Josiah. I have to admit that just for a moment I was tempted by your idea of a shop, because I'm fond of you and after all these years it's hard to think of life without you. But can't you see? If I do as you say I'll just become the crippled old woman in the sewing shop. At Palmer's they don't even think of my legs. At Palmer's, I am who I am. I make my contribution and now will do so even more when Hermione is away. That really suits me, Josiah. And if you profess to love me you'll understand that. AJ needs me now just as much as Pippa does. I have things to do here.'

'I need you,' Josiah said too loudly. 'I need you by my side.'

'Darling Josiah, you can be by my side,' she said gently. 'But to do that you must stay with Palmer's.'

He scowled.

'Look, if you need to settle down, my darling, you must do it. But how old are you? Forty-five? No matter how old you get I'll always be older than you. I'll end up in my dotage with my crippled legs and you'll be in your prime. Look! You still have time to find a nice young woman and have a family, my darling. There were some fine young women at chapel on Sunday. Perhaps that's really where your thoughts are leading you.'

'Is that where you want me to go?' he said sharply.

'Don't be silly, Josiah.'

'It's not that, Abi. It's you I want, not some chapel girl. Always was.'

'Well, you can't *have* me. You've never *had* me! You and I were never like that, Josiah.'

They were interrupted by a thunderous rattle on the door followed by the looming presence of AJ Palmer. 'Oh, there you are, Mr Barrington. I've been looking everywhere for you. There's a problem with one of the spots. I told Mr Ramsden you'd see to it.'

He stood aside while Josiah slipped past him, then turned to Abigail. 'I thought we might have a bit of a pow-wow, Miss Wharton, about this business of Hermione going off to London.'

He ushered Josiah out of the room and shut the door behind him. 'Old Barrington gets more dour by the day,' he said. 'Good job you can handle him, Miss Wharton . . . Abigail, if I may?'

She moved Joe Zambra's accordion off a chair so AJ could sit down.

He stretched out his legs in front of him and told her that good old Cameron would be taking over the bookings and correspondence, so she need not worry about that. What was required of her was her expertise and her ability to deal with people. In addition, each and every day, the two of them would have a pre-rehearsal pow-wow and a post-show debriefing. He would value her views in the day-to-day running of the troupe.

'Apropos, Abigail,' he said, 'two things I want you to think about. One – I have an idea that I might put the mesmerist top of the bill after the dancer goes. That business with Roy Divine makes it rather more than a straight mesmerist act. I can smell success around those two. A potent combination. Two sides of a coin. And this leads me to the second thing I want you to consider. I want you to go to Marie Divine and tell her that there must be no more of this nonsense of haranguing her brother in public. It upsets people, gets the rest of the company out of sorts.'

'Very well, AJ. I'll speak to her. But shouldn't Hermione deal with it? She's not away until next Sunday. I don't want to tread on her toes.'

'No. I think you should do it. Of course, if anything goes wrong she can pick up the pieces later. If she's around,' he said gloomily. 'Always off with that Jacob Smith chappie at present. Something about dress fittings. New clothes for London.'

She looked across at him. His body appeared to have shrunk in his clothes. He seemed a much smaller, older man.

'She's bound to be excited, AJ,' said Abigail gently. 'This London jaunt will be a bit of a change from the routine, the common round.'

He coughed. 'That common round, that routine, Abigail, has been our life. Up till this week I'd have said it was our delight. Palmer's was our creation. Without Hermione there would have been no Palmer's. Without Palmer's I'd have been an ageing bit-part player in someone else's company.' He sniffed, then took out a white handkerchief and blew his nose loudly.

'AJ!' Abigail was suddenly very urgent. 'This will only be for a short time. Do you think Hermione will survive without you? Without Palmer's? She's carried away now with this enthusiasm with Tesserina. She spotted your potential and she has spotted Tesserina's potential. And for that Pippa and I, as Tesserina's guardians, are grateful. But as soon as Hermione has obtained proper patronage for Tesserina she'll leave her in London with Joe Zambra and that little pianist and then come back. Tesserina has that tough fellow Joe Zambra to watch over her. She'll come to no harm. Hermione will be back with Palmer's in no time. You can count on it.' She didn't know whether all this was true but it seemed to be the thing to say. She hoped it was true, for AJ's sake.

He tucked his handkerchief away. 'Right. Right. I'm sure you are right, Abigail.' He stood up very straight. 'Now there is something else I wanted to mention to you. The Hernfield boy came and had a word yesterday morning. He says he would like to join us for a year. He's a good chap. Could be useful. Offers to do anything, but asks for some help and opportunities with his dramas.'

'A year?' Abigail found herself pleased at the idea but tried to think like Hermione. 'Of course, AJ, you'd have to consider the extra wage involved.'

'That's the beauty of it, Abigail. The boy asks no wages. Has funding from indulgent parents, as far as I can see. I have told him he must act like any member of the company and do as he's told, when he's told it. No special favours.'

'Well, if you ask me, AJ, you have nothing to lose and at least you will gain another pair of hands. You might come to be grateful for them.' If Josiah followed through his notion of a shop, AJ would be further disappointed.

He frowned at her. 'What's that? Is there something else?'

She shook her head quickly. 'No, no. Just a general point, AJ. Another pair of hands would always be very useful.'

Later, as the door closed behind him Abigail decided she would have to work on Josiah. AJ couldn't take another defection. If he lost Josiah Barrington the company could very well collapse altogether. And that wouldn't do at all.

All in Order

Abigail surveyed the Divines' pristine dressing room. Two chairs were placed neatly under the shelf. The mirror glittered bright and clean and the make-up tubes were in neat rows. Combs and brushes lay to attention. The big jar of gold paste stood at the ready, beside a pile of the clean folded squares of gauze that the Divines used to apply it to their bodies. Their costumes hung straight from wall hooks, as did six pairs of the soft pumps they used for their tight-rope walking. A guitar stood in the corner: a surprise to Abigail, who had never heard anything other than shouts and bumps coming out of any of the Divines' dressing rooms.

'You got an eyeful then?' Marie's sour voice came from behind her.

'Oh. Hello . . .' Embarrassed, she stood aside to let Marie and Blaze into the small room. They were in street clothes; Marie carried a shopping bag and Blaze a hat box. They put their burdens on the shelf, sat in their chairs, and turned to survey their visitor with identical cold blue eyes.

'Well?' said Marie abruptly.

The air of threat in the small room made Abigail uncomfortable. 'I wondered if you knew that Tesserina is off to London on Sunday?' She laughed nervously. 'To seek her fortune, as it were.'

'So we heard,' said Blaze.

'Good riddance to bad rubbish,' said Marie.

Abigail failed to rise to the bait. 'Well, Mrs Palmer will be accompanying her—'

'Likewise,' put in Marie.

'Well . . . er . . . AJ has designated me his helper in her place.'

'Though not his bed, I bet,' said Marie, her thin mouth twitching.

'Marie!' warned Blaze.

'I can see no need to be uncouth,' Abigail ploughed on. 'And in this role he's asked me to tell you to stop haranguing your brother Roy in public, all about the place. It's upsetting the company. AJ doesn't like it. So you are to stop.'

'Or what?' demanded Marie.

'Or he'll terminate your contract with Palmer's.' Abigail paused. 'He's clear on that. You'll be out on your ear.'

Marie stood up and Blaze pulled at her and made her sit down again. 'She's an old bat, Blaze,' she said. 'The pair of them. Him and her. Both ugly old bats.'

'Shut up, Marie,' he said wearily. 'Do you want to work or not?'

Abigail had her hand on the doorknob. Then she turned and said, 'Did you hear about Roy?'

'You mean him and his stupid act with that old queer?' Marie sneered.

'Well, Marie, after Sunday when Tesserina leaves, that stupid act will be top of the bill.' Abigail got out of the room quickly and shut the door behind her, saving herself from the shoes that were thrown against it. The usual shouting started up but, standing there, she could only hear Marie's voice railing against AJ, against 'that old cripple', about 'that bloody traitor Roy', and 'the little French whore' who had started it all. There was no sound from Blaze. He was taking it all in and saying nothing.

Walking back to her own room Abigail found herself hoping that Marie did make a fool of herself and end up banished by AJ. It would make all their lives easier.

Josiah was waiting in the room for Abigail. 'I've decided,' he announced.

She sat down in her chair and stretched her aching legs before her. 'What have you decided then, Josiah?'

'I've decided to stay with Palmer's . . .'

'Oh, good,' she said, genuinely pleased.

'. . . but I've been thinking about what you said.'

'Good,' she repeated.

'That our . . . friendship should stay just that. Mebbe I should be looking around for someone younger, like. Someone to settle down with . . . eventually,' he said. He looked into her eyes. 'Sorry, Abigail.'

She felt as if someone had slapped her with a wet fish. But she said cheerfully, 'That's the best thing I've heard in ages, Josiah. We all need you here, especially now. But you're right to think of the future. No one could blame you for that.'

Then, quite awkwardly he shook her by the hand. 'So . . . friends, then?'

She stretched her mouth into a smile. 'Friends, Josiah. Always friends. After our years together, what else is possible?'

When he had gone, she stamped her foot on the floor. So that was that. The last love, the last swain, the last person in whose arms she might lie, and know herself for the woman she was. Poor Josiah, she thought. And poor Abigail.

She looked at herself in the mirror. Then she shook her head and ran her hands through her grey hair, making it look even wilder.

'Now then, where's that Pippa?' she said out loud. 'Off on her wanders again, no doubt. This new dress for Tesserina will never be finished at this rate.'

360 REST FOR THE WICKED

Pixie Molloy

Louis and I were relieved of any need to talk about the events in Laurel Avenue by the concentration required to make our way through the bustle down on the wharfs. To our right, boats and ships bobbed and clicked on the wide, dark mouth of the river. No matter how grand Fawcett Street may be, no one could deny that this river was the great main street of this town, the centre of its commerce and the source of its wealth. This was so, even in these hard days.

This time I was not so disturbed by the looks and genial comments thrown at us from the workmen about their tasks. I felt part of all this. After all, did this not all happen under the bridge, so familiar from my jug? Had not my father worked in the sight of these cranes as a young man? I felt comfortable in this place.

Finally into the silence between us dripped some neutral talk from Louis about a threatened strike here during the war, which led to talk of treason and issues about what counted as just and right during a war. He started to talk about how it would be good to make a play of those events, counterpointing them with the looming crisis of the present day.

Louis had such good ideas. Not only that, but these ideas blossomed in his mind into a whole new thing: a play or story that had something further to say. 'There would be this fellow who is proud of his work and is torn between the immediate injustices in his life and the greater injustices of a war against tyranny . . . What's that?'

He pointed towards a crowd who were leaning over a wall, staring down into the river in a space between two ships. I wriggled through the crowd of heavy-set workmen to look over the sea wall. The river was low: regular lines on the sea wall showed the pausing places of the retreating tide. To our left, flopping over a sodden seaweed-hung staithe, was what looked at first like a discarded rag doll with mud-streaked streaming red hair. But this was not a doll: it was a child. Her legs and feet were bare and she was wearing only a shift.

Her painted face bulged painfully but I still recognised her. It was Pixie Molloy. Her skin shone bluish-white and she was very dead. I know this even though I have only twice in my life seen a dead person. I turned my head to look more carefully at the swollen, upside-down face. Yes, it was the pert little girl who so worshipped Roy Divine: the girl from Spitalfields, London Town.

A policeman and a beefy workman were climbing down the staithe to get a closer look at the flopping body. The policeman looked up at the men on the wall. 'We'll need a rope, lads. A canvas cradle of some kind.'

'Is the bairn alive?' A deep male voice emerged from the crowd behind me.

The policeman shook his head. 'No chance,' he said.

I closed my eyes and on the inside of my eyelids saw Angelo Zambra bruised and swaddled in bandages in his hospital bed, then white-turbaned and chill in his elaborate coffin. I thought I had forgotten that face but here it was in front of me.

I felt cold then hot, and sick enough to vomit, all at once. I swallowed hard and wriggled my way to the back of the crowd to Louis.

'A dead body, Louis,' I gasped. 'Drowned. It's one of ours. One of Madame Bunce's Pixies. Pixie Molloy. A cheeky little thing. Lots of spirit.' I pushed him. 'Don't just stand there! Run! Run! Go and tell Madame Bunce, tell AJ. Tell Mrs Palmer. Run!'

He grasped my arm tightly and I threw off his hand. 'I'll stay here and wait for them to lift her. She'll need someone.'

He hared off, passing three policemen on bicycles who were hurtling down towards the dock.

They found a canvas sling and hauled Pixie Molloy up on to the dock, passing her from hand to hand like boys with a wrapped, fragile bird. They laid her on the dock and we all stood there for a moment in silence, looking down at her battered body. It smelled of seaweed and rotten fish.

The policeman pulled her shift down to her knees.

'It's a shame,' said one man behind me. 'That young.'

'The sea's bliddy unforgivin',' said another.

Then a policeman spread his cape over the poor body and there was a kind of breathing out of relief from all standing on the dock. The sight of her was hurtful to our eyes.

At that point the crowd started to loosen out, ready to drift away. Another policeman halted them. 'Anyone know this child?' he said. 'Does anyone know this child?'

Please, child, please.

The workmen shook their heads. 'Never seen her afore, marrer,' said one, turning away.

'I knew her,' I said. 'Her name was Pixie Molloy.'

The crowd slowed its retreat. The policeman got out his notebook and pencil. He licked the lead. 'Pixie? A funny name, that. Where might she live? Her parents will need tellin'.'

I couldn't explain why they were all called Pixie. I told him that she and I were with a troupe at the theatre, just moving through, and there were no parents anywhere near here. 'Just Madame Bunce, her teacher.'

'How do you spell that?'

Reminded of the obtuseness of the Bishop Auckland policeman, I spelled it out carefully for him. My sense of *déjà vu* was overwhelming. 'She's Pixie Molloy's guardian. The dance leader.'

'We'd better send for her.'

I looked beyond him. 'Here she is already.'

Mr Ramsden's motor car drew up, driven by A.J. Palmer. Out tumbled a weeping Madame Bunce, and Miss Abigail, followed by Louis Hernfield. AJ strode forward and shook the hand of the policeman and introduced his female companions. He was very comfortable, centre stage, even in the midst of this chillingly real tragedy.

The policeman leaned down to lift back his cloak from Pixie Molloy's face, but as he did this Madame Bunce started to scream and shudder.

Miss Abigail stepped in front of her and peered at the face. She grimaced. 'We do recognise her. She's one of our company. Pixie Molloy. One of our young dancers.'

He nodded and made a note in his book. Then he leaned down again to cover the face. Another policeman started to shoo the crowd away. 'Go about your work now, lads, will yeh? Leave these folks in peace.'

Improvements

'Very good, Roy! That's so very much better,' Hermione called down from the upper circle. 'But remember to slow down, dear, and separate the words. Make them distinct. Don't shout. Project! You really must watch and listen to AJ. He could throw his voice to Hartlepool if he so wished.'

Hermione was teaching Roy Divine to project his voice. His performance last night as Stan Slater's golden stooge had (she commented to AJ) been very good from the point of view of glamorous mime. But he had to agree with her that Roy rather lacked voice. Apart from the front row of the stalls, not many of the audience had picked up the rather heavy humour in the exchanges between Roy and Stan Slater.

Unfortunately AJ was not on hand to demonstrate this morning, having left Roy in Hermione's hands, to dash down to the docks to investigate this accident to one of the dancers. He had asked her also to take the opportunity to listen to Joe Zambra, who had asked AJ to assess his accordion skills for the stage. According to Joe, he had played in cafés here in England, and in France when he was in the army. But, as AJ had told him, to perform on the stage was a different kettle of fish altogether.

Hermione and Jacob Smith – always at her side these days – made their way down to the stalls and Joe set himself up centre stage with his gleaming instrument. Tesserina was hovering, well within sight, in the wings. Roy Divine stood just behind her in the shadows, watching.

The accordion squeaked and snuffled like a living animal as Joe set it against his body. Then he began to play, rendering, note perfect, the piece that Hermione normally played for Tesserina's first dance. He certainly had a good ear. At first the mood was tender and sweet, then more urgent and passionate as the tempo mounted. In Joe's hands the music was muscular rather than sensual, although the sheer passion came through.

As he drew the last chord from the accordion Tesserina clapped, whistled and shouted '*Bravo!*' Roy joined in the applause.

'Surprising,' murmured Jacob Smith. 'He has a very good touch.'

'Well!' said Hermione. 'Well, I never!'

Joe stood quite still, looking down at them.

'Do you read music?' said Hermione.

'No,' he said. 'I just listen and play.'

'Well, you certainly play in tune,' she said. She looked back at the big auditorium. 'But I don't know that the sound is big enough for a place like this, Mr Zambra. If there were two of you, perhaps . . .'

'I thought mebbes Tesserina could dance to it. It would save you . . .' he said.

She was already shaking her head. 'No. It simply must be the piano with the orchestra, Mr Zambra. Tesserina's dance needs the delicacy of the piano. The mood would be wrong. Either Mr Smith or I *must* play for her.'

Joe glared at her for a moment then shrugged his shoulders. 'Well, it'll have to be the cafés for me when we get to London, then.' He closed up his instrument, returned it to its box, and made for the side of the stage where Tesserina was waiting.

'There are some accordion orchestras around,' called Jacob Smith to their retreating backs. 'Perhaps you could try . . .'

'Save your breath, Jacob,' said Hermione. 'The boy won't stray far from that girl's side. We have ourselves a little watchdog, Jacob, if not a chaperon.'

Roy made his way along the row to sit beside her. 'Thank you for that help, Mrs Palmer. I'm very grateful that you took the trouble.'

'You are very welcome, my dear. AJ has high hopes of your act. Very different. Improving by the day.'

Roy stretched out his long legs under the seat in front. 'I hear our exotic dancer is going off to London.'

'Yes. We have news of one or two people who are eager to see her work. So we intend to take her down there and show her off.'

'You'll be her agent?'

'Something like that.'

'Is AJ going too?'

'No. He has his responsibilities here. Mr Smith and myself will take her.'

'I see.' Roy leaned back further in his seat to watch his brother Blaze adjust the hawser and then test the tension on the tightrope that passed above their heads to a fixing on one of the columns supporting the circle. 'Oh! Now here's a treat for us.'

He sat there with them and watched as Marie and Blaze, without their music, went through their complicated tightrope routine. They incorporated some new, dangerous moves; their execution was flawless.

Jacob and Roy pattered their applause and Hermione called, 'Well done, Marie. Those new moves make all the difference.'

Leaping gracefully on to the stage, Marie graciously acknowledged her praise, then treated Roy to a withering look before sweeping off into the wings, followed by Blaze.

'I think perhaps you are not your sister's favourite person, Roy,' said Hermione.

'It's a long time since I was that,' said Roy, his colour high. He leaned down and kissed Hermione on the cheek. 'Thank you again, Mrs Palmer,' he said.

Hermione put her hand to her cheek.

Stan Slater was hovering by the door, waiting for Roy, who flung an arm round his shoulders and said something in his ear before they went through the swinging doors, leaving Hermione and Jacob alone in the auditorium.

'That one needs watching,' said Jacob Smith suddenly. 'Something of the dark about that feller.'

'He's certainly gained a lot of confidence since he left Marie and Blaze behind. He was so quiet before. I think perhaps she stifled him.' She put a hand on Jacob's hand where it lay on the chair arm. 'You are so sensitive, Jacob.'

'It's you I'm looking out for, Hermione,' he said gruffly.

She squeezed his hand. 'We're going to have such fun, Jacob, when we get to London. Such fun . . .'

Fitting the Pieces Together

We returned from the riverside all crammed together into Mr Ramsden's motor car. It bumped over the cobbles and jarred our bones. Miss Abigail didn't complain and Madame Bunce was so well upholstered that she probably didn't feel the jarring. Of course, she may not have noticed it because she was so busy bawling and crying out, 'Molloy, Molloy, my poor little Pixie! Such a naughty Pixie.' You'd never have known that this was the woman who had beaten the child for years and cursed her to hell just this last week. Maybe the despair was not put on. It was hard to tell. People were very strange.

I sat back in the bumping car, wondering just when – or whether – I could tell Miss Abigail of the thoughts that were welling up in my mind about Roy Divine. I have to admit the advent of Louis Hernfield, the bridge on the jug and visiting Laurel Avenue had helped to push that business in Bishop Auckland away from the front of my thoughts. But now, when I saw the lifeless body of Pixie Molloy, the memory of those events was alive again, reaching out and biting at me. What if I told her about him saying, 'Please, child, please?' Pixie Molloy was a child, much more of a child than I was. But would Miss Abigail believe me? Would the police believe me? Hadn't I recanted my statement in Bishop Auckland? They would all think I was mad. Roy Divine was the grown-up, after all.

What about the 'Please, child, please'? It was a child who had died there on the staithe. What about Pixie Molloy?

Then it occurred to me that I should talk to Louis. He had existed outside of all these events. He might make some sense of it all, just like he could make sense of a shipbuilders' strike in the depths of war.

Disclosure

'What did you say? Tell me that again.' Louis frowned.

We were sitting in Miss Abigail's cubbyhole, me sewing my way through a pile of black armbands for the company to wear at that night's performance, Louis sitting on the dressing shelf with his feet on a stool. AJ had decreed that the show would go on and Miss Abigail had conceded that this – the armbands – was at least something we might do for poor Pixie Molloy.

She told me AJ would make an announcement before the show. His line would be that the show would proceed because this was what young Pixie Molloy would have wished.

I said I thought if I were Pixie Molloy I'd have felt somewhat slighted by the merriment and light-heartedness that is central to Palmer's shows. Miss Abigail quoted AJ. 'He said, "It's our bread and butter, after all, Abigail."'

There was something new here. I had never heard him call her by her first name before.

There had been a very fraught moment when we came back to the theatre from the river, when the chief policeman thought perhaps the show should be cancelled. AJ was suddenly very tense. But Mrs Palmer had put a hand on the policeman's arm.

'The other young dancers are grief-stricken, Inspector. We are at a loss to know what to do with them. As I said to my husband, perhaps the best thing would be to dedicate tonight's performance to dear little Pixie Molloy. A tribute, so to speak.'

Obviously mollified, the sergeant pulled at his moustache. 'There is that, of course. Well, I'll get on. As far as I can see it, it's a simple question of did she fall or was she pushed?'

Having delivered this he went off to ask questions of Madame Bunce and the little girls, and Miss Abigail set me the task of sewing the black armbands while she went off with AJ and Mrs Palmer to discuss just what they should do further in the light of this tragedy.

'He attacked you?' said Louis later in the cubbyhole, after listening very carefully to my tale. 'The fellow attacked you?'

'It was all over in a minute, the first time because Angelo, Joe's brother, saved me. Then the next time, which I can't remember properly, Angelo was injured, then he died.'

'Divine killed him?'

'I don't know. I think so. But Roy made me reassure the policeman there that he didn't do it.'

'Why d'you do that? Reassure them.'

'I don't know. I was frightened of him. I wanted to get here, back to Miss Abigail,' I said miserably. It suddenly occurred to me that it would have been better for Pixie Molloy if I'd had more courage.

'And what about the little dancer?' He picked up my thought.

'Well. Don't you see? She was always hanging around him.

He always seemed to have a cluster of those little girls around him. But she was among them. He encouraged it. Something not right about that, if you ask me.'

For a minute we were silent, absorbing the terrible implications of what I was suggesting. Then Louis said, almost wistfully, 'She could have just wandered off and fallen into the dock.'

'*Did she fall or was she pushed?*' I shook my head. 'Madame Bunce kept the children locked in. Pixie Molloy couldn't have got out without some help. She was starry-eyed about Roy. Followed him round like a dog.'

'But that doesn't say—'

'Louis! I told you. That thing that happened to me came back to me in bits. One bit I remembered was him saying something. When I was struggling he kept saying, "Please, child, please". Those words keep coming back to me.' I was sewing furiously to keep myself from crying. 'And Pixie Molloy was a child!'

Louis kneeled down before me. 'You might be small, Pippa, but you're not a child.'

'But Pixie Molloy – she was a child, Louis. She *was* a child.'

He sat back on his heels and gave a long whistle. 'That's what you really want to say, Pippa? That Roy Divine killed her? Because she was a child?'

I put in the last double stitch, bit off the thread, smoothed out the armband and put it on the finished pile. 'That's what I'm trying to tell you, Louis.' My voice was trembling. 'I think it is that.'

Then Louis kneeled up and looked me straight in the eye. 'Oh, my dear, brave Pippa.' He reached out and pulled me towards him. 'You are unique.' Then he kissed away the unshed tears in my eyes, before placing his lips on mine, making a ripple of prickling feeling sweep through my body right down to my feet, along my arms to the very tips of my fingers. I put my hand on the back of his head and pressed him to me, so that I could feel the bony contours of his face. I wanted that burning feeling of his lips on mine to last for ever.

In the days I had known him I had felt with certainty that Louis would kiss me some time, some time in the misty future, if he were round long enough. It seemed inevitable, even after my sadness over Angelo. How strange that it should happen now because he wanted to comfort me about poor little Pixie Molloy.

The door crashed open and Miss Abigail's voice came to me through the wheeling stars. 'Now, now, dears,' she said calmly. 'No time to play. These are grave times.'

I wanted to protest that it wasn't play, it was deadly serious. Louis scrambled to his feet, and pressed his hands down his jacket to smooth it. 'I'm sorry, Miss Abigail,' he said. 'Pippa was upset.'

She looked him in the eye. 'I'll see to Pippa,' she said. 'AJ was looking for you, Louis.'

'Yes . . . yes.' He glanced down at me and made for the door. 'I'll see you, Pippa.'

Miss Abigail sat down beside me. 'Pass me one of the black bands, Pippa darling. I'll help you finish these. Then you can go off and talk to Louis Hernfield in some more public place.'

Full House

That night the performance was a sellout. When I looked through the hole in the curtain I could see that there were even people standing at the back of the stalls. Josiah said there were people crowding the box office complaining of the shortage of tickets. As AJ always said, word got round. You might say the only question tonight was whether 'the word' was how good a show A. J. Palmer put on, or of the dramatic death of one of his company. Whatever the cause, he and Mr Ramsden would be equally pleased. There would be good takings tonight.

After a shortened overture, AJ – wearing a black ribbon on his sleeve – stood before the curtain and made an affecting little speech about the unfortunate accident that had befallen their young dancer. There was a muttering, a murmuring of sympathy from the large audience. 'And,' he said in conclusion, 'in consultation with her young friends in the troupe, we have decided that the show must go on in tribute to our own – our very special – Pixie Molloy!'

United in borrowed grief, the audience, not knowing what

else to do, applauded loudly but without the stamping, whistles and halloos that usually accompanied such enthusiastic applause.

Beside me in the wings fluttered the Pixies, enduring the fiercely muttered exhortations of Madame Bunce that, on pain of good hidings all round, they must *not* cry and ruin their make-up. She wore an outfit in black sateen topped off by a cloche hat with an organdie veil. Miss Abigail remarked that she looked like a cross between an undertaker and a bad fairy in an English pantomime. (I had never seen one of these but looked forward to doing so. They were supposed to be unique.)

One of my jobs that night was to stand in the wings with my basket of black ribands and hand them to the performers as they waited for their cue. Tom Merriman demurred, muttering about unnecessary sentiment. However, one glance from AJ had him pinning it on his oversize jacket.

At last the orchestra struck up some chords and the curtains opened to reveal Lily Lambert, dressed in a slender black gown. Very slowly she began to sing:

'I'm a young girl and I've just come over,
Over from the country where they do things big;
And amongst the boys I've got a love,
And since I got a lover I don't care a fig!
The boy I love is up in the gallery.
The boy I love is looking down at me.
There he is! Can't you see? Waving his handkerchey,
As merry as a robin that sings on the tree.'

She sang the song at a much slower tempo than the music ordained. When she finished, there were tears flowing down her cheeks and a rustle in the audience as both men and women reached for their own handkerchiefs, to wipe away tears shed for a child they didn't know.

The Palmers had been, I thought, very clever. What should have been a tasteless exercise became as moving a tribute to Pixie Molloy as any church oratorio.

The applause for Lily Lambert was deafening, and the audience began to clap again when the curtains swished back to reveal the Pixies in their places, ready for their dance. This time there were cheers and whistles from an audience relieved not to have to feel sad.

The Pixies performed their dance with their usual well-drilled efficiency, then blushed and hung their heads at the tumultuous applause. As they came off three of them started to cry, undeterred by cuffs from Madame Bunce.

After their first dance the show floated along on a sea of goodwill and applause, undercut by a peculiar sadness. Perhaps many people here had children who had died. Certainly many of them would have sons and brothers who died in the war. Perhaps this thing that had happened to Pixie Molloy brought to their minds forgotten sadness and allowed them to weep again. Angelo was certainly in my mind.

We had to skip Cissie Barnard's turn as she was dead drunk in the dressing room, having used the news of Pixie Molloy's demise as an appropriate excuse to drink most of a bottle of whisky and strip off in the hallway of her digs. AJ had to reinsert his Waterloo speech to make up the time.

Tesserina, usually oblivious of most things around her, seemed to be very distracted by these events. She stood still and stiff as I arranged her dress around her.

'Sad, Tesserina?' I asked. And I waited for her to say something about the little dancer.

She pouted. 'I am not pleased,' she said. 'I want Joe to play for my dance but Hermione, she says it must be her and the little man.'

Her brutal self-centredness made me smile.

'Do not smile, Pippa. I am sad.' She sighed heavily. 'How can I dance when I am sad?'

'Well,' I said, no longer smiling, 'Lily Lambert sang beautifully, and she was very sad about the poor little dancer who died today.'

Tesserina frowned, irritated perhaps at having to think about someone else.

I sighed and pulled the line of her arm so that its extending wire touched the floor and arranged the fabric in its swirling pool around her feet. 'You have to dance your very best, Tesserina,' I whispered. 'This is what you're here for. They're waiting.'

'I know this,' she said sadly.

Her sadness showed. Her dance was as efficient and perfectly executed as the Pixies' routine but tonight the audience was unmoved and their applause was perfunctory. Miss Abigail was very disappointed. She said Tesserina's swirling dance, mechanically executed without her usual passion, was 'small beer' compared with the other excitements of the evening.

I resisted the desire to ask her about 'small beer' and explained that Tesserina wanted Joe to play for her.

'Yes. Hermione Palmer mentioned that to me. But Hermione was not keen. She thought the accordion would make the whole thing too bucolic, not sophisticated enough for London. Thought it would ruin it.'

Despite the fact that I was angry with Tesserina I had an inspiration. 'Why can't Joe be on stage as well? Perhaps Tesserina could start off with the piano and the orchestra, then Joe can take over, there on the stage with her. It can all be about them. They love each other so much,' I ended lamely.

Miss Abigail nodded. 'You might have something there, Pippa. I'll talk to Hermione.'

Back in the wings I dipped into my basket and handed Mr Slater and Roy Divine their black ribands.

'What's this?' said Mr Slater. He was already halfway into the trance that sent him on to the stage a foot taller than his real height.

'It's for Pixie Molloy,' I said. 'For respect.' I turned to Roy, who was already pulling his black riband high on his bare golden arm. 'You heard what happened to Pixie Molloy?' I said.

'We all heard. AJ told us,' said Mr Slater. 'You were there, he said.'

I was still staring at Roy. 'What do you think of it, Mr Divine?'

'A tragedy,' he said, his eyes blank. 'Such a young kid. A tragedy to have an accident like that.'

'They haven't said it was an accident. Just that she was dead.' I locked his gaze with mine. 'Who knows what happened?'

Mr Slater looked from one to the other of us. I could hear him taking heavy breaths. He clapped a firm hand on Roy's shoulder. 'Stop chattering, man. You need to concentrate! Listen! That's our music.'

Miss Abigail told me later that the mesmerist's act brought

the most applause of any that night and that AJ was smug, claiming that his idea of adding Roy to the act had made a crucial difference.

I didn't see any of this because I had gone backstage to the Pixies' dressing room. I knew Madame Bunce wasn't there because I'd seen her being fed brandy by Mrs Palmer. She was still riding on the wave of sympathy that had surged around her since the discovery of Pixie Molloy. On my way to the dressing room I passed Louis, in his rags, all dressed up for the role of corpse in his own play. He winked at me as he passed but we didn't speak.

In their dressing room the five remaining Pixies had stripped off to their vests and knickers, their faces cleared of make-up except for the residue of painted eye-lines that had sunk into their eye-sockets and made their eyes shine in their mirrored reflections.

I offered round a packet of lemon drops that I had bought just for this purpose. 'How are you all feeling? I have been worried about you. It must have been hard, hearing that about Pixie Molloy.' I looked from face to face, looking for someone to say something.

The thin, fish-faced girl called Pixie Smith shrugged. 'It's awful. We keep looking for Ginny, don't we? Behind us. Around us. In the line. We keep thinking she's there, in the corner of our eye.'

The other girls chorused their agreement.

'Ginny?'

'Pixie Molloy. I'm Violet. And her . . .' she pointed to a small frizzy-haired girl whom we knew as Pixie Corbett, '. . . she's Gwen. We told the policeman that Molloy's name was Ginny. Her proper name. Madame Bunce couldn't remember. And we had to give him Ginny's suitcase and the letters from her dad so they can write to tell him.'

'He said they'll take her home on the train. In the goods van,' piped up Gwen Corbett. 'She'll get home before we do,' she added mournfully.

I hadn't thought of the Pixies as having homes. I'd always supposed their home had to be wherever Madame Bunce happened to be. Poor wretches. I dragged myself from this grim thought to concentrate on my present purpose. 'What do you think happened to Pixie Molloy . . . to Ginny . . .?'

'Ginny fell into the dock,' said Violet. 'The policemen said so. He said she drowned. Battered by the tide. That's what he said.'

'But how did she get there, out towards the docks at night? Madame Bunce keeps you all in.'

Gwen nodded. 'Ginny climbed out of the window. Buncie always locks the door but Ginny liked to get out. She was a bright spark. She could pick locks and this one wasn't too hard. Sometimes she'd bring us back sweets and meat pies. Once she brought us a bottle of beer. We always waited for her to come back, 'cause she always had something for us.' She sniffed away a tear. 'But that night we waited and waited and she didn't come.'

'We got the strap from Bunce for not running to tell her that Ginny had not come back. But we'd have got the strap from her if we'd told her, for letting Ginny go. Can't win,' Violet sighed.

'What did Ginny do, when she went out?'

'She sort of went around the streets. Talked to people.'

'She got caught out once,' said Gwen, 'but she knew the man. So he set her free. Didn't tell on her. She said he was very kind.'

'Who didn't tell on her?'

'Mr Divine. Like I said, Ginny said he was very kind. Gave her black bullets, these shiny sweets they have here. Ginny said he promised to show her some mesmerism tricks he's learned from Mr Slater. Promised he'd get her into that act somehow.' Violet sighed. 'Get her away from Bunce for ever.'

'I told her not to go,' said Gwen suddenly. 'There was something funny about him. He tried to kiss me on the mouth once. Ugh! Horrible.' She shuddered.

'And he tried to get her to bring me with her, out into the streets,' Violet chimed in. 'But I wouldn't go.'

'I tell you what I think, *mam'selle*,' said Gwen. 'I think he mesmerised her and made her jump in the drink.'

'But had his Wicked Way first,' announced Violet. 'Like it says in Miss Cissie's song.'

'Poor Ginny,' said Violet, and behind her the other Pixies murmured their shocked agreement.

These children, more knowing than I was, and so close to Ginny, had worked it out. I knew Violet was right. Roy Divine had done this thing to Pixie Molloy.

I said, 'You should tell the policeman all this, about Ginny getting out.'

Violet shook her head and the others followed suit. 'No. No. Buncie'll kill us if we say a word about any of that. T'in't worth it.'

I looked at the cold, hard little faces and handed over the whole bag of lemon drops to Violet, with instructions for her to share them out fairly. Then I made my way back to our own cubbyhole, to digest what the Pixies had told me.

Now I had him! Now I had Roy Divine. Even if he didn't push Pixie Ginny Molloy into the dock he knew what had happened to her. He'd have to tell now. But how would I be able to tell the police this? Wouldn't all the stuff from Bishop

Auckland come up and put me in the wrong? He could easily make a fool of me again.

There had to be a way, though. It would just need thinking through.

Theatre Bar

In the theatre bar after the show, Josiah Barrington sat with Tom Merriman and Lily Lambert, who was flushed with her success as the sad songstress of the evening. Though she lacked the diamond-hard star quality of Cissie Barnard, Lily had a fine voice. And tonight, riding on the tide of sentimental sadness over a dead child, she knew she had caught the mood of the audience. Once in a while this happened and she enjoyed the intoxication of tuning properly into her audience. Sitting at the small table over her second glass of port she vowed to herself to hold on to that feeling, inject it into all her performances. She saw herself bowing to rapturous audiences in London, in Paris, in Johannesburg, in Melbourne.

Her thoughts were interrupted by the sour voice of Tom Merriman. 'So where's Cissie Barnard slunk off to? Sleeping it off, is she?'

'Poor Cissie,' said Lily. 'Poor Little Pixie Molloy. Cissie was quite overwhelmed.'

'Well,' he said, 'at the very least a tragedy like this gives her an excuse. Not that she needs an excuse. She's in for the sack, that one. No doubt about it.' He drank off his whisky and attended to his pint of ale. 'The beer is very strong in these parts. It's like drinking—'

'That's enough of that, Tom,' grunted Josiah Barrington. 'Ladies present.'

Tom cocked an eye at Lily. 'Well, if you think that's a—'

Josiah curled one of his big fists. 'I told yeh. That's enough.'

Tom's eye returned to his pint of beer and he slumped back down in his chair.

Lily raised her glass to Josiah. He was a good-looking, well-set-up man really. And very kind. He was usually hanging round Abigail Wharton but something must be up there. That relationship had always been a hard one to reckon. Abigail was a sweet enough woman but she was fifty-five if she was a day. And those awful legs. What a cross to bear. Lily found herself crossing her own trim ankles. She smiled at Josiah.

'I heard you came from round these parts, Josiah . . .'

At the other end of the bar Abigail suppressed the twinge of envy she'd felt as she watched Lily flirting with Josiah. After all, she had brought that about herself. But she had envisaged Josiah going for one of the demure ladies of the chapel, not another woman in the company. Still, she'd always liked Lily, admired her as a real professional. Not as talented as poor Cissie, of course. But steady, reliable and very pretty, looking young for her thirty-odd years.

Cissie had already been mentioned at Abigail's table, where she was sitting with AJ and Hermione. Jacob Smith was, for once, not with them, having been called home by his sick sister. Cissie had just been rescued from outright dismissal by Hermione, who was worried about so many changes in the cast. After all, she asserted, when she was on form Cissie could hold an audience in the palm of her hand.

Then Tesserina – sitting in the far corner of the bar, chattering twenty to the dozen with Joe Zambra – became the topic of their discussion.

'The dancer was a bit of a damp squib tonight,' said AJ. 'Not quite the wonder you make her out to be, Hermione. Not at all.'

Hermione frowned. 'A small dip in her performance, AJ, that's all. The girl's got this bee in her bonnet about the Italian boy playing this blasted squeezebox for her. From the sublime to the ridiculous, if you ask me. It would be no better than some cheap Italian adagio café dance.'

'Just so. And we know you're not going to make your fortune with such an act, Hermione,' said AJ. He went on smoothly, 'The whole attraction of it was your delicacy, your classical playing with the . . . er . . . physical expressiveness of the dancer's style.'

'Exactly!' said Hermione glumly. 'That was the whole beauty of it.'

'Do you want me to talk to her?' said Abigail. 'Though, remember, she can be stubborn. I have to say she has great determination. She wouldn't have survived without that.'

'Well, if she's determined to do this with the Italian boy, there'll be no London, I'm telling you.'

AJ met Abigail's glance. 'Now that would be a pity, darling,' he said glibly to Hermione. 'Such a disappointment for you.'

Abigail smiled to herself. Cunning old boy. Then she said, 'I could talk to her, Hermione. But whether she's to dance to your music or to Joe Zambra's accordion, perhaps she needs a bit more time before charging off to London. She needs to be sure of herself as a performer, don't you think? I did have this idea of Joe Zambra in performance, supplementing your piano. Part of the staging, so to speak.'

'But she's so good just on her own. I'd set my heart on—'

'And it will happen, my darling,' said AJ. 'But perhaps not just yet?'

'I don't think you'll get Tesserina now without Joe Zambra,' said Abigail. 'They are like two spoons in a drawer. No parting them.'

'But . . .' Hermione stopped, having spotted Mr Ramsden making his way towards them, flanked by a young woman with short hair wearing a forest-green wool suit, and a middle-aged man in military uniform, who walked with the aid of a stick.

AJ stood up. 'Ramsden! Good to see you.'

Mr Ramsden introduced his companions. 'This is Captain Benedict, AJ, an old comrade of mine, and his daughter, Miss Philippa Benedict.'

They all shook hands. The captain removed his cap and hooked his stick on the back of his chair before he sat down.

'Captain Benedict is on a mission,' said Ramsden, ordering drinks all round and signing the waiter's chit with a flourish. 'He wishes to confer.'

Captain Benedict coughed. 'I'm looking for a young French woman called Mademoiselle Valois and a young man called . . .' The captain glanced at his daughter.

'Louis Hernfield,' she said. 'I wrote it down.'

AJ, Hermione and Abigail glanced around the room. 'Not here just yet,' said AJ. 'They are with us but not with us, so to speak. They may well join us but sometimes the young ones find a different place to unwind after the excitement of the show. May I ask the nature of your mission, Captain?'

'Well, these two young people called at my house this

morning but unfortunately I was away. My daughter dealt with them, but I was disappointed not to meet them myself.'

'They called on you?' Abigail's voice rose to a squeak. Pippa and her secrets.

AJ coughed. 'Miss Wharton is by way of being the girl's mentor, her foster mother.'

'Her foster mother? Is there no mother?' The captain glared at Abigail, his voice sharp.

Abigail, defensive, shook her head. 'She is an orphan. But I assure you she's like a daughter to me, Captain Benedict. She joined me in France and we've been together ever since.' She paused. 'But why would my Pippa call on you? She knows no one here.'

'Pippa?' The captain looked at his daughter. 'She was called Pippa?'

'Barbara Philippe Valois . . .' said Abigail.

Captain Benedict's daughter rushed on. 'It seems she and the young man were walking around the streets and they happened upon our house, which has the same name as this town in France where she was born. This appealed to Miss Valois, I think.'

'She called uninvited? Pippa?' said Hermione, disbelieving.

'That's of no consequence,' said the captain irritably. 'I just wish to talk to them. To the girl.' He placed a card on the table. 'Would you ask them to call on me?' He closed his eyes. 'Where are we? Wednesday tomorrow. I'd be obliged, Mr Palmer, if you'd ensure that they call on me on Saturday morning at ten o'clock. I have written a note to Mademoiselle Valois requesting the same.'

'To what purpose, Captain?' said Abigail, still bemused about Pippa's private quest here in Sunderland. 'Why should Pippa call on you?'

The captain looked at her blankly. 'To the purpose of talk, Miss Wharton. I think Mademoiselle Valois and I may have interests in common. We were both in Carcassonne, a place I have loved.' He stood up, put his hat on his head and glanced at his daughter. 'I think we should go, my dear. I'm not used to keeping such late hours.' He bowed in the general direction of the company at the table, took up his stick and made his rather painful way to the door.

His daughter stood up, blushing. 'I hope you may forgive my father. He was very keen to meet Mademoiselle Valois and is now disappointed. He was very struck by her coming from that town, the town after which our house is named.' Then she fled after her father.

The waiter came across with a drinks-laden tray.

'Just set them down, Jerry,' said Mr Ramsden affably. 'We'll deal with them in turn, to celebrate a very successful evening.' He turned to AJ. 'Don't worry about old Benedict, dear boy. He's a good chap. I went to school with him. Had a bad time in the war, which left him a bit short in the leg as well as temper.' He picked up his glass. 'Now, let us toast a very good evening's business.'

They raised their glasses and all except Abigail put the captain from their minds. She picked up her glass. 'I'd rather make a toast to a young girl, a poor little girl,' she said. 'Pixie Molloy. May she rest in peace.'

Marie

'What? What are you saying?'

Marie Divine had scoured off the gold paint and was in her street clothes. Dressed like this, she looked smart, fashionably boyish, and remarkably untheatrical.

'Pippa Valois wants to talk to you about Roy,' said Louis, leaning against the doorjamb of the Divines' dressing room.

I scowled at him, not wanting him to speak for me, even though coming to Marie had been his idea. 'I need to tell you about Roy, to—'

'I know all about my brother Roy. It was you who caused his trouble. Then he went off and came back and he's lording it all over us with that pansified mesmerist.' She glanced at Blaze. 'We don't need him any more. We're doing very well without him, thank you very much.'

I looked around. 'Please will you sit down and not say anything until I've finished? You're the only one—'

She picked up her snakeskin handbag. 'If you think I'm gonna sit—'

'Marie! For God's sake, sit down and listen. Stop interrupting the kid.'

We all looked round in astonishment at the rare sound of Blaze Divine's voice. Then we waited for Marie to throw something at him but she sat down on one narrow chair. I sat down opposite her.

Blaze put an arm on her shoulder. 'Now let the kid have her say, Marie.'

She turned to glare at me. 'Well?'

I began at the beginning, starting with how I'd thought Roy was nice and friendly. About how he attacked me and how he knocked Angelo against the parapet. About little Ginny Molloy being besotted with him, and Roy being extra friendly towards the little girl. How she must have thought him very kind and friendly. And now, as Marie knew, Pixie Molloy had suffered this accident at the wharf.

'So,' I ended lamely, 'I thought there might be some kind of a connection. Between Angelo and Ginny Molloy. That was her name. Ginny. Ginny Molloy.'

Marie glanced up at Blaze. 'So what kind of connection are you thinking about?'

'I think Roy might have led her, or pushed her, or frightened her so that she ran into the dock,' I said miserably. Then I said the worst thing in my mind. 'I think he likes hurting children. That night he hurt me he said, "Please, child, please." I keep hearing his voice saying that.'

Marie's cheeks had turned bright red. Blaze whispered something in her ear.

'Have you spoken of this to anyone else?' she said.

'Just my friend Louis here.'

'Not Miss Wharton?'

'No.'

'Why not?'

I couldn't say that I'd embroidered the truth in the past to Miss Abigail, and she might not believe me now. I couldn't say that I was worried that Miss Abigail might think I'd led Roy on in some way, when she heard that I recanted the story I'd told to the policeman.

'I thought she might be worried,' I said. 'She's had much on her mind, having to get Tesserina ready for performing and now helping AJ because of Mrs Palmer's leaving.'

'So, what do you want me to do?'

'Get Roy to tell you what happened. Perhaps make him go to the police.'

Marie Divine laughed: a very mirthless sound. 'Get him to tell the truth? My dear, the truth and my dear brother Roy are strangers. You can't beat the truth out of him. I should know because I've tried.'

I suddenly knew now that she'd tried to do this many times. That was what all the shouting and bruises were about.

'She's right,' squeaked Blaze Divine. 'Brother Roy's the cat that prowls alone and is a stranger to the truth. If he's done wrong – and I'm not saying he has – you won't get a single word out of him. Not one.'

I shivered at his words. It dawned on me that these two, strange as they were, knew all about their brother and his unusual ways.

Marie opened the door. 'Now get out, the two of you.' Her voice followed us. 'And stay away from him, or the police. We'll deal with him.'

As we made our way down to the bar it occurred to me that we might have misunderstood Marie Divine. What if Roy Divine had always been the bully? What if the noisy public rows had been her resisting his bullying, protecting poor Blaze and finally heaving Roy out of the nest like some mother bird getting rid of the cuckoo? Perhaps the version with her as the bully was just *one* version. Of course she was nasty and aggressive. But now I knew how hard Roy was to deal with, how changeable his moods. What would it be like living with that day after day, year after year?

The theatre bar was bustling and hot. Miss Abigail was in full conversational flight with the Palmers at one end of the bar. For once, Mr Barrington was not beside her. He was at a smaller table with the singers and the comedian and the man who did the new act with the snake and the rabbit. Roy Divine was up on a bar stool, laughing and talking with Mr Slater. The mesmerist turned and nodded, a slight smile on his face. I caught Roy's glance in the bar mirror and he raised his glass of beer towards me.

Louis and I joined Tesserina and Joe at their table in the corner. I sat down but Louis remained standing, saying he needed to talk to Mr Palmer. 'But have one first,' said Joe with unusual affability. He put up a hand and the waiter came across to take his order. Joe seemed very happy. 'Tessa and me have been talking about the act. I have other tunes . . .'

I wondered if he was leaping ahead too fast. Even I could see that the delicacy and power of Mrs Palmer's music was a great setting for the extreme feeling in Tesserina's dancing.

But I could not give this opinion here.

Here is Angelo, swathed in bandages. But now lying beside him on the hospital bed is a smaller figure, her wet shift clinging to her tiny bud-like breasts and black seaweed draped across her narrow shoulders. Her rusty hair moulds itself to her small head and her carmined lips and outlined eyes make her face the face of a doll. Clutched in one small hand is a white cloth, which she lifts into the air. I can smell a sweet smoky smell. Now we are backstage in the small theatre in Toulouse and the doctor is there clamping a white cloth round the mouth of a dancer who is screaming. She goes limp and he starts to pull on her arm which becomes as long as a leg. No arm can be that long.

I glanced again at Roy Divine, lounging at the bar. I was certain now that I was right about him. He was dangerous. The thing was, what could I do? Make a fool of myself again? What would ordinary people, people who lived in the real world, make of that genial fellow at the bar being involved in two deaths? One the death of a little girl who was just looking for kindness.

Louis drank off his lemonade and nodded towards the Palmer table. 'They're not so hard at it now. I want to talk to AJ. I'll see if I can get a word in sideways,' he said, and made his way purposefully towards them.

Now I had become what the English call a raspberry, or a gooseberry. I was not quite sure what kind of fruit that was, although Miss Abigail had described it as very sour, which was quite appropriate that night. Joe and Tesserina were holding hands under the table and only had eyes for each other. And they spoke in their own language. Perhaps I was both a raspberry and a gooseberry.

Joe caught my eye. 'Tessa here says Hermione Palmer wasn't happy tonight, that her dancing wasn't on the ball. I've said it'll be right when I play for her, but Mrs Palmer'll have none of that. Then we're saying now Tesserina's not going to London unless it's with me. An impasse, as we used to say in the army.'

I had an idea. ' You know lots of tunes, Joe, don't you?'

He laughed. 'I've been playing tunes since I was the height of this table. I know thousands of tunes.'

'Well, why not put a dozen of them together and make your own independent act? Then you can have your own set in whatever show Tesserina's in.'

He looked at Tesserina and she nodded her head. 'A good idea,' she said. Then she added something else to him.

He turned to me. 'She says that if we're to go to London on this Monday, that's too short a time and, anyway, would that London feller take me as a separate act? She says I need some time. She's got a point.'

'Tell the Palmers Tesserina doesn't want to go to London until you've built up your set, and have a following here. Then you'll go to London together.'

Tesserina had followed this. 'But Hermione is not pleased, Pippa. She wishes to go to London.'

I shook my head. 'It's about you, Tesserina. Not about Mrs Palmer.'

Joe struck the table with the palm of his hand. 'You've got sommat there, Pippa.' He turned and said something to Tesserina, then translated to me. 'I told her you know this company better than either of us. If you have thought of it, it's a sound idea.'

To my dismay the two of them dropped back into their own private world and I sat there feeling angry until I was relieved from my sense of isolation by Louis bounding back across the room. He thrust a thick deckle-edged card in my hand. 'The Carcassonne man was here, Pippa! And that girl Philippa. He says we're to call on him on Saturday.'

I read the card:

Ambrose P. Benedict
Carcassonne
Laurel Gardens
Sunderland

On the back, pencilled in hurried script, it stated '10 a.m.
Saturday.' Underneath, almost as an afterthought, he had
scrawled 'Please! APB.' I closed my hand around the card. I
felt his hand on the card; the hand that had clasped the door-
handle in the apartment I shared with my mother. The hand
that had clasped my mother's hand with some kind of
affection.

*I can see the back of the soldier as he goes through the arch. He turns
and waves. My mother's hands grip my shoulders tightly. I can smell
the scent of fresh lemons. Who is that,* Maman? *That is your father,*
Pippa. *That is your own father.*

I asked Louis, 'Did Miss Abigail say what he looked like, this
man?'

He frowned as though this were a silly question. 'She said he
was rather short-tempered and that he walked with a stick.'

'Well . . .' I held up the card to the light. 'Ten o'clock
Saturday morning . . . I'll have to wait till then.'

Joe butted in. 'Tesserina says, what's this about?'

I'd forgotten them. 'Tell her it's nothing,' I lied. 'Nothing at
all. Just a person who wants us to meet her father.'

At the end of the evening I turned down Louis's offer to
walk me back to my lodgings. I sent him home by himself
and walked back with Miss Abigail. I'd noticed Mr Barrington
leaving the bar with Lily Lambert on his arm, and thought
perhaps Miss Abigail would need me.

The Glass Bottle

The next day two policemen came to the theatre to talk to us all about Pixie Molloy's accident. At first they gathered us on stage and told us that Ginny had died by drowning. There were no marks on her to indicate otherwise. That said, they were puzzled as to why the child, a ward of the troupe, after all, had been out unsupervised and allowed to wander to such a dangerous spot.

Madame Bunce was flustered by this and talked of how disobedient Pixie Molloy had always been. 'I told her again and again . . .' her voice faded away and she glanced uneasily at AJ.

The senior policeman nodded. 'We'll have to talk further, Mrs Bunce.'

'Madame Bunce!' she corrected him wearily. 'Madame Bunce.'

The second policeman was moving through the group, taking names and addresses. This was a bit of a vain exercise, as the only address was the theatre here and the next theatre in Newcastle. Few members of the troupe lived in their homes, even if they had them. Tom Merriman had a house in a place called Cricklewood, and I heard several people giving the address of their mothers or siblings in faraway places: Lancaster, Havant, Dumfries and Grimsby. And, of course, Sydney, Australia.

Through the turned backs of the crowd my eyes caught those of Roy Divine. He was staring at me with a thin smile on his face, just a twist of the lips. I glared back but was not inspired to draw the attention of the policemen or chase after Roy as he slipped into the wings with Marie at his side. The surprising thing about that was that they were not shouting or quarrelling with each other.

Miss Abigail noticed too. 'They seem unusually friendly. How very odd.'

I told her the sight of those two, heads together, made a chill to ripple right through me. Miss Abigail told me the English call it someone walking over your grave.

By the time Friday came round I was in a bit of a daze. Things seemed to be happening to me at a strange distance, as though they were taking place in a clear bottle that I held in my hands. It was closed to me and I could see it all happening but could do nothing about it.

This matter I was embarking on was much more real to me than this tragic drama over Pixie Molloy, than Roy Divine's smirking glances or even Louis's anxious looks. Tomorrow I would meet Ambrose Benedict, who might be – who probably was – my father. What if I took one look at him and hated him? I was already angry with him because he had left us to the life that led to my mother's death. But that was not all. I felt excited and curious. He too must be feeling curious. Why else would he leave the card with such a message?

In the end I decided that I would dedicate tomorrow to my mother, at her best: alive and well and enjoying good company. Today I was flooded with thoughts of her: swinging her shopping basket as we walked along; adjusting the buttoning on her suit before she placed her hat dead centre on her lovely hair; ironing the fluted organdie collar of her blouse; chuckling at something I had said or done as she ruffled my hair. Today the only bad things I could remember from those years were when her sad profession poked its grubby fingers into our life together: that nasty Belgian whom she nearly married was one case in point.

My thoughts moved to those earlier, eerier memories of the sight of the soldier through the doorway, then being out in the streets, looking, always looking for that particular soldier and never finding him. Then there was something about a group of soldiers again, throwing me from hand to hand as though I were a ball. There were gaps. There had always been gaps. But these days I was remembering more.

My mother is there now in the midst of the soldiers, laying about them with her umbrella, then hustling me away, asking, 'Are you hurt, are you hurt?' She keeps muttering the words to me as she hurries me through the archway and up the steps to our apartment. There is no beating today, just her tears falling into my hair.

Louis tried to talk to me several times that Friday but I could hardly hear the words he was saying. After three tries he gave up and sat hunched in a corner, scribbling in his notebook. I knew I should ask him what he was writing, but I didn't. He too was inside that bottle and I couldn't quite touch him.

As We Were

The Friday night performance was a *tour de force*. AJ told us it was our best in England. The press coverage of the tragedy had meant a sellout at the box office every night since. That night everybody was giving the performance of their career. Tesserina recovered her grace and dazzled the audience with her seductive dance; Cissie stayed sober and was very funny; Lily sang like a nightingale; AJ was at his magisterial best and Mr Slater and Roy's act achieved gasps and laughter in equal measure. The new touch tonight was that Mr Slater hypnotised Roy at the beginning of the show, so as they went through their routine, whenever Mr Slater coughed, Roy stopped what he was doing and did an acrobatic back flip. The audience loved it.

Backstage, Hermione and AJ gloated over their success. AJ thought perhaps the response of the audience was sharpened by the dramatic fate of Pixie Molloy. 'But then I think perhaps we are welding ourselves together again into the new, larger Palmer's Varieties. We must take some credit. Hermione darling, we are girding our loins to raise ourselves into a leading travelling troupe, prepared to step on to the largest stages in the country,' he said enthusiastically, 'with resounding success.'

'All down to your Herculean efforts, my darling,' murmured Hermione, who had been obliged to play for Tesserina tonight without the benefit of Jacob Smith to turn her pages. Unfortunately her old friend had been confined to home again by his sister's illness. Still, she felt she'd managed very well, though she said it herself.

He read her thoughts. 'You coped very well on your own, darling. Better, if anything. Tesserina was right back on form. That Smith feller seems none too reliable, if I may say so, darling. I know he's something of a pet of yours, but . . .'

'His poor sister,' she said faintly.

'Do you think there will be any possibility that the benighted sister will let him go to London with you?' he said. 'These illnesses of hers are something of a windfall, don't you think?'

She stared at him for a moment. 'You've read my mind, AJ. It might prove to be very inconvenient.'

'Perhaps that's the reason why, unlike you, the feller has no adventure in his soul, never got out of this town.' He added thoughtfully, 'Though, as you say, he is very talented.'

'Top of every class,' said Hermione. 'Beat me in some.'

AJ let the silence run.

'I was thinking, AJ . . .' said Hermione.

'Yes, darling?'

'Perhaps I have been just a bit precipitate about Tesserina.'

'Do you think so?'

'She is so very volatile. That is the quality, well harnessed, of course, that makes her a good performer.'

'Especially in the dance,' he supplied. 'Temperament is so important.'

'Just so,' she said. 'Especially in someone who will be great, like Tesserina.'

'And now we have the problem of the accordionist . . .'

'Do you know what I was thinking?' Her face lit up with a wicked grin.

'So what were you thinking, my darling?'

'I was thinking of those tales I'd heard about great racehorses who had to have a favourite goat or donkey in their stalls for them to win their races. That's Joe Zambra. That's why we have to tolerate him.'

AJ was smiling broadly. 'You are a terrible woman, you know, Hermione.'

'Well,' she said, 'it's ridiculous. To think she could dance properly to that hurdy-gurdy sound.'

'Of course, the chap has quite a facility,' AJ said thoughtfully. 'We might find a place for him somewhere; playing between acts, perhaps, or during scene changes. That might keep them happy.'

'As long as he doesn't want to gallop alongside her. That's all my concern. She has a way to go yet before she wins her particular race.' She reapplied her lipstick.

'Agreed.' He picked up his coat and hat. 'So, we'll keep him, as you say? And you can work further magic with her.' At the door he turned. 'So I take it that nobody will be going to gallop down to London?' he said innocently. 'We'll wire Mr Terrance?'

'Perhaps you would do it, darling?' She smiled up at him and tapped him quite vigorously on the arm. 'You manage things so well, AJ. No wonder I took you on.'

'As we were, then?'

'As we were.'

When they got down to the bar the first people they saw

were the Three Divines sitting at a corner table, deep in conversation, and Mr Slater sitting up at the bar staring quietly into a small whisky.

'Ah,' said AJ. 'Negotiating a Divine armistice, no doubt.'

Hermione hugged his arm to her side. 'AJ! As usual you have everything in a nutshell.'

Washing Hair

I didn't go to the bar with the others. I pleaded a headache to Louis but promised to meet him at his house at nine the next morning.

Miss Abigail volunteered to walk home with me, saying that she was tired: it had been that kind of week, after all. 'Quite a rollercoaster. First the London proposal is on, and I'm queen bee, then the whole thing's off . . .'

As we took off our hats and coats she asked me about the army captain and I repeated the fiction about the coincidence of the name of the house. 'The old man obviously wanted to talk about my home town.'

'I wouldn't call him old, darling,' she said. 'He might have had a bad leg and a few lines but he wouldn't be even as old as me. And I don't think of myself as old. Not quite.'

This was said with such heavy emphasis that I hauled myself out of my stupor and protested, 'You'll never be old, Miss Abigail. Never in the whole world.'

This made her laugh. 'Very kind of you to say so, my dear.

But, to be honest, this week I feel . . . well . . . quite a bit older than I felt last week.'

'Well, you don't look it.'

'Very kind of you,' she repeated drily.

At least she'd brought me out of my self-centred haze. 'Have you had a disagreement with Mr Barrington?' I said, suddenly inspired. I remembered that in the bar this week Lily Lambert had been flirting with him. 'I hope not. He adores you. Anyone can see that.'

Miss Abigail waited a while before she answered. 'We've not disagreed, darling. It is more that we've come to an agreement. Or to agree to disagree on a certain matter. Josiah has wanted me to marry him for quite some while. Then he wanted the pair of us to retire to a shop selling nails and chisels. I did hesitate. But to retire! Leave the company! It all seemed unthinkable, ridiculous. So we agreed to go our own ways.'

I thought of my mother and the soldier. They went their own ways. Was it unthinkable, in those days, for them to be together? I tried not to think too hard of tomorrow when I would meet this old-young man with a limp.

I dragged myself back to the present. 'To be honest I *can* think of you in a shop!' I said suddenly.

'Oh, you can, can you?'

'But not selling nails. I can see you in the back shop on Bond Street, drinking tea with Miss Dina Brooks. I can just see you choosing trimmings for fine hats.'

The thought was cheering. It certainly made her smile. But then the smile faltered. 'Sadly, I just had a letter from Dina. It seems her friend Mr Brown wants, for reasons to do with his loving wife, to withdraw his backing for Dina's shop. The shop makes money for her but not quite enough. So poor Dina might have to come out of the shop. Such a pity. It was so much her *thing*.'

The sadness in the air was broken by the appearance of our landlady with two water-carriers of hot water. 'Saw you comin' in early. Thought you'd want your water to make a start.'

I'd forgotten it was Friday. Miss Abigail and always I washed our hair every Friday night, no matter where we were, no matter how late it was. This was much to the disapproval of Tesserina, who had only washed her hair once since we'd been together. And for the week after that she'd muttered on, and brushed her hair for hours, railing in her own way against the wispiness and waywardness of her long curly locks.

Miss Abigail's grey locks were equally wispy and wayward but she seemed to like it that way. When first washed, her fine hair lay close to her head, moulding itself to her delicate skull, and snaked down her back in a loosely linked plait. It took an age to dry before the fire but when it dried it increased in volume a hundredfold and became an ill-disciplined cloud of grey for the whole of the next week. Normally she wore it 'up' in the old-fashioned way. But it was fine and slippery and soon escaped its pins.

My hair, being short and thick, was much easier to deal with. Washed once a week and towel-dried, it took up its usual glossy helmet shape almost instantly. When it grew, Miss Abigail cut it with her dressmaking scissors and her fine eye for shape meant it always looked the same, which pleased me.

That night, I sat on the floor before the fire with my back to her while she towel-dried my hair. Usually we did this in silence, enjoying together the peace and quiet. But tonight, rubbing away, she said, 'Are you feeling all right, Pippa? You've seemed quite broody for some days now.'

'I'm fine.'

'Is it Louis Hernfield? I thought you two got on very well. So nice for you to have a young person in the company.'

'Tesserina's young.'

'But she doesn't really count, does she? She will go and make her own way.'

I knew what she meant. Tesserina was out of time, out of any sense of age. And now she had moved away from us into Joe Zambra's shadow.

'I do like Louis,' I said finally. 'I admire him.' I thought of the kiss. 'I like him a lot.'

'I'm pleased about that. He's a theatre kind of person and now it seems he's joined us, so we'll be seeing a lot of him.' She paused. 'But I was thinking perhaps Angelo might still be on your mind.' She combed her fingers through my drying hair. 'Not that that is surprising, of course.'

'Yes, he's still on my mind. But not every minute. Do you know I was only with him twice? I've spent much more time with Louis than I spent with Angelo.'

'But the dreadful thing that happened to him must have fixed those times in your mind . . .'

'Yes. I know what you mean. I cannot really explain it. But I will try.' For the first time in months my English failed me. I could think of the French words, not the English. Then my brain cleared. 'It is as though Angelo made a space in my heart and mind, and Louis filled it. I was entranced with Angelo's beauty and that sort of woke me up, so that it's very easy now, to be with Louis.'

'Does Louis know you feel this?'

'No. I would not tell him.'

'Good. That would be quite a mistake, I think. Discretion, as they say, is the better part of valour.' She took up her brush and started to brush my hair, turning the brush at the end to make my hair turn under. 'You seem to have that worked out. So it's not about Louis and Angelo that you're brooding. So what is it?'

Even now, in this intimate setting I could not talk to her about Ambrose Benedict. I turned to my other worry.

'It's about Pixie Molloy. I have been thinking about her. Did you know her name was Ginny? None of them can use their names. She doesn't let them, that horrible woman . . .'

'No, I didn't know her name. Poor girl. AJ was saying earlier today that they have sent her down to her home in Spitalfields for burial. In her coffin. What a shock for her family. I didn't even know the child came from there. Madame Bunce kept them so apart.'

'That awful woman. Cannot the police arrest her for being so cruel?'

'I don't think so, darling. D'you know, she's not that much different from many dance leaders. They're a ferocious lot.' Miss Abigail sounded resigned. 'I endured all that myself. But of course I survived. Unlike poor Ginny Molloy.'

'Cannot AJ get rid of the horrible woman?'

'I have to say there was talk of that. But it would be very cruel to her and to the other Pixies if it's done now, don't you think? To leave them high and dry after this terrible accident?'

The fire dropped a bit and I leaned forward and put on some more coal. 'I think it might not have been an accident,' I said, settling back against Miss Abigail's knees.

'But dearest Pippa! You heard what the policeman said. It was a clear case of drowning.'

'But what . . . who . . . got her down there to the docks? How did she get into the water?'

'That's a mystery that will never be solved,' sighed Abigail.

I took a breath. 'I think it was Roy Divine.'

The brushing hand stilled. 'Oh, my dear, I know you had a terrible experience with him at our last stop. But this . . .?'

'The other Pixies said that Ginny climbed out of the house to go walking with him more than once.'

Miss Abigail began to brush my hair again without speaking.

'She could have got out, gone walking with him and he . . . played some game with her and she ended up in the dock.' The words burst out of me.

She turned me round to face her. 'Don't you think you should go to the police, if you think this?'

'It's almost nothing. It's less than there was about Angelo. And they didn't believe me there. Look what I had to do about that. I had to change what I said. He'll tell them that but he won't tell them it was he who made me do it. The police will never believe me. I am from the outside, a foreigner; they see me as a nuisance. I will not – cannot – go to them.'

Her bright glance was boring into me, piercing into my very soul. 'We theatricals too, you know, are outsiders. We are seen as a nuisance. In these small towns we're like foreigners even in our own land.' She turned me back round and started again to brush my hair with firm strokes. 'I don't know. Perhaps we should just let Pixie Ginny Molloy go to Spitalfields and rest in peace.'

I closed my eyes, mesmerised again by the strokes of the brush. Her voice came to me from a distance. 'Don't worry about this, my Pippa. And don't worry about that soldier. *We* are your family. Me. Now Louis. Even Hermione and AJ. This soldier may have something for you, my darling. You may take it, whatever it is. You must take it. But remember that this is where you belong. We are your family.'

Carcassonne

At the house in Laurel Gardens Philippa Benedict makes us welcome. This time she doesn't keep us in the hall, but shows us straight into a large back room which is half dining room, half study.

The man standing in a soft smoking jacket in front of the fireplace doesn't look like a soldier. He looks like any middle-aged man with bright eyes and a head of thick grey curly hair. His face is kindly enough, but etched deeply with lines as though he has flinched in pain many times. He smiles a slightly lopsided smile and shakes hands with both of us. My own intense worry flees when I realise that the hand that shakes mine is shaking. He keeps my hand in his.

'Pippa?' he says. 'Your name is Pippa?' His voice sends ripples down my spine.

'Really it's Barbara Philippe Valois.'

He leads me to the deep window seat and sits me beside him. 'I was so sorry not to be here when you called. I have a regular visit every month to a hospital near York.' He looks at his daughter. 'Perhaps you would show Mr Hernfield the conservatory, Philippa?' He turns to me. 'This daughter of mine has a wonderful understanding of plants and is even growing new species out there.'

This is obviously a plan, as the daughter leads Louis away without demur. Once they have gone the room is filled with a silence so heavy that I feel impelled to break it. 'Carcassonne, *monsieur*. Why do you call your house this?'

He smiles slightly, the corner of his mouth drooping. 'Well, Mademoiselle Valois, I named it so because I have admired that beautiful town in France, so modest and immensely grand at the same time. A town I never wish to forget.'

'You were there? You visited Carcassonne?'

'Six times in all.'

'Did you visit a person there?'

'Only twice. The other times I was looking for this same person but she was no longer there.'

Another heavy silence. I am burning to ask him who was that person but I don't have the courage. Finally he says, 'Tell me about yourself, Miss Valois . . . Pippa. Tell me about your life.' I like his voice. It comes from somewhere deep in his chest but is still very soft.

Then – stumbling at first – I begin to tell him all about me and my life. I tell him all the things that whirl around in my head about my life with my mother. I tell him about her. All the good things, of course. How she was pretty and well liked. A good teacher, although not in a school. 'She only taught at home when I came along, *monsieur*.' I omit the comment that a woman with a bastard child was not respectable enough to teach in a school. I don't tell him about the Belgian, and all my mother's other callers. I tell him of the good food she cooked and how she knew where to get the best bread. I tell him how people were cruel to her and how we had to move to other towns to escape their wrath.

I tell him how she caught influenza, although I don't tell him about the baby born dead that weakened her and made her susceptible to it. I tell him how she and I lit candles in a church to get her better – but all in vain. I tell him of the hospital ward in which she died, and the rosary in her hands.

'So Barbara is buried in Paris?' His voice is like lead.

I have to admit I don't know. 'I fear it is a pauper's grave, *monsieur*, unmarked, unrecognised. I had to run from the hospital as there was this gaoler-nun who would have thrown me in an orphanage. It is a matter of regret that I left *Maman* to be buried without me being there. But I was very young.'

His hand tightens on mine. 'Poor Pippa. Poor Barbara.'

I tell him about surviving on the streets and learning the skill of sewing by a kind of enforced accident, how I was rescued from the sweatshop by Miss Abigail, my foster mother and mentor. 'So this, *monsieur*, is how I became what Miss Abigail calls "a theatrical" and make my home at her side, on the railway or in lodgings, staying in no city or town long enough to call it home.'

During certain parts of my story Captain Benedict holds his hand up to shade his eyes. When my tale comes to an end, we sit in silence. At last he takes his hand away from his eyes and looks at me. The piercing nature of his gaze makes me think of Miss Abigail.

'I don't think you found this house by accident, Pippa.'

I shrug. '*Non, monsieur.*' I reach down into my bag and pull out the jug with the picture of the bridge. 'My mother always kept this jug with her, even in the hospital at the end. I rescued it the second before I ran away. Then by coincidence this year we found ourselves performing in this town. I made friends with Mr Hernfield, who lives here, and together we discovered that jugs with this design were made by your company before the war. Laurel Avenue was the address in the newspaper article about you when you returned from the war. Then, when we came here, the name of your house jumped out at me.'

He smiles slightly. 'Detective work! Splendid.'

Then another silence in which I suddenly become angry. He has sucked all this out of me and is still sitting there saying nothing.

'Now you,' I say.

'Me?'

'Now you must tell me why you bother to invite a total stranger inside your house. Even if I did recognise the name on your gate.'

He looks startled, then coughs. 'Well, as you've guessed, there is a story.' He sits up straight. 'I was travelling in France in 1905 on what you might call a wild-goose chase, trying to drum up some business for our pottery. I tried my trade in Caen, St-Brieuc – silly places. Paris and Toulouse . . . not so bad. Then, for selfish reasons, I made my way to Carcassonne. From my reading I had always been interested in the crusader castle and the medieval town, d'you see? Once there, I needed a pamphlet translating into French and a priest introduced me to your mother. That was when I knew really why I was drawn to that place. Once I had met your mother I stayed in Carcassonne for three whole weeks, two weeks more than I had planned.' He pauses, then clears his throat, frowning. 'Barbara Valois.' He says the name very slowly. 'Oh, she was clever and so beautiful! I was intoxicated.'

I try to fill the space. 'I thought about it, *monsieur*. My mother must have been only twenty then, just four years older than I am now.'

This thought startles him into continuing. 'I was thirty.' His cheeks become ruddy. 'I have to tell you I'd been long married and already had children but your mother – well, she bowled me over. So lively. So intelligent. Such a free spirit. I had never met such a woman . . . never . . . like her.' His voice is low now, almost impossible to hear. 'And never since.'

'But you left her!' I bang my hand against his. 'You left her there. You left us.'

He groans. 'I know. I know, Pippa. I saw you then and I see you now, and I know how very much I have missed, how I would have loved to see you as you grew into your grown-up self. But when she discovered the truth of my life here Barbara would not have me stay. She said . . . she said . . .'

'What did she say?'

'She said we'd been drawn together from our own choice, as our natural selves, not some contrived social contract. I told you she was clever. So clever with words. So persuasive. She said that blissful interlude was a gift out of time and now we must get on with our lives. I would have stayed, thrown everything away. But she convinced me. I didn't know then—'

'Didn't know what?' My voice is shrill. I glance at the door in case Louis and Philippa come running in to find out what is the matter. They don't.

'I didn't know about you, Pippa. That you were already there.'

'How can you be sure of that?'

'I only discovered ten years later, during the war. I was in the army and had ten days' leave just before the Battle of the Somme, and instead of coming home I went south to Carcassonne. Barbara was still there. I could not believe it – to come away from the front and find her still there in the same apartment. I was overjoyed. But she had this child. As soon as I saw you I knew you were mine.'

'How could you know? That you were my father.'

He stands up stiffly, makes his way across to the desk and comes back with a framed photograph. It is a portrait of a child of nine or ten with a short dress tied by a broad sash. She has a mop of dark curls and bright mischievous eyes. It is like looking in a mirror at myself.

'It's my mother,' he says. 'She always had that photograph of herself on her mantelpiece. Look at the back.'

I turn it over. It says, 'Philippa Jane Barratt, aged 9.' 'How is it that you saw me? I have this memory of seeing you in your uniform, going through the archway. But I never really saw you.'

'You did see me. Barbara didn't say I was your father but we were introduced. She said I was Philip and our names were the same. You climbed on my knee.'

How can this be? Have I wiped from my head every time I climbed on to some man's knee? It was only after Mr Slater mesmerised me that I even remembered the Belgian. Perhaps that event made me forget every time I climbed on to any man's knee, even the knee of the man I now know to be my father.

Suddenly Captain Benedict is laughing. 'Your mother said I was very honoured because the last time you'd been persuaded to climb on to a gentleman's knee you had beaten him over the head with a lamp and half brained him.'

'Did I kill him?' I say.

He actually laughs at this. 'Absolutely not. Your mother said you sent the feller away with his tail between his legs.'

He coughs. 'There was this other time. Your mother had sent me out for bread and I came upon some soldiers teasing you, throwing you about. I gave them what for and picked you up and brought you all the way home on my back. Your mother made this joke about you being the crusader and me being the horse. We all laughed so much.' He chuckles.

His easy laughter tells me that he has no idea about my mother: what she was driven to, for us to survive. He thinks he knows her, after all these years, but he doesn't. It dawns on me that while we tell some truth to the people we love we also communicate with them by lies of commission and omission, just to keep their image of us more or less intact.

Would the captain have talked of her with such love all these years later if she'd told him of her profession? She was right not to say, just as I'm right not to say anything now: not about her, or the fact that I couldn't remember seeing this man face to face. I could have passed him in the street and not recognised him.

Now I say, 'So even then you went off and left her for good?'

'No. No. I was determined to come back to see her. She knew I had the family here and would never . . . but she did not mind. As I told you, she was a truly free spirit. But I knew I'd go and see her again and again . . .' he coughs, '. . . until I died. That's how I felt.'

'But you didn't,' I say. 'You didn't do this.'

'Well, I went back to the front after that visit and was badly injured by a shell. I was sent back here and spent many months in hospital. And even when I got here my poor wife nursed me for nearly a year before I was back on my feet.'

'And then . . .?'

'And then after the war I went back to Carcassonne. I went back three times. My wife was understanding about it. She knew my obsession with the crusader castles and considered such historical trips to be recuperative. I went three times but I never found my lovely Barbara. Or you.' He takes my hand in both of his. 'I loved her, Pippa, and I want even now to show my love for her,' he says softly.

The clock ticks.

Finally I stand up and, holding my hand, he stands up too. 'Captain Benedict . . .'

He puts his hands on my shoulders and looks me in the eye. 'Captain Benedict? I'm your father, Pippa. Philip might seem too informal but it's all we've got. Call me Philip. My friends and my family call me this and so must you.' He puts his arms right round me now, and hugs me so hard I think my ribs will break. After a second I hug him back.

'Philip,' I say, 'I am so glad you were in Carcassonne and I know she never loved another man. She left me the jug so perhaps she knew I'd find you, one day.' My heart is brimming with a sense of rightness. I know my father now. Whatever else happens in England, this is what I·have come for. There is sense in it.

Smiling, he stands back and takes my hand in his. 'I have something to show you. Come and see.' He leads me across to the big desk. There, laid out in neat rows, are the treasured objects of memory of his time with my mother. Railway tickets, postcards of the scenes of the South of France, of the food-market in the great square, and many views of the great crusader castle of Carcassonne. A ribbon in the particular blue I know my mother favoured. A small battered book entitled *En Croisade contre les Cathares*. A battered notebook with 'France Journal' scrawled across the cover. And then, in neat lines, like men on a chequerboard, small square much-handled photographs: some of the castle; one of the mill race; many of her, usually in a white organdie blouse; some of him.

Three photographs show the two of them together. I imagine him asking a passer-by to take it. Even as I thrill at the sight of my mother's youth I know I could never aspire to her beauty. When I look at the photograph of this man smiling happily alongside my mother, I could never escape the fact that I am Philip's daughter and his mother's granddaughter.

'Well?' I say.

'Well?' he echoes.

'I can see that you loved her.'

'O-oh, yes. I told you that. Now, d'you see this box? I bought that in Paris, years later, when I came to look for her and failed to find her. We can put all these things in it and you can take them all with you.'

I'm already shaking my head. 'They're yours. Without them she'll be gone from here. She's inside my head, inside me. I don't need them.'

Still he insists on giving me a selection of them, in a stiff brown envelope. Then he reaches into a drawer and brings out a small, blue notebook with gold lettering. 'Well then, you must take this. It's a bank book. In it I have deposited fifty guineas for each year of your life. And I will continue to do so.' He puts up a hand to stop my protest. 'Your mother would have nothing from me but you must indulge me. It is merely a small token. If you know me as your father you must take it.'

I am at a loss for words.

'And you must take this also.' 'This' is a photograph framed in a small leather carrying case, of the two of them, leaning against the Pont Vieux.

Now his arm is around me again. 'And I want you to come to see me many times, Pippa. We can make up for the years and we can remember dear Barbara. I have been fortunate in my life in some ways but now I count it as the greatest good fortune that you have found me and I have found you.'

I break away to take the bank book and the photograph, and put them in my bag beside the bridge jug. 'Thank you, Philip.' I am trying not to cry. I want to get away now. It's all too, too much.

On cue the door swings open and in bursts Philippa with Louis. She is beaming. She comes across the room and hugs me.

'You must know?' I say, struggling out of her grasp.

'Pa has told me. So very romantic.'

'There is so much to understand.'

She stands in front of me, looking me straight in the eye, just as her father did before. They are very alike. 'Welcome to our family, Pippa,' she says. 'Always remember we are here.'

I nod rapidly and glance desperately across at Louis. 'We must go,' I gasp. 'We have an extra rehearsal this morning.'

Louis starts to protest and I glare at him.

She steps aside. 'Will you call again before you leave?'

I am already shaking my head. 'There is so much to do at the end of the run. Miss Abigail depends so much on me.'

Louis butts in. 'I am going with the troupe on to Newcastle, and further on the tour. But I'll certainly be back to see the ancients. My parents, that is.'

'Good.' Ambrose Philip Benedict shakes him by the hand. 'Well, you must see that Pippa comes with you.' He limps across to me and puts his hands on my shoulders. Then he kisses my brow, just under my hair. There is the faint scent of tobacco on his breath. 'I know you will come, Pippa. You and I have time to make up. And write! I can't tell you how I longed for letters from Barbara. You must write to me and tell me what you are doing.'

'Yes! Yes! I will do that, Philip.' Thinking I might faint, I grab Louis by the arm and flee. I don't stop running until we get out on to the Ryhope Road, when he hauls me to a stop and asks me what the heck this is all about.

I can't tell him that this is the beginning of the rest of my life. I know who I am. I know now who my mother was and can love her and not blame her. After being hugged and kissed by my father I am no longer either afraid of Roy Divine nor perplexed by Mr Slater. Having finally understood my mother and father's strange tale of love and steadfastness I feel ready to look at Louis with new eyes.

I put my arm through his. 'Let's sit on this wall and take a breather,' I say.

Pep Talk

On that Saturday afternoon we were all called to the theatre for band call and announcements. Most of the members of the troupe gathered in the front rows of the stalls. AJ came to sit on the edge of the orchestra pit, one leg elegantly trailing. Hermione stood beside him, hands clasped delicately under her bosom. Her make-up was exquisite.

Louis and I sat next to Tesserina and Joe on the very back row, watching the proceedings. Louis was still recovering from the sight of the bank book, which credited me with nearly a thousand pounds' sterling.

'You're rich,' he'd grinned as we sat on a garden wall there on Ryhope Road. 'You'll be looking down on a poor old printer-playwright soon.'

I had pushed the book into the depths of my bag, muttering, 'It's nothing, nothing.'

'So the old boy really did acknowledge that he was your father.'

I scowled at him. 'Why would he not do that? He not only acknowledged it, he embraced it. You are so bourgeois, Louis.

Philip Benedict was really pleased to see me and learn of my mother. I was pleased to talk to him who knew her when she was young. He was very sad about her. Me, I've never had time to be properly sad about her, so I am glad he is. He has time to be sad.' I was almost shouting at him, there in the street. 'He loves that I am here. That I am his daughter.'

He put a hand on my arm. 'Don't take on so, Pippa. I can see you are delighted. Don't make a bad thing out of a good thing, there's a dear.'

To make amends for being bourgeois he took me for coffee and cakes at his parents' house, where the old man talked to me about his uncle, who had fought against Napoleon. That seemed to get things back into proportion, somehow.

Now at the theatre AJ was doing his usual end-of-engagement speech about a wonderfully successful week. He ended with a dramatically sorrowful aside about the tragedy of Pixie Molloy. Mrs Palmer had sent flowers to her family and AJ himself had taken the liberty of offering the sympathy of everyone in the troupe.

'However,' he cast his firm but fair gaze around the whole company, 'I am pleased to say that Madame Bunce has girded her loins, shown herself for the true professional she is and declared she will accompany us to Newcastle and complete her contract.'

There was the barest of cynical silences before the expected polite mumble from the people gathered there. At least nobody booed.

AJ stood up very straight, put back his shoulders and went on in the manner of Henry V in his speech to his soldiers before Agincourt. 'And now, ladies and gentlemen, let us look forward to tonight's show, which will be the very best in a good week. And on to Newcastle! Our reputation has gone before us and we have much to prove. But Palmer's Varieties is up to the challenge; we have strengths we have not yet tapped. The best days are yet to come.'

(*We few, we happy few, we band of brothers* . . . I had seen him do that speech so many times . . .)

There was a round of applause, even a few *Hurrahs*! from Cissie Barnard, who had already started drinking.

AJ coughed. 'One final announcement. There has been some discussion that Tesserina, accompanied by my dear wife, Mrs Palmer, may go down to London to promote her career in the metropolis. On purely selfish grounds I am pleased to announce that they will both be with us for some considerable time yet . . .'

Another *Hurrah!* from Cissie Barnard.

'. . . to grace our show with their presence. However, Mr Cameron Lake and Miss Abigail Wharton will continue in the tasks assigned to them in anticipation of Mrs Palmer's departure. This will allow Mrs Palmer to concentrate on the music for the whole show.' He paused. 'In addition to this, Mr Joe Zambra has agreed to explore ways in which his accordion music may contribute to Palmer's Varieties.'

Tom Merriman, in front of us, muttered something about the old boy swallowing a dictionary, but his comment was covered by the general buzz as the company relaxed at the end of Mr Palmer's speech. The seats clattered as they stood up, ready to disperse to their various corners and cubbyholes in the theatre.

Louis and I sat tight in the tenth row. Louis wanted to see AJ about a new short play that he thought might go down well in Newcastle. I stayed because I didn't want to see Miss Abigail until I had properly digested what had happened in

Laurel Gardens and made up a story that had enough of the truth in it to satisfy her.

Down at the front AJ and Mrs Palmer were in conference with the Divines, including Roy. Mr Slater was lolling against the orchestra stalls, looking on with interest. Roy was gesticulating angrily.

Their voices came across the empty stalls.

'I'm sure we can do it, Mr Palmer,' said Marie Divine in that curious hard voice of hers. 'I know the act's changed. But Roy's an old hand. He'll pick it up.'

Roy was standing at her shoulder. 'I can do it, Mr Palmer,' he said earnestly. 'Just give me this one chance to prove it to you.'

Mr Slater hit the edge of the orchestra pit with the side of his fist. 'I would have thought that he couldn't do both things, AJ. He needs all his concentration, all his energy to work with me. It could be dangerous.'

'Dangerous?' squawked Marie contemptuously. 'You don't know the meaning of the word, you silly little man.'

'Steady on, Marie,' said Roy. He went across to Mr Slater. 'I've gotta do it, mate? I've gotta try again with them? Family, after all. But I can do both, believe me. Your stuff's dead easy? All quackery, after all. But I was born on the high wire . . . Stan, mate.' But Mr Slater was already gliding away through the side exit.

Roy turned back to AJ Palmer. 'Don't worry, sir, I'll change his mind. But please let me get back up there with my brother and sister. I'll show you I can do it.'

AJ hesitated.

Marie intervened. 'Look, Mr Palmer, you'll be here in the theatre at three o'clock?'

'I am always here at three o'clock.'

'We'll have it ready then, to show you. And by then Roy will have got round that old sourpuss, Slater, I promise you.'

Mr Palmer shrugged. 'Nothing to lose. I'll see you all here at three o'clock.' He bustled away with Mrs Palmer. Louis got up to follow them. I stayed there in the shadows in row ten, and watched the Divines as they followed Louis out, Marie and Roy with their heads close together first, then a good yard behind them came Blaze, with his head sunk low on his shoulders.

Later, as I was sitting mending with Miss Abigail, I gave her an edited version of my visit to Laurel Gardens that morning. Like Philippa Benedict, she thought the whole story very romantic. Of course, I didn't show her the embarrassing bank book. But I admitted that Captain Ambrose Philip Benedict was my father and I was pleased about it. I showed her the photographs. She declared my mother very beautiful and she took one look at the photograph of Philip Benedict's mother as a child and declared that here indeed was proof positive. 'No doubt about it, darling.'

She became very busy again with her sewing. 'So what will you do, now you have found your family?' Her head was down. I couldn't see her eyes.

'Do?'

'Now, you have this family and to all appearances they seem to like you, to want you with them. A good thing too.'

This made me laugh. 'But you're my family, Miss Abigail. You and Palmer's. Didn't we say this? I am marvellously changed by meeting and liking my father but I am still me.'

'But this man, Pippa, is your father!'

'Yes. And he wants me to write to him,' I said. 'I have promised to write to him, to keep in touch. And I will do that. I have read much English but written little. It will be good practice.'

She looked up at me. 'So you won't go and live with him in his fine house?'

'No fear. Isn't that what you English say? But I am pleased, excited he is there. He is in my life. He is my good English part. I will continue to be me. But I now feel properly planted in the past, so can grow on.'

She laughed out loud at this. 'You are a strange girl, Pippa, but I do so love you.' She held up her sewing. 'Now, darling, we must get on or the dancers'll go on tonight in rags.'

A minute later she said, 'That was good news about Tesserina! I knew it was far too early for that London adventure. The trouble is, Hermione was getting restless. It's all about her. But she's settled down again so now our little family is safe.'

'There's Joe, of course,' I put in. 'It's different now.'

'Oh yes, there's Joe. I have a feeling there will always be Joe. And anyone can see Tesserina has moved on now, that she doesn't need us any more. But for now she is still part of our family. Anyway, Hermione wants a rehearsal with this dress at two o'clock, to iron out these new difficulties. So we must stay around.'

Perhaps I should have known better, but at that moment I felt things returning to normal, that we would be going on our customary theatrical paths and doing the next thing that Palmer's demanded. But there was one more test to face.

Fall

In the afternoon rehearsal Tesserina's dance retrieves all its passion and natural grace. Mrs Palmer is alone at the piano. There is no sign of Mr Smith. Mr Palmer has taken Joe away somewhere to test out his repertoire on the accordion.

There are small differences in the dance today, as there are at every performance. This instant creativity is what marks Tesserina out from Madame Bunce's Pixies. They are drilled so hard they would do their routine in their sleep. Tesserina's genius lies in her reacting to the whim of the moment with grace. Therein lies her success and her weakness. If the whim of the moment is disturbed or preoccupied, then the dance is not so successful. But at its best it is magical.

'Excellent,' breathes Miss Abigail, beside me in row ten. 'So much better.'

I look for comment from Louis, who is sitting to my left but as usual he has his head down over his scribble-pad and has hardly noticed Tesserina's dance. AJ's going to read through the new play with him, after the high-wire rehearsal, and he's still changing parts of it.

NO REST FOR THE WICKED

Roy Divine has been up a ladder twice to check the hawser fixing of the end section of the high wire, where it comes out over the stalls. He must have seen me but has taken no more notice of me than if I were a fly. Marie has been up the ladder; Blaze too. None of this is unusual. They are always quite rightly obsessive about their safety.

Miss Abigail hauls herself up from the chair. 'I'll go and see to Tesserina's dress.' She puts her hand on mine. 'No, you stay here, darling. Give Louis the benefit of your advice.' She has been very kind about Louis and me. She likes him and nurtures our friendship.

In the doorway she passes AJ, who comes to take his place in the front row with Mrs Palmer.

Even Louis's head raises for the acrobats. Marie walks along with one long pole, then another shorter one. Then she walks without the aid of the pole, appears to fall, then retrieves herself. This always gets a big gasp from the audience.

Then she does a kind of high-wire dance with Blaze, where it's only through falling against each other that they stop themselves from falling. Then on comes Roy and after one or two steps to balance himself he runs up and down the rope without any pole. Even I gasp. There is a patter of applause from Mrs Palmer and shouts of *Bravo!*

Then Roy makes his way to the centre of the rope and stands there, leaning forward on one leg, the other behind him. He is as graceful as a bird. Then he twists round and does the same on the other leg. He appears to lose his balance and retrieves it, bouncing back up on to the rope and to safety.

Then he works his way along the rope to the point where he is over the orchestra pit. He stands very still, then does a kind of slow-motion somersault. Hand-foot-hand-foot. We all hold our breaths. Then he stands up easily and smiles down at us, almost swaggering there on that fragile wire. He bows, acknowledging the patter of applause and the murmurs of appreciation from AJ and Mrs Palmer. Then from behind me in the shadowy space comes a short sharp cough.

Roy puts his head up and his hands out, performs a perfect back flip and comes crashing down into the orchestra pit. Even in that split second I swing round, but there's no one behind row ten in the darkened auditorium. I know, though, that a second before, Mr Slater was standing there.

Mrs Palmer, Marie Divine and her brother Blaze are all screaming. AJ is scrambling to get over the barrier into the orchestra pit.

'My God!' breathes Louis beside me. 'Can you believe that?' He goes forward to see how he can help.

I stand up to see more clearly. Roy's body is folded over the narrow end of the grand piano like a rag doll. Like Pixie Molloy across the staithes in the dock, only his eyes are open and blood is seeping from his mouth.

I went back through the theatre and outside. There I found Mr Slater leaning against a wall, smoking a cigarette. 'It was you! You did that thing to Roy Divine.'

As he spoke, cigarette smoke streamed from his lips. 'Me? What did I do?'

'You coughed!'

He chuckled. 'I'm always coughing, Miss Pippa.' He waved the cigarette in my face. 'It's the cigarettes. They clear your chest.'

I shook my head. 'You coughed and he did the back flip like he did when you hypnotised him in your act. But you didn't reverse the mesmerism.'

He shook his head. 'I can't think what you're talking about!' he said blandly. 'It's all quackery, dear. Didn't you hear him say so before? I noticed you paying close attention.'

He knew exactly what I was talking about. I stared at him. Then he threw his cigarette down and stamped on it. Then he came so close I could smell the tobacco on his breath. 'He told me, Pippa. All about you and the Italian boy. Boasted. And he told me about the Molloy kid. D'you know what he said? He said he was trying out hypnotism on her and she walked into the dock. Can you believe it?' His soft voice was laced with anger. 'I do lots of things on the stage for entertainment, you know. And I could do much more. I see things in people that they don't know themselves. For instance, I know that you were in pain, searching for something you have now found. I knew that I had to reverse the thing in you or you would have gone mad. The gift can be dangerous.' He paused. 'Of course, it can also be dangerous to call a man's lifework quackery.'

'You should have gone to someone about what he said.' How could I say this? When had I ever managed to talk properly to anyone about Roy Divine?

He shrugged, lighting another cigarette. 'Roy said it was an accident. Both of them, accidents. As you found, he can be very slippery. But he was good in the act. He was not bad company. We were set to make our fortunes. For a day or so I forgot that it's our fate in life to walk alone. So I protected him. And *then* Marie Divine crooks her little finger . . .' He leaned back against the wall and took a very long draw on his cigarette. 'They do say pride goes before a fall, Miss Pippa.' Again as he spoke the smoke poured from his mouth. His watery blue eyes gazed into mine. 'So, are you going to tell on *me*?'

From my heels to the very top of my head all I felt at that moment was relief: I felt not just relieved but happy that that man was dead. Angelo and Ginny Molloy could rest now, as some justice was done here today, even if the means by which it came was threaded through with the blackness inside Roy himself.

At this point Louis came out of the theatre, clearly looking for me. He had my coat and my beret in his hand. He spared Slater barely a glance.

'Pippa, Miss Abigail says I'm to get you as far away from here as possible while they . . . deal with everything. I thought we could go to a place called Roker, further along the coast. We can walk and watch the waves and talk to each other about . . . anything that's not to do with what's happened here today. We'll just be together.'

He held out his hand and I took it. As we walked away I could feel Mr Slater's gaze boring into my back. He called out my name: 'Pippa! Mam'selle Pippa . . .'

But I don't turn round to meet those eyes. I squeeze Louis's hand and we start to run.

Epilogue

Lordship Hotel
Bayswater
London
15 February 1933

My dearest Philip,

I hope you and Philippa are well. We have just had a letter from Janey Doby, who takes care of the ancients (parents of Louis). She says the weather up there is nithering. That means very cold. Is that not expressive? English is the most wonderful language.

This letter is an apology for not calling on you when I was in the North last week. As you know, I always love to see you when I can. All the time I have with you is very precious. We had to be in Hartlepool for the funeral of A.J. Palmer. You remember him? He was a real character – an actor of the old school.

The church in Hartlepool was packed. So many faces, familiar and unfamiliar! Many from that troupe that I knew so well, before it was disbanded when the acrobat died. Lily Lambert and Cissie Barnard are rather older and more worn now. Cissie, who is now active in the Temperance Movement (her earlier acquaintance with the demon drink was very intimate!) told me with irreligious satisfaction that the Palmers' comedian – Tom Merriman – had drunk himself to death. And Lily Lambert – now long married to Mr Barrington and a shopkeeper – told me that Mr Slater, the mesmerist, had been arrested for some dark deed and had spent some time behind bars.

We travelled up with my dear friend Miss Abigail Wharton and her friend Miss Dina Brooks, the ones with the milliner's shop in Mayfair. Do you remember it was your money gift to me that allowed Miss Abigail to invest in the shop? Well, it is now flourishing and very well patronised. Miss Abigail enquired after you and sent her regards.

The widow, Mrs Palmer, was magnificent in black with a huge black mantilla. She put on a great show, but was obviously very sad. She had arranged the service and her friend Mr Jacob Smith played the organ. Mr Cameron Lake, whom I also knew from the troupe, sang the 23rd Psalm. It was very moving. Everyone had their handkerchiefs out.

Palmer's London Agency has done very well in recent years. Mrs Palmer confided in Miss Abigail that the tragic break-up of the troupe was a happy accident for her. She'd always wanted to try her hand in London and this forced them both to make the move. They could have started a new troupe but she prevailed on AJ to move to London and set up the agency, and they never looked back. She mentioned that the Divines – sister and brother to the tragic acrobat – are now working in America in the moving picture industry.

Tesserina and Joe sent a huge array of flowers from Italy. Tesserina has now just had her fourth child and, according to Joe, is not missing the dance a bit. I have since thought that the success of Tesserina's dancing was not about performance, more about her finding herself. Joe now runs a big café in the village of Baveno on Lake Maggiore, and plays his accordion in the square on Saturdays.

My beloved Louis and I are very well, as are young Angelo, Benedict and little Tessa. I hope you received their photographs to add to your collection. At school Angelo is called Sam. Just why that is, is a long story – I will tell you about it some time.

As you know, Louis's play about the Treaty of Versailles caused a lot of argument in the papers but is still doing well here in London. There is talk of it going on in New York but I think that might be what the English call a bit far-fetched. Louis has started to talk about another war! He feels sorry for the Germans but he does not trust them. I hope he is wrong. His talk worries me, as I know that Germany peers over the shoulder of France towards Britain.

All this made me think about our beloved Carcassonne. I would so like to take the children there, to the place where I was born. I have this plan that we might go next summer – you, Philippa and me and Louis? And the children, of course. Do come, dearest Papa! It will be such good company. And we could buy the finest wine and drink a toast to Barbara and the young Ambrose Philip Benedict. My French will be very stumbling, I think, after so many years.

Dearest Philip, we will make our way north again very soon and I will have the pleasure of continuing our long conversation.

With the best love in the world from your daughter, Pippa